FATES CHOSEN

Teresa L. White

Order this book online at www.trafford.com
or email orders@trafford.com

Most Trafford titles are also available at major online book retailers.

Printed in Victoria, BC, Canada.

ISBN: 978-1-4269-2258-9 (sc)
ISBN: 978-1-4269-2900-7 (hc)

Library of Congress Control Number: 2010902464

*Our mission is to efficiently provide the world's finest, most comprehensive book publishing
service, enabling every author to experience success. To find out how to publish your book, your
way, and have it available worldwide, visit us online at www.trafford.com*

Trafford rev. 3/15/10

www.trafford.com

North America & international
toll-free: 1 888 232 4444 (USA & Canada)
phone: 250 383 6864 ♦ fax: 812 355 4082

For Tony, your encouragement is admirable.

ACKNOWLEDGMENTS

I ORIGINALLY SAT DOWN with my laptop intending to write a short story that had been stuck in my head to post on an internet forum. What I didn't know at the time was that I had the ability and focus to create an entire book.

Tony, thank you for your belief in me and for being the proud husband who wasn't too shy to tell everyone, "My wife's writing a book!" The support and faith you've given me is probably what motivated me to continue until the end.

Taylor, thank you for the constant writers block that you provided me with, with your endless chattering about your friends every day after school. I love you kiddo, never change.

Megan, you're my little comedian. Thank you for all the funny things you do and say that always manages to break the monotony.

Lacey & Hope, I'm proud of you both. Continue to move forward in life and take control! Lacey, my one eyed girl your courage and strength still amazes me. Hope, your smile is addictive please never stop smiling for the world will become a sad place without it.

Mom, I love you thanks for always being a simple phone call away and for believing in me through all of this.

Vicki & Howard, thank you for taking the time to read the original script (unedited) and giving me some much needed feedback. I love you both.

Uncle Don and Aunt Cora, I love you both very much thank you for always being there to play a hand of cards, talk politics and golf, and enjoy a good meal together.

To my cheering squad…. I.E. All of my family and wonderful friends who encouraged and sent me constant texts asking if 'I was done yet?' Yes I'm finally done (with this one!) and yes I will sign all of your books. I love you guys.

CONTENTS

CHAPTER 1

Life in Furlin

A S I SIT OUT in the sun feeling it warm my face in the early morning hours, I wonder about how we came to be in Furlin. It is my traditional day off, I turn sixteen today and my calling upon will come later in the day. I'm excited yet, nervous. I know what I want them to say, I've thought of nothing but my calling since I was a small boy first set out to see where I'd best fit in within our village.

Furlin is organized fully by our Liaison. They make all callings amongst our village. A Liaison is replaced every three years, there's a panel of ten men and every three years the eldest gets early leave to live in solace. This is a year three, and all sixteen year olds are on edge wandering who will be called to fill the new Liaison seat. Being a Liaison is an honor to all and it means a life of ease.

Most of the time; you know well before your sixteenth birthday where you'll be placed. But there are some like me who have been put through many different internship's since I started them. An internship here means a trial period in which you're set to work in a specific job area to see if you can do the work and how efficiently you can do it. I've been sent to the fields, the blacksmiths, the healers, the cook stations, and many more. I've been with each job close to six months then sent to another internship. I never felt at the time that I was doing a bad job. I never got complained to or reprimanded, so I didn't understand the constant changes in my internships.

Our life isn't a complicated one. Everyone has a job, a home, and food enough to sustain life. Our village isn't large compared to the bigger villages such as Breakstone, we have over five hundred people and with the way things are done there isn't usually much time for socialization.

Our marriage partners are set when we are young, sometimes as young as three or four years of age. Our education starts at three and it is teachers who will suggest matches for marriage. The suggestion is taken to the Liaison and they watch all matches, then they go to the families and negotiations begin. There are very few rules about matches, one being the ages. Boys must be older but no more than one full year. And once a match is made both families are expected to groom their child for the event that will take place, they can never choose to break the match. My match is with Elora, we live in the same row of cottages and we've been playmates since we were small children. I'm happy about our match and I know this time next year our ceremony will arrive. All marriages are bound in a ceremony when the girl reaches the age of seventeen; Elora and I are only a month different in age.

Amongst parental negotiations comes the housing for a new marriage. Our cottage ring was laid out many years ago and the families get together for a small time each day and build a small piece of our home. It is a very modest cottage, a sitting room, a kitchen and two small sleeping rooms. In an early discussion over how to keep the sleeping rooms warm without building two fireplaces and chimney's began a new idea of putting one fireplace in each room with their backs sitting together and sharing one chimney. This idea is now implemented in all new cottages. Elora and I sit together most evenings and watch the building of our home. We're not allowed to take part in the building of our own home. We're also not allowed to place items within in until our marriage day. So it's customary that all gifts and finds be given to the others parents to be safely kept until we are married. .

At twelve years old when we start our internships we are also no longer allowed to be alone with our matches. We must always have an escort; our escort is usually my friend Kyan. He also lives on our row and is just a couple months younger than I. I sometimes escort for him and his match Leta, not that there is really much time to spend running around with no purpose in our village. As I mentioned our village is an organized one, and those who choose to break the routine face the Punishers. They do exactly as their name states; there are punishments for every rule that can be broken. There are times for everything and everyone is expected to keep in time with the rules. It's really not as difficult as it sounds though, and maybe I just feel that way because now it's just a way of life for us all.

It's still early and the sun feels warmer as time drags on, the village is waking up and beginning their normal day. I heard my mother calling to my younger sister Myka to let me sleep. I let them believe that as I wanted to see Elora as she goes for her morning milk ration. I know Myka will be out soon to do the same, and she'll of course break my peaceful morning.

I heard Elora's door open and I glanced shyly over her way. She knew I'd be out this morning to see her go by, so my being here enjoying the warm morning is no surprise to her at all. She is beautiful as always, I know I've loved her many years and I become happy when I see her. Her hair is golden in color and even with the curls it reaches all the way down her back, her eyes are the most vivid green I've ever seen on anybody. When we sit at our daily cottage gathering I may only hold her hand in mine. I'm not allowed to touch her hair, although I'm tempted constantly. It looks so soft and smells always of the magnolia's that grow in the forest beyond our cottages. Our talks are kept very quiet for if our siblings hear they'll poke constant fun at as. We're excited about our callings coming, though neither of us is sure of my destiny.

Elora expects she'll be put with the one and two year olds. As she walked by she gave me a shy smile and whispered good luck to me. I felt more relaxed as I rose to go help with the morning chores.

I expect the Liaison's to call for me after mid-meal, they will also call on my parents to attend as well as Elora. Elora is invited as she'll be a part of my life and their choice affects her as much as it does me. I plan to take my meal with my parents. My father is a wood worker; he helps make all the furniture and many other items needed in town. My mother is a healer for the women and children in the village; she delivers babies and cares for their ailments through their childhood. They have already made arrangements to have mid day off from their work. And Elora will still in internship but they will release her when the Liaison's clerk comes to call on her.

There was some protest from my mother when I offered to put together our meal but I wasn't giving in. I made roast venison sandwiches with potatoes and gravy made from the meat. I even made small cherry tarts from the cherries in our small garden.

"Happy Birthday!" My mom sang as she came through the door.

My father, always hungry from his hard work goes right to the table. "What smells so good son?" He asked as if the day wasn't the least bit special.

"Are you nervous Davin?" My mother asked as she looked over the table to look over our meal.

"No… yes….just a bit. I have no idea where I'll be working, everyone always knows!" I just can't believe that on the day of my calling I have no idea at all, and I'm excited. I hoped for a position as a hunter or maybe follow in my father's trade so I can make furniture for our cottage. But I have no idea really. I'm not sure how Elora will accept me if my job is not one of honor.

CHAPTER 2

The Liaison

W E ATE QUIETLY AS we waited. As I got up to help my mother clear the table we heard the knock we had all been waiting for. "I'm here for Davin Hewit." The clerk said. His name is Jobe and outside his job I've known him since I can remember. He is close to my parent's age. His family sends us preserves at holidays; they make the best preserves but they have kept their recipe a secret.

It's nice to be picked up by someone I know but I still felt very nervous, I noticed that no one was following him to get my parents. I also saw no sign of Elora or someone headed to get her. The walk was nerve racking and the idle small talk with Jobe wasn't helping any.

The Liaison's building is bigger than the cottages we live in but built much the same out of stone with small amounts of wood. The door's are wooden and have intricate carvings of ivy and small delicate flowers. Inside the walls are covered with red velvet drapery. I'm asked to sit and wait, this relieved me some figuring it was time to wait for my parents and Elora to get here. After only a couple minutes the inner double doors are opened and I'm called in.

The room is very large and the walls here are also covered in velvet, but the windows are not covered and the early summer breeze is wafting in. In front of me is a very long table almost the width of the room and all the Liaison's are sitting on one side of the long table. Many have papers and cups of ale in front of them. They seem in a pleasant mood and the eldest of the Liaison's, Wan asks me to have a seat near the large table. In the room around me there are many chairs, which are mostly empty except a couple clerks to record the meeting. My family is not present nor is Elora, I'm so afraid and I wonder what I have done wrong. Have I somehow insulted the Liaison's? Am I about to be cast out of the village?

I watched as Jobe closed the windows and drapes to allow the meeting to go on in privacy.

"Davin," Wan started out. "I'm sure many things are running through your mind; let me assure you there is no trouble for you."

"Yes Sir." I managed to choke out.

"We asked you here alone for many reasons, your calling will require the utmost privacy, and thus why your parents and match are not here. Your match is being taken to your parents now and our clerk Wes will assure them all is fine, that we just had some questions before your placement." Wan's voice is very soft and I relaxed as I listened to him although I think I am still shaking some.

"This session will take a small amount more time than most, we have questions for you." Wan began again. "They will help us further in our choice of your placement." I nod as if I understood everything thing that was happening.

"We've spent much time discussing your placement over the years, I'm sure you've noticed how often you were switched in your internships. What are your thoughts on why that is?"

I thought for a moment almost lost wondering what they were looking for, I decided I'd just answer honestly as I always want to be honorable.

"I at first thought maybe I wasn't getting along with people or doing my job right, but as I thought about it I felt I always did as I was instructed, I never complained nor was I ever reprimanded for doing a task wrong or too slowly. So to be honest I'm unsure why I was switched so much."

They all seemed busy writing, I almost felt like I was just talking to myself. Wan cleared his throat, "your match with Elora, how do you feel about how that's coming together?"

I wondered why my match with Elora has anything to do with my future work, but again I attempted an honorable yet honest answer. "I am happy with my match, Elora is beautiful and smart, I must confess it's a year before we are bound and it still feels too far away, I'm sure I love her and that she feels the same for me."

Again they were writing and it seemed many minutes passed before Wan looked up smiling seemingly pleased with my answer. "How do you feel about your father's trade?"

I'm almost relieved at this question, I feel as if they are leaning toward making me a wood worker. I think maybe this is normal and my parents and Elora will be brought in as a surprise once I answer this question. "I feel it is an honorable job, I enjoyed my time learning wood working and have thought many times how pleasing it would be if I could make our own furniture for our cottage once we are bound."

There was a small chuckle out of a couple of the Liaison's but a stern look from Wan quieted them quickly. "Was there any one job in particular liked more than others?"

Am I getting a choice? That is the only thought that runs through my mind. "I very much enjoyed hunting Sir."

"You were taken to punishers once for being late; do you feel your punishment was just?" Wan asked in a very serious tone.

"Yes sir, I've never been late again." I said with a small laugh. I've never thought much on it; at the time I felt more embarrassed than feeling as I had been mistreated. I once got caught being late to internship and I was taken to the punisher's. I got scolded and a minor whipping from Skullmaker, no worse than my father gave me for sneaking into the cookies really. But I was sure to watch my time better afterward.

"Davin you may step back into the waiting room we would like to discuss a few things, I'll have a clerk bring you some ale while you wait."

After what seemed like a very long wait I was called back into the room again. This time the entire Liaison's seemed very at ease, they looked at me directly with warm smiles upon their faces. I almost wandered if I had been chosen for Liaison. I was again invited to have a seat; one nearer to the main table this time, as I sat a clerk brought me more ale and a plate of pastries.

Wan seemed to be the speaker for the Liaison, he started by welcoming me back.

"We are very pleased with you Davin. And we have watched you close over the years." This startled me a bit but I refuse to cower or seem afraid. The Hewit's have always carried themselves with honor over the generations, I didn't want to be the one to break this great trait.

"We are the ones who made the decision to move you from job to job, after seeing you learn to work so well and so quick in the first internship we wanted to see if you could do it again just as quick." He was smiling as he spoke to me as were the others. "You never let us down, whatever internship you were sent to you mastered quickly and worked efficiently. We even started betting on you to see how quickly you could do it because some would say it was too much of a task." He said almost laughing now.

I was almost upset that my hard work had become somewhat of a joke. It was hard not to show a hurt face; I think Wan sensed my feelings. "I apologize; I know it feels that we have made some joke at your expense but that's not the case at all I assure you." He looked down at his papers again, maybe to remind himself of where he should continue.

"We have created a new sort of job for our village and you were chosen shortly after you began your internships. The job is called {The Watcher} and that is exactly what you'll be doing Davin."

I was confused, no trade, no laboring? "Watching what Sir?" I asked.

"Watching everyone, everything. We want to be assured of the village's happiness, we understand everything just runs based on choices we make for the people, but are they happy? Do changes need to be made?" Wan seemed very sure that he wanted me challenging the Liaison's choices. I don't think in all the years of Liaison's that one has ever challenged them and now I'm being asked to do so?

Wan began speaking again this time very guarded and careful in his words, "Your title is to be secret, known only to us and the few clerks here. You're to tell your loved ones your new title is clerk and leave it at that. Clerking is an honorable position, so no need to worry about your honor." He seemed very assured that he had no worries with me, I wasn't sure I felt the same but very honored by the choice.

"I'm very honored to be asked to such a delicate calling Sir." Was all I could manage to stammer.

"As you're aware this is a year three and we all know it's time for my leave. Soon you'll be among us and be there for the for this event. It's a rather huge event this time as I'm last of the first Liaison's and the choice is very important." He looked almost sad as he spoke about his leaving Liaison position.

"Davin you're to report here in the morning. You still have much learning to do as you become acquainted with your new position. Your first few months your days will be full here but as time goes by you'll find yourself having more free time. In this free time you're free to do as you wish. You can hunt, woodwork anything you would like. We just ask that you do something that makes it seem that you're not idle. As you know we are strict about idleness." I knew all too well the way time in our village worked.

"You're free to go home and celebrate your birthday as well as your new clerkship. This large book here is yours but it must remain here, this office is open to you always to study or speak with us. And if need be we'll have your own room built out back for your work." The book was very big and looked handmade, it was leather bound with Gold writing on the cover. It said: "The Watcher Davin Hewit" I was in awe of how beautiful the craftsmanship of the book was much less the fact that it said my name on it.

All the men stood and put out their hands for me to shake; I started with Wan and thanked him for such blessings. Each was about the same a welcoming handshake and thanks from me.

"The clerk will show you to your new horse as well, feel free to choose what tack you'll feel most comfortable using, we look forward to seeing you in the morning."

I followed the clerk out in a daze. I also get a horse too? It was a beautiful horse he was almost black in color very noble looking. I picked all leather tack with small amounts of silver trinkets on them. I knew how to ride a horse, my father taught me many years ago, but most in our village have to either breed horses or save their share of coin given out from the sale of wares to other towns. I had no idea I'd be getting a horse so soon in life. The clerk also informed me Icould keep in here as long as I needed to.

I rode home on my new horse I decided to name him Blitz. I went directly home knowing everyone was probably worried about me, I'd been gone a long time. They must have heard the footsteps of the horse as I saw three faces poking through the small kitchen window as I turned into our yard. Elora was the first to greet me and in all my excitement I swept her up in my arms with a great hug. The smell of her hair engulfed my senses for a moment and as I looked up I noticed my parents looking very upset yet relieved to see me.

As I walked toward the house I was flooded with questions, I finally had to hush everyone so I could tell them what happened. I explained that I had somewhat of a small training course but was chosen to be a clerk for the Liaison. This made them all smile with pride, I told them the reason they were not sent to witness was because of a questioning process that was long and dull. I assured them they honestly missed nothing exciting.

"I must go home to help prepare supper and do chores before we meet at the cottage." Elora told us, I'm instantly sad to hear she is leaving. I walked her to the door and took her hand. "I look forward to this evening with you; we shall celebrate with a fire and wine." This is the traditional celebration amongst families when it is a birthday. I want so much to walk her home but it would be against the rules of courting.

"Davin." My mother said in a voice that I know means I'm in trouble. "You may not hug Elora like that, especially outside where others can see as you just did!"

"I know mother, please forgive me I was caught up in my own excitement and lost my manners." I begged in my best good son way to which I knew mother can always forgive with a smile.

"Wash son, Myka will be in soon for supper and we have things to prepare for your celebration."

My chore before supper was to go to the well to bring in water for washing. I know my father also gets many more buckets throughout the evening. And Myka always helps with supper.

We feasted on roast pheasant, turnips and fresh warm bread. It was one of my favorite meals and I know mother planned it for my birthday. We also had butter which we don't get often, it just depends on how the cows are doing. Sometimes we are lucky if we get our daily ration when they get stingy with their milk. I think to myself that's the first thing I'd like to work on changing, working a bigger area so we can have a few more cows for the people. Some families own a cow but I know how hard they had to save and the extra work they have to do to provide feed for them.

My mother filled our travel basket with wine and fresh cherries for this evening. I sat quietly waiting I'm excited to be with Elora tonight and even more so to learn about my new position and what I'll be doing.

My father is quiet almost sad this evening, I went to sit with him before it was time to go. "Are you happy with your calling son?"

"Yes, I guess I'm surprised, I know it's an honor to be called to work in the Liaison's office."

He smiled at me and almost looked relieved. "It's an honor, although I was hoping you would join me in my trade, I'm very proud of you for your calling to the Liaison."

I gave him a pat on the back "Thank you, it means a lot to know you're proud."

"It's time to go!" Myka said as she ran for the door. Usually after an hour of working on Elora's and my cottage we go with Myka's match to work on her cottage. But tonight is different and we've agreed with Jake's family that tonight we would celebrate and they were invited to join us. Jake was an only child so his family only had one cottage to build. I know Myka was hoping they'd joined us.

Elora's family had arrived before us and had the fire lit as we arrived. Early summer evenings are still chilly. Jake's family was also here. I didn't think we had run so late. I certainly wasn't trying to as I just wanted to be sitting with Elora.

There was a chorus of happy birthdays as we came upon the gathering. I hugged, kissed cheeks, shook hands until I really was ready to just sit and relax. I took my place next to Elora and instantly our hands joined. "Good evening my love," She whispered so I only I could hear.

"I've missed you since you left my cottage and I apologize for sweeping you up publicly earlier today." She blushed instantly.

"No apology necessary, I rather enjoyed it." I gave her hand a small squeeze to reassure her that I felt the same. It is funny how when you love someone and your words and actions are limited how you can communicate with just a looks or small touch and know that is enough. We have heard and seen many matches go bad. I never fear this with Elora and I.

As the wine got passed around and we all started talking it all became a blur. The only thing I wanted to do was sit and enjoy the breeze that brought me the smell of her hair and enjoy the feeling of her tiny hand in mine. I felt like I have a million things to say to her and yet I said very little.

There is talk of my calling but I diverted it as much as I can. I know I have to remain vague. Everyone wants to know about Blitz. I told them he was a bonus for the work I'd be doing.

Kyan wondered in to give his congratulations and ask about my calling. I again said as little as possible. He told us that Leta can't make it as her mother was ill but sends her well wishes.

Our celebration was drawing to a near. We all have to go to our work and internships as normal. Before she left, Elora slipped a small sea shell into my hand.

"Happy birthday my love," She whispered. "Be sure to smell it when you're alone."

I slipped it carefully into my jacket pocket. We are only allowed to give a small kiss on the cheek as we say goodnight.

"Sleep sweetly my love." I whispered as my lips met her cheek. I could feel the heat rise on her cheek as my lips touched her. I again felt the angst again at the thought that I have just more than a year before I make her my wife.

I said my goodnight's to all, my family went in ahead of me knowing I enjoyed being alone when our evenings were drawing to a an end. I stood and watched Elora as she walked home until she disappeared inside and slowly walked into my own cottage. As I put on my nightclothes I took the sea shell and get into bed. I remember her telling me to smell it, expecting the smell of ocean I put it to my face and it smelled of her hair. That shell is the best gift of my whole day I fell asleep holding it near my face enjoying the smell.

CHAPTER 3

The Book

Iawoke early this morning, and I was engulfed by the smell of Elora's hair. I instantly thought she had snuck in my window, but as I opened my eyes I saw the dawn was coming and I felt the tiny shell in my hand. I brought it to my face to enjoy the smell that almost tortures me every time I'm with her. All I can do is smile, such a tiny gift and it meant more to me than anything I have. Usually any gifts that we trade have to be put away for our cottage but this is our secret, besides what could this shell do for our cottage? Now I'll have to quest to find her a small gift.

"Davin!" My sister nagged at the door. She always has a knack for ruining a perfect moment. I'm well aware I have to bring water up so morning meal can be made. I rose slowly and dressed quietly. The shell never far from my reach, I put it in my pocket and headed out to start my day.

I stopped in to see Blitz; we don't have a proper barn I'll have to build a small pen for him soon. Extra hay had been delivered though I ordered none. I fed him quickly and ran to get the water.

"Father, did you order extra hay?" I asked as I came in with the water.

"No, it was delivered last night after we were done celebrating." He seemed happy about this, extra hay comes from our savings although I have my own share saved he knows it would be costly for us to keep an extra horse when we could use a cow more.

Coin is only passed in our town for extra supplies, and only came to our village within the last ten years or so. Once a month all materials are gone through within each work area. Anything that is bid as an extra we gather and meet in the grove about twenty miles from our village with other villages. We trade for things we may need, the village of Gabby has honey bees so we are always able to get honey and wax. Sometimes trades can't be made and coin is exchanged. Market days are fun for all the families each will bring a tent and stay one night. We are also allowed to sell items we make within our homes with our own items. The Liaison trust in the honesty of their people, when we arrive home all the coin goes to the Liaison with lists of what brought the coin in. Ten percent goes to the town fund which is used to purchase livestock and other items needed, although we are very self sufficient and make most all we need. The rest of the coin is divided to each family. If a family doesn't show their fair share on paper they are called to the Liaison's and asked why, sometimes it's just a busy month. If it isn't a constant problem they will get their fair share, if it's a constant problem they will be shorted coin. Sometimes there are even small bonuses if a family does very well at market. The Liaison feel if we all strive together we all prosper together. And thus far it works very well with very little scuffle amongst the people.

The clerks deliver the coin share to the people. It's always in a small box, with the family name on it. You remove the coin and a paper with small notes of thank you and sometimes an explanation. It's up to the man of the house to distribute the coin. Our father always gives us a share, which we have to keep put away for our marriage. Sometimes we are allowed to bring a bronze or silver on market day. When I do, I always buy something for Elora to be put away. Bits of lace or a small vase, simple things like that. My mother says I spoil her already, but that it's not bad. Once I found some green material and my mother loaned me enough coin to purchase enough for a dress. This I never told Elora about. I plan to hire the tailor to make her a gown and it will be my wedding gift to her.

I ate quickly this morning I was very excited to get to my new work. I've wondered what exactly I'll be doing since I left yesterday. I hope whatever it is that I can make a difference and help where we struggle as a village.

As I rode through town there were many whispers about my new found fortune. I can see how my having a new horse can create a moment for idle gossip. I left Blitz with the stable boy and headed for the front doors when I noticed Wan waving me in through the back entrance near the stables.

"Good morning Davin, are you ready to get to work?" He asked with a mischievous grin on his face.

"Yes sir!" I'm truly excited.

He took me to a small room with a beautiful dark wood desk; the chair is of the same style and has a red velvet cushion which matches the drapes that hang on the wall. The book was in the middle of the desk along with paper and an ink well and a beautiful dark green feather quill. I wondered if they know I'm drawn to the color green. The desk has a back piece which sits against the wall; it contains small slots and drawers. There is also a dark wood box on the floor below my desk, it has a metal lock on it and there is a key sitting in the lock. There's a small box in one of the slots on the desk, much like the boxes used to hand out coin, it has my name written on top.

"The small box will contain your wage; all who work in the Liaison's receive a small wage." Wan said as he picked up the small box, "you have the lock box down below as well, you may keep your savings in there if you wish. The box is for the book though, when you're not in here that's where the book belongs." He handed me the small box and nodded toward my hand for me to open it. I opened it slowly; it felt heavy in my hand, inside it held two gold pieces and five silver.

He opened the lock on the big box then handed me the key. Then he opened a small drawer from the upper part of the desk and pressed the bottom of the drawer with his finger, it popped open to reveal a hidden compartment. He took the key back and put it inside the compartment then pushed the pop up piece down and closed the drawer.

"That will be your monthly wage until your leave comes. We have set your leave age at forty-six like ours. I expect when you're forty you'll start looking for your replacement. We all choose our replacements, even the clerks." I listened to him very carefully. "You'll actually take your leave at forty-seven, you'll get one year to train your replacement. Also your wage will immediately transfer to your replacement, but there has already been a leave fund set up for you many years ago so worry not." I nodded with amazement as he reached down and opened the box; it was green velvet lined and had dividers making compartments.

"The big one is for your book." He reached to the lower left compartment which is the next biggest one but the velvet sat higher than the rest, he lifted the velvet pad and there was a small wooden plank with a tiny key. He used the key to open an empty space and took my wages and dropped them into the tiny compartment, locked it and put the key back into the hidden compartment.

"What are the other slots for?" I ask in awe, I've never seen so many secrets hidden in one small area.

"You may keep what you like in there; this is your box, only you have the keys or knowledge of where the keys are. I had all this built for you many years ago when your father was a young man." This surprised me. "I knew after your birth what I intended for you, and your workmanship had proved me right time and time again. This is your office, I know I said we may build you one but this was my office and I decided you would need your privacy so I've moved out. You need to be sure the door is always shut and locked when you're in here and that no one ever sees where your keys are hidden. The blueprint for this box is under the velvet where your book hides. When you choose your student, have a wood worker you trust make you one."

"Now, open your book." He instructed me, I did as he asked.

"The first page is only what I wish of you to do, the rest is blank, I want you to keep accurate records of everything you do." I looked down on the page, it didn't have much written:

Always strive to keep our village running fair for the people.

Fight when there need be, battle to keep things just.

Always trust the Liaison to hear you fairly before jumping to swift conclusions.

Always remember to stay true to your feelings.

That was all that was said, it didn't explain much but I'm sure my training will bring more as days go by.

"Also one other thing," Wan began again. "There has been a locked box placed on the table in the main hall. In your top drawer you'll find wax and your new seal. Any inquiries to Liaison gets put in the box, they will call on you when they are ready to discuss it."

I thanked him for everything I was feeling somewhat overwhelmed. He also excused me for the day. I was hungry, so I decided I'd go to the town kitchen for mid-meal. I was careful to put everything away including both of the keys, Wan watched and smiled with pride.

CHAPTER 4

The Cottage

A FTER I ATE, I returned to the stable for Blitz. I planned to get some of my saved coin so I could purchase the wood I needed for Blitz's pen. I know I can build it behind our private garden near my father's small pen it sat very near the river. When I arrived home I heard hammering, I rode out behind our cottage to see my father with another wood worker putting together another pen.

"I was commissioned to build a pen for that massive hunk of horse you happen to be sitting on." He said as he laughed at the sight of me on Blitz.

"Wow, I was just coming home to get coin so I could get wood to do it myself." I said surprised. "What can I help with?"

"Nothing at all, but when you're in your own cottage you'll be doing this yourself." He answered still laughing. "Why not bring us some cold water though please."

I ran to get the bucket and headed to the well. We're lucky our well is not far from our house. As I came up to the well I noticed that Elora and Kyan were there.

"Why are you two here?" I asked them.

"We came to help deliver things for your new pen and your father sent us after water." Kyan said with laughter in his voice.

"Funny he sent me here as well, coincidence? I think not!" I took Elora's hand and pulled her close for a quick kiss. Kyan and I have a small agreement he lets me give her small kisses without reprimand but that is it, and it usually costs me a cup of wine.

I asked if they were off for the day, but they were only sent to help deliver items. We walked slowly back to my cottage holding hands and watching for others so we weren't noticed. We were careful to let go before my father noticed, I also showed her the shell she gave me the night before.

"You like it then?" She asked shyly.

"How could I not? I'll see you at our cottage tonight my love, until then miss me."

"I always miss you my love." She said, her voice is so quiet and soft, I could listen to her talk all day and not get tired of it.

"Farwell my love." We both whispered as our hands grazed one last time

My father was smiling big and proud as I brought both buckets of water to the pen.

"You really love that girl don't you son?"

"Yes father, I ache when she is away and I yearn for our evenings together watching our cottage come together."

He laughed, "That's wonderful you two are a true match indeed. You know your cottage is about done?"

"Heh, how would I know such a thing when I'm outside while you all work inside?" I said laughing at his question.

"I just thought it would do you good to know." He said.

"It does and it doesn't, of course I'm happy our cottage will be done in plenty of time for our marriage, but will we be allowed to see each other each evening anymore?" The despair in my voice must sound pitiful I'm sure.

"Well we'll work something out, remember we still have Myka's cottage to finish as well."

"I remember father, can I ask you a question?"

"Of course son, you may come to me about anything."

"Did you feel like this with mother? Does everyone feel like this?"

"It's said to only be like that with true matches, some people have to learn to love their match, it does not always happen like it did with you and Elora loving each other so naturally. That's why your match happened so young; we weren't the only ones who noticed you two always being drawn to each other."

"What about you and mother?" I asked again not sure if he was dodging the question or simply forgot it was part of the question.

"Our match didn't happen until I was ten and it was a strained match for some time. The first couple years we barely spoke a word to each other. But when I was just about to receive my calling we were sitting for our cottage building and I looked at her and the sun was setting low behind her and something in her smile just did something to me. I think it was that moment for her as well, she put her hand in mine and well the rest is history I guess you could say."

"Wow, what would have happened if that moment never happened?"

He smiled slyly, "well you can't break a match so we would of had to of learned to live together no matter what. Ha! Look at the Peirce's; she throws dishes at old Foster every time he angers her! But the next day you always see him coming back with wild flowers for her ready to make his apology until next time. Everybody's different son. I think you and Elora have been blessed. Always remember to treat her with love and compassion and she'll never change her love for you, and hopefully never throw a dish at you!"

We both laughed hard at that. I could never picture her being angry at me, nor I her.

"Oh yeah," My father started again. "I'm to give you this letter with instructions for you to take it to the tailors and wait for them to read it."

"Thank you father, I'll be home at supper, if I get some time I'd like to take Blitz out and see what he has in him."

"Have fun and be careful son."

I rode right over to the tailors with the letter and waited while Mr. Foley took the letter and looked it over.

"Well let's get you measured properly young man." He said as he fold the letter back in place.

"Pardon sir?" I asked quizzically.

"I'm to measure you for three riding pants, shirts and two riding jackets. Also two new black suits, according to this letter."

He measured me quietly and then handed me yet another letter to take to the boot makers. When I got there I was told I'd be receiving riding boots and dress boots. I guess it's all per request of the Liaison's. I'm assuming my suits will be somewhat the same as all of theirs.

Finally I think I'm done with all the errands and I didn't have to build my pen, I got on my horse and headed out of the village. There is a path we have made in our travels for market and I just want to go a distance and get a feel for Blitz. I started him at a trot; his gait was so smooth I was instantly comfortable, so I took him into a run. He transitioned smoothly and he ran for a few minutes. The cool summer air felt good on my face and my mind felt free as we ran to nowhere in particular, I slowed him down and turned him around and headed back to the village. I know it was short, but I didn't want to push him too hard. I'll learn his limits as time goes by. I decided to turn just outside of town and go to the small river that runs behind my cottage. I got off of Blitz and walked him into the water he seemed comfortable and even took a drink. So did I, I was thirsty and realized I have not stopped for a break since mid-meal.

As I leaned down to scoop a drink into my hand I seen a very small rock, it was almost green in color and it's shaped like a heart. I picked it up out of curiosity and I quickly realized I had found my gift for Elora. I had admittedly forgotten with all the excitement of the day. Now I'm excited for this evening when I can give it to her.

I rode slowly home, all I can think about is giving Elora my gift, hoping she likes it as much as I like my shell. I was tempted to put the shell in my small box under my new desk for safe keeping but then I couldn't enjoy the sweet smell when I'm alone.

My pen for Blitz was done, it's bigger than I had planned to build, but then he's a big horse. There's also a fresh stack of hay and a bag of oats off to the side. There's a barrel for water and my father wisely put it where both horses can reach it for drinking. I led Blitz into his new pen and began to remove his saddle. They also built a small shed where I could keep my saddle and tack. I carried my father's in there as well. Then I set forth to brush and feed Blitz. As I brushed him he seemed to enjoy it, he constantly used his nose to nuzzle my neck and made soft noises in my ear. It's a good thing I didn't ride longer, now I have little time to get ready for supper, and I know I'll need to run to the river to wash and put fresh clothes on.

"I heard a bit of news on my way home this evening." My mother announced as she sets supper on the table.

"What's that?" Myka asked her.

"The traveling side show is setting up north of town!" My mother exclaimed.

The traveling side show comes every year. When word spreads that they are setting up the Liaison's act quick and allow everyone an early day so the festivities can be enjoyed by all. I'll have to remember to bring some extra coin from my job tomorrow. There's always plenty of sweet stuff to eat, games to play, and shows to see. I've always enjoyed the strong man, even as a young boy I'd beg my mother to let me see him. I also enjoy all the different animals in the cages, I'm sad to see them caged but they're animals we would never see around here, so my enjoyment is bittersweet.

After our supper we left to go work on my cottage, I picked a small yellow tulip for Elora out of our flower bed and hid the small stone inside of it. I'm allowed to bring her flowers, but if the rock is seen it will be put in Elora's box of our marriage things. The families were so quiet working on the cottage tonight we were able to speak in private.

"When you're alone look in the petals, I've hidden a trinket for you." I whispered when I gave her the tulip.

"Thank you my love, I'm sure I'll treasure it." Elora's voice is so small she needs not even to whisper.

"Have you heard the traveling side show shall be tomorrow evening?" I ask in my normal voice, so the nosey family thinks we are simply conversing.

"Yes, but I'm sad we'll lose our evening together."

"I am as well my love. It seems so far from our ceremony doesn't it?" I asked hoping to hear that she is just as excited to be with me as I am to be with her.

"Yes it feels like forever to me!" She exclaims almost too loudly I saw my sisters nosey eyes peek out the front window.

To hear this from Elora makes me so happy I'm almost afraid to give her the news my father passed to me earlier today, yet I know I must.

"My father says work on our cottage is almost done." I told her with sadness filling my words I watched as tears came to her beautiful green eyes, her sadness hurts me so bad.

"I've heard the same from my mother, Davin I thought we would have every night together like this."

"My father says we'll find ways to be together, we still have Myka's cottage to finish too. She is only twelve so it's still small work, I'll have some time in the evenings."

She smiled at this news, I'm sure my father is right in his prediction that we are a true match. I gave her hand a small squeeze to reassure her of my love. The door of the cottage opened quickly and both of our families came out, everyone was smiling and they were holding small cups of wine.

"We sit out here alone while you all get happy on the drink?" I asked as I helped Elora to her feet.

"We are done!" Myka yelled as our mothers brought us wine.

Elora looked at me horror stricken and I felt my heart crash with emotion.

"Done already? You can't be! I'm sure you have forgotten something?" I asked hoping to prolong our evening together.

"No son, we are done and if I must say it's a most beautiful cottage, all the way down to the curtains your mothers worked so hard on hand stitching in the late hours of each evening after you have gone to sleep." My father announced with such pride that I didn't want to disappoint him with our sadness.

"A toast! To our beautiful children, and a marriage that has made these families friends." Elora's father announces as we all raise our goblets in unison, "To friends!" Everyone cheered.

I bid my farewell to Elora and her family as we left to go to Myka's cottage.

"I'll see you at the side show tomorrow my love." I said as I I kissed her cheek I whispered, "Do not fret we'll find a way." I promised with my kiss.

Elora's sad tear filled eyes haunted my dreams all night and my sleep was fitful. There must be a way that we can still see each other without breaking the rules. It's so unfair to just cut off our evenings after so many years.

There's so much excitement in the village as everyone prepares for the traveling side show this evening, everybody is working hard as they all know they have to try and get a full day's work into a half a day. The people of our village are always eager workers and so a day like this with so much excitement it's hard to ignore the feeling of it, even with the sadness that I felt right now.

I went straight to my little office this morning, I didn't want anyone seeing my sadness and thinking that I'm unhappy with my calling. I heard a small knock at my door, It was Wan.

"Davin?" Wan called out to me.

"Yes sir?" I asked as I opened the door to let him in.

"There's really no time to get into much today with the events this evening." Wan announced as he took a seat next to my desk.

"Yes, the excitement has Furlin in a busy buzz of activity doesn't it?" I asked, not really looking for an answer.

"Why do you seem so sad on such a joyous day then Davin?" He asked me. It's almost like Wan is in my head. It's not the first time he has spoken my thoughts.

"Our cottage was finished last night." I'm sure my answer is full of the sadness that has seemed to take over me.

"And this is sad news for you?" He asked in amazement.

"I won't get to sit with Elora every evening, and we have over a year until we can be bound!" I told him with my voice full of despair.

"That's interesting." He said quietly. When I looked up at him he looked as if he was in deep thought.

"So, it appears we may have a true match?"

"Appears?" I almost yelled at his realization. "My heart is so heavy at even thought of not seeing her every evening that I almost want to cry! My heart hurts when we bid farewell each night! I dream of her and wake looking for her to be by my side! I love her and have loved her since I was a small boy."

"Calm down son, you'll be able to see her each day. I'll arrange for you to have mid-meal with her in the village kitchen. It's public so you mustn't do anything to make me regret that I'm doing this for you, but I can't have a heart broken watcher on my hands!"

"You can do that? Isn't against the rules? H-h-how?" I'm almost in tears with the excitement of such a gift.

"Of course I can do it." He says like I'm requesting an extra ration of milk or something.

"I'll speak with the Liaison today, we'll have the clerks deliver a letter informing both of your parents of our decision and it will be done." He said with authority. "We have done this before; it won't be such an unusual request really."

"I don't know what to say, this means so much thank you!"

"You're welcome." He said as if he hadn't just given me a great gift. "Now I have a few things to discuss with you before I excuse you for the day, it will be much easier now that you don't look like someone just stole your most prized possession." He said with laughter in his voice.

"Wan, she is my most prized possession!" I said a laughing with him. I feel like a fool a little bit, men are supposed to be tough and honorable and here I'm sulking over a cottage being finished.

"I can see that," he said thoughtfully. "Now I hear you got all your fittings done yesterday, after you're done here go see if anything is done for you. You need to show you work in the Liaison's and being properly attired is important. Also tonight at the side show you have your first task. Part of your job is seeing that our village is running smoothly and determining if changes need to be made to keep it this way. Just listen to the people Davin. Listen for complaints of unhappiness or suffrage. We need to know all that is happening with our people." His instructions are so precise I always feel like he says just enough but never too much. He doesn't seem a man who is free with his words.

He handed me two silver coins. "Consider tonight work and enjoy yourself."

Before I left I put the silver I had yesterday back in my box and took a few bronze pieces, locked everything back up and headed for the tailors to see about my new clothing. Just my riding jacket was done, so I left it there until more was ready.

It seems the entire town is having mid-meal at the town kitchen today. It's probably easier than trying to prepare and clean after a meal before they run to the side show. I saw Elora in the back of the line and I quickly went to her so I could give her the good news, she still looked very sad but smiles when she sees me coming.

"I have good news my love!" I announce as I take her hand and slip two bronze in her palm. "In case I don't see you before you want to do something fun."

"Many thanks my love, what news do you bring me?" She asked in her sweet quiet voice.

Quietly I told her about my talk with Wan and how we can have mid-meal together until we are bound. She was happy but worried her parents will not let it be allowed, I assured her it will happen. We stayed together through mid-meal and I reminded her many times it was our first of many. Looking around I noticed more today in the kitchen than I had before. There were many like us waiting for their ceremony to come that were dining together. I suppose Wan was right when he said it has been done before, I'll have to dine here tomorrow and see if it's the same.

CHAPTER 5

The Traveling Side show

I WALKED WITH MY family to the side show instead of riding Blitz, events like this are a treat and should be enjoyed with family. There are a lot families walking near us, and the excitement of the young children is spreading to everyone else. The smell of food around us is intoxicating.

I felt someone grabbing for my hand, pick pocketing isn't tolerated in our village but you can never be sure if people from other villages have followed the caravan across the countryside to make profit on unsuspecting people. I turned around quickly to find Elora.

"You walk too fast my love; excited to see if you're as big as the strong man this year?" She teased.

"No! I should have never let you see me admire how big he is!" I said laughing at her teasing. "Where is your family?"

"They're back a little bit, when I saw you my mother gave me permission to catch up with you and your family." She looked back at her mother who was smiling.

"Elora, I'm so glad to have you join us." My mother said as she gave Elora a hug. I'm instantly jealous I want to hug her too. I think our parents are conspiring to give us time together. I wonder that maybe it is suppose to be this way, why not just tell us so we don't feel as if we are sneaking around and fear punishment.

"I can see tents!" Myka yelled, she adored the monkeys and that's all she talked about afterwards.

As we walked into the side show we saw tents of yellow, blue and red. There are men standing outside the tents yelling things like, "Come one come all see the fat woman eat a pie!" They set up a large fence around the show and it cost a bronze to get in. That way you can go in all the tents and the side show freaks get paid for their small shows.

"I'll pay this time." I told them proudly.

The man taking coin is very tall and he is wearing a suit that is red and white striped with a tall black hat on his head. His moustache is long and curled at the end and he has a small patch of hair on his chin that he has combed into a point, he's almost scary looking. Every year I think they should get a more cheerful person to greet you and take your coin.

I gave him one of the silver coins. "We have a rich man among us!" He yelled, I felt the heat rise to my face I put out my hand for my change.

"Five bronze, have fun rich man!" He said as I continued walking into the gate.

"Let's just invite the pick pockets over!" My father said as he walks past the gate keeper.

"Don't worry father I have deep pockets, I'll feel if anyone tries to take it." I laughed. The man tried to give a small apology but my father pushed us all forward.

The show is set up in a big circle and made so you can walk from one thing to another without getting lost. It seems bigger this year, I wonder if there were some new shows to be seen. In the middle of the circle you can find food and drinks as well as some games where you can win little trinkets.

The first tent is small and is bright blue in color. The man outside is yelling like all the others. You can't really hear what they're saying, the noise is so loud. There's a hand drawn picture of a sea lion on a box with a ball on his nose. As we went inside the tent the air was cool and the smell of fish was over whelming.

"Look how cute it is!" Myka said. "Can I feed him a fish?" A tall skinny boy handed her a fish and instructed her how to feed it. My mother warned her if she got bit she'll not feel sorry for her. We all roared with laughter, as she now looked regretful for asking to feed it.

"Go on feed it!" I told her. "You'll be fine, now you're just teasing the poor little guy!" She gave him his fish without incident he took it to his little pool and ate it. He was pretty interesting but the smell of fish was bad enough for all us and we took our leave quickly.

Elora's family came up behind us, finally catching up. Our fathers shook hands and we all stepped away from the line to the next tent to talk.

"Did you get a note from the Liaison's?" Mr. Dover asked my parents.

"Yes we got it, I expected it though. Don't you remember getting the same letter when you were courting?" My father asked.

"Yes, but back then it wasn't my little girl." He said laughing.

"It'll be fine it's only a meal in a room full of people." My father said reassuringly.

During this whole exchange Elora and I kept quiet and our mothers had big knowing smiles on their faces.

"Well; you two lovebirds have permission to take your mid-meal together on work days at the village kitchen." Mr. Dover said to us.

"Thank you Sir." I said as I reached to shake his hand. Elora remained quiet as that is her role she is to be passive in the presence of men. It is one rule I don't care much for but it's a tradition.

"What shall we see next?" My mother asked trying to end the uncomfortable situation.

"We can go to the next tent." I offered and took Elora's hand in mine again.

The next tent was red and bigger than the one that had the seal in it. The man outside is inviting us in to see some of the side show freaks. He is yelling about a fat lady, a tiny man, a woman with a beard and a man who swallows fire. "Come see the freaks!" The man yelled louder as we get closer.

The fat lady was huge and she has food all around her. She looked sad as we enter the tent but she put on a smile as she saw us come inside. Elora's little brother Eldon who's also twelve, looked at her his eyes so huge and I could see sorrow in his face.

"You're not a freak." He told her. She got tears in her eyes, I almost felt ashamed not only for myself but for her to be put on display like so.

The tiny man is very small, maybe the size of a three year old. He has a moustache and is wearing tiny little overalls. His area shows all things that make life difficult for him being so little. There's a table with a mug of ale sitting on it, he reached up to grab for the ale to show that he couldn't reach it. Also a horse that he couldn't even get his feet up in the stirrups to climb into the saddle; in fact he could walk under the horse. We all laughed at that.

The bearded lady just sits in a blue velvet chair combing her long, dark beard which reaches down to her chest. In our village not many men wore beards, so to say she is a sight to see just doesn't explain the shock of seeing her sitting there combing her long facial hair.

The fire eating man was very exciting there were a few people gathered around him watching him perform his freakish talent. He was using what looked like an arrow and dipped it into a jar of liquid then he touched it to a torch to light it. He did some twists and turns to show the fire and make it look more exciting then he opened his mouth and put the fire in his mouth and when he took it out the fire had been put out. There were a lot of Oooh's and Ahhh's from the crowd. Then he dipped the arrow in the liquid again and took a small drink of the liquid, he touched the arrow to the torch again and then slowly brought it to his face and turned slightly from the crowd, he then blew at the fire and the fire exploded forward in a big burst of fireball. Everybody clapped with excitement, the liquid he used smelled like the oil we use in my fathers' shop.

We left the tent and headed to the food and drink booths. My father and Mr. Dover went to get drinks while Myka and Eldon ran to get us a place to sit at the tables. The rest of us were in search for the new treats that the side show always brought. We found rum soaked cherries that were dipped in white sugar before they put them on the plates. And peach bread with dollops of butter on them. They also had maple hard candies that we could take home. I bought an extra bag of the candies to keep in my box at the Liaison.

We joined the others at the table to enjoy our little trove of treats. The ale at the side show is a lot different than what we brew in our village. Our ale is light and pale in color, side show ale is thick and almost a brown in color. They kept it cold and the flavor was very strong but good, but any more than two and you were drunk. I'll stop at one; it's so heavy I don't think I could drink much more.

I was listening to the talk of the villagers as we ate our treats. The most complaints I heard was that people wanted more flour, if they wanted bread at night they couldn't have biscuits in the morning. There were also complaints about the lack of butte, I'll talk with Wan and let him know what I've heard.

We went to the strong mans tent next; I endured the quiet teasing from Elora. But it was an exciting little show he lifted very heavy objects in the air. He even picked up people to show how strong he was, his arms are huge as is the rest of him. Elora can tease me all she wants it's still my favorite part of the show.

There were a lot of wagons that had been opened on the sides to reveal caged animals. They all have big red words painted on them announcing what they are. There was a lion and of course the monkeys that Myka loved so much. We also saw an alligator, it was so big and scary that Elora wouldn't look. And there was a lady walking around with a huge white and orange snake with pink eyes around her neck, she said it was a python, and that it ate rabbits. She let us touch it, I thought it would be slimy but it felt like leather, it was so soft and smooth. Even Elora and my mother touched it admiring its beauty.

We went to play some games afterwards. One bronze got you three tickets for games. I spent three bronze and shared my tickets with Myka and Eldon, Elora didn't want to play. We all won a few trinkets; I won a small bracelet that was made of knotted string and beads which I gave to Myka, because it was blue her favorite color. She won a couple lemon candies playing a game where you throw balls at metal bottles and try to knock them off a stool. I was just putting a lemon candy in my mouth when I heard shouting toward the front gates. At first I thought it was a pick pocket being caught. I quickly realized it was not.

"There's a fire in the village!" I heard a woman yell.

I let go of Elora and told her to keep Myka and Eldon safe with her and ran following where the men and women were running to. As soon as I got out the gate I could see the flames and smoke as I ran towards it. I was trying to figure out where it was coming from when I realized it was near our row of cottages, I ran even faster worried about Blitz. As I got closer I became painfully aware of what was on fire.

It was the Dover's cottage, I watched as the men ran for buckets and formed a line from the river and began passing the buckets of water towards the cottage. The fire is in the entire cottage, I could feel the heat on my face and the smell and smoke was burning my nose and eyes. When my father saw me amongst the crowd that was gathering he ordered me to go get Elora and the kids. My walk back to the side show wasn't festive at all I couldn't imagine how I was going to tell Elora and Eldon that it's their cottage on fire.

"What's on fire?" Elora asked as I walked up to them.

"I'm sorry Elora; it is your family's cottage." I watched as tears came freely out of her eyes. Eldon also began to cry silently. Myka took his hand and tried to comfort him. He only looked silently into her face, looking as if he was a lost child.

"How could this of happened? I put the cook fire out myself; I even put my hand in the ash to make sure it was out." Elora sobbed as we walked slowly back towards their cottage.

"The men are working hard to get the fire out; they have formed a line to the river and are pouring buckets of water on it. Maybe it can be saved." I told her trying to sound hopeful, although I knew not much would be saved. The fire had taken the entire cottage and was starting to burn itself out as we had all arrived back with our parents.

CHAPTER 6

Devastation

THE FIRE HAD LEFT the house in ruins, but the men had it out in about an hour. My mother and father offered to let the Dover's to stay at our cottage until they could figure out what do next. Eldon will stay in my room; I gave him clean sleeping clothes and took him to the river to wash with me. We were all covered in soot from helping put the fire out I also brought soap and linens to dry off with. We cleaned up in silence, though I heard Eldon sobbing I did not want to embarrass him by pointing it out.

"It will be alright Eldon." I tried to reassure him. "We'll figure out what to do tomorrow."

"I know it's just sad. That was our home and everything we worked for is gone like it was never there." It's so profound to think how happy we were just hours ago without a care in the world.

When we got back to our cottage it broke my heart to see Elora's face black with soot, and the tear stains that ran down her cheeks are proof of her pain.

"My love, go with Myka and go clean up. I'll get some sleeping clothes from my mother for you." I went to my parent's room where they were getting together sleeping clothes for Elora's parents.

"Mother, Elora and Myka are going to the river to clean up do you have sleeping clothes Elora can use?"

"Here son," she said handing me a thick night gown. "Give her some clean linen's and soap as well please.

"I will mother, I helped Eldon get cleaned up and I'm going get him settled in bed while everyone cleans up. I'll get some wine poured as well." I told her, she looked relieved for the help.

After everyone was cleaned up we sat to have some wine. Elora and I sat in the window seat silently just looking toward what use to be her cottage, I didn't even know what to say to her.

"Elora dear, get some sleep we'll go early and see if anything is salvageable." Mrs. Dover told her.

"Good night and thank you for the sleeping clothes Mrs. Hewit." She said not even looking at anyone or anything just moving silently to Myka's sleeping room.

"Good night for me as well, I'll do all I can to help tomorrow." I told them, I'm sure it went unheard everyone was in a daze even me.

I woke early, even before the sun. I heard noises in the kitchen and even some laughter as the women worked to make morning meal. Eldon was just waking up too. .

"In that chest are clothes I've grown out of, find yourself something to wear. I'm sure it won't take long to get you some more clothes."

"Thank you Davin you're a good friend; even to a kid like me." He looked exhausted, I'm sure he didn't sleep much.

"You're my little brother kid, how could I not be there for you squirt?" He hated when I called him squirt but this morning it made him smile.

I went into the kitchen to get the water bucket, as I looked over to Elora she was sitting in the window again. She was also wearing a dress made of the material I bought at market months ago for her.

"Mother, when did you make the dress?" I asked confused, as I had planned to have the dressmaker's do it before our wedding as a gift for her.

"I've worked on it over the last month, something told me to, I just can't explain it son." She said almost apologetically.

"It's beautiful mother! I could never have the dressmakers make a better one, thank you." She smiled softly to me and gave me a hug.

"Go tell her how beautiful she looks; maybe you can get a smile on her sad face."

I walked slowly across the room as she looked up there was still tears in her eyes. I smiled for she is truly beautiful with or without the dress or the tears.

"Good morning beautiful!" I said and pulled her up for a small hug.

"There's the smile I've been waiting for all morning." My mother said from in front of the cook fire, even Elora's mother had to smile. Our fathers were at the Dover's burnt cottage already to see what could be done.

"Come eat before these biscuits get cold children." My mother likes our meals to be served and eaten as soon as she takes it off the fire. As we ate the room is very quiet, there wasn't much to be said and we were all weary from last night. Our fathers came in as we were finishing.

"I have good news and bad news." Announced Mr. Dover

"The bad news first is best, makes room to enjoy the good news." My father said to break the ice.

"Well," began Mr. Dover. "The cottage is not usable it will need to be torn all the way down. But our coin did not get ruined I even found Elora's and Eldon's so they have their savings as well." He did sound somewhat relieved as he let it out, it was not easy news to bring to a family you loved so much.

"Well that is wonderful news!" Exclaimed Mrs. Dover, she is a cheery woman anyway, I know she is trying very hard not to let the fire ruin her spirits.

"Is there anything else that was salvageable?" She asked, I'm sure she was hoping for something else to be saved.

"Well the pots for cooking could use a cleanup and they will be fine. I'm sure there are a few small things here and there as well, we'll have to pick through as we get the old cottage torn down."

"No one was hurt and that's the most important thing to me." He says as if that finishes the conversation.

I left for work so I could try to get done early and help with the cleanup. I also had a note asking for a day off for the Dover's to settle their business before returning to their work. As I came around with Blitz a clerk from the Liaison's was walking towards me. He simply told me to tell the Dover's to take the day off without worry.

I went back in the house to return the note and tell them what the clerk said, they were relieved. Missing work is a big deal it means your share gets put onto others. I said goodbye again, and looked one last time at Elora, she seemed to be cheering up a bit. As I came into the stable at the Liaison's Wan was waiting for me.

"Was anyone hurt?" He asked with his voice full of concern.

"No sir, just sad over such a loss." I can't think of any other words to describe it.

"We are planning a meeting, the Dover's and your parents will be there, I also expect you and Elora to be there as this will concern you both as well."

"There's a meeting?" I asked feeling confused.

"Yes, remember we work together in this village I'll not have a family left to struggle when something like this happens. We have never had something like this happen, so we'll all learn from this together."

"What time will the meeting be?" I asked now full of curiosity, I can see he has something planned.

"Before mid-meal, I have the hall being set up so we can all dine after we discuss this situation. I'll have a clerk deliver a letter in just a few moments he is preparing it now; I want it delivered before your family leaves for work." He said walking towards the back door. "Your office, so we can do some work before the meeting."

I followed him inside and we go to my office, before he stepped in he told a clerk to bring us some ale.

"Did you do as I asked last night at the side show?" He asked as he took the mugs of ale from the clerk and closed and locked the door.

"I did listen, it was a festive mood and the people seemed happy, there were some complaints of not enough flour in the weekly rations and the lack of butter amongst some families as they enjoyed the foods though."

"What do you think is the problem?" He asked.

"I know for families if they have biscuits in the morning then plan on having bread with supper it becomes difficult stretching it out and getting butter with daily rations is becoming harder, they aren't complaining of the shortage on the milk rations but it has been noticed by some." I tell him from what I heard the night before and seen in my own household.

"The cows are getting old we'll need to refresh our stocks soon." He said more thinking to himself than speaking to me. "How would you feel if I sent you with a few companions to buy some stock in the next week?"

"Where would I go?" Other than market I've never been anywhere else. I'm a little nervous but I tried not to show it.

"I would send you to Breakstone; I hear they have a very fair market on cattle. I'll send you with two clerks and a punisher most likely Sid, he's the most intimidating and will help deter thieves while you travel." He said and took a drink of his ale.

Sid is the biggest punisher of all; he is very intimidating looking simply because he stands over a foot taller than most grown men in our village. The people have nick named him Skullmaker, I don't think he minds, he does after all have a reputation to keep.

"Just let me know what I need to do to plan for our journey and I'll be ready." I told Wan almost excited that I could do something to help.

"I'll have everything put together and leave the instructions on your desk when I've finished. As for the flour I'll check in at the mill and see how our supply looks, if we are doing well I'll have an extra pound of flour added to weekly rations." He said thoughtfully.

"Thank you Wan, I'm sure the extra flour will be a big help to most everyone."

"I think that is all for now, would you like to come see how the hall is coming along with me? You need to get to know everyone in these offices in order to do your job properly anyway." He said as he got up to leave the room, I followed him as he had asked.

In the hall tables have been put in and the chairs set around them so we could dine later. The clerks and Liaisons were busy coming in and out checking to make sure all is set up according to someone's plan. The windows have been opened to allow the breeze in and fresh wildflowers have been placed on the tables. It looks cheery in here, maybe I'm getting used to it, the first time I was summoned here I was alone and unsure of where my future stood. Now I know and the room isn't as scary as it seemed before.

"We'll be meeting in about an hour, I expect everyone to be in place when the families arrive." Announced Wan, it was an order more than a request.

I went quietly behind the stables and picked some wildflowers to surprise Elora with. I had planned to do it for her mid-meal with me if she came; I even brought a green ribbon to tie around the flowers. I set them in my office and went to the hall for the meeting. When I entered the hall Jobe called for me to come to him.

"For normal Liaison meetings your seat is over there." He stated pointing to a table that runs down the length of the room. "That's where all clerks sit you'll be taking the first seat near the Liaison's table. Today though, we'll all sit together at this table I've placed cards with everybody's name on it as to where they will sit. Find your place and your families now so when they are announced you can help them find their seats."

"Also before I forget we'll be standing together by that wall." He pointed where there is no furniture. "When the families are announced, I also put one of your finished suits and boots in your office please get changed quickly as we'll be announcing the families very soon, a clerk has just left to get them." He walked away before I could even respond.

I took the flowers I had picked Elora and set them where the place card said her name and looked how they had placed our fathers together and worked the families to their sides.

I went quickly to my room and started putting on my new suit. I put my hand in the suit pocket and found a small note it simple read "Please bring suit to the tailors once a week for cleaning and repairs and it will be returned the following day." My mother will be happy to hear she won't have to clean this heavy suit I think to myself.

The suit is black like the others in the Liaison office it's very heavy just picking it up. I dressed quickly in the suit and felt dreary it was heavy and stuffy. Before now my clothing was a lot simpler.

Within a few minutes there is a small knock on my door, it was Jobe and he simply told me. "It's time."

CHAPTER 7

Solutions

I STOOD WITH THE clerks as my family and the Dover's were announced into the hall they all looked confused. I walked over to take my mother's arm and directed everyone to follow me. They all seemed relieved to see me but their quizzical looks to me are of no use, I knew nothing of what is about to take place. After everyone was seated, Jobe announced the Liaison's. Eldest to youngest they entered and took their seats. I'm still learning their names but I know all their faces and even know a couple from around the village. Wan is the only Liaison left standing even the clerks had dutifully taken their seats.

"It's with great sorrow that this meeting has come to be." He began slowly, looking as sad as the Dover's, he has always been known as a caring man and many know he works hard for the people and can be trusted to do right by his decisions that affect our village.

"Dover's; I'm truly sorry for what has happened to your cottage, and that is why I called you all here today. You cannot remain without a cottage, although we are all grateful the Hewit's have given you shelter."

As I looked around at our two little families I noticed my mother seemed very uncomfortable. Like she didn't want to be in this room, maybe she had a bad experience with her calling and I've just never heard of it.

"I have a solution in mind, the Liaison and I talked it over and we feel it's the only way, and I just want to ask that you all hear me out before you protest." He asked sympathetically.

Everyone nodded to show they agreed. Though, they looked even more nervous than before.

"Davin tells me your families work on his and Elora's cottage has been finished. Is this correct?" He asked the parents.

"Everything but the furniture and personal belongings, Sir." My father said with pride.

"We have decided that the best solution is for the Dover family to take the cottage just finished." Every one of us gasped at this.

"We are not trying to take away the hard work that both your families have put into this getting the cottage ready for the ceremony. But we also know the importance of each family having its own cottage. We'll have the stone layers go in immediately to add an extra sleeping room for Elora. It should be done by this evening with the full man power we have headed out there." He seemed regretful he had to make such a decision, this has never happened in our village.

"There are just a few other things I'd like to discuss with you, then I've arranged mid-meal to be brought in so we can dine together. Now we have always made sure to keep within job areas extra items set aside in case there ever be a need. JD knows all too well how we keep the woodworkers busy." JD is what they call my father; his given name is Jacob Davin Hewit. They have called him JD since he was a baby though. My father laughed and nodded as if to say he knew all too well.

"I've sent word around to all the work places. We'll get together anything that can help." He said with authority. "Also last night after the people at the side show heard of the bad news the gatekeeper came to me with a wonderful idea. Tonight we'll call the whole town out to help in any way they can, clothes, dishes, coin anything they can donate will be given to the Dover's, of that anything they don't need or want will be put away in case this ever happens to another family. The gatekeeper also asked me to give you this on behalf of donations given last night by all the workers of the side show." He handed Mr. Dover a small velvet purse heavy with coin. "The side show is also staying a few extra days and they have all offered to help you get moved into your new cottage."

All of this news was so overwhelming everyone was in tears. "Is there any questions I can answer for you?" Wan asked us as he saw the tears on our faces; he gave us a look of pure understanding.

"Where will Elora and Davin live if we take their cottage?' Mrs. Dover asked over her tears.

"Leave that to us, we promise that this beautiful match will have a cottage by the day they are bound." Wan answered her, I'm sure they shouldn't be worried about that at this moment.

"Mr. and Mrs. Dover you have done so much in our village, you always do your share and a little extra, let the village help you as you would help any other person if they had been put in such a terrible situation." Wan plead with them; he knows he has a village full of proud people.

"There are no words for such kindness and for the people of the side show to offer help and give us coin when they don't even know us!" Mrs. Dover said to Wan with tears in her eyes.

"When the gatekeeper requested to see me last night I was just as surprised. He said of all the villages they travel to each year this one is a favorite of his people. They say they have never been robbed here, that families send out jars of preserves and other goods to them he says it's their duty to help. I'm happy that our village has been so kind to them." Wan answered her, hoping that she will have the same understanding he has also came to.

"Now if that's all of the questions, the hunters got a turkey yesterday and those in the village kitchen have been working hard to prepare a feast to show they are also thinking of your families."

"Call in the kitchen!" Wan told Jobe.

Within minutes the table is set as we sit there and a feast fit for the king was brought in for us. There was turkey of course, bread and butter, roasted potatoes with onions and herbs, cherry tarts, and cherry wine, which according to Wan had been sent in from a family in the village. We all ate quietly I think more than anything we were shocked of how quickly a tragedy is turned around in a village that cares about each other whether they are family or not.

After we all ate, it remained quiet until Wan stood up and announced that it was time for things to begin.

"All the clerks have been instructed to set out around the village and notify everyone of the gathering tonight, and what it's for. Just so you all know we'll meet as dusk, the gatekeeper has brought in a wagon for our use along with a driver and a few friends to help us move things. So first thing we need to do is go to the woodworkers shop, JD can take you through of course, get your tables and beds, anything you'll need from there feel free to take it."

He picked up a sheet of paper and gave it to my father. "Jd I'll need an inventory brought to us after all is taken care of. Make sure the Dover's get everything they need."

"Yes Sir." My father said with a smile.

"I've had the wagon taken over there and they should be ready for you to tell them what to move and where to move it." Wan concluded. "I shall see you at dusk, thanks for dining with us it has been enjoyable."

We all went quickly over to the woodworkers shop and my father showed Mr. and Mrs. Dover around and helped them pick everything they would need. The side show people were there as promised, ready to help. The strong man was amongst them to help with the heavy stuff. They were all very nice to us all and seemed so happy to be there helping us out.

My mother excused herself and went to the town kitchen to ask if cool water could be brought to those helping us.

Even Elora had become happy again. She looked even more beautiful in her dress when she smiled.

"I forgot to tell you thank you for my stone." She said when we were waiting for the furniture to be picked and moved.

"I found it washing in the creek it was perfect, later I'll try to have it made into a necklace for you." I told her quietly.

"I'd like that very much."

"Are you happier now, knowing you'll have a cottage again?" I ask her.

"I'm sad we are losing our cottage."

"Elora, the Liaison is right, it's the only way, they'll figure our cottage out later. I trust Wan, he'll see that it's done. I'm not upset, I'm happy for your family and hopeful for our future together. If I have to build our marriage cottage myself I will, I promise you we'll be bound on time for I can't wait a moment longer than I already have!"

"Then I'll be sad no longer, I promise. Do you have a bronze I can use until I can get some coin later?" She asked me.

"What do you need? I'll take care of it right now." I'd walk across a fire for her if she asked me to just to see her happy.

"I lost my hair soap in the fire I'd like to get some from the common before we go back to your cottage." I did notice her hair didn't have the smell that usually engulfs me when we are together.

"Stay put I'll be back shortly and it won't be like a gift that has to be put away this time no one will think twice about it." I lightly kissed her cheek and ran towards the common.

The common is a building where we go pick up our weekly rations of food and other needs. As I entered I noticed the shop is in a flurry of work. Isabell, a lady who treats everyone like they are child of hers came over to help me.

"Davin, I'm so sorry about what has happened. Please anything we can do to help, don't hesitate to come to us." Isabell married but never had children; her husband died just three years after they were bound. She isn't as old as our parents but she has never had another match made for her. She never seemed bitter or angry, but in her eyes we are all her kids, she'll even scold us if need be.

"Isabell, Elora has nothing left; can you help me with any personal items she gets here normally like her hair soap that smells of magnolias?" I asked her and offered her the coins I had left from last night.

"Put your coins away young man! I'll have none of that at a time like this. Give me ten minutes and I'll have Elora restocked with all her needs from us." I'm sixteen and she still scolds me like a five year old. It's endearing though, to be cared for by someone you sometimes only see once a week to fulfill the ration list.

She came out a few minutes later with a box the size of a bucket. "If she needs anything else come right back and I mean it!" She hugged me tight and told me to pass it to Elora for her.

"Farewell Isabell." I called back as I opened the door to leave.

"Farewell my handsome Davin." She has called me that since I was six when I fell and bruised my forehead. She said no matter what was on my face I'd still be the most handsome boy she knew. Isabell always makes you feel special when you're with her.

I ran all the way back to Elora, when she looked at me she laughed and asked, "Isabell?"

"Well who else would go to all the trouble to make sure you have everything you need or want that is in the common?" I teased and we both were laughing. "Now promise me you'll make your hair smell of my shell again or I'll have to plug my nose when I'm around you!"

Your terrible Davin, you would never do such a thing even if I washed my hair in fish!"

"Alright, I think I might actually have to hold my nose if you did that!" I enjoyed teasing her, her face turned pink and her smile got so big. I think she enjoyed it as much as I enjoyed doing it.

"It looks like they're about done I guess we'll get to see the inside of our cottage before we are bound after all!" She said with a sd tone in her voice.

"Davin, head over to the cottage so you can help us unload everything." My father told me.

I decided to leave Blitz and walk with Elora to the cottage. It's a beautiful day, I love early summer months everything feels so fresh and alive. I know it should be a somber sad day but when I'm with Elora and see her smile I forget everything that is troubling me

As we arrived at the cottage I could see five men busy working on the extra room for Elora. They had the stone walls up and I could see the chimney coming up as one of the men was working on it. The others were putting the shingles on the roof. The room from outside looked very large, much larger than the average sleeping room.

We all worked hard throughout the rest of the afternoon. My mother and Mrs. Dover were in and out, either bringing us cold water or arranging furniture. When supper time came my mother and Myka went to our cottage to make us all a quick supper so we could wash and run to meet with the villagers as Wan instructed.

The evening was nice; a big bon fire greeted us along with the entire town, everyone with gifts in their hands and smiles on their faces. I knew then even more that the Dover's would be able to overcome this tragedy.

They received coin, jars of preserves and honey, candles, clothes, even small pieces of furniture. Mr. and Mrs. Dover thanked everyone over and over. By the time everyone had given their gifts the side show wagon was almost full again. We were excused early from the gathering so we could help unload the wagon again and the Dover's could get settled into their new cottage. It was dark by the time we were done and we were all exhausted, the Dover's thanked everyone in our family so much I think they were losing their voices.

"Davin, tell Elora goodnight quickly as I'm sure she is as tired as we all are." My mother whispered as she headed toward our cottage.

"Yes mother, I'll be right behind you." It seemed to me they are leaving Elora and I alone more than before I'm not sure if this will become normal or if it's just because of the events that have happened over the last two days.

"My love I bid you the sweetest of dreams in your new bed." I whispered as I took her in my arms.

"Sleep well my love and thank you for the beautiful dress." She said softly with her lips touching my cheek. "How did you know?" I asked thinking my mother might have told her.

"Only you would pick something this beautiful to match my eyes." She kissed me lightly on the cheek and turned to walk back into her cottage.

I know she'll enjoy her new sleeping room a lot; it was larger then I thought. There was also a small table with a mirror and drawers brought in so she could sit and brush her hair. It's a beautiful room fit for a princess. I can't help but wonder if Wan had anything to do with it. I feel like he goes out of his way for me and the ones I love.

CHAPTER 8

Planning the trip

I HARDLY KNEW WHERE I was when I first woke this morning. I don't even remember getting in my own bed. I knew I was exhausted but didn't realize how much until this morning, my body was so sore and yesterday's events are still running through my mind. Now my biggest worry was what would Elora and I do for a cottage, I know Wan did his best for the Dover's but I'm feeling somewhat selfish about losing our cottage. I know he said he would take care of it and I shouldn't worry but I'm just so afraid they will make us wait longer to marry.

I walked to the Liaison this morning wishing I had at least walked Blitz back to his pen last night, I felt bad I didn't even feed or brush him before nightfall. I walked around to the back of the building he had fresh hay out and seemed fine. I gave him a carrot that I had slipped in my pocket this morning and he nuzzled my chest as if to tell me good morning.

"I'll take you out later boy, I promise." Why I talk to him is beyond me, I know he won't answer me, I just feel he listens to me maybe even understands me. I've grown rather attached to him over the past couple days, I never felt this way towards my father's horse.

"Good morning." I said to Wan and Jobe as I walked in. It seemed like they are the only ones I know in this place and yet maybe that's because they're always here when I am.

"Good morning Davin, how did the move into the cottage go?" Wan asked as he gestured me towards a chair to join them.

"It went well; they seemed very comfortable when I bid them good night."

"That's good, be sure to let me know if the Dover's need anything while they get settled." Wan instructed me.

"Thank you I will."

"We're working out the details for our trip to Breakstone." Jobe interrupted as if he is in a hurry.

"Yes, we'll want you to be leaving first thing in the morning tomorrow." Wan added.

"Why so quick?" I asked nervously again only thinking of being away from Elora.

"I spoke with the side show gatekeeper last night he asked if our village had any other needs they could help with." Wan started, "truth is the trip would be much easier if they went with you with their animal wagons to help you bring the cattle home. So as long as their people can use the village kitchen for meals they will lend three people to drive the wagons and help with the cattle."

"How long will the trip take?" I asked, now almost excited for the trip.

"Three days and you'll be home, Breakstone is a full days travel and that will give you a day to make your purchases and a day to travel home. Davin be sure to ask you family as well as the Dover's if there is anything they need from Breakstone. I'm sure your family has savings but if you need coin for the Dover's be sure to let us know. I'll also compile a small list of items I need and I'll leave it to you to see that I get them." Wan instructed me with a knowing look.

"Who will be making the trip with us?" I asked curious if he knew who in the side show would be joining us.

"Jobe will be accompanying you, he'll see to the needs of the Liaison, as well as Sid for protection and I'm not sure yet of the side show people but I'm sure they will be adequate. I'm also sending a herder and he'll help you choose good cattle." Wan informed me.

"Also I want you to just take a day to relax to get ready for your trip in the morning. I know the past few days have been very busy for you and the next three will be the same. I'll have the kitchen prepare meals to take with you and set your horse up with a carriage so you don't have to ride so far on your own. Also your clothing and boots are done so be sure to pick them up after mid-meal so you have them for the trip into Breakstone. So, do anything you need done today and the caravan of helpers will be at your cottage at sunrise." Wan told me, he always has so much to say and he always says it with a matter of fact tone that I have to absorb it quickly.

I excused myself and went to my office as I sat I noticed two small boxes on my desk. The first was Wan's list. Maybe he didn't want Jobe to know he had already made it for me. The list was specific even listing which shops to visit for the items. The second box held twenty gold coins and another list; it simply said ten cows one bull. I took this to mean that's what I was to look into purchasing for livestock. Ten cows would provide more than enough milk and butter for our village with the livestock we already had.

I took out the book and on the second page began to write out what was needed and being done for the town. I'm still am unsure of exactly what my job is but if this is it I want to be sure that it gets recorded for future reference. I also grabbed the two gold coins from it's hidden compartment. That left three silver in case I need anything, not to mention the savings my parents have for me, they kept it put away but always will allow me some if I need it. I don't know how much I have in savings and I've never asked. I know it will be given to Elora and I when we are bound, as will what Elora's parents have saved for her.

I waited until it was time for mid-meal before I left the Liaison, it was a little early so I decided to sit in the sun and watch for Elora. The village is always busy at mid-meal a lot of the villagers met with their families to have mid-meal together some use the village kitchens others go to their own cottages.

Elora and Eldon were walking towards me together. Eldon was smiling and so was Elora maybe the fire hadn't ruined their spirits.

"Good afternoon to you both!" I greeted them as I stood up and brushed the grass off my pants. "How did your new cottage treat you last night?" I asked.

"Good afternoon my love, the cottage is perfect but is missing just one thing." Elora answered.

"What's that?"

"You!" She said with tears coming to her eyes.

"My love don't worry we'll have a cottage in time for our wedding." I'll try to reassure her no matter how much I worry about the same things she is. "Let's go eat , I have some news to share."

We got our meal of wild turkey stew and bread and found a quiet place in the corner to sit so we could talk freely.

"I'm to make a trip to Breakstone tomorrow." I announced after we said a small blessing for our meal.

"Can I go?" Eldon shouted out of nowhere. He had been so quiet this afternoon; I thought he had lost his voice.

"HAHA! No Eldon, I've to go for work not fun, besides I've never been to Breakstone and I wouldn't dare take you somewhere I didn't know myself."

"How long will you be gone?" Asked Elora, trying not to sound sad that I'd be gone, I know she'll be sad as I am. We have never been apart in all our years.

"Only three days, my love." I assured her as I took her hand into mine and gave it a small kiss. "Don't worry it's just to get some supplies we need in the village, and I won't be alone."

"I'll miss you Davin." She whispered quietly.

"I'll miss you as well my love, is there anything either of you would like me to bring you from Breakstone?"

"Candy!" Eldon said like he knows everything that is sold there and it's just a town full of candy.

"I need nothing, Isabell really did take care of all my needs, and she even sent new combs and brushes." She says laughing.

"Isabell loves you of course she would be sure you have everything you need."

As we finished our meal I did everything to assure Elora that I'd be safe. And promised Eldon I'd find him a candy he has never had before. I bid them farewell and walked slowly to my cottage.

The people of our village aren't allowed to go to other towns, the reason is the towns outside our village are governed by the King and the church. Our village sits outside the Kings territory which is how we are able to govern ourselves without the King or churches interference. If a family wants to come to Furlin to live they have to go to the Liaison's, then they make the decision if they will be welcomed into our village. I'm not sure how it comes about; I just know not many have been allowed to stay as it upsets the balance of our village.

At supper I asked permission to go to the Dover's to find out if they needed anything from Breakstone, and also asked my family to get their lists ready for my trip as well. Myka's request was similar to Eldon's of course.

The Dover's were finishing their supper as I knocked on the door, Mr. Dover let me in. I explained why I was there and Mrs. Dover got up and brought me two silver coins and asked me to get her some new linen's for their cottage, and to get Mr. Dover a new smoking pipe as his was lost to the fire. I told them when I'd be back and bid them goodnight.

"Elora, walk Davin out please." Mrs. Dover said and Mr. Dover gave her a look of disapproval.

"Yes ma'am." She said as she got up and walked towards the door.

"Promise me you'll come back safely." Elora pleaded with me as we closed the door.

"I promise you my love, please don't worry yourself." I told her wondering if maybe I should at least tell her I'll have protection. "There will be many with me and even Skullmaker will accompany us to keep us safe." I told her hoping to ease her worries.

"I'll try hard not to worry, but if I don't see you on the third day I'll burst!" She told me, her hand trembling in mine.

I looked up into the windows to see if we were being watched, we weren't. I pulled her close to me and brought her face to mine slowly I brought her lips to mine and kissed her gently at first. As our breaths quickened she pressed her lips even harder to mine, her lips are so soft and I had to respond to her fevered kissing. She quickly pulled away from me and I looked towards the windows, no one was there.

"Why did you stop?" I asked her breathlessly.

"I'm sorry I shouldn't have risked the punisher on you." She whispered now crying.

"I'd take a hundred whippings for another kiss like that my love." I told her pulling her close to me again. "Never say you're sorry for kissing me like that again!" I demanded. "Promise me!"

"I promise, I just can't bear the thought of you at the punisher's." I quieted her with my lips and again our breaths quickened as we kissed. She let out a small moan, one like I've never heard before and it awakened something in me I've never felt before. I opened my eyes quickly to see a shadow come towards the window and pulled away quickly. I don't have to tell her why; just my look is enough to know our farewell may draw attention to ourselves.

"Sleep well my love I shall be back with you in three days." I told her, glad she couldn't see that my face had flushed.

"Farewell my love, three days and you have a promise to keep to me." She reminded me and turned towards her cottage. I watched her until she was in the door. Something in her walk had changed, she looked even more sensuous then before and I just wanted to run and stop her from going all the way inside and kiss her again. I felt a sudden agony as she closed the door. A year! I think to myself, how can I take it if she keeps kissing me like that?

I walked home very slowly so I could calm down from what Elora's kiss had done to me. I felt so confused about the feelings that have been stirred in me, I wanted her now so much more than ever. I've always wanted her as my wife there is no question about that, but the way that I want her now makes me feel shameful. And I don't know who to ask if it's wrong, if I go to my father he may know that we have kissed and send me to the punisher. I can't figure out if I want to be joyous or cry and I'm overcome with a feeling of despair, like I just needed to go back and be with her.

I got in bed and just laid there with the shell in my hand smelling the scent of her hair, wishing she were with me kissing me like that again.

My sleep was fitful all night; all I dreamed of is Elora and her kisses. I heard the knock on my door to get up but I just laid still and smelled the shell and thought of last night.

"Son," My father said at the door. "Come eat before your traveling party gets here and has to wait on you!" He demanded. I got up and dressed quickly, grabbed the bag I had packed for my trip, put the shell in pocket and headed out to face my day.

CHAPTER 9

The Trip

JUST AS I SAT down to eat I heard the caravan pull up outside the cottage.

"Guess, I'll eat as we drive out." I said as I scooped my eggs and ham into a biscuit.

"Davin, here's our list." My mother said handing me a list and two silver.

"I'll remember to get it mother don't worry, I'll see you in three days!" I said as I ran out the door.

The caravan was a sight to see. Blitz was hooked to a small Black carriage and being driven by Sid {Skullmaker} the punisher. I'm feeling a little apprehensive about this, guilty about last night and possibly being found out.

The side shows wagon has been covered with a dirty white tarp to cover the bars inside. The strongman was driving the wagon and the gatekeeper and one of the men who stands outside the tents inviting people to see a show were sitting next to him. Jobe was in a black carriage with another clerk sitting with him, I think his name is Garran. He is older than Jobe and I've not ever talked with him before. In the back of their carriage sat Wes, he worked in the barns and I'm assuming he would be the one sent to help me choose the livestock.

I climbed up into my carriage with Sid; I'll let him drive it as I've never driven one before.

"Good morning Sid." I said as cheerfully as I could muster.

"Mornin Davin." He said, his voice was deep, he's a tall guy standing I'm sure over six feet tall. His hair is light brown and is cut short, so short you can see the skin on his head.

"Bring everything you'll need?"

"Yes Sir, I'm ready."

The ride was smooth; I figured it would be very bumpy in a carriage. At first we were both quiet, I was too afraid to speak and Sid was busy concentrating on keeping Blitz on the road.

"So…" Sid began after about an hour of silence. "How are you coming along with your new calling?"

"I like it a lot, I'm still learning about it though." I answered him.

"Most clerks seem happy when they are called." He told me.

"I am happy, just the last couple days with what happened with the Dover's I'm a little bit worried about my future with Elora." I confided in him, hoping he had heard a bit of news from the Liaison's this morning.

"Yes, I heard your marriage cottage had to be given to them." He said, "don't worry so much Davin, I'm sure things will be taken care of before your bound."

"I hope so; I couldn't bear it if we had to put off our marriage because we had no place to live." I told him, I'm sure the despair in my voice could be heard but it doesn't matter to me now, I felt comfortable with Sid and I'm not sure why.

"You really love that girl don't you?" He asked with laughter in his voice.

"Why does everyone keep asking me that? Of course I love her!" I said not sure why everyone is so worried about Elora and I.

"Well there has been some talk of you two." He told me, like he knew some huge secret.

"Some talk? What do you mean by that?" I thought I had been caught. I felt hot all of a sudden and my stomach felt like someone punched me there.

"Well.." He said slowly, "they say you're a true match, that it has been known all along." I'm so relieved that he said that and I relaxed again.

"My father said the same thing a couple days ago." I confessed to him.

"Well true matches are very rare Davin, and you can just see it, we've all seen it since you were both small that's why your match came so early."

"Well to be honest Sid, I'm so confused." I said hoping I wasn't opening the door to a whipping.

"Why would you be confused? I've seen the way you look at her; I now hear the despair in your voice as you speak about her."

"I'm confused because the feelings I have for her, I want to be with her all the time, when I'm away from her I feel empty inside like part of me is missing, and truthfully I have feelings of wanting her like I've never felt before, she stirs something in me that makes me feel shameful inside. And I have no one to ask about it, Kyan is younger than me so he wouldn't know, I fear my father will punish me if I speak with him. I just feel lost." I told him quietly trying to hide the tears that had come up.

"Davin what you feel for Elora is natural. We all get those feelings." He told me very seriously, I'd never come to expect to be having this talk with Skullmaker. I'd have never thought him capable of it; maybe I should look past his calling and realize he's as human as the rest of us.

"You love her that is good it means a long life with your match. And what you're feeling is normal you want to be with her in ways you feel are sinful, lustful, but it is ok to feel that way. You just have to learn keep those feelings under control until you're bound." He warned me.

"A year, I have to feel like this for another year?" I exclaimed.

"Yes a year." He said laughing now. "The feeling will not always be so strong; it may be that way now because you have to leave her for a few days. And it could be because of the emotional past few days you have spent taking care of her and her family." He explained still with laughter in his voice, although now his laughter wasn't as frustrating as it had been before.

"Sid, can I confide in you?" I asked him looking into his face.

"I thought you were already Davin." He said laughing

"Well yes I was but there's more." I said trembling, but I had to know and I felt Sid was the only person I could talk to right now. "Last night Elora walked me out after I had a talk with her parents. No one was watching us and I kissed her, not on the cheek like I'm allowed to, I kissed her lips for a long moment."

"Davin it's alright that you sneak kisses like that, we all have done it. You just have to be careful not to get caught." He explained without sounding like he was ready to stop our carriage and give me the whipping I knew I deserved.

"Well when she walked away she looked different to me, more sensual and I wanted her in a way I'd never truthfully thought about before she kissed me like that." I admitted.

"Again Davin it's normal. What your feeling is your manhood awaken. When you're bound you may act on those feelings all you want, but for now suppress them, and be careful that your kissing her doesn't lead to you acting on your feelings of wanting her like that." He told me not laughing any more, more like a father and son would speak.

"So I'm not in sin?" I asked like a little boy.

"Not at all Davin, you're a young man in love with a beautiful girl. I'd have thought you'd of felt that way before now."

"No never. We have never stolen a kiss before we always obey the rules of courting." I told him honestly

"When Kyan escorts you also?" He asked me curiously.

"We kiss more when we are with Kyan but just small kisses on our cheeks, or I'll touch her hair. But that has been all there ever was before last night." I told him truthfully.

"You respect her a lot. I can see that Davin, as long as you continue to treat her that way she'll love you for as long as she lives." He told me knowingly.

It got quiet again and I just sat watching the scenery go by thinking about everything Sid and I talked about. I no longer felt guilty for the stolen kisses last night or the feelings that came with them. I felt like I understood now what's happening to me. And the shame I felt was gone.

"Are you getting hungry yet?" Sid asked me

"I'm starved!" I told him.

"It's time to eat everyone." Sid said as he stood up and yelled and he slowed the carriage to a stop.

Everyone slowed to a stop and hopped down from the carriages and wagon.

"Thank goodness!" The strong man said looking weary. "I thought I was going to starve an hour ago." He stated laughing.

"You're always hungry." The gatekeeper told him as he walked to as tree to relieve himself.

"And you drink too much ale Fin!" The strong man yelled towards him.

At that we all laughed hard. Jobe called us all to his carriage where he began handing out roast venison sandwiches and jars of water and wine to each of us. He gave the strong man two just in case.

We all sat and ate quietly under the shade of a huge magnolia tree. Which only made me ache even more for Elora as the scent of magnolia flooded my senses.

"We'll push on until we are close to Breakstone then stop and set up camp for the night." Jobe told us.

"Just holler when we get there." Fin the gatekeeper said cheerfully.

The rest of the ride was quiet, Sid and I talked some but nothing as important as the talk we had earlier that morning.

We even talked about him being called Skullmaker, he told me that he liked the nick name and knew for a long time that people called him that. Then told me if I admitted that to anyone he would whip me, we laughed hard at that. I was really enjoying the ride with him though.

As the sun started to go down and the air was getting cooler Jobe stopped us all for the night. He asked us all to help get some wood so we could have a hot supper all of us ran willingly toward a long ago fallen tree to gather what we could hold. The strongman was showing off as he grabbed the tree trunk and said he had his share. It was fun talking with everyone while we waited for our supper. The strong man's name is Harry and the other helper is called Colt. I'm not sure if that's his real name it's just what they kept calling him.

Jobe had the fire going and had a big pot of stew on it stirring it occasionally as we sat around the fire waiting to eat and talking with each other. The talk was mostly of our task tomorrow, the plan was, I was to ride in with Harry and Wes in the wagon and get the livestock at first light. The rest would follow us into Breakstone, then we would go in pairs to do our shopping.

"It's important that we stay with someone in Breakstone. Davin and Sid will stay together while Davin gets all his purchases taken care of." Jobe told us.

"I've also put a pillow and blanket in my carriage for each of you." Jobe said

"We brought a tent." Chimed Fin. "at least we can sleep with some comfort."

"If we get done early enough we can head out and get some of the ride out of the way." Jobe said hopefully.

"That sounds good to me." I piped in enthusiastically.

Everyone laughed at me. "We all know why you're in a hurry young one." Sid roared with even more laughter.

"Hey now!" I said defensively.

"Don't be so defensive, I think we all know about your true match by now." He proclaimed.

Everyone nodded to agree with him. I felt myself flush with embarrassment.

"Don't be embarrassed lad." Harry said, "some of us only get to wish we had someone to run home to." He looked sad as he said that. I no longer felt embarrassed, I felt like I just learned a part of side show life I wanted no part of. I couldn't imagine life without having a loved one.

After supper the side show guys had the tent up in a matter of minutes and we all got settled to sleep, all of us except for Sid. He had guard duty for the first half of the night and Harry would take the second half. After a couple hours of restless sleep I was happy when Harry woke for his half of the watch, he snored so loud I couldn't sleep.

Jobe woke us all at dawn; he had been up before us and had morning meal cooking already. We all joined in putting away the blankets and tent as Jobe finished morning meal for us. We ate our meal and listened to Sid as he told us about a thief that had come upon our camp last night. He didn't get into details just said the man left with a red behind and apparently in the future he'll need to find a new way to steal without using his hands. I wasn't sure what he meant by that all I knew I hadn't heard anything and no one else mentioned hearing the scuffle either. Now that I thought of it bringing Sid was a great idea.

After we finished eating our morning meal I climbed up into the wagon with Harry and Wes for the ride into Breakstone. We rode for about three miles and then saw wagons traveling towards the town. We joined behind a man bringing in a wagon load of fresh hay.

"Bet he's headed to a place with livestock." Wes told Harry.

"We'll follow him in then." Harry said.

CHAPTER 10

Breakstone

THERE WAS A STONE wall standing at least eight feet tall surrounding Breakstone. As we neared the gate I could see there were gatekeepers on guard. There were tents pitched outside the walls with what looked like very dirty people living in them, small children stood dangerously close to the road asking for food and coin. Wes told me they were poor and the children begged to help feed the families, he told also me that this kind of life has become common under the kings rule. I felt sad for the children; I didn't know this lifestyle even existed. Wes warned me to expect to see more as we got further into the town.

As we entered the gate a guard stopped us.

"What is your business here? I don't recall seeing any of you before." He asked sternly.

"We come from Furlin to purchase livestock and supplies." Wes told him very quietly. "The two carriages behind us are also with us."

"Go ahead, any trouble and we'll toss you in the dungeons, you hear?" He shouted up at us.

"Aye Sir we understand." Wes replied, as the guard stepped aside and waved us through.

"Wow that was scary." I said taking a deep breath.

"It's normal Davin they have jobs to do just like us." Wes told me.

The town was huge there were small shops all over most of them had small children with their hands out begging. We followed the load of hay all the way across the big town it stopped at a very large stable full of cattle, horses and pigs. Harry, Wes and I walked up to the fence together when a man wearing worn out work clothes approached us.

"How can I help you men?" He asked in a deep voice.

"We're looking to buy some cattle Sir." I informed him.

"Cows are one gold each, bulls are one gold and five silver." He told us.

"Sounds good, how much are the pigs?" I asked.

"Pigs will run six silver or two just weaned for one gold."

"Thank you, please give us a moment and we'll start picking them out." I said.

"No, first you'll tell me what you're buying, then you'll pay me, then you can take your pick." He rudely informed me.

I looked over to Wes and Harry they both nodded and I agreed.

"If I pick out some pigs how much will it be for a crate to transport them?" I asked.

"How many pigs do you want?"

"I'm thinking four weanlings." I answered.

"A couple silver added to your bill then." He told us.

"Great then I'd like ten cows, a bull and four weaned pigs, three sows one boar please." I informed him. "I also need a white horse, a mare preferably."

"I have a couple you can come take a look after we pick the rest of what you need. We can talk price then." He said looking towards the cattle. "So far you're up to thirteen gold seven silver."

I paid him and instructed Wes to pick the cattle he liked while I went to look at the pigs. They all looked healthy so I told him to let his hand pick the four and crate them up for me.

"Are you ready to look at the horses?" He asked. The horse was on Wan's list so I wanted to be sure to pick a good horse. Harry followed us through the gate. There were a lot of horses and they all looked good. He had three studs and one mare that was pure white with big dark eyes.

I walked up and felt her legs and looked her over real good then I looked to Harry.

"She's nice looking, strong and healthy too." He confirmed for me.

"How much does she cost?" I asked turning back to the stable master.

"Two gold five silver, and I'll throw in some tack to get her home safely." He told us.

"Take her around." I said to Harry as I handed the man three gold. "You've been a great help."

After we had everything loaded up we went to the different shops. I took Wan's list first. Sid followed me quietly offering to help carry items back and forth to carriage while Harry watched our carriage as we shopped. Wan wanted some simple things, some blue parchment paper, new ink and quills. Then the final request on the list a gold necklace with earrings that match. It wasn't very specific so I did my best. Fortunately between what he left to pay for livestock and his personal items I had plenty of coin to pay for everything.

I took all Wan's items to our carriage and joined Harry, Fin and Wes at the general shop. There I found many candies I thought Eldon and Myka would enjoy. I settled on cinnamon hard candy and cherry soft candy, I picked up enough so Eldon could share with Elora. I picked out the items on the list for the Dover's and for my parents in that store as well. I decided to get them each a present since I was shopping. I bought Mr. Dover honey tobacco, I found a nice candle holder for Mrs. Dover. My parents were hard to shop for though. I looked all through the store until I settled on a new water pitcher for my mother and a new pair of wood working awls for my father.

I also bought a bolt of cloth for Elora as I knew when her sixteenth birthday arrived her clothing would change. All the girls got new dresses that looked more like what our mothers wear than what the smaller girls in the village wore. I also found her new combs for her hair, they had yellow butterflies on them and I thought they would be beautiful in her golden hair. I finally headed back to our caravan just as Jobe had arrived with our meals and a barrel of ale for the ride home.

"Is everybody ready?" He asked us.

We were all ready to get out of this noisy town full of beggars and thieves. I checked to make sure the mare was tied properly; she'll be walking next to Blitz on the way home. They were nuzzling each other as I came up to them. "Don't get any ideas Blitz; she isn't for you." I told him quietly.

We rode out for about three hours before stopping to set up camp for the night. Harry was watching closely to make sure we weren't followed out of town. As soon as I stepped out of the carriage I went to look for wood. I was hungry even the dried meat I bought in town didn't help much.

"What's for supper this evening, Jobe?" I heard Harry ask as I was heading back towards camp.

"We are having roasted chicken, potatoes and ale of course." He told Harry. This made my stomach groan with even more hunger.

We all sat by the fire long into the evening, talking of the things we had seen and the deals we had made on our trip. I know how much I had been dreading being away from Elora and that she is never far from my mind, but I've really enjoyed this trip and I hope I did well with my purchases for the Liaison, Wan and everyone else.

I had to figure out a way to have Elora's dress made without it looking like it had come from me as well. Maybe I can bribe the dressmaker into making and delivering it with the rest of her new attire she'll receive on her birthday. Maybe I could speak with Sid for an idea, since it doesn't seem he is out to get me. I have enjoyed the time I've spent with him, I really thought at first it would be bad having him drive me but I'm glad he did.

The next morning we headed out at dawn, Harry and Wes watched the camp last night and I even got some sleep during Harry's watch. We had some distance from the other carriage so I decided to try and talk with Sid about Elora's dress.

"Sid, how would I go about getting a dress made for Elora's sixteenth birthday without getting it taken away until we are bound?" I just came right out with it, if it got me in trouble then I'd just have to take it.

"Is that what the bolt of material is for?" He asked looking as if he may strike me down.

"Honestly; yes I want her to have her new attire, I had bought her material before and my mother had been working on her dress as a wedding gift but then she had to change it after the fire so Elora would have proper clothes." I explained.

"I'll take it home with me." Oh no I did it now I'm losing the material I thought.

"I'll have my wife make her a proper gown for her sixteenth birthday and deliver it to her myself, I'll also tell her it is from you but to say it's from our family." He told me. I couldn't believe it.

"I'm at a loss; you have been so kind on this trip how can ever repay you?" I asked full of emotion.

"Just keep our village's interests in mind when you make all those decisions in your new office." Was all he said and I didn't need an explanation. All I want to do is do right by the village for it affects us all if I make bad decisions.

We rode straight to the Liaison barns and unloaded the cattle into the new pens that were built why we were away. I had missed mid-meal and I couldn't rush off to see Elora till after supper, so I went into my office to see Wan and give him his left over coin and the items he requested.

"My boy I'm glad your back!" He said with a big smile. "How did it go?"

"I think it went well Wan, I was able to finish everyone's wish list including yours. I also decided to buy four new pigs while I was there, they had good price and I figured it wouldn't hurt to add to our current stock." I told him hoping he wouldn't be mad about the pigs.

"Good thinking Davin. There's a lot of coin here are you sure you got everything?" I handed him a big box that held the paper and other supplies for his desk. Then I took a small box from my pocket which held the necklace and earrings. "I hope this is what you had in mind." I said as I handed him the tiny box.

He opened it slowly and gasped as he looked at it. The necklace had a very thin intricate chain and the charm had an emerald with an intricate gold setting that made it look as if the emerald was sitting in a bed of gold lace. The earrings were small emeralds with the same type of gold lace setting.

"Davin, this is perfect, thank you I couldn't have picked a better one if I had gone myself. What did this cost?" He asked almost breathlessly.

"It was two gold's and five silver, I figured since I did so well with the other purchases that the cost of such beautiful jewelry was well worth it." I explained quickly.

"Wonderful my boy, how about the horse I asked about?" He asked as he closed the little box and put it in his jacket.

"Come out to the barns, I'll show you!" I told him almost running for the doors.

Everyone was still out working on unloading the livestock and their purchases. They stopped as Wan came out so they could see his reaction to what we came back with.

"The cattle are very lovely let's hope they produce as good as they look, good job Wes." He said as he walked near the pen.

"What a magnificent mare! Davin you did well." I beamed in his praise. "She will due perfectly." He said admiring her.

"What will you name her?" Harry asked.

"She isn't mine to name." Was all Wan said and walked towards the small crate holding the pigs. "These are lovely pigs as well, you all did well, I think the next time we need things from Breakstone the traveling party will be you all." He said proud that he had chosen this team himself.

"Well, if you would all excuse me I need to get Blitz unhooked from this carriage and be on my way so I can make supper time with my family." I said heading towards the front of the carriage.

"Davin don't worry about the carriage; you may take it home or leave it here." Wan told me.

"Thank you, I think I'll take it to our cottage tonight so I can unload the gifts for my family." I told him.

"Take a day off tomorrow and get some rest, that goes for all of you." He announced to us.

"I bid you farewell then." I said to the men.

I was able to handle the carriage with ease, which surprised me I thought it would be much harder to drive a carriage. I went home and emptied the back of the carriage out. I set everything for my family on the table and took the Dover's stuff to my room. Then I went to wash up by the river before supper.

The afternoon was warm enough that I could get in the river and wash and swim a bit before I went back to the cottage. My thoughts were full of Elora, I couldn't wait to see her tonight, to smell her hair or even hope for another forbidden kiss. I was just resting near the bank day dreaming when I heard rustling in the bushes on the bank.

"Who's there?" I demanded. The river was usually private this time of day, I heard more rustling but no one spoke. Again I asked who was out there but no one answered me. I jumped out of the river and grabbed my linen to cover myself and walked towards the bush, I knew as I got closer who was there.

"My love come out of there, the scent of your hair gives you away." I said laughing.

I'm sorry, I saw you come into town and I just couldn't wait to see you, I didn't know you would be doing more than a quick wash, when I saw you were in the water I tried to sneak away but I tripped and gave myself away." She said with her face flushed.

I tied the linen at my waist and pulled her into me. "I've missed you so much beautiful." I told her, "I'm not angry you were trying to see me naked." I teased.

Her face flushed even hotter as she leaned forward to give me a kiss, I quickly looked around and pulled her behind the bush. We kissed so fervently I was afraid I'd hurt her, but she continued kissing me pushing her body even closer to mine. My desire for her was becoming more of a need than a want I tried to pull away from her as she pressed closer to me. I realized that my desire for her was now showing, my manhood had given me away. She stepped back quickly looking afraid.

"I'm sorry Davin, I didn't mean too." She whispered her eyes welling with tears.

"It's alright my love, I can't always hide the desire I feel for you, especially when you kiss me like that." I said trying to assure her she didn't do anything bad.

"Sit here and let me get clothes on then we can just sit and talk." I told her. "No peeking either." I teased at her.

After I got my clothes on I went to sit with her on the bank.

"I'm sorry Davin." She started to say.

"Listen here Elora, if you apologize for kissing me one more time I'll find myself feeling like you don't want to kiss me." I said to her, I didn't want her to feel bad for wanting to kiss me because I refuse to feel bad for wanting to kiss her.

"I rode with Sid on our trip." I started to tell her.

"You rode with Skullmaker?" She asked looking scared.

"Yes, he isn't really very scary once you talk with him. We talked a lot about how I was feeling about you." She looked at me confused. "He told me it's good that we felt such passion and desire to be with one another, but he warned me to be careful." She nodded to show me she understood. "He also said something that I found kind of funny, he told me that all matches sneak away for forbidden kisses before they are bound, he says that it's almost expected." We both laughed feeling a little more ease about our stolen kisses. I told her a lot about the trip holding her hand tightly to calm her down.

"Kiss me again my love." I commanded her.

She leaned into me and kissed me softly and slowly at first as our breaths quickened our kiss again became hard and fast. I tried to slow her down again but even at that moment it was hard for me to slow down myself. Slowly we pulled away from each other.

"See we just have to learn to stop my love, and never again say you're sorry for kissing me." I said quietly in her ear.

"I won't I promise." She said with a small kiss on my lips to seal her promise. "Will you be over later?'

"Yes I have things to deliver from the trip; you think your mother will let you walk me out again?" I asked mischievously.

"By the sounds of your story; I almost expect it." She answered me with laughter in her voice.

"I'm happy to be home again, I missed you my love." I told her as I pressed my face into her hair.

"I missed you too my love, I felt as if I my heart would burst until I got to see you again." She told me as she brought her lips to mine again. This time we just kissed slowly, both of us fighting not to let it turn into the hard passionate kisses that we had moments ago.

"I must go before my parents get home, I'm always the first one home." She whispered in a voice that said she didn't really want to go. I didn't want her to go either, but I also didn't want my parents or Myka to come out here looking for me.

"I'll be with you soon my love." I told her kissing her again." You go first, the back way so were not seen coming out of the same area." I instructed her. I watched as she went the way I told her to make sure she made it safe, and then I gathered my dirty clothing and linens and headed to my own cottage.

Everyone in my family enjoyed the gifts I brought them. My father really loved the awls I got him, he said he didn't have any like them and couldn't wait to put them to use, and my mother put her new pitcher to use for supper. Myka really enjoyed the cherry candy I brought her; she said the cinnamon candy was hot but that she also really liked it. I also bought her some new hair pins with blue butterflies which she adored.

After we had supper I asked my mother if I could deliver the Dover's items to them. "Of course you can." She told me. "Take your time I know it has been days since you have seen Elora." If only she knew I thought with a smile.

I carried the box of goods over to Elora's and knocked on the door. Eldon almost knocked me over in his excitement to see me.

"Davin how was your trip?" He asked as he closed the door behind me.

"It was good, we did all our business spent some time shopping to fill the lists from everyone and headed home." I told him.

I sat and talked with the Dover's for over an hour, they served cherry pie as we sat and talked about Breakstone. Mr. Dover sat puffing on his new pipe and tobacco and Eldon stuffed candy into his mouth until I thought he may burst.

"Elora, walk Davin out and don't keep him too late I can see how tired he is." Said Mrs. Dover, she was clearing the table and trying to get Eldon to stop eating candy.

Elora and I walked out to our old log and sat together awhile in silence.

"Are you alright my love?" I asked her, she seemed so quiet tonight.

"I just keep thinking about this afternoon by the river." She said solemnly.

"Your thinking about seeing me naked again aren't you?" I could feel the heat rise to her face.

"Davin you're bad, I was not thinking about that."

"I don't believe you." I told her trying to ease her mind. We both laughed and relaxed a little.

"My sixteenth birthday is coming soon, and then it's just a year until we are bound." She reminded me.

"I know, does it feel like forever until we are bound?" I asked her hoping she didn't say no.

"I'd marry you tomorrow if I could my love."

I felt my heart quicken at the thought of it. "I wish." I said quietly.

We sat for a few more minutes and I looked back toward her cottage to see if anyone was looking and again, we were left alone to sit and talk. I kissed her quickly and told her how much I loved her. Then I helped her up and bid her goodnight. My heart and head couldn't take another chance at a forbidden kiss, I felt like I'd give in if I tried.

"Sleep well my love." I whispered as I walked toward my own cottage.

CHAPTER 11

The Invitation

THE NEXT DAY I enjoyed my time off. I took Blitz out and rode outside of town for a long time. I decided I'd ride over to the side show the see Harry, Fin and Colt. I wanted to be sure to thank them and be able to say goodbye before they were gone. As I got closer to their camp I could smell a fire and hear faint talking.

"Hello?" I shouted at the gate so someone could let me in. Fin came running towards the gate.

"Davin, it's so good to see you." He said as he opened the gate.

"We are just sitting down to eat if you would like to join us." He invited me.

"I'll sit with you for a few minutes I actually came to see how much longer you would all be staying." I told him as we walked towards the circle of people.

"Well we're thinking of pulling out tomorrow actually." He told me, I thought I heard sadness in his voice.

The entire group greeted me by name. The world's smallest man offered me a mug of ale, and Harry offered me the empty space next to him. I really felt a sense of belonging as I sat there talking with all of them, listening to them tell stories of traveling around the country side putting on their shows. I felt like they really enjoyed coming to Furlin as they told Wan.

I didn't want to be late meeting Elora for mid-meal, when I realized how late it was getting, I told them I had to go for now. Harry invited to me to bring Elora and our families out tonight for a goodbye celebration. I told them I'd do my best to get everyone to come tonight, I'm sure we could all use some fun after what has happened over the last week. Harry walked me back to the gate so he could let me out.

"I enjoyed the time we spent together." Harry said as we reached the gates.

"I did too Harry, you guys were so nice to me thank you for letting me see a part of you most don't get to see."

"Davin you make me wish I had settled down years ago, found me a beautiful wife and had me a boy just like you." He said with sadness in his eyes.

"Maybe it's not too late." I suggested.

"Son, it's been too late for years, but don't you worry about me go meet that beautiful girl of yours before you're late and she smacks you with a rolling pin!"

We were both laughing as I mounted Blitz. "See you tonight." I called back to him.

I ran Blitz all the way back to town. I could see by the look on Elora's face that I was late. "We still have time to eat if you wish." She said looking up to me.

I tied Blitz up and joined her to get our meal. "I'm sorry my love, I rode out to the side show to see Harry and Fin and lost track of time. I won't ever let it happen again I promise." I gave her my best I'm sorry face.

"I forgave you the moment your rode up my love." She told me as we took position to bless our food. It was customary to bless our food even though we didn't take rules of a church we all still believed in God.

As we ate I told her about our invitation to the side show tonight. She was excited and was sure her family would love to join in the goodbye celebration she also knew they had thanks to give.

"I'll come get you all after we get washed this evening." I told her as we left the kitchen. "Until then I bid you farewell." I said as I kissed her hand.

After I left Elora I went to let my parents know about our invitation the side show for a celebration, they seemed very happy we were invited. I also asked my father to let Elora's family know that they were also invited.

I still had the afternoon to myself, so I rode Blitz over to the river. I didn't have any linens but all I really wanted to do is put my feet in the cool running water and enjoy the quiet. As I sat and removed my boots Kyan came up behind me. I haven't seen Kyan much lately with all the events that have taken so much of my time.

"Hey Kyan, what brings you out here on a work day?" I puzzled.

"I've been finishing work at the bowery a little earlier so they just let me take some time off today." He told me proudly. Kyan's internship is to make a lot of the weapons that the hunters use. I did an internship there for a small amount of time I really enjoyed the work there.

Kyan removed a flask out of his jacket and offered it to me.

"Brandy?" He asked.

"Where did you get this?" I asked as I took a small swig.

"It was a gift from Liam, he liked a bow that I made him a lot I guess." He shrugged.

"That was nice, must have been a very nice bow this is some very good brandy." I told him after I took my second swig.

"It was my best bow yet." He beamed with pride, "I made him a cedar bow, it barley has any bend to it and the arrows fly further than any I've seen."

"Well good job, will they expect you can make more like it?" I asked him.

"It's not a matter of making more, every hunter wants one now. The wood is difficult to work with, I feel like I was lucky to get that one." I guess this explained the tired look on his face.

"I'm sure you'll figure out an efficient way to make more Kyan, your smart and you make great bows, I still use the one you made me. When I get the time to go out and use it that is." I told him almost sorry I'd brought up how busy I've been and the fact that I haven't been able to spend time with him lately.

"You've been pretty busy lately. I suppose that happens when you turn sixteen huh?" He asked actually not acting like his feelings were very hurt.

"Yes very busy and the fire didn't help much. How is Leta doing?" I asked, I haven't seen her in a couple weeks at least.

"She is doing well, her internship is working out well she is sure that her calling will be in the flour mill."

"It's good she likes it there then, I didn't care much for the work there, but then the boys did all the heavy work." We both laughed at that.

"How are the Dover's settling into the cottage?"

"They have everything they need." I told him sadly.

"Sorry you had to lose your cottage Davin, have they told you what will happen yet?"

"Not yet, they said at the Liaison that it would be taken care before we are bound." I told him.

We sat quietly for a few minutes just passing the flask back and forth. Usually we would be trying to drown each other in the river but I don't think either of us is feeling young and playful as of late.

"Want to go get something to eat?" I asked Kyan, I think after all that brandy we both could use a bite.

"Yeh sure, bring anything new home from Breakstone?" He asked me as he got up and offered me a hand.

"I brought some candy and some dried beef." I told him, I knew I forgot to bring him something from Breakstone and I didn't even realize it until now.

"That sounds good to me!"

We walked over to my cottage and he helped me put Blitz in his pen. "Nice pen, did you have to build it yourself?"

"Actually no, my father built it for me." I told him as he laughed.

"That explains why it's so nice then." He teased me.

"Let's go already; I have to get ready to help with supper soon." I told him blowing off his sad sense of humor.

After we enjoyed some candy and some of the dried beef Kyan bid me farewell to go do his chores. I went out back and brushed Blitz down then I fed and watered both horses. I also took care of the water buckets for the cottage and started making supper for my family. I really enjoyed fixing meals, but my mother doesn't like me to cook, she says that its women's work. I hope Elora won't feel as strong about it; I'd enjoy cooking for her.

Soon after we all had supper I went to get the Dover's so we could go to the side show. My parents and Myka waited in our yard for us so we could all walk together. Elora and I walked behind the others so we could quietly talk and hold hands as we enjoyed the cool evening air. The feeling wasn't as festive tonight as it was last time we went out to the side show.

As we got closer to the side show the familiar smells of food was on the breeze, not the food we commonly ate but the treats we yearned for all year waiting for the side show to arrive. As we came up to the gate Fin was waiting to let us all in.

"Good evening fine folks of Furlin, welcome to our celebration!" Fin greeted us. He had a smile that warmed us, not a smile that we would see on the nights that the sides show was open for everyone.

There was a big fire burning in the middle of the encampment and all the side show workers were sitting around it talking, laughing and eating. I could smell the fresh peach bread that we had all enjoyed the night of the fire. Harry jumped up when he saw us coming towards them.

"Davin so glad you came!" He said as he rose then lifted me off my feet to show off his strength for the others. "Come walk with me for a moment before we get comfortable and full of ale."

I excused myself and we walked towards the trailers that held the animals used in the side show. We stood next to the elephant silently for a long time; I was grabbing handfuls of hay feeding her quietly as she used her trunk to bring it through the bars to her mouth. I think really there was no choice for me to stand and feed her because she kept putting her trunk all over my face until I reached for more hay. It was just out of her reach and I could see why.

"Ellie leave the man be, it isn't his job to stand there and fill your never ending stomach." Harry scolded her; funny thing was she stopped putting her long trunk out of the bars towards us. I wondered just how much she understood.

"Well Davin, I wanted to ask you about something." Harry looked troubled and not at all the happy jovial guy I traveled with just yesterday.

"What's troubling you Harry?" I asked him hoping he wasn't about to give me his goodbye.

"I was talking with Wan, he suggested for me to stay and live in Furlin. He tells me of a widow named Isabell, that I might be able to be bound to." He almost looked hopeful as he confided in me.

"Isabell is a great friend of ours, have you met her yet?" I asked curiously.

"Yes I met her this morning after speaking with Wan. I was happy to see she is the very same woman I'd noticed the night of the side show. I know we talked during our trip and I told you I'd love to have a life like what you have here in Furlin, I just never imagined one would be offered to me is all." He truly looked torn about making such a big decision.

"Why are you questioning it if it's what you want?" I asked him.

"These people are my family, I feel like I'd be abandoning them Davin. I've been with the side show since my parents abandoned me as a small boy. I started working with the side show very soon after, at first cleaning after and feeding the animals then adding chores of the show as time went by. Fin is like a father to me, I feel like I'll hurt him if I choose to stay."

"Have you ever talked with Fin about your desire to have a home and a wife?" I asked him quietly.

"Yes, he always laughed at me." Now I could see tears welling up in his eyes.

"Why not let me talk with Fin, maybe I can help him see that this is what you want and need." I offered.

"No, I'll have to do this on my own. I just wanted to talk to you about it, and to let you know you may be seeing me after the side show leaves tomorrow." He informed me.

"I have work in the Liaison's tomorrow and I dine in the town kitchen for mid-meal, meet up with me whenever you need." I told him feeling very secretive.

"Well Davin, no matter what I choose, I just wanted a minute alone with you to tell you how much I enjoyed our time together. You really let me see a world I didn't know was out there, I used to think you men with their hearts set on marriage were fools, you made me see that I'm the fool."

"I didn't mean to make you feel so confused." I stammered unsure if he was upset with me.

"Davin it wasn't just one thing you said or did, it was the love I saw in your eyes when you spoke of Elora and your future with her. I want that and I think I always have." He admitted. "Let's head back to the fire before were missed."

As we got closer to the fire I could see the ale was flowing freely as was peach bread and sugared cherries. There was laughter in the group and I could tell stories were going at full speed, much like the night we spent on our way to Breakstone. I sat near Elora and just watched her, she was listening to a story being told by the little man and her face was glowing with laughter.

After some time passed when the fire and conversation had died down some Fin and another worker went to get a surprise to show us. They came back with a small lion cub and all the girls of the group were just in love with him, his name was Ace and he was very newly born.

"His mother had twins but the girl died. She is still taking care of Ace here and that's why she isn't in the show right now." Fin explained to us.

"Won't she be angry you took the baby from her?" Myka asked full of curiosity.

"We raised his momma she knows us all and she lets us play with her cubs when she has them." Fin answered Myka knowing more questions were coming.

He let us hold the cub and play with it for a little while. He really was neat he liked to gnaw on our fingers and made little growling noises when we pulled them away from him.

"What will happen with him?" I asked as I rubbed his fat belly.

"The same thing that happens to all our animals of course, he'll become part of the show very soon. The tamers are already trying to work with him. We have lost all the litters from his momma so we have a lot of hope for this guy." He told us as he plucked him from my hands to return him to his momma.

Soon after we all said our farewells to each other, it was later than I thought and as I stood I realized I had drunk too much ale. My head was dizzy and I stumbled forward, everyone laughed, I'm sure I looked funny, I caught myself quick and laughed with them. I was sad to say bye. I had become good friends with some of these people and it was difficult knowing it would be close to a year before they came back. As Fin was walking us to the gates he gave each of us a small box that had been painted with the bright colors that all the wagons had been painted in. He explained that the people of the side show spent today making each of us a necklace for luck; he also told us these weren't the little trinket type jewelry given out when games were won either. Mine was a tiger's tooth as the charm and the necklace was made of tiny silver rings all entwined together. And Elora's was a carved magnolia painted white on the same type of chain that held mine. Myka's was a hand carved seal; I'm guessing that the boy in the seal tent had something to do with hers. Eldon's like mine was a tiger's tooth only a smaller tooth.

We walked somberly back towards the village, we all had a great time but it seemed so hard to say farewell to our new friends, and I wonder what will become of Harry. I'm sure he'll make a decision of what he feels is best for him, but no matter what he'll feel as if he's letting people down.

I slowed down some so Elora and I could fall behind everyone a bit so I could tell her about my talk with Harry. She was so excited that Isabell might have a match that she almost let the secret out with all her questions.

"Quiet now, it's still not decided my love." I told her hoping she would sense that it was to be kept secret.

When we got to her cottage we sat quietly on our log together, since we get to have mid-meal together now there isn't much to say in the evenings now. I just enjoyed sitting with her holding her hand and catching the scent of her hair when the breeze comes through. I leaned over and kissed her carefully so it didn't appear inappropriate if anyone had been watching. Slowly I turned to peer at her windows to see if anyone was watching us, but again no one was, I pulled her close and kissed her soft and deep. I've wanted to kiss her like this all day, our breathing quickened fast this time and our kisses became heavy and quick. I felt like my head was spinning, in between the ale and her lips I didn't know if I could restrain myself this night like I had before. I quickly pulled away and got up.

"I must go my love for if I don't now I may never be able to stop." I told her trying to hide my embarrassment.

"I understand for I feel the same, I desire you and I don't think I can wait much longer much less a year." She told me with tears running out of her eyes.

I pulled her close to me and hugged her tight to my chest. "We can't do anything that will cause them to break our match my love, promise me no matter what you'll wait as I do." I whispered with my head buried in her hair. Just that scent alone is enough to begin to stir my desire for her again.

"I promise Davin I'll do nothing to hurt you ever, I just don't know what's happening to me." She admitted to me with tears still running freely from her eyes.

"You'll be fine my love, as I will be. We have to be careful but being careful will not end what we feel now, it will grow as we do." I assured her, repeating what Sid had talked with me about. Even though I had that advantage my own feelings still confused me and I didn't want Elora to know that. We stood for a long time just holding each other, I was truly afraid to kiss her again for the fire it would stir in me tonight may not be doused as easily as yesterday.

"Farewell my love I must sleep off this ale." I told her as I gently pulled away from our embrace. I have no idea how long we had stood like that. I brought her face close to mine and gave her a small kiss on her lips and turned away. She did not bid me farewell tonight, I felt as if I somehow let her down but I can't stay any longer, my will is giving and if I stayed it may only cause us more pain.

I went quickly to my room not in the mood for talk any more tonight. As I laid with the shell in my hand I felt my own tears coming; the pain in my heart is too much to bear tonight.

CHAPTER 12

Talk of the village

I ROSE SLOWLY WITH a pounding in my head that quickly reminded me of last night. I'm feeling the shame of hurting Elora worse now than when I laid down last night. I dressed quickly hoping I could catch Elora as she went by this morning. I waited only a few minutes when I seen her coming toward me.

"Good morning my love, I'm sorry I hurt you last night." Was all I could get out as she came towards me. She was smiling and wearing the dress my mother had made her. I loved seeing it on her.

"You didn't hurt me, I cry for the love I feel for you the desire I feel for you. I worry about our cottage and I worry we'll be caught and torn from one another." She confessed.

"Don't worry about any of that, we'll be careful I promise we'll control our desire. We have to or face the punishers and the Liaison's; that alone is enough to make us more careful."

She knew I was right and nodded as she continued to walk and start her day. I'm so relieved that she is not upset at me and that it wasn't I who made her hurt. I walked around back to Blitz and got him ready to go so I could arrive at the Liaison's early. My head was still pounding hard but I had to ignore it and get on with my day.

As I rode towards my job I tried to listen for the sounds of the side show pulling out though I heard nothing but the normal hustle and bustle of town. As I got closer to the Liaison's I noticed that all the drapes in the building were still pulled closed. When they were closed it usually meant that there was a meeting in progress. I went in the back quietly to my office so I didn't intrude something private. I took out my book and made some notes on how the new livestock was doing and wrote the date to show when the side show left the village.

After a short time Jobe was knocking on my door. "Your presence has been requested in the main hall Davin." He told me sounding urgent.

I picked up my book and quill and followed him into the main room. I could see the Liaisons and clerks all sitting in their proper seats and before them sat Harry. He looked exhausted his eyes were red but he looked somewhat relieved.

"Good morning Davin." Wan greeted me standing from his chair. "Harry has decided he would like to join us in our village, the vote has been made and I must say he's a very welcome new comer." Harry looked up and smiled at me.

"I'd like you to go get Isabell for us as this meeting concerns her as much as it does the rest of us." Wan instructed to me, he picked up a letter and held it out for me to take.

"Have her read this then bring her back please." He said as I took the letter.

"Yes Sir." I said as I took the letter and ran for the door. Forgetting the pain in my head with the new excitement I ran to the common. I don't think I noticed anything or anyone on my way there.

"Isabell this is for you." I said handing her the note. As she opened it her face beamed with a huge smile. They must have hinted they had found her a new match before now.

"You need to come with me to the Liaison's." I told her putting my arm out so I could escort her properly.

"Davin there's a new match for me? I never dreamed it would happen I've been alone many years now, who is he?" She asked excitedly.

"That I can't tell you but I'll say I think you'll be happy with the match." We walked back quietly, I didn't want to give too much away and I'm sure Isabell was nervous and excited all at once.

We walked into the main room of the Liaison's but only the Liaison's and the clerks were in the room. I wondered where Harry had gone. Wan looked happy as we entered the room. Isabell was still a very pretty woman and I'm sure it is a relief that they have found her a match.

"Please take a seat Isabell." Wan invited her. "We know you've waited many years for a suitable match. Losing your first husband was difficult I'm sure. Do you feel ready to try with another match?" He asked her.

"It was hard to lose my husband but I've had many years to heal. Yes, I'm ready to move on with my life." She told Wan confidently.

"Isabell this match we have picked for you is a new comer to our village. But he has never married and would like very much to be bound to you and become an active part of our village." Wan said, he is again to the point when he spoke. The only doubt left in her head by now was who this mysterious new comer he's speaking about is.

Wan stood up again and walked to the door behind the main tables and called Harry in. Isabell recognized Harry immediately and could only smile in agreement with the Liaison's choice. He had flowers in his hand and a smile on his face, Iit seemed like it would be a great match.

"Davin will be your escort during the days and the evenings you may spend with friends, just never alone." Wan told the three of us. I was excited by this news; I enjoyed Harry and Isabell's company. "He'll report back to us how the match is working out. This match is unlike any we have ever done. When we match as children we are sure their love will grow as they do, especially if it's not already showing. But to match two adults is risky. Take your time and seek us for any counsel you may need."

I think it will be a good match, the look I'd seen in their eyes said a lot and it was a look I've never seen in neither Harry nor Isabell before this moment.

"Harry will stay in my cottage until other arrangements are made for him. I'll get to his calling during the week you two may dine with Davin and Elora at the kitchen for mid-meal. I'll also free up all of your afternoons for the time being for courting, it's turning summer so the time should be enjoyable. I'll also free up Elora's time from the children's center until it's time for her calling." Wan told us, I was excited for this news I didn't know how to react.

"Isabell, if this match works and you're to be bound to Harry, is your cottage sufficient for you both?" Wan questioned her.

"I think I may need taller door frames." She said with laughter in her voice, this caused everyone in the room to laugh.

"Well if that's all, I need to speak with Davin for a few moments about what is expected of him. Then you may all go enjoy the morning until it's time for mid-meal."

Wan and I walked to my office quickly. "I think we have a good match." Wan said to me as I closed and locked the door.

"Yes Sir, I think you have chosen well." I told him as I took my seat.

"I want you to go with them courting for a few reasons Davin. One it will be part of your job and I want you to consider it part of your job. I need to know how well it works making matches like this, of adults who have lost their spouses and such. It could be very important to our future. It seems wrong to make one wait for another match when sometimes one never comes for them. I want to know how they get along if it comes naturally or if it seems forced, anything that seems out of place. I also want you to record important facts as well. I've asked to have Elora join on these courting sessions for two reasons one is for you both I know you need and want time together but I also want Harry and Isabell around people they are comfortable with so they are not afraid to show affection to each other."

"I understand Wan, is there anything specific I should do for them or with them?"

"No, just go places where you enjoy spending time with Elora and let nature take its course for Harry and Isabell. I'll have Isabell's friends around the village invite them to suppers or wine to help them socialize into the village as a couple." He told me. "Go on now show Harry around town and introduce him as not only a new comer but as Isabell's match, I'd also like to know how our people react to the match."

"I'll do my best Wan, and thank you for allowing me extra time with Elora." I told him.

"Just remember your job son." He said as he got up and left my office.

I joined Harry and Isabell in the main room and asked them to come with me. We walked around the village visiting with the people. I took my job seriously and paid attention to the reactions of our people. So far everyone seemed happy to have Harry join our village and even happier that Isabell would finally have a husband.

I took them to see my mother; she was taking care of a new baby that seemed very angry to be there. Lily, the baby's mother looked tired and red eyed. Lily had just turned eighteen and it looks as if the baby had come quickly after she was bound, although the baby was very tiny, smaller than most babies born in our village. We sat and watched my mother as she checked the angry infant over. Harry and Isabell both had a look of yearning in their eyes and they watched the baby.

"Looks as if she isn't gaining much weight Lily, how often are you feeding her?" My mother asked with concern in her voice.

"She doesn't stay on Mrs. Hewit, I try a lot and she lets go as quick as she gets on." Lily answered my mother we could hear the exhaustion in her voice.

"Alright, she was an early baby, some early babies do have problems to begin with and she is just hungry that's why she is crying so much. I have a couple wet nurses and I'll send one home with you. But I want you to continue to try and feed her every other feeding. Wet nurses are so experienced sometimes they can get them going quickly, it should only take a few days. Be sure you're eating and drinking plenty as well, that will help." My mother is very good with babies; I always wondered why she only had Myka and I. She left the room for a moment and came back with another lady and introduced her to Lily, they left together.

"Now what do we have here?" My mother asked turning to the three of us. I quickly explained what had happened this morning.

"That is wonderful! You both can join us for supper to celebrate, and I'll have JD take you both home afterwards." My mother had a way of talking people into things quickly before they had a chance to say no.

"Davin when you see Elora for mid-meal have her invite her family as well. We can have a big fire and supper, this is the greatest news." She was already conceiving plans as we excused ourselves to go to mid-meal.

"Your mother is great Davin." Harry said as we left her office.

"Yes, she gets excited when there's good news, I'm sure her and Mrs. Dover will scheme all evening to keep you two together." I said laughing.

"I'm very happy." Isabell told us both. "I've waited a long time I hope to make you as happy as I feel right now over our match."

"I must admit Isabell, when I saw you at the side show and seen you wore no husband on your arm I asked Wan about you, he told me your story and right then I knew I wanted to be the one who brought you happiness again." Harry told her with tears welling up in his eyes.

"I'm happy that you chose me and I'll never forget this very moment." She reached up and touched his rough cheek as he bent down towards her to give her a small kiss on her cheek.

I'm sure this match will work now; I can see a love blossom right before me. It's so good that they have each other now. I felt warmth inside me like the warmth I felt when I thought of the love Elora and I share.

We walked towards the kitchen and I could see Harry had put out his arm to properly escort Isabell through the village. I'm sure there was much gossip as the people watched us walking towards the kitchen, not everyone knew the news, but in our village it would spread like wildfire. I was distracted during mid-meal just trying to get the reaction of the people over Harry and his new match. I didn't hear anything bad, most people just talked of his size.

Elora and Isabell chatted excitedly over the match while Harry and I talked over what his calling might be. He was excited to think he may have the life he only dreamed of a short time ago. I asked him how his parting with the side show went and he told me that it went well. He said it was very sad for a few moments but they all had wished him well and sent him with trinkets to remember them by. I was relieved to hear they weren't angry with him, I know this would have been much harder if he hadn't gotten good blessings from his loved ones.

The four of us walked together to the Liaison's after mid-meal. I wanted to update Wan on this morning before went out to the river to soak our feet and waste the day.

"How's it going?" Wan asked as I entered his office.

"It's going well Wan, I think they are a good match they both seem happy and comfortable with each other."

"How are the people in the village reacting?"

"They are responding well I've not heard anything bad. They seem to like Harry and are happy Isabell finally has a match." I told him.

"Good then, what are your plans for this afternoon?" He asked me I almost wonder why he wants to know so much but it's not my place to question him.

"We are going to walk to the river and soak our feet; I don't know how long we'll be there yet. My mother has invited Isabell and Harry to join us for supper and a celebration this evening."

"Go to the kitchen before you leave and have the workers pack you a basket for the four of you, so you can have refreshments if you get hungry or thirsty. You might do well to bring a couple blankets also." Wan said as he dismissed me from his temporary office. "Enjoy your afternoon."

I went to join the others and told them about needing to go back to the kitchen. They walked with me over and waited outside while I went in to get what we needed.

"Didn't we feed you already?" Mary teased when I put in my request. Mary is my aunt, my father's sister.

"Yes you did, but I'm a growing man." I told her and she burst into laughter. "Actually, I have to escort the new match this afternoon, I'm sure you have heard all about it through the gossiping hens around this village."

"I did hear about it, how exciting it all seems he's so huge and Isabell so tiny. Are they happy with the match?" She asked I'm sure so she would become a gossiping hen like the rest of the ladies in the kitchen.

"I think it's a perfect match." I told her helping add fuel to her fire. My aunt is a great lady and I love her dearly but I know she'll gossip away. I might as well give her something good to gossip about.

She left to the kitchen and came back shortly with a basket packed full of food. It was so heavy I struggled to pick it up. "I said a snack not a week's worth of food." I told her as I took the basket.

"He's big, he's bound to be hungry I'm sure his mid-meal couldn't have been very filling for him."

"I'm not even going to give you a lesson on the rudeness of that." I said as I walked out of the kitchen.

Harry took the basket from as I came out of the kitchen. "Did they put an entire cow in this basket?" He asked as he felt the weight of it.

"I'm sure they did, it was my aunt who packed it, and you know women they always think we don't eat enough." I mused as Elora and Isabell both shot me a mean look.

"I'm kidding my love; don't be angry at my small joke, for that's all it was." I said taking her hand in mine.

"Sometimes Davin your humor is not all that amusing." She informed me.

"Let's get going to the river so we can cool off and enjoy our afternoon in peace." I said trying another stab at my humor. This time it worked, Elora was filled with laughter as she pulled me towards the path to the river. There is a common area at the river that the entire town can use, not every cottage has a private area like we do. When we got there the spot was empty as I'd expected it to be so I decided it would be alright to set ourselves there for the afternoon.

Elora and I were the first into the water splashing and playing quietly. Harry and Isabell went a bit away from us and spoke quietly to each other. I'm glad to see they already want to be alone.

"What do you think about the match Elora?"

"I think its wonderful Davin, look at them smiling at each other and laughing together. It seems like they were meant to be." She seemed as excited about it as I was.

"Are you happy to have free afternoons with me until your calling?" I asked hoping she was.

"I prayed to have more time with you and it has come, I'll enjoy every moment of it I get." She beamed.

We calmed down and settled on the bank with our feet in the cool water. It was nice to just to sit with Elora I've always enjoyed the time I get with her, I never felt pressured to keep up conversation we are just comfortable sitting holding hands and letting the world pass us by. I occasionally glanced over at Harry and Isabell and they were holding hands like Elora and I only they were talking up a storm. I could hear them burst out with laughter once in a while.

"Are you ready to have a bite to eat or drink?" I asked Elora as I got up from the riverbank and took her hand to help her up.

"I could use something to eat and drink I think."

"Hey you two, join us for a bit of food if you'd like." I called over to them. They both got up quickly and joined us at the basket.

The basket was packed full of treats for us. There were fresh baked cookies with oats and dried peaches in them. There were also fresh corn cakes and dried beef to put in the cakes. They also sent us small cherry tarts and fresh milk to drink. They had put the milk in preserve jars with lids so we each had our own portion. It was a great little feast we had in front of us.

"I wonder how long they will make us wait to be bound." Isabell said hoping to start a conversation.

"I hope it's not long, I've lost so much time in the side show and I just want to get to living our life together."

"I hope it's not long either, I'm so happy with all that has happened today I'd marry you tomorrow if we had permission." Isabell said, almost so quietly we barley heard her.

"You have waited a long time Isabell; don't be ashamed for feeling the way you do." Elora told her confidently. "Hopefully you won't have to wait as long as Davin and I have to."

That made us all laugh, with all the talk about Elora and I in town not to mention the talks I've had with Harry it's become common knowledge how impatient I've become over these last couple weeks.

"What kind of work do you think they will give me?" Harry asked me.

"I think they may put you through some internships to see where you'll fit in, I'm not sure though it's obvious you're strong so they may already have something in mind for you." I answered him as best as I possibly could, I had honestly been wondering the same thing myself.

"I suppose we should all head back, Elora will you please extend my mother's invitation to your family?" I rose slowly feeling so full of food, I could have sat and talked until the late hours of the evening but I knew I still had to get Blitz and do my chores at the cottage tonight.

After walking Isabell back to the common Harry and I walked over to the Liaison's stable. We said our farewells and I went in to saddle Blitz up so I could ride him back to the cottage.

"Davin?" Jobe called towards me.

"Yes Jobe, what can I do for you?" I asked walking towards the back of the building.

"Wan would like to see you before you ride out." He informed me.

"I'll be right in let me finish saddling Blitz."

I finished getting Blitz ready to go and tied him to the fence on the outside of the pen. I also gave him some hay to tide him over while he waited for me, he always seemed excited when I saddled him and he tends to just want to go for his ride.

I don't really need to wonder what Wan wants I'm sure just an update on the afternoon with Harry and Isabell. Wan's office was empty as I went in, I also checked to see if he was in my office. Then I heard voices in the main hall so I went in.

"Davin take your seat please." Wan instructed me. All the Liaison's and clerks were in their seats also, I seemed to have come in during a meeting.

"We are discussing a couple important matters and we would like to hear your opinion on them. So we would like for you to answer as honestly as you can, understand?" Wan was standing now looking towards me as the rest of the room was also looking at me. I hoped I didn't do anything wrong as I took my seat.

"First thing is Harry's calling, where do you think he would best fit in within our village?" I was so relieved the meeting wasn't about anything I had done that I almost let a sigh of relief escape from my lips.

"I think he is very strong obviously; are there any areas where we lack the need for someone with strength like his?" I asked looking towards Wan.

"Not than any of us can think of at this time Davin." Wan told me.

"Well I'd suggest sending him out with the hunters in the mornings and see if he fits there. I wouldn't tell him it's a permanent calling yet though." I suggested.

"Why would you suggest he not be put in a permanent calling?" Wan asked me with a surprised look on his face.

"Well when children are sent to do internships the point is to see where they work well, some of the children get sent to different internships until they are put in one that they fit well in. I don't feel we can just throw Harry into a permanent calling and just assume it will work out for him." I explained hoping that what I said was making sense.

"So young yet so full of wisdom this boy." Lee said, he's the man who would be taking Wan's seat when his work was done.

"That's why I wanted to wait to get his opinion before we took a vote. How do you all feel on putting Harry on trial to be a hunter for the time being?" Wan asked looking for the vote. "If your vote is yes please raise your hand now." The entire Liaison's on the panel were in agreement.

"I'll let Harry know this evening before he goes out to celebrate where to check in the morning, Jobe can go speak with the hunters and let them know it will only be until mid-meal for now." Wan instructed.

"Next item up for discussion is a delicate matter. Harry and Isabell, were unsure what amount of time to allow before we see to them being bound." Wan said as he took his seat again, he seemed relaxed now that he got some of what was troubling the Liaison taken care of.

"I'd say wait a few days, let's see how they get along and if they are wanting to just get on with their lives or take their time. I know we discussed it a little bit earlier this afternoon and as of now they seem to want the courting to be quick. I can see something in them I've never seen before. I think they may be a true match, but I'd think it would be good to wait a small time before making a decision this soon." I told them with confidence.

"A true match at their ages, I never thought it possible." Lee said to Wan.

"It's possible Lee, we know they happen rarely but these two have been lonely, maybe that is what draws them to each other. I think we'll wait a week or so and discuss the progress of the match again. Davin, please continue to keep us updated on their progress. I've informed everyone of the way the village is handling the changes, we are pleased it is going smoothly." Wan was talking to us all but he looked at me a lot.

"I agree with the village it seems a welcomed change." I agreed with Wan.

"Be sure to keep your book updated as well Davin. What is taking place here is a big change for our village and it's important we keep careful record of it as we never know when we may have another similar situation."

"I will, Wan and if there is anything I can do please just speak with me about it, I'll do all I can to help."

"Davin, you're helping us a lot and don't think we haven't noticed you." Lee said looking at me. I've never heard him talk so much during these meetings.

"That's all we had to discuss you're all excused for the day. Davin, go to your office for a few moments before you leave please." Wan said as he got up to leave the room.

I followed him to my office quickly wandering what this would be about. He took the chair he always sat in when he was in my office and I took my chair. I noticed a letter on my desk that wasn't there when I had come in earlier looking for Wan.

"I just wanted to have a few private moments with you before you left." Wan started out. "The letter is from Sid, he left earlier for you."

I opened the letter quickly and all it was said was "See me about your gift." I'm assuming the dress is done or something is needed.

"I had a long talk with Sid this afternoon. He seemed very impressed with you. I can see he has put full confidence in your calling, he is one of the very few that know what exactly your calling is. I just want you to know as I've learned in my years working with Sid; he can be a trust worthy person to confide in." Wan said in almost a whisper.

"I enjoyed the time I spent with Sid and I found him easy to confide in I must admit." I told Wan.

"I'm happy you're comfortable with him, it's important you become that way with those that will be running the Liaison when I'm gone Davin. Lee will be replacing me and you'll spend a lot of time with him during your work here. I've worked with him many years Davin, he has never done anything to make me feel mistrust for him and I hope that you'll feel the same about him." I really enjoyed my talks with Wan. I feel like he makes me a big part of something that usually makes me feel like an outsider.

"I'll take some time with Lee as I can."

"That's good; you'll need to learn to speak your opinion comfortably with the Liaison, just like you did today. Just because we spent years making decisions doesn't mean they have always worked out for the best. That's why your job here is so important. Whether you opinion differs from ours or not, you see things differently and it's important for them to have new fresh opinions. The world is changing around us, we can't always remain the same village changes are coming, and having your fresh and honest opinion can make a difference. The Liaison also know that they need you and will never just overlook your opinions."

"I'm just so confused at times, but I'm learning why I'm here. And I promise to always keep my job with honor and respect." I promised Wan.

"I know you will son that is why you were chosen, now go take care of your business with Sid so you don't upset that beautiful girl of yours by being late again." Wan told me with laughter in his voice.

"How did you know about that?" I asked him, are they watching me that much.

"Jobe saw her waiting for you, and spoke with her briefly. He mentioned it to me as he found it funny; her irritation at your tardiness. It seems to me like this town has been so tightly run that when someone is late is a major irritation." I laughed at him; I remembered seeing her face when I came up late, she was rather annoyed with me.

I left quickly so I could see Sid before he left the punisher's office. We always called it the dungeon when we were small kids. The office was small about the size of a cottage without sleeping rooms. The heavy velvet curtains were black as were the chairs covers. Sid was sitting at his desk with a quill in his hand writing something very long by the looks of it. There were three wooden paddles of different sizes hanging on the wall. The room was meant to look intimidating but I no longer felt that way. The two other punishers were already gone and I hoped I hadn't kept Sid from anything important.

"Hello Davin, how are things going for you?" He asked as he put away what he was working on.

"Things are busy with the new match and new comer." I told him.

"Yes I'm sure it's exciting for everyone, it's not like the new comer is just a normal man looking for a home." He said laughing. "How do things look for his and Isabell's match?"

"I think they are good for each other, I spent the afternoon with them and they're already hoping for a quick courting so they can be bound."

"That's wonderful, I spoke with Harry some while we were on our trip he spoke fondly of Isabell and I could tell he was ready to start a life here in Furlin." He spoke fondly of Harry I think they will become good friends.

"What was it you needed of me about the gift?" I asked him remembering I had to get on my way.

"Lynne has been working night and day to make that gown. She has some lace that she made many years ago while she was with child with one our boys, she was always hoping for a daughter that never came. Anyway she would like to use the lace for Elora's dress if it's alright with you?"

"I think Elora would like that very much Sid. Please send my thanks to Lynne I really appreciate what she is doing."

"I know you do otherwise I wouldn't have asked her to take on the task lad. By the way how are you two doing since our talk?" He asked as he got up to walk me to the door.

"We are good as always, confused more than ever but we're working through it." I told him as I opened the door to leave. "Oh I forgot to tell you there will be a small celebration at our cottage for Isabell and Harry, stop by if you can."

"I'll speak with Lynne we may come by for a few minutes before we go work on our son's cottage this evening."

"Great I hope to see you then and thank you again for everything." I told him as I got on Blitz.

CHAPTER 13

Hope and despair

M Y RIDE HOME WAS uneventful until I could see our cottage busy with a bustle of activity. My mother, Mrs. Dover, Myka and Elora were busy hanging lanterns from a rope someone had hung from one tree to another. There was a fire built with a spit set over it. A turkey was roasting as it was turned slowly by Eldon. The smell was incredible, as was seeing Elora working in our yard.

"Good evening ladies!" I said as I rode Blitz towards the yard.

"Good evening Davin." My mother called. "Get off that horse and start getting water in the barrel." She ordered me.

"Got it mother, do you want it full?"

"Of course fill it please I expect it will be used quickly tonight."

As I went in the cottage to get the buckets I could see that the fire in the stone oven was going and the fire in the fire place. It was so hot I could see why they were working so hard in the yard. There were sweet potatoes roasting in the oven and a huge pot of venison stew was in the fire place.

"Where's father?" I asked my mother as I was headed towards the well.

"He went to get Harry and Isabell, and hurry up Jake and his family will be here shortly."

Jake is Myka's match, his family have become good friends with us although lately with everything going on with the Dover's we haven't spent much time working on Myka's cottage. Although Myka is only twelve we have a few years to get the work done. The main part of her cottage is done though; all that is left are the little things like carvings in the fireplace wood, fine detailing, windows and such.

After I finished with the water I went in to get some clean clothes and linens and went to the river to bathe quickly before everyone arrived. Eldon walked down with me to clean up some as well, he was covered in soot from being so close to the fire. He is always so quiet and shy, much like Elora is when were not alone. When were alone she loses her shyness to some degree. We washed quickly and I offered Eldon fresh linens to dry off with. He was a good kid I enjoyed his silent company a lot. I'm sure the fire is still fresh on his mind which has made him even quieter.

"Thank you Davin, and in case I didn't tell you before thank you for everything you did to help our family last week." He told me quietly.

"Any time kiddo that's what big brothers are for, and since I'm the closest thing to a brother you'll have until your bound you're stuck with me." I told him as I rustled his hair walking past him.

"I hate it when you do that!" H said and chased after me.

"I know; that's why I do it." I slowed so he could catch up with me. "If you ever need me you know you can come to me right?" I asked him.

"I know Davin, your good to my family and we love you I just want you to know that." He told me shyly.

"Eldon you're my family I'd do anything I could to make sure you had all you need, not only you but your whole family, and it's not just because I am to be bound to your sister either." I told him as I gave him a pat on the back.

We joined the others in front of the cottage, Jake's family had arrived and everyone was taking seats on the logs my father and Mr. Dover brought out for the celebration. Harry and Isabell haven't arrived yet, which is good because the women are still trying to make everything look perfect. There was a small table set near the cottage where some presents were set. It's customary to send a gift when a match is announced. I was waiting to give a gift, actually I had nothing to give yet, we'll be going to market soon and I'll look there.

"I had a nice afternoon with you my love." Elora said as she sat next to me on the log furthest from the fire. It's too warm yet to get comfortable near a fire.

"I must say it was a pleasant surprise to find out we would get to spend more of our afternoons together until your calling. Do your parents know of it yet?" I asked her.

"I think they must but they have not objected as of yet."

"I hope they don't because I could sit next to you on that river bank every moment of everyday and not tire of it." I whispered softly as looked into her beautiful green eyes.

"I love you." She said softly. It was something we rarely said but we knew how we felt.

I heard a wagon coming and looked up to see my father arriving with Isabell and Harry. In the back of the wagon there were many jugs of wine. My father told me they were a gift from the kitchen and had me unload them.

Harry and Isabell were greeted warmly by everyone, even a few people from the village had stopped by to leave a gift and give their congratulations. Most of the night was spent with villagers stopping in to welcome Harry and congratulate him on being matched with Isabell. He was now the biggest man in town even taller than Sid. His muscular build made him appear even bigger. Some of the village children were nervous to shake his hand but he was great at easing their minds that he might want to squish them. Isabell was all smiles, I've always known she was a very cheerful person but seeing her this evening she seemed happier than I've ever seen her.

Sid and Lynne arrived and Lynne was putting her gift of hand embroidered linens on the table. I went over to her as quietly as possible. Not that there was plenty of distraction

I just didn't want anyone think that I was up to something. "Thank you so much for what you're doing for me." I told her quietly as she turned from the table.

"It's my pleasure Davin, as you know I have no daughters of my own this is a true joy for me to do." She said with her soft voice full of admiration.

"I appreciate it Lynne, if there is ever a way to repay you for all you're doing please tell me."

"Repay me by keeping your promise to Sid lad." She said quietly and walked over to rejoin her husband in congratulating Harry and Isabelle. Knowing that Sid knew what my real calling is, made wonder if he had mentioned it to Lynne as well. Things rarely are kept secret in this village.

I seen that Wan had come as well but left before I had a chance to greet him. When my mother came out of the cottage she asked me if he had left. When I told her yes, she sighed and walked away shaking her head.

The evening went by very quickly. Before long everyone was saying their farewells. The Dover's stayed late to help us clean up, Elora and I moved slowly in the cleaning trying to prolong our time together. Our mothers knew what we were doing and they excused us to sit at our log by Elora's cottage. We walked quietly hand in hand to our favorite spot.

"It has been a weird couple weeks hasn't it?" She asked me.

"Yes, life sure has changed a lot since my calling."

"Are you overwhelmed with it all my love?"

"Not as long as I get to sit here with you and enjoy your company." I whispered as I put my head to her hair, it was still something that just drew me to her. I don't imagine it ever changing. I even remember when we were still small I would play with her hair. That was before I wasn't allowed to touch it though.

I moved her hair away from her neck and kissed her neck with tiny soft kisses. I heard her moan softly as I kissed her ear. She pulled gently away from me, I knew we're both afraid, but when we're alone it's become increasingly difficult to resist each other. She softly took my hand in hers and kissed my fingers very lightly, I can feel my body tremble with excitement. I don't understand how tiny kisses on my fingers can excite me like this. When she stopped kissing my fingers she just looked into my eyes, I could see the desire in her face and the fire that had lit in her eyes. I felt like I was drowning in her gaze, I'm not sure whether I should get up and go home or sit here and continue to feel the torture that is now consuming my entire body.

"Kiss me." She whispered, I could feel her breath on my lips already as she had come so close to me, never breaking the gaze that had me feeling as if I'm in a trance.

"I can't my love, I'd lose any control I may have left in me if I do." I said quietly, our gaze never breaking. She came even closer to my face this time so close our noses were touching and again she whispered for me to kiss her. I again pleaded with her to stop and as I was pleading she kissed me hard and passionately. I couldn't pull away and I could feel my heart pounding so hard I thought my chest would burst. She was the first to pull back.

"I knew you couldn't resist me my love." She teased, her voice sounding different there was a sly sexiness about it that made my heart beat even faster, my stomach was in knots of emotion and I'm afraid my body gave way and my manhood and was now making my sitting very uncomfortable. I was afraid I'd give myself away and I had to sit here and endure her teasing so she wouldn't see my body's betrayal to me. I couldn't take it any longer.

"I can't resist you my love I never could. Why are you intent on torturing me like this?" I asked my voice barely a whisper.

"I'm not trying to torture you, what I feel in my body I don't want to deny, it's like something wild has been released in me and I just feel reckless. When that feeling takes over me I forget anything or anyone but you and my desire for you. I don't know how to stop it." Her eyes were filled with tears now and she moved back some her gaze was still on me even with her tear filled eyes.

"I feel the same desire and want for you Elora don't ever think I don't. I'm just afraid we'll do something that may take you away from me forever and my heart would die if that were to happen. It's very difficult to resist the feelings I have for you, my body betrays me every time you kiss me like that and I don't know how to stop it." I told her with pleading in my eyes, I didn't want her to be hurt by me and my resistance.

"Does it hurt you like it hurts me when you don't act on your desire?" She asked me begging for some understanding of what happening to her.

"Yes, I feel like I'll explode if I don't give in to you and to my feelings." I assured her.

"It feels the same for me, I don't want to wait another year to be bound to you Davin, I want it now, I want to start our life together and I don't want to feel shame when I desire you like this." Her words have turned into small sobs and my heart was breaking to see and hear the pain that's in her now.

"I don't want to wait any longer either but what choice do we have?" I asked her praying maybe she had the answers I couldn't come up with.

"We don't; our lives are not in our control never have been." She said unhappily.

"We'll control our lives when our time comes my love. Then you can have anything you want and I'll do anything that assures your happiness. But I can't risk us right now, if we give into our desires now even if we weren't found out other things could happen. You know babies don't only come to those happily bound." I told her in a way that still sounded like pleading.

"I know that Davin, I've thought of the consequence honestly I have. But when that feeling takes over my body there is no consequence that can calm it."

"I do understand my love, quiet now all will be ok. I promise you and you know I don't break my promises to you ever."

"I'm going to hold you to that promise, because ever since we lost our cottage all I feel is fear when I think about us being bound. I couldn't bear to have them make us wait longer. I look every day but I don't see a new cottage going up at least even if it wasn't ours it would still give me the sense of hope I've lost." I knew she was feeling this way I've felt the same desperation since that day after the fire. But I have to trust the Liaison when they say we'll be taken care of.

"Don't lose your hope and give up your will out of fear. If the day comes when we are due to be bound and there's still no solution presented to us, I'll pitch a tent and we'll still be bound." I promised her.

I heard voices coming our way. It was Elora's family, at first I was startled but then I realized we were just sitting calmly like we were supposed to be. I've been so nervous when Elora and I are alone now I can see why they make us have escorts now.

"Go in with your family my love, I'll see you tomorrow and we'll have all day to enjoy each other."

"Sleep well my love." She said as she rose to walk with her family.

"Sweetest dreams to you, I love you." I whispered as I kissed her cheek good night.

I fell into my bed exhausted, not only from the busy day but from my time with Elora. I always felt drained after the excitement left my body. Sleep came quickly but my dreams were of Elora and me on our log. I felt like she was near me but so far away I couldn't even touch her hand. I woke feeling such despair like she would never been within reach.

I got up and dressed quickly and ran to do my morning chores. I didn't eat with my family as my stomach was still in knots over my restless dreams. My parents were worried that I wouldn't eat but I just told them I think I had too much last night. It worked and they excused me to go to my job.

I walked in this morning hoping to shake some of the despair that was consuming me. As I came up the Liaison's I noticed the curtains were drawn again, and villagers were coming and going looking very angry.

I went right to the main room where I learned what was happening. The people are complaining of things coming up missing. They say their gardens are being raided and some have even lost chickens. I could see the liaison trying to calm everyone down, sending them all with notes to replace the things that had come up missing.

Wan ordered the clerks to keep seeing those who were wronged and be sure to ask if they saw anything unusual, and summoned me to my office.

"What's the matter with you son?" He asked me as he shut my door quickly.

"Why would you thing something is wrong?" I asked him hoping he was speaking of the problem in the village.

"You look terrible, almost tortured. Has someone brought you bad news?"

"I had a rough night is all Wan, it's nothing to worry over."

"I can see your worried now tell me, I just can't have one of my workers walking around looking like he just lost his best friend."

"Well; I really don't know where to start Wan. Since the fire things have changed so much with Elora and I. We are both frightened about losing our cottage and we feel like our marriage will be put off." Wan laughed at my despair, wonderful now I'm a joke as well.

"I told you I'd be sure you're taken care of, do you not believe me?" He asked now serious.

"I want to believe it really I do. But something has stirred inside of us both since the fire and our feelings for each other are of desire and the more we try to suppress them the worse the situation feels, and fear has set in us both."

"I do understand that feeling you're both feeling and I'm sure the tragedy of the fire and losing your cottage has just

made it stronger. Have you two acted on your feelings?"
I couldn't believe he asked me that but I knew he had the
right.

"NO!" I almost yelled at him.

"That is good." He said quietly trying to calm my tone
down.

"How is it good? I feel tortured I feel like my heart is going
to be ripped from my chest Wan."

"Son, you love her and want her I do understand. I had a
wife once you know. We went through the same thing only I
think it was not so strong for us."

"I just want the time to pass so I can know our future and
hold and kiss Elora without guilt and worry that we'll do
something wrong."

"Your answers will come soon Davin I've not forgotten
my promise to you both, please be patient and trust me."

"I'm trying to be patient, last night just got to me. I now
can't kiss Elora for fear I can't stop and fear of my body
betraying me desire for her."

"Sid and I talked a little about what you're going through;
now don't be mad at him. Much like I have you telling me
how Harry and Isabell are doing I have others letting me
know your progress. I worry about you two, I know we have
a true match and have known that since you both we small.
I need to know what's happening; I need to be sure you two
aren't growing apart." I laughed at him when he said that.

"Growing apart is defiantly not an issue for us." I said
kind of defiantly.

"And I never want it to become an issue, it's why I ask
those around you what they see and hear. I know you confided
in Sid but be assured he didn't tell what he told me to get you
or Elora in any trouble."

"I just don't know what to do, when we are at the kitchen
or around friends and family this doesn't happen with us. But
something as simple as a kiss is like building an out of control
fire."

"Just be careful, you seem to be keeping it in control now. It's not bad to feel desire for her, it's just how you act on it. Have faith in me; assure Elora all she needs and enjoy what you have with her. You two will be bound and you'll get to act on your desires, it just can't happen now. You understand that right?" He asked me, I was feeling calmer now maybe he was right I just had to keep my faith.

"Yes, I do understand completely Wan. And I'll respect your wishes and have trust in you." I promised him. I was growing very fond of my talks with Wan and I found them very enjoyable. And he always had a way of calming my nerves when they seemed to get the best of me.

"I'd like you to take some time around the village this morning looking into this thievery that has been taking place. I had some complaints a couple days ago now the complaints have doubled. What I thought might have been some rabbits or something may not be."

"I'll do my best, I don't know if our garden was hit or not I didn't even ride my horse in today."

"Well fetch him and ride down the river a few miles, I noticed all the complaints are coming from those living close to the river."

"I'll see what I can figure out then, thank you for helping calm me down. I feel better about everything."

"Things will get easier for you Davin; you just have to trust in me for now."

"I do, I'll see you later this afternoon with my reports on the thievery and the new match." I told him as I left my office.

I headed straight towards my cottage so I could saddle up Blitz and be on my way. I just about walked right into Elora in my haste to get home.

"Are you in a hurry?" She asked. She looked as beautiful as ever this morning. I think she gets more beautiful every day.

"Yes, my love I have to ride out a few miles on the river. Someone has been stealing from the gardens and hen houses; I'm just going to see if I can see anything out of place."

"Will you back in time for mid-meal?"

"I don't know, if I'm not please go in without me and take Harry and Isabell out this afternoon. I'd hate to be the cause of them not getting their time together."

"I will; be safe my love." She said looking disheartened.

"Wait one second before you go running off like a shy maiden." I demanded her laughing.

"I have some news for you. I had a long talk with Wan this morning; he assured me we are not being overlooked. Now will you not worry so much?"

"I'll do my best Davin, I promise."

"Good because I cannot bear to see you as sad as you were last night. Have a good day my love, I'll see you as soon as I can." I gave her a small kiss on her hand and continued on to my cottage.

CHAPTER 14

Thieves

I T WASN'T LONG BEFORE my journey up river began. Blitz of course was always ready to ride though. His ears perked when he saw me coming towards his pen. I headed out towards the river and remembered that I skipped breakfast so I turned him around and went to the cottage. I grabbed some dry meat and some biscuits from breakfast. I figured I'll be near water so I can drink from there.

It was difficult keeping Blitz from running. I wanted to take the ride slow in case I found anything that would lead me in the direction of the thieves. The only thing I did notice were bare foot prints maybe belonging to a child. They stopped soon after I found them, and then there was nothing. I rode a good mile from the last prints and I thought I heard soft crying across the river. I stopped Blitz and listened very carefully. I did hear crying, I tied blitz to a tree near the river and waded across. I was walking very carefully I didn't want to scare anyone. I came upon a small ragged tent; I peered inside and looked at the faces of two young children. Both were crying and holding on to each other. I also saw what was left of a chicken and some fruit.

"I won't hurt you." I told them cautiously. They certainly looked frightened enough as it was.

Both of the children were dirty and I could see some bruises on their arms and legs. They looked as if they had been through a lot. My heart hurt to see them in such poor conditions.

I sat down on the outside of the tent. "Who are you?" the boy asked me looking more frightened as I sat and peered in on them.

"My name is Davin; I live in the next village down the river."

"Are you going to hang us?" The skinny little boy asked.

I laughed at him, I know in the bigger towns they hang thieves but in our village it was never a form of punishment in our village, nor did we have issues with our people being thieves.

"Now why would you think I'd hang a fine boy such as yourself?" I asked knowing why he thought it.

"We stole food from your village." He admitted, the little girl began crying harder.

"Why are you two here?"

"Our father died when a bull rushed him, our mother got the sadness real bad in her. She killed herself with a rope in our cottage only a few days later." I was stunned by his answer.

"Why didn't the people in your village take you in, why are you here?"

"They said mother was crazy and they told us to leave the village before we went crazy too." He told me sadly.

"What village are you from?"

"Breakstone, Sir they threw rocks at us until they couldn't reach us any longer. We ran till we came to the river and followed it down."

"What are your names and how old are you?" I asked him, my heart was breaking for these two innocent children who not only lost their parents but their homes and people that should have loved them.

"I'm Luke and my sister is Maggie, she is four and I'm seven." He said proudly, he is so strong for a boy so young.

"I want you two to come with me." I said to Luke, they both looked terrified. "I'm not going to punish you, but I'd like to take you to my town. Come on I'll get you something to eat and a bed to sleep in tonight."

The poor children looked terrified but they slowly got up and walked towards me. I picked little Maggie up so I could carry her threw the water to Blitz. She was so frail I was afraid I'd break her. I put both the children up on Blitz's back and slowly walked them back down the river.

I promised them over and over that they were not in trouble that I was only trying to help them. I could see why they were so terrified though. We talked small talk, Luke was full of questions, and he wanted to know about Blitz and Furlin. Maggie said very little, I'm sure she is weak though and it takes much of her strength just to sit on Blitz.

I cut away from the river before we came into town. I wanted to take the children into the Liaison's before the town started gossiping. I tied Blitz to the fence and took both of the children down, but I kept Maggie in my arms I don't think she had the strength to walk anywhere.

I put both the children in my office and went to get Wan. As he followed me in I explained what I found, he was mortified by the tale I told him. He was even more mortified when he set eyes on Maggie.

"Davin, take these children at once to your mother's office. I want a full report on their health. I'll have Jobe go to the kitchens and get them something to eat. Go now!" He ordered me. I could see he felt the same urgency for these small children as I did.

Little Luke said nothing but looked relieved that Wan hadn't ordered him to his death. I picked up both children with ease and headed to my mother's office. Before I made it in Isabell saw me with the frail children, she took Maggie from me and followed me into my mother's office.

My mother looked as horrified as Wan and Isabell did when they set eyes on the children. I quickly explained what had happened with them as she took Luke from my arms.

She lifted him with ease and Isabell took Maggie and set her down next to Luke on examining table.

"Jobe will be here shortly with something for them to eat." I told them both.

My mother got right to looking the children over. She removed their ragged clothing and the children were covered in bruises. My mother and Isabell both gasped at the sight of their frail bruised bodies.

"Isabell go them fresh bed clothes; don't worry about shoes for now they will have to be in bed at least three days if not more." My mother ordered, Isabell didn't even stop to let her finish she was out the door and running towards the common.

I watched as my mother gently washed them and checked all their injuries. Maggie has a broken arm, I thought it looked funny but honestly thought it was just her frailness that made it appear so odd looking. Luke has a lot of bruises and scrapes but no broken bones. Both of their feet are raw and red from having no shoes on when they were chased from their home.

Isabell returned as my mother finished setting Maggie's arm on a board and securing it with thin bands of linen to secure it. She helped my mother put the bed clothes on them. None of us spoke much; we were in shock over the condition of the children. I looked out the window and seen Harry and Elora waiting. It must have been time for all of us to meet.

Wan followed Jobe in with a small basket of food for the children. They had brought them soup, bread, and tiny cherry tarts, along with small jars of milk. My mother told us they would have to eat it slowly. She was worried that such a large meal would make them sick if they ate it too fast.

"How long have you been living on the river?" My mother asked Luke.

"They chased us away I think maybe six days ago. I've lost count." He told her.

"How bad is it?" Wan asked my mother.

"They both have many bruises, Maggie has a broken arm, their feet are raw and very infected, and they are very malnourished." She informed him this information was enough to set Isabell into tears. I know she has longed for a child for so long to see these two just cast off hurts her more than most will see.

"They will stay with us until they are healed." My mother began. "We can worry about the rest when we need to."

Wan nodded his head to show he agreed with my mother. "I'll need plenty of socks for their feet and some extra bed clothes for them. The rest of what I need I already have or can get. Davin bring in Elora and Harry." She ordered and she went into the other room.

I opened the door and called to Elora and Harry. "My mother needs you both in here." They came quickly and when they saw the two children their looks were the same as the rest of ours on first sight of them. My mother came out of the room with a jar full of white cream.

"After I get this on the children I need Isabell and Harry to carry the children to my cottage, let them eat and put them in beds until I get there. Try not to let them walk anywhere, so we can start their little feet healing." She put a thick layer of the cream on the children's feet and wrapped clean linen around them.

"Now quickly get them to my cottage. Isabell put them together in Davin's room, his bed is bigger." I walked them out the door and assured them I'd be with them soon that Harry and Isabell will be good to them. I gave Maggie a small kiss on her forehead and shook Lukes hand.

"Wan may I request that Harry and Isabell be relieved of their duties while the children heal, they are adults and I think maybe the escort rules may be removed for this situation, I think they will handle themselves with respect." My mother said looking straight into Wan's face with a urgency I've never seen from my mother.

"Yes Mrs. Hewit I think you're right. I trust them both and I can see they will take good care of the children. I'll let the Liaison know that things have changed. Also thank you I know you're expecting three babies soon and I appreciate you taking control."

"No, I can't take time off right now, but with their help I can manage the children's health and well being in the evenings. Of course I'm sure Myka will be happy to help fuss over them as well." She told Wan not looking as upset as she had moments earlier. I think she was afraid he would deny her request.

"I'll have mid-meal delivered to your cottage for Isabell and Harry, as well as extra socks and clothing for the children. Please keep me updated on their health. And thank you again." Wan said as he and Jobe left the office.

"Davin, Elora I'll have to make a lot more of this cream, it may be the only thing that will help save their feet." She took a leaf from a drawer in her desk. "Out where the side show was camped towards the trees there are small patches of this plant. I need to two go gather every leaf you can. And use a rock or something to mark each plant it takes seven days for the leaves to grow again and we may need more." She handed us each a basket with linen laid on the bottom and told us to go.

We ran all the way to the camp site then headed towards the trees, the leaves were easy to find and there seemed to be an abundance of them. As we hurried to gather as many as we could Elora asked me what had happened to the children. I told her the story that Luke had told me and watched her weep in disbelief. It only took a few minutes to stuff our baskets full and there were still many more plants if we had to get more. We turned around and ran all the way back to my mother office and gave her the leaves.

"Now I want you to go to the common get them each their own blanket and pillow, also try to find them some toy or something they can call their own. They will need a lot of security and love, what they have been through will make it very difficult for them to trust any of us." My mother said as she turned to go in the door behind her office.

We walked quickly over to the common, both us feeling exhaustion from the run out to campsite to pick the plants. Neither of us said much, we were so focused on Luke and Maggie there was nothing else to speak of.

At the common they were already told of the children and that some of us would be coming in and out to get supplies for them. I'm sure Jobe had filled them in and told them to help us. They took us into the room where all the supplies were kept hidden from the villagers. Elora found Luke a soft yellow blanket with a small pillow for his little head. I found a handmade pink blanket with lace sewn around the edges for Maggie and a pillow that matched it. We looked through the toys and found Luke a stuffed rabbit and a rag doll for Maggie. We also found some maple hard candies, probably from the last market day and took some for them. We told the ladies of the common thank you after they wrote down what we got for the children.

We walked quickly back to my cottage. I wanted to get with them quickly as I'm sure they were frightened. As we went into the cottage and saw Luke on Harry lap sleeping very soundly, Harry just sat silently rocking him gently. Harry was so huge and to see him sitting there rocking that tiny child was amazing. Isabell had Maggie swaddled in a blanket so she didn't injure her arm any worse and was also silently rocking her. Maggie was not asleep but she looked so at peace I almost felt as if we had intruded on them when we came in.

"We got them some blankets and pillows, and Wan will have mid-meal delivered to you soon." I told them as I walked over towards Maggie and gave her the rag doll.

"Thank you." She said with a voice so small I could barely hear her. I leaned over and gently kissed her soft tiny cheek.

"Tomorrow we'll bathe them; I'll bring a basin big enough for them to sit in. Harry and I can boil water so it will be warm water for them." Isabell told us.

Harry just sat silently rocking Luke. I know that Harry was abandoned at a very young age, I think him seeing these kids really brought back some bad memories for him. Elora and I went to my room to put fresh linens on my bed along with their new blankets and pillows. Since Luke was sleeping we set his stuffed rabbit on his blanket. For a long moment Elora and I just stood and gazed at each other. The horror of what those children had been through sinking in to both of us. We went out and silently sat at the table with Harry and Isabell. Maggie had finally fallen into a restless sleep crying out every few moments for her mommy. Isabell calmed her as best as she could.

Soon there was a knock at the door, it was a clerk he had a basket of food and another basket full of socks and fresh linens for the children. Elora took the food and set the table for us, she served us all and we sat silently picking at our food. Luke woke up as Harry leaned forward to take a bite.

"How are you feeling Luke?" I asked him as he sat up in Harry's huge lap.

"I feel tired and hungry." He said in a very weak voice.

Elora moved her chair near Harry and began to feed Luke some stew from our mid-meal. Luke only took small bites and it looked like he was struggling to swallow his food.

"Are you an angel?" He asked Elora as he stared into her face.

"No, I'm not an angel but I'll be your friend if you want to be mine." She told him as she smiled at him and ran her hand across his forehead to get his hair out of his eyes.

"I'm Luke." He announced and put his hand forward as if he were a little king.

"Nice to meet you Luke, I'm Elora." She introduced herself and shook his hand.

Harry handed Luke to her so he could go out back. She rocked him softly and asked me to get his rabbit. He loved it, he held it close to his chest and fell asleep quickly in her arms.

"Poor kid is tuckered out, sounds as if the past six days has been very hard him. He did so much and took care of Maggie as best as he could, he sure is tough." I said.

My mother came in shortly after Luke had fallen asleep. "I hate to do it but I'm going to have to wash their feet again and put this cream I made on them." She said as she looked at them. "So sad what's become of these perfect little angels."

I got up and warmed water for my mother and Isabell and Harry took the linen off their feet. They didn't cry but they looked afraid and in pain. The whole time Harry and Isabell spoke softly and lovingly to them. My mother was careful washing their little feet, she told Isabell to watch as she would have to help do this over the next couple days. She also told them of the favor she was granted for their help with the children. They both thought it was wonderful news. I could tell already they loved these children as much as I did when I found them by the river.

The next couple days passed quickly, we were all very caught up in the care of the children that nothing seemed to matter. I went into the Liaison's daily to update them on how the children were healing and to also update them on how well Harry and Isabell worked together giving all their love and devotion to Maggie and Luke. Elora was still given afternoon's off and we just spent the days out by the river playing with the Luke and Maggie and enjoying our mid-meals and time together. We all cared for the children with love and compassion and we all loved them like they were our own. My mother came in a couple times a day just to check on the children's feet. After three days they were almost healed. Maggie's little broken arm almost looks as if it will heal straight as well.

Before I realized how many days had come by my mother reminded me that we were leaving for the market in the morning tomorrow.

"What about Luke and Maggie?" I asked quickly, the little ones were never far from mind anymore.

"I've already spoke with Isabell and Harry they will stay at our cottage while we go, they have both given me a list of things to look for that they need. And I spoke with Wan and he is fine with it. He doesn't feel the need to meddle with this match since the children got here." She pointed out.

"They sure have taken to Maggie and Luke that's for sure." I told my mother.

"Yes they have, it will be good for them to have some time alone with them when we go to market."

A short time later I heard a knock at the door I was surprised to see Jobe standing at the door. "Wan needs to see you as soon as you get some free time." He informed me as he turned and walked away as quick as he came.

I've already been to see Wan this morning I can't imagine why he would need me again. Blitz was already saddled from my first trip in, I went around to his pen and led him out and around to the front of the cottage.

Luke was sitting in the window looking towards me. He looks happier now than he looked when I found him in the tent. My mother still wants them off their feet for another day, though they are healing great and the infection is gone. I waved to Luke as I mounted Blitz and headed towards the Liaison's. When I went in towards my office I could see my door was open and Wan was sitting in his normal chair waiting for me.

"What trouble's you Wan?" I asked him as I closed the door so we could have privacy. I knew by his look that whatever he had to say it would be important.

"How are Maggie and Luke today?" I really despise when he answers a question with a question.

"They are doing well, their appetites have increased more every day, and they are itching to go run and play. Their feet are almost healed so maybe only one more day and they can. And Maggie's arm looks to be healing straight"

"I'm slightly troubled about Isabell and Harry staying at your cottage with just the children, what are your thoughts on this situation?" He asked me showing his grief.

"I don't feel that they will do anything to ruin their reputations. I can see they love and respect each other. And they are different when they are with the children, in fact they act much like my father and mother when they are in public."

"They aren't doing anything more than holding hands?" He asked quizzically. He hasn't been asking much about Isabelle and Harry just if they are getting along he has been more interested on the children and their health.

"They don't even sit next to each other when they are with the children. Maggie is very attached to Isabell she'll sit in her lap for hours she really enjoys the love Isabell gives her. And Harry and Luke are also inseparable. Harry has been teaching Luke how to carve little wooden animals much like the ones we win at the side shows. Silly kid has almost a whole zoo already."

"I'm relieved to hear that, are you still feeling good about their match?"

"Yes, they treat each other with love and respect, and they carry themselves that way as well. I can honestly see where they are good for each other and for the children. I wonder if the kids would be thriving so well if weren't for the love and compassion that Isabell and Harry have given them." I really believed that too, when they wake in the mornings the first thing they ask for are Isabell and Harry.

"I'm happy to see you speak so fondly of them both, I have some things to think over and after you return from market we can meet again." He spoke quietly as if he was troubled by something that had happened. I don't think Isabelle and Harry did anything wrong, I'm not going to worry myself over it.

"How are things going with you and Elora? I haven't seen you at the kitchen for a couple days."

"We've been taking mid-meal at the cottage with the children when we do the children enjoy the attention we give them. Maggie doesn't swim yet Elora and I've promised to teach her when her feet are better." I told him hoping he could see how well the children are taken care of and loved by us all. He still hadn't told me his plans for the children once they get better. I just hope as does everyone else we'll still be able to see them.

"That's good I'm glad to see it's been good for everyone. You can go now I just wanted to speak with you about Isabell and Harry before you left for market." He said as he got up to leave my office.

I unlocked my box and took a few silver coins out I was hoping to buy the children some candy at market if anyone had any. This year we are riding out on the morning of the market, my mother doesn't want to be away the three days like we usually are. I'm not sure if it's worry over the children or the adults though.

CHAPTER 15

Market Day

I SLEPT HEAVY LAST night, my parents in such a rush to pack the carriage with things we needed to take to market, we won't even have a booth this month but my mother is hoping she can make some trades. I haven't done anything for market this time. I usually make belts to use for trade. I have coin now so I'll just buy anything I may want or need.

Elora's family left last night, I was so sad to hear her family would be there the two days. Hopefully we get to see them for mid-meal or supper today while we're there. They were able to save some of their preserves from the fire so they will be able to trade for some things. I gave her a couple silver coins last night when I saw her leaving just in case she needed anything. Her birthday is next week maybe she'll treat herself to some sweets while she is out there.

My father woke me quietly before the sun had even started to show in the sky. Harry and Isabell were already sitting at our table looking as tired as I felt. We all got ready quietly as we didn't want to wake up the children. I dressed in my grey riding outfit, I wanted to ride Blitz out there and back, I really didn't get time to do more with him then ride around town so I think it will be good to take him for such a long trip. It was about twenty miles to the grove where we all meet. About four different towns usually come, but it's sometimes different who will be there. I'm hoping the people from Gabby that have the honey will come. Sometimes they make candies out of the honeycomb and they are everyone's favorite.

The ride to the grove was uneventful, we did come across others traveling to the grove like we were. I didn't talk much with my family as we rode out, once the sun started to shine I was so busy looking at all the animals hiding off the path. I noticed a lot of deer just beyond the tree lines and a lot of quail on the path as well, we practically ran some over they didn't want to move from some corn that had fallen from someone's carriage. Even Blitz tried to stop there for a nibble, I just laughed at him as I pulled him from the mess.

"Not much further." My father yelled towards me.

"Can I ride ahead, please?" I asked like a little kid.

"Go ahead just look for us in a little while." He instructed me. Usually I rode in the back of our carriage, it's nice having some of the freedom I've gained over the last few weeks.

I brought Blitz to a trot and headed to the lively sounds I heard coming from the grove up ahead. I could hear horns in the distance playing music and the sound of laughter. As I got closer I could see people with their small tables of wares set up everywhere. I looked for the Dover's so I could tie Blitz up with their horse and look around. They had their wares set up next to the people with the honey, this made me happy for two reasons, I could see Elora and I'd be able to take home fresh honey and candy.

"Well hello Davin, have a good ride?" Mr. Dover asked as he helped me down from Blitz.

"It was a great ride, how's things been going here?"

"Busy as always we've sold most of our own wares and not much left of what we brought from work either." He told me.

"Wow hope there's stuff left when my parents get in."

"There's always stuff here you know that by now, for as the piles get smaller by the day the evening brings out even more wares." We both laughed at that, the evenings during market were great, people always had homemade wines and liquors to trade with. I'm hoping to find cherry wine for when they announce when Isabelle and Harry can be bound.

"How's that lovely daughter of yours?" I asked him hoping he wouldn't catch that I had been missing her like I was.

"Oh she is probably wandering around aimlessly looking for her lost love." He said laughing. "She's been sad since we left lad, go look where they are selling ribbons you're bound to find her there, I got your horse go on!" He had a big smile on his face as he walked away from me with Blitz.

It didn't take long to find my love she was wearing my favorite green dress. I secretly told her one day about where the material came from she wears it often since I told her. She was standing at a table full of hair pins, ribbons and jewelry. I walked up behind her quietly; I'm sure she hadn't seen me coming.

"What's your fancy pretty little girl?" I asked standing behind her.

"Oh I don't know; a tall boy with thick dark hair and blue eyes with a penchant for trying to be sneaky." She said as she shrugged never looking back at me.

"Well maybe; if you turn around slowly... Really slowly, you'll find what you fancy." I don't think I have the ability to be seductive like she is but I gave it my best.

She turned slowly towards me with her eyes closed and kissed me right on my chin. She does have terrible aim, so I bent down and told her to try again, this time she got me quickly and softly on my lips. She opened her eyes and gazed up at me for a few moments and said:

"Yes, I've found what I fancy."

We were so happy to see each other we became quickly inseparable during the entire day. Kyan joined us shortly after we found each other as did Eldon and Myka. I asked Kyan if Leta's family had come but he told me Leta's mother had been really sick and they decided not to make the journey.

After we walked around and looked at all the tables set up I went and bought honey and candy of course and headed to where my parents had set up.

"I brought meat and biscuits if any of your hungry." My mother called to us all, she has quickly become accustomed to feeding large amounts of people lately. Fortunately the Liaison had agreed to up our food share while we had the children and Isabell and Harry to feed now.

I grabbed a blanket and the food basket and set us up under a shady tree so we could all eat together. I also grabbed a jar of the honey so we could enjoy it on our biscuits.

"Don't start without me, I'll get water." Said Eldon as he picked up the bucket and headed for the well. Someone many years ago put that well in here, it's nice to always have fresh water especially now when the weather has turned so warm.

Our talk was just mostly about the children and what a sad story they came with. Kyan had met them only once and he even took to them immediately. After we finished eating we all went our separate ways to shop and spend time with our family.

I picked some hair pins and ribbons for Maggie and I found small jars of paints with little brushes that I had to get for Luke. I also found some lace, not sure what I'd do with it yet but I'm sure one of the girls in my life will need it for something. I also found the cherry wine I was looking for, some people also from Gabby make it and for one silver I got two big jugs of it. After I was done shopping I put all my purchases in the back of my parent's carriage and walked over to the river.

I was sitting under a shady bush with my feet in the water when I not only heard but smelled Elora behind me. I was excited instantly but I know that with us being alone like this can only lead to trouble.

"I just wanted to soak my feet." She said as innocently as she could muster. Only I heard the seductive way her voice had turned.

"We are going to be in trouble if we get caught alone my love." I tried to warn her, I was so full excitement yet I was terrified.

"Caught how? My mother knows where I am, she also knows you're here." She told me her voice so low I could barely hear her over the rushing water.

"She let you come anyway?" I asked in astonishment.

"Yes but I only have a few minutes, Eldon will be right behind me she gave me a small window so I could enjoy a kiss."

"She didn't?" Now I'm shocked.

"She knows we kiss silly man." She said laughing at my fear.

"Then we should hurry and kiss." I told her pulling her close to me. We didn't let our kisses get out of control, we knew Eldon would be with us soon and we didn't want him getting in trouble when he finally got his match because of something hesaw us do.

Elora took her boots off and put her feet in the water next to mine. Sometimes when our feet touched she would turn red and look away. I think only because Eldon was there. We all just sat quietly enjoying the shade and cool water. After you did your shopping there wasn't much to do but enjoy some time to relax. When other people started showing up at the river it got loud and rowdy so we all decided it would be best to go back. When I got back to my parents they were packing to leave.

"Already?" I asked

"Yes son we have finished our shopping and all our wares have been sold or traded. It was a good day but we need to get home to the children." My father said as he handed me a crate to put in the wagon.

"Can I go tell Elora farewell?"

"Yes; don't be long though your mother is getting anxious to get out of here." He said with a look that said he meant business.

I ran clear across the market and Elora was at her parents table. "We are leaving." I told her, "I just wanted to bid you farewell before we rode out."

"I'll be right back mother." She said as she came to help me untie Blitz. "We are leaving soon as well my love. Don't worry, I'll be home tonight you can come bid me good night."

"I will, if you promise to not torture me like you did the last time I bid you goodnight." She looked hurt but I knew she understood my trepidation.

She gave me a proper kiss on the cheek and we bid farewell. "Be safe on your journey home my love." I said as I got on Blitz. "I love you."

She blew me a kiss as I turned around to leave. I heard her call I love you to me but she said it softly so her parents didn't hear her.

The ride home was hot and dusty. It would have been better if we waited till evening, but my parents didn't want to ride through the night with only the four of us. We are bringing more with us then what we left with and the carriage seems to be moving a lot slower. I can't wait to get home to the river so I can bathe and get some sleep. Doing market in one day rather than two or three are very difficult. My father's horse is tired and moves slower as each mile passes us.

Finally I can see the edge of our village coming in to sight. "Go on boy!" My father yelled knowing how impatient I had become with the slow pace. I rode ahead to our pens and took the saddle off Blitz and brushed him down. He enjoys being brushed as much as he enjoys going out for a ride. As I was headed over to the stables I could see Luke and Maggie in the window waving at me. Isabell and Harry must be making them stay in the cottage. After I finished up my chores I saw my father and mother coming in the carriage. I helped them empty it as I was eager to give the children their presents, I also helped my father put away and feed his horse.

"Davin!" I heard Maggie shriek as I walked in the door. "What did you get us?"

"I found no candy at the market little lady." I tried to tease but she had already seen the bag sticking out of the top of my crate.

"Come tell me what you did today while I find the treats."
I instructed her, Luke had already crawled up in Harry's lap
so he could see into the crate as I unpacked it.

"We played at the river, and we worked in your garden,
all the weeds went away." As she said it she put her hands
in the air and in a wave like it was just that easy to weed the
garden.

"Well that was very nice of you, and for all your hard work
I brought you ribbons and pins for your pretty blonde hair."

"They really were out of candy?" She asked shyly. Everyone
in the room laughed loudly at how cute she was.

"No silly of course I got you candy, how does honey candy
sound to you?"

"It's my favorite!" She squealed.

Honey candy is broken up pieces of the honey comb that
has almost crystallized. It's very sweet and I've loved it since I
was a boy. The candy is very popular too and the people from
Gabby have mastered making and selling it. We've got honey
candy from other people and it's never the same.

Luke loved his paints and he can't wait to start painting
the animals he and Harry have been making. He also gobbled
up so much candy that I thought he wouldn't eat for a couple
of days. He already looks like he has gained some weight in
the time he's been with us. We have also found out Isabell is
a great cook, it's no wonder he is already starting to look like
a normal seven year old. Maggie still looks tiny but she has
color in her cheeks and her face looks fuller. I wonder what
would have come of them if I hadn't found them by the river.
The thought of it scares me really bad, as bad as the tale they
told of what had happened to them.

"Now if we are all happy with our candy and presents,
may I please go bathe in the river?" I asked the kids laughing
at their enthusiasm.

"Go Davin you stink!" Maggie joked with me.

I went to my room which has become quite crowded with
all the presents everyone constantly brought them. I've been
sleeping on the floor in here for over a week now. I don't mind

though, I'd give those kids anything I had just to see the smiles that light up their faces. I gathered up fresh clothes and clean linens and headed to the river.

The sun was just starting to set as I got into the water, it's still very warm out and the water was cool. After I washed up, I swam to the bank and just sat in the water and watched as the sun went down. I smelled supper cooking all the way out here, as I much as I didn't want to get out of the water my stomach reminded me that it was time.

Isabell was cooking with my mother, and my father and Harry were playing with the children at the table. My father is surprisingly good at doing little girls hair and he had Maggie looking like a little princess. Myka has become pretty quiet lately she mostly sits by herself in her room when she is home and not doing chores. I've talked to my mother about it and she says she did the same thing when she was Myka's age. I had started thinking she didn't like having all the extra company in the cottage, but when she was out with everyone she fussed over making sure the children were happy as much as we all did. I'm not happy with how withdrawn she has become, maybe I can speak with her and cheer her up.

Dinner is a noisy affair in our little cottage now. Maggie likes to chat away with anyone who will talk with her. I'm starting to think that's why she is so tiny she never stops chattering to get a full meal in on her. Little Luke gobbles his dinners down like he hasn't eaten all day. Mother says he will slow down when he becomes sure that food will always be available for him. She says the kids will always have hidden fears due to the tragedy that they went through. She says they may never overcome some of the problems they have.

Isabelle made a wonderful dinner as usual, venison steaks, with fresh sweet potatoes and fresh hot bread. We also had butter tonight so with the honey the bread was the best. We ended up with about five jars of honey, and with the kids here I'm sure it won't last until the next time they have market.

"I have big surprise for the two of you if you finish all your supper." My mother told Luke and Maggie.

In unison they both asked. "What is it?"

"I was thinking of taking the bandages off your feet for good this evening and maybe we can build a small fire and play in the cool of the evening."

"We can finally play and walk?" Maggie asked looking as if she was not sure if mother was just teasing her or not. They longed to play outside so bad that they would stare out the window for hours.

"Yes you may little lady." My mother answered her.

They were so excited they could barely sit still much less finish their supper. My mother took their bandages off carefully and looked their feet over. "They look great I think we'll go play outside after all." She said smiling at their little faces.

My father and Harry went to gather up wood for a small fire and had it lit and going as we brought the kids outside to play. As we all settled down around the fire to watch the children play Harry brought two pieces of rope out of his pockets.

"These are called jump ropes, when we were in Stormhaven I seen the children playing with these and I thought you two being as smart as you are might be able to figure them out." He gave each of them a rope then took a seat near Isabell. They twirled the ropes and swung them around their heads and snapped them on the ground. But this isn't what Harry had in mind for them. He got up and went over to Luke where he stood behind him and had him take an end of the rope in each hand. Then he told him to slowly bring the rope over his head and when it gets down to his feet to jump over it. After a few time both Luke and Maggie were able to do it, even with her arm still in bandages. They laughed and giggled as they jumped the rope. After a while my mother called us into the cottage for dessert. She had made strawberry tarts with the strawberries she got at market today.

After everyone had eaten their tarts Isabell and Harry helped me tuck the children into bed and my father took them to their cottages. The kids fell asleep very quickly I'm sure the jump ropes wore them out. I sat in my window watching for Elora's carriage to pull into their cottage. I've seen a few families arrive hopefully she'll be home shortly.

I must of fallen asleep sitting in the window I woke with the sound of tapping on my window. I jumped up really quick and looked out. She looked like a dream standing out in the moonlight in her night clothes. It took me a few seconds to realize she was really there. I opened my window quietly and the smell of her hair told me that yes she really was standing there.

"What are you doing out there?" I asked her, I was in shock from being startled awake then to see her standing there really confused me.

"I saw you sitting in your window when we came in. After everyone was asleep I looked out and you were still here. I thought maybe something was that matter."

I laughed for a moment and she got a very hurt look on her face. "I must of fallen asleep waiting to see you come home is all my love."

"Oh I see, and here I thought you were pining away for me, but you were simply napping in your window." She teased.

"I was pining away for you there is no doubt about that, I just happened to be doing it in a very sleepy state is all. Will you forgive me?" I asked her.

"Your forgiven, but only if you come out here and kiss me goodnight."

"I'll do one better than that, I'll come walk you safely home. Did you sneak out your window?"

"Yes, I did and thank you for the offer a girl like me shouldn't be wandering alone at such a late hour."

We walked quietly over to her cottage and went to the back where her window is. She turned towards me and kissed me so fast that I didn't even realize that she was going to kiss me. In my sleepiness I relented to her easily, it wasn't too long before our kisses grew increasingly urgent and she was pulling my body into hers. Our breathing was heavy and desperate as she held tightly to me never bringing her lips away from mine. Before I realized it was happening we were sinking to the ground onto our knees. I could feel my excitement growing and the more she pushed the more excited I became. She was pushing her body against mine so hard there was no way to hide what was happening to me. This just made her become more aggressive with her kisses, and her hands were now pulling at my shirt and even at the button that held my pants. I moved from kissing her lips slowly to kissing down her neck to her breasts. I was so frightened yet feeling brave. I've watched her blossom into a beautiful woman in agony over the last few weeks I couldn't control myself from her anymore.

I couldn't pull away from her and I couldn't stop my mouth from kissing her breast that I had brought out of her nightgown. She moaned quietly with excitement, she didn't even sound like the girl who had just been talking to me at my window. She reached down and touched me this time lightly but her touching became quicker her grasp harder. I felt like I'd explode right there, my heavy moans of pleasure were smothered by her swollen breasts. Suddenly we heard a footstep, we froze; didn't move anything, her hand still down my pants and my lips still on her breast. Then we seen what had taken the step it was her father's horse. We both jumped up and dusted off our clothes. We were so frightened we didn't say anything only just looked at each other as we straightened our clothes.

"Elora I'm so sorry I should have never touched you like that." I was stuttering and still out of breath from being frightened so bad and from what had just happened.

"I wanted you to touch me like that Davin don't you understand that?" She pleaded quietly still looking into my eyes trying to control the tears that were coming.

I pulled her close to me this time only burying my head into her hair and holding her close to me. "I love you and don't want to lose you my love. I'm also afraid I'm going to hurt you and I never want to hurt you."

"You're not going to hurt me."

"You don't understand what I'm feeling though. I feel different when I get like that and it frightens me." I pleaded with her.

"It doesn't frighten me, it excites me more."

"We have to wait until we are bound, if we don't we'll either be caught or you'll become with child. If either of those things happened we'd lose each other forever. Don't you understand that?" I pleaded with her hoping with all I had to hope with that I'd not hurt her.

"I do understand that Davin, but I also understand what I want and that's you, and you stop me every time."

"Because I love you and I can't bear the thought of being without you, so I have no choice then to be willing to wait, no matter how intent you seem on making it difficult."

"Would you have stopped if that horse hadn't moved?" She asked me with that seductive voice she now can bring out at will.

"I didn't want to." I admitted to her.

She leaned in to kiss me again, this time I didn't open my lips as easily and she backed away slowly.

"I love you, sleep well Davin." She said as she jumped into her window and shut it before I had a chance to bid her goodnight. I watched her in her window for a few seconds when she seen my face she smiled then she lifted her nightgown over her head and stood naked before me, she was beautiful and I couldn't take my eyes off her. Then she blew me a kiss and turned away and got into her bed once she was lying naked in her bed she used her finger to call me in. She just laid there staring waiting for me to come to her and for every part of me that wanted to go in the window and take her and relieve the torture she was causing; all I could do was turn and walk away. If I went in there I couldn't have stopped myself, in fact if she had stayed out here any longer I may not have been able to stop either.

I walked to the river and took my clothes off and got in. The cold water felt good on my body. My excitement from what I saw in her window was going down finally as I just sat there replaying the whole thing over and over again in my head. That only caused me to become excited again, at this very moment the only feeling I have is agony I want to give in so bad. I want to just go to her window and go to her it's all I can think. How could I have walked away from her like that, and why is she making it so hard for me? In some ways I was angry at what she did to me tonight and in some ways it excited me so bad it was all I could do to resist going back. I got out of the water and laid on the bank to dry off. I was feeling a little more relaxed as I stared at the stars above me wondering what would she do next and if I'd have the strength to resist her. If it wasn't for that horse I don't think I would've stopped and that kind of frightens me.

After I was dry I got my clothes back on and walked quietly back to Elora's cottage I just needed to see that I hadn't hurt her. When I looked into her window she was sleeping, she had put her nightgown back on and she lay uncovered on her side facing the window. She didn't look upset as she slept I hoped she felt that way tomorrow at mid-meal.

I tossed and turned on my floor all night, I had nightmares that it had been Wan who had taken the step when we were outside Elora's window. He broke our match and sent Elora away from the town the villagers threw rocks as she ran away. When I woke I knew where the dream had come from but there wasn't anything I could do to change my fear of Wan or what had happened to the children.

CHAPTER 16

A surprise in the making

ELORA'S BIRTHDAY WAS NOW two days away, yesterday she didn't leave her job to take mid-meal with me or come be with us at the cottage afterwards when we relieved my mother so she could go to her job. I seen her once but she only looked away. I could see the hurt in her eyes. I didn't mean to hurt her I try so hard to make her happy but only end up hurting her. I talked with Wan about it and he assured me she would come around, he also commended me on stopping the situation before we did anything we would regret. I didn't tell him just how far we had actually taken it though.

My days at the Liaison were becoming routine, I always talked with Wan and updated him on how the two situations were coming along. I also helped hand out the coin that was the villagers share from the market. Wan told me it had been good month for our little town. My wage was the same and I tucked it away with the rest of what I had saved. I also wrote in my book about the progress that was being made with the children and the match.

When I seen that Elora wasn't waiting for me again for mid-meal I just went back to the cottage, I could handle the children for my mother until Harry and Isabell got there to help. She was relieved to see me because she had to check on one of the women who was about to give birth. She told me as long as everything was alright she may be home early.

I was sitting on the floor helping Luke paint a horse when Elora, Isabell and Harry came in. None of them had taken mid-meal at the kitchen and Harry was carrying the basket that Isabell used when she brought us all a meal.

I stood up and dusted off my pants and welcomed them in.

"Elora, come speak with me now please." I said with urgency, I could not stand for her to treat me with silence that hurt me more than anything she had ever said to me.

"We have lunch here Davin." She said trying to get out of the talk she knew I was about to have with her.

"Oh you two go talk, we'll get lunch together." Isabell offered.

She followed me out the door and behind the pens near the river. I didn't want to be over heard and the river is good for keeping secrets.

"Why are you not speaking to me?" I demanded from her.

"I'm embarrassed Davin, I feel rotten for what I did to you the other night, it was unfair for me to do that to you."

"Well, not speaking to me made me feel so much better about everything." I said, my anger becoming apparent everything that had happened was welling up inside me.

"I was trying to give you some space honestly I feel terrible over what happened the other night I hurt you and tried to force you to do something that I knew was wrong. I should of never came to you like that," She wasn't crying but her eyes were pleading with me to understand her.

"Elora I love you; and all I want is to be with you and make you happy. Don't you understand how hard it was for me to walk away from you the other night?"

"I do understand I'm sorry."

"If it hadn't have been for that horse we could be dealing with a lot worse than some hurt feelings. I don't want to lose you, I've wanted you to be my wife since I was a small boy and now all I can do is fear I won't be able to resist you and it will in the long run cause me to lose you. I feel like a caged and tortured animal!" I was almost shouting but she stayed strong and didn't run from me or yell back at me, she stood and listened to me never losing the look of love she held for only me.

"I don't mean to torture you and I understand all that you're saying really I do. When we are alone I just can't seem to stop myself it's like my body and mind aren't mine anymore and all I want is to fulfill a need that comes from so deep inside of me that it almost is painful to not fulfill it. Do you understand that?" She was standing up for herself but not in a combative way in a way that yearned for understanding.

"You don't think it feels like that for me? You seen the other night what happens to me when you turn into a seductive enchantress, do you think it's easy to make that go away? Do you think I don't have a need or a desire to fulfill the excitement that we created?"

"Seductive enchantress?" She asked as if she didn't know what I had said.

"You're different when you start getting excited your voice changes your breathing changes; you touch me and your touch is like fire on my skin." I tried to explain to her.

"You're different to Davin, and your body says yes to all my touches and desires then your mouth says no." She said looking hurt again.

"Then what do we do Elora? I'm at a loss, I want you, you know that more than anything after the other night, but I'm terrified and you know that, what do we do here? Do you want to risk losing everything?" I'm so lost, it shouldn't be this hard.

"I don't know, but I promise I'll try to make things easier on us both.' She pleaded with me.

"I promise you too, I just don't want to lose you my love." I said as I pulled her close to me and kissed away her tears that were now flowing freely from her beautiful green eyes.

We both apologized over and over. I kissed her tenderly on the lips being careful not to light a fire that neither of us were going to be able to put out.

"Should we go eat something?" I asked her worrying that Harry or Isabell would come looking for us.

We all ate our mid-meal together, Elora and I stayed very quiet while we ate. Harry and Isabell both must of sensed something was wrong but they both kept themselves busy tending to the children. While the ladies were cleaning up dishes Harry asked me to take a walk with him. We went almost to where Elora had stood only a little while ago and stopped. I guess we weren't the only ones to use the river to hide our secrets.

"What's going on boy?" He asked me sternly.

I sat near the bank and watched the water for a few minutes then out of nowhere tears flooded my eyes as the emotions all ran through me and I felt as if I was being ripped apart.

"Is it really all that bad?" Harry asked as he sat down next to me and put his big hand on my shoulder.

I poured out my soul to Harry I felt like I could trust him, where I'd normally hold back with Wan or Sid I told Harry everything. I had to let it out to someone besides Elora I had to have a man's help.

After I let it all out we sat quietly neither of us saying anything, Harry let me calm down some before he began to have what he called a man to man talk with me. He told me that what we felt for each other was alright, and that there were ways that we could relieve what he called the sexual tension between us.

I had never talked with my father about what would happen when I became bound with Elora, I had an idea of what I wanted to do with her just by our passionate meetings but to be honest I didn't know how things worked. Harry told me all the things we could do that wouldn't involve making her become with child. And he told me how to touch her and make her feel good without having intercourse with her. Intercourse sounds like a medical word to me but he explained it to me and also explained that it should be saved to the night we are bound. It was wonderful to get some understanding of what not only my body wanted but what hers wanted as well. I'm so grateful to have Harry here with me now. I asked him if he and Isabell were doing those kinds of things and he was not offended, he spoke candidly with me and told me it had been a long time since either of them had been with someone but they did fulfill their needs carefully with each other. He said Isabell had told him that all matches do it and that it was almost expected. Funny how that's not the first time I heard that kind of statement.

"Harry you have no idea how grateful I'm to have you as a friend. I'm so happy to know if things go like that with Elora again what I can do with her so I don't hurt her anymore. The last couple of days has been so bad I didn't know what to do."

"I'm happy to have you as a friend as well Davin, come to me anytime you need to talk. I'll keep our talks between us you won't have to worry about getting in trouble."

We got up and went into the cottage, I honestly did feel better about things and by the looks of it Elora and Isabell had talked as well, Elora looked as happy and relaxed as I felt. The rest of the day went by with ease we were relaxed around each other again like we had been before. I was grateful because I love her so much and it hurt to know how bad she was hurting.

We had all been watching the kids jump rope outside in front of the cottage when I seen my mother, Myka, and Jobe walking towards us. My mother looked very irritated as she ran into the house to put her things down.

"You've all been summoned to the Liaison's office Myka will watch the children until you're done." Jobe announced.

We all looked at each other with confusion and got up to follow him. My mother came out of the cottage and told Myka to take the children in and make them a snack and followed the line of us headed to the Liaison's office.

The drapes were pulled closed so I could tell we were in for a meeting. As we went in, the door that lead to the main room was already opened for us. I could see my father sitting inside looking as lost as all of us. I knew it couldn't be anything to do with Elora and I as Harry and Isabell wouldn't be there. Soon after we all took our seats the Dover's were also escorted in.

Lee stood up and welcomed us and thanked us all for coming so quickly.

"This meeting is about the match between Isabell and Harry." He began. "We feel that since the children came to over village a lot has been changed, and not for the bad. Wan tells us of how much time you both have spent nursing the children back to health and how the children have taken to you."

Harry and Isabell only sat in silence nodding as Lee spoke. "After a lot of talking we have come up with an idea that we would like to run across all of you. We want your honest opinions so please do not be afraid to speak up." We all nodded towards Lee in agreement.

"Since your match has been less than the traditional way we do things, we feel that trying to keep it traditional will work against us, you're both adults and know what you want we don't see a need to prolong your courting if you feel it is not necessary to do so." He is a lot like Wan when he speaks, I'm not sure if it's because he's watched Wan direct meetings all these years or if just how it's suppose to be done.

"Harry, Isabell do you have any objections to being bound within the week?" We were all stunned by this but it didn't seem like it was bad, everyone looked happy.

Harry stood up and helped Isabell stand up. "We would be pleased to be bound as quickly as possible, we have wished for it since the first day we spent together." He said honestly as Isabell smiled to show she agreed.

"And do any of you object to this taking place so quickly?" Lee asked the rest of us. We all said "no" at the same time.

"Alright then it will be done. The next thing we would like to discuss will be the children. Wan spoke with Mrs. Hewit today and he tells us the children medically are well. That's where again Harry and Isabell come in, we would like to place the children permently with you both." By this time the happiness that filled the room showed our support of their plan.

"Well I guess then it's decided. Mrs. Dover and Mrs. Hewit will you help Isabell make the plans for the ceremony?" They both answered "yes" together.

"During this week Isabell we'll have some workers out to help make your cottage big enough to help accommodate the children, is there anything specific you would like done while they are there?" He asked.

"Just for enough room for the children, the cottage is adequate for us otherwise." She said modestly.

"Well I guess everything is set if there is anything needed come see us. You may all leave and start planning, Davin we need you stay behind for a few minutes." Everyone got up to leave and I assured them I'd be along shortly, I kissed Elora on her hand and quietly told her I loved her.

Wan got up from his seat and motioned for me to follow him. Lee also joined us. This time we went to Lee's office. He closed the door and we all sat down.

"What do you really think of the choices we made today?" Wan asked me bluntly.

"I like the decision I feel like Harry and Isabell really love each other and the children have become a huge part of them. I don't honestly see where else you could have placed them. And as far as them being bound so quickly, I think for the children's sake it's the only right way to do this." I told them as honestly as I could.

"I like the decision we made but I worry how the village will react." Lee said to us both.

"I think if it comes to a lot of argument we can use a tactic rarely used in this village." Wan said.

"What tactic is that?" Both Lee and I asked.

"We'll tell them that is a simple answer for an awkward situation and the decision is final; if they don't like it they are free to walk away from this village at any moment." Wan told us.

"If it has to be that way than so be it." Lee agreed.

"Another thing I'd like to discuss is my leaving the Liaison. I'd like you Davin to get to know and trust Lee and learn to speak as candidly with him as you do with me. He understands what position you're in because it was him and I who worked out your title and everything that came with it."

"Do you know when you'll be leaving?" I asked Wan.

"I had planned on staying on to train my year that was required, but I honestly feel that Lee can help with training once the new Liaison is chosen. I don't feel that you require training you have caught on exactly what this towns needs of you. Our goal for your job was to help a committee of old fools look through the eyes of the younger generation. They depend on your word to help them make decisions that wouldn't normally be an issue. Look at Isabell and Harry we have never brought a man of that age being single into our village to live. But the opportunity it made for Isabell made it worth the try and we may not of tried had we not had all the input you gave us."

"I understand what you want of me, will you just retire and stay in town, or will we still be able to see you?" I asked afraid I may be losing someone I found as a friend not only my instructor.

"My plans will be made known as soon as I know them, as of now nothing has been decided on my part yet." I don't know if he just looked tired to me or if it was his age showing itself some.

"We need to make sure you have your mother and Mrs. Dover try to include in the wedding plans something that also binds the children to Isabell and Harry. We think it's very important that they know they are part of a family. After the ceremony we'll get the kids into the school and get Harry's calling figured out. I know he has been going with the hunting party in the mornings and they report that he is wonderful at hunting. I'd like you to speak with him and find out if he's happy with hunting as a calling or if he would like to try something else." I felt like Wan was a walking book of instructions sometimes.

"I can do all that for you, how long before you want me to let you know on Harry's calling?" I asked.

"Just let them be bound that's fine I won't move him around until after the ceremony, but let me know as soon as you find anything out."

"That will be no problem I come in daily anyway and I'm sure we'll talk before the ceremony."

"I've talked with Lee some about you and Elora, and I noticed yesterday that you didn't take mid-meal together yesterday. Is there a problem?" He asked, I'm unsure why he is always so interested in what happens with Elora and I. Maybe it's because he feels we are a true match.

Just some hurt feelings I guess, things are alright now we talked earlier this afternoon." I told them.

"What will help ease the tension for you two Davin? I don't like seeing you looked so tortured over these last couple weeks." Again I just don't understand why he is so concerned about us.

"Well unless you can speed the calendar up then it's just something we have to bear, correct?" They laughed at that. Glad that I amuse people while I sit feeling tortured again at my feelings of not being able to make my own decisions in life.

"Just bear with it son, it will all work out for the best, before you leave will you be sure to update your book on the decisions we made today?"

"I'll do that Wan, nice speaking with you both this afternoon. If you need me you know where I'll be." I walked away feeling agitated with both of them. Maybe they didn't have feelings like Elora and I have before they were bound, but I'm in agony over all this, even after Harry's talk earlier I'm still feeling like somehow it's going to get screwed up.

When I got back to the cottage everyone was so happy and celebrating the news it was hard to hold onto my bad mood. I got out the cherry wine I had acquired and poured everyone a cup.

"To Harry, Isabell, Maggie and Luke. May you all live a happy loving life with eachother, if anyone deserves it it's you four." I toasted as everyone raised their cups and said "cheers" at the same time. The wine was really sweet and strong. Of course that didn't stop us from enjoying it. We ate and celebrated outside in front of a fire until late in the night. Many villagers came to inquire what the celebration was about. Some seemed very happy about the quick progression of things some seemed rather bothered. I remembered what Wan said and wondered if it will really cause people to leave the village. Some villagers even returned with a gift for the happy couple.

Elora and I danced around the fire and sat together, we seemed right again after our talk this afternoon. Since it was so noisy I quietly whispered to her about the talk I had with Harry and she told me Isabell had a talk with her as well. I felt very comfortable talking with her about what I had learned earlier although I did not give her the full details about what Harry had told me could be done. I was hoping for my sanity that we might cool off a bit so we aren't put into that position again.

We drank more wine together and talked about how happy we were about the Liaisons decision today she confided that she was jealous that they didn't have to wait so long to be bound and I told her how I felt the same. But I never wanted Harry or Isabell to know that we felt that way, neither of us wanted to make them feel bad about their lucky decision.

After awhile everyone began to feel tired, Harry and Isabell went to tuck in the children and our mothers were cleaning the dishes. Our fathers had walked to the river for a drink of water and to clear their heads, I think they had drunk more than even Harry had put away. Elora and I were both feeling the wine as well. We were still sitting by the fire, she looked beautiful with the fire lighting up her face and making her hair look more golden than it already was.

"Will you sleep by your window again?" She asked me with her voice taking that change that scared and excited me all at the same time.

"Why?" I asked trying not to get lead into another night of what had happened a couple nights ago.

"I'd like to come kiss you goodnight later." I really wanted to be with her tonight, but I'm so afraid.

"Won't we get caught pressing our luck again like that?" I asked trying to get her to see that it wasn't such a great idea.

"My door locks my love, no one would know I'm gone, besides everyone is so liquored up they will sleep soundly." She had it planned out all the way, and all that ran through my mind were things Harry told me today, the liquor and her invitation has me finding it hard to resist her.

"Will you behave and only ask for a kiss?" I asked trying to see her true intentions for later.

"I'll only ask for a kiss I promise." She said her voice now more seductive.

"I think you'll want more." I said hoping I was getting my point across about how nervous I was.

"I'll want only a kiss."

"Alright I'll go to your window though; I don't like you being alone at night." I was trying to work out a compromise with her.

"If you fall asleep and forget to come see me I'll never forgive you Davin Hewit." She swore.

"I promise I'll come kiss you goodnight." As I said that our fathers came around the house. Mr. Dover went in and told Mrs. Dover he was ready for bed, they said their goodnight's left quickly. When I told Elora goodnight I pulled her closer like I was going to kiss her cheek but instead I whispered that I'd see her later. She gave my hand an excited squeeze, I wasn't really sure of what would come of tonight but I was really excited now to go to her.

I went into the cottage and told my mother I'd finish cleaning up for her and she went to bed with my father. They were both stumbling so I knew they would be asleep quick. Harry and Isabell had the kids asleep and were on their way out the door. Harry was allowed to drive Isabell home now that their date had been made so soon. They bid me goodnight with huge hugs and thanked me for the great celebration. Myka had gone to bed while we were still drinking and dancing around the fire.

I cleaned up for my mother and went into my room, grabbed a blanket and a small jug of wine I had hidden from a different celebration. I quietly opened my window and went towards the river I walked beyond my house a bit and laid the blanket out by the river where bushes blocked the view from the river. I walked slowly over to Elora's window hoping that she simply just wanted a kiss and I wouldn't have to use the blanket. I had drunk some of the wine before I left; I was enjoying the reckless feeling it left me with.

Quietly I tapped on Elora's window and she was out of it with one swift jump. "Kiss me." She said as she wrapped her arms around me. I was easily persuaded and I leaned down and took her in my arms, picked her up and headed towards the river. The whole time never letting her let up on kissing me to ask where I was taking her. As I neared the river her kisses became wild and her breathing was so heavy I thought I may need to stop and let her catch her breath. As I laid her on the blanket I pulled from our kiss causing her to moan in argument of being stopped, I think she thought I'd try and fight her again.

I picked up the jug and took a big drink of the wine and offered it to her.

"Are you trying to get me drunk, Davin?" She asked her voice was back to that seductive enchantress that made me wild with desire for her.

"I think you're already drunk my love, for you must be to have let me sweep you away from the safety of your bed knowing my dishonorable intentions."

"Can we go in the water?" She asked slyly.

"Are you trying to get me naked my love?" I asked her, mocking her tone as best as I could.

"Maybe." Came her sultry answer.

We had more of the wine and she leaned over and began kissing me again, this time she met no resistance from me. Her hands were trying to pull away my clothing and my hands were exploring her body, her skin was so warm and soft I was losing all my will power quickly. I let her pull off my shirt in between our hard heavy kisses, her lips tasted of wine and were so soft and supple I could go on kissing her like this until dawn. She got my pants undone and down never taking her lips off mine. She knew all too quick that there was no turning back now. Nor did she try, I pulled her nightgown off her and picked her up and walked into the water with her. I buried my face into her breasts kissing each one and enjoying the soft moans coming from her throat. I brought her face to mine and began kissing her even more wildly than we had been before. She was trying to put me inside of her but I knew I couldn't let her go that far. I put my hand down into the water and began touching her softly, she relaxed and stopped trying to get me to enter her.

I was so glad we came to the river if we had stayed near her window we would have been caught for sure. Her cries came louder and faster and she pulled away quickly from me. She reached down and took me in her hand I felt waves of pleasure surge through my body, my moans increasingly getting louder. I put my hand down and began touching her softly again. She had me pushed up against the bank of the river we were almost completely out of the water. Our bodies were tangled together and our moans came in sync with each other.

"Don't stop." Was all I could cry out to her and soon I had the relief I had waited for so long for. I brought my hand away from her and we kissed slowly calming down together.

"Let's wash off in the river." She said quietly and lead me back into the water. We began stealing soft kisses and washing each other off. She came closer to me and our bodies wrapped together again. "I love you." She whispered so soft I could barely hear her.

"I love you Elora." I said as I began kissing her again. I picked her up and carried her out of the water. We laid on the blanket silently looking at the stars for a long time.

"I'd better you get home my love, before we fall asleep and really get in trouble."

She didn't fight me, and dressed silently and let me lead her back to her window. There was no sign of life around us and I was feeling very relaxed as I helped her into her window. She kissed me one more time and closed her window, no words needed to be said.

I went back to the river and finished the wine, and took the blanket to the front of our cottage and laid it out near what was left of the fire. I looked up into the stars thinking of what happened at the river. I was full of contentment, and I didn't feel guilty for what we'd done. I felt like a man now, I couldn't explain it I just knew I felt different.

I woke to the sun in my face and my mother standing over me with her hands on her hips. Alarms instantly went off in my head.

"So you had so much to drink you couldn't make it to your own room?" She asked laughing at me.

"Something like that, it was warm in my room and cool out here." I said joining her laughter as I got up, picked up my blanket and went into the cottage.

CHAPTER 17

Controversy

I GRABBED SOME CLOTHES and went out to the river to wash up and get dressed, since the children had been sleeping in my room it was just easier to go out to the river. As I stood in the water flashbacks of the time I spent with Elora ran through my head, I had a lot to drink but I remember everything we did last night. I still feel no regrets, I love her and I was careful, and we didn't get caught which makes it that much more exciting. I don't think we can meet like that often, I'm still feeling we both are having a hard time completely controlling ourselves. I'm still worried about making mistakes with her.

I ate twice the normal amount I usually do in the morning, I'm not sure if it was because all I had to drink or if it was from my time with Elora. Afterwards I helped Maggie with her hair ribbon as my mother tried to get her to eat more. Mornings were the hardest with Maggie, she wanted Isabell and Harry there and she couldn't understand why they were never there when she woke up.

After I ate and helped my mother clean up I saddled Blitz and rode across the village to the Liaisons office, the drapes were drawn closed yet again. This time I went directly around to the back and put Blitz in a pen. When I opened the door I could hear shouting in the main room, I walked quickly over to the room and took my seat.

Wan and Lee were there with a couple other Liaison's and only two clerks. There were three couples from the village all older with children that were grown one woman was yelling at Wan that he has disgraced our village by allowing a stranger in town and marrying him off to a widow within weeks of him being there. She continued to rant and rave for near ten minutes; she even brought the children into it calling them orphaned bastards. Everyone with her nodding to show they agreed as she went on and on. Finally Lee stood and asked her to stop.

"The Liaison spent hours upon hours trying to make a fair decision, I'm sorry it doesn't please any of you. Our biggest concern was for those involved, namely the orphaned bastards you speak so lowly of. We can't always make decisions that are going to make everybody happy, what we can do is look at the situation and make a decision based on our opinion and the opinions of those involved. To make this quick and simple, our decision is final and there will be no changing it. Simply if you really can't live with a decision we have made you're free to leave our village. This meeting is over please go about your daily work.' He left them no room to comment or argue, he turned around and walked out of the room and the others that were also there followed him out, as did I. I was glad he spoke so harshly to them it hurt me to hear them speak so terrible of the people I cared about so deeply.

We all followed Lee into a back room, it was small but big enough for all of us to sit and talk. We heard the door at the front of the building slam shut hard. Wan stood up and called a clerk to the room we were in.

"Please go inform Sid of those who were just here and have him act accordingly if they don't go to their work now." Wan ordered the clerk.

"We shall know soon enough what they decide to do with their options." Wan said looking at Lee.

"How many have come in to complain like this?" I asked.

"Just them, and this is not the first time they have stormed in here and argued a decision that we have made." Wan said looking towards me. "How did the celebration go over last night?"

"It went well; many villagers came out and congratulated them on being bound and even brought gifts for them." I informed everyone.

"That's good I expected the younger villagers to accept this well. As far as the children go, I certainly didn't have anyone coming to me to ask for the children so I think we made the best decision we could for them." Wan said, he was angry and we could all feel it.

"There is nothing else we can do about them, if they don't go to their jobs they will deal with Sid. If they decide to leave that's their business, I'll no longer allow them to come in this way arguing with things that honestly have nothing to do with them." Lee said as he walked out of the room.

Wan got up and asked me to join him as he got up to leave the room. We went to my office.

"Are you alright?" I asked him

"Yes son, I'm fine just frustrated with everything that just happened." He explained.

We sat quietly for a few moments he looked as if he had something important to say but just didn't know where to begin. "Son there are some big changes coming to our village, you're going to have to learn to stand up for your beliefs and stick to them."

"Like what?" I asked him curiously.

"I can't say much right now, Lee and I have been working on it for a long time. The Liaison doesn't even know all that will be happening."

"I understand, please just let me know when it's something that I can help with." I offered to him hoping to alleviate some of his worries.

"We have Elora's calling tomorrow you know." He said thoughtfully, I've tried hard not to think about it, not that I'm worried I just don't want to fret as bad with hers as I did with my own. "Your not even going to ask me about it?"

"I figure if it was something I was suppose to know, someone would have talked with me about it. So I wait patiently like she does."

"Very good then." He said with a smile. "What are your plans for the day?"

"I suppose much like they have been over the last week or so, although I'm sure my mother has plans to work me to death over this ceremony coming up." I said laughing at the thought of it.

"Yes I bet she does nothing funnier than watching women put together a party. Any plans for Elora's birthday?"

"I think her parents are planning a small dinner to celebrate her calling." I told him.

"You look happier this morning I take it you both were able to talk your troubles through last night?" If he only knew how we fixed our tensions.

"Yes last night was relaxing for both of us, I think the finality of the kid's future helped that a lot and the wine I found at market." We both laughed.

"Wine has a funny way of helping clear your troubled head. I hope you both realize we haven't forgotten you or put your courting on a back burner."

"I've felt better about all that since we talked about it the other day. We are just both in a hurry to start our lives together I guess. Hearing that Harry and Isabell get to marry so quickly was a little hard on us both but we don't blame anyone because we understand the need for the urgency."

"I'm glad you brought that up actually, I meant to ask you about that yesterday. Just curious to your reaction is all."

"We just wish it were us, we bear no ill feelings to anyone honestly." I told him hoping he knew I was being completely open with him.

"I felt the same when it was getting time for me to bound as well, I felt like it would never happen. I had her for only a short while though and I've vowed to die with only her in my heart. We were a true match and I miss her every day." I hadn't heard Wan speak much of his wife before, I knew she died in their second year of marriage during child birth but that was all I knew. "I've always wanted to have the rules changed on when the young could be bound, like to let them decide for themselves as long as it was done between sixteen and eighteen. Some couples like you and Elora are in a hurry and some wouldn't mind waiting the extra year."

"If the rules worked that way Elora and I'd marry tomorrow on her birthday whether we had a cottage or not." I told him proudly.

"So it's that bad is it?"

"It is to us, yes we get to see each other daily but we can't show the affection we feel for each other. We have to hide and sneak around for a small kiss here and there. I can't run my fingers through her beautiful hair if I choose. Sometimes I can just be sitting near her and the scent of her hair touches my nose and it sets off feelings of desire for her like you wouldn't imagine. I've been told that she'll be my wife since I can remember yet after all these years when I feel I'm ready for her to be exactly that, I feel like a door gets slammed in my face." I was trying to be careful what I said, but I felt more comfortable with Wan today.

"I do understand how you feel Davin. We went through the same thing you two are going through. Sneaking around when others were busy working to steal a kiss or a caress. I felt as if I'd die waiting for her. Now all I can think if only they had let us become bound earlier, I could've had her that much longer." He said regretfully with sadness in his eyes that I had only seen once before when Isabelle had spoke of her dead husband.

I didn't know what to say, I didn't want to plead for his help with Elora while he was hurting from speaking of his wife.

"Well go get on with your day, there isn't much for you to do around here. If we need you I'll send one of the clerks to go find you."

"Thank you Wan, I'm going to go check on our new animals since I have some extra time this morning. I'd like to see how they are growing. I've noticed we are getting butter more often so the cows seem to be helping a lot."

"Have good afternoon and I'll probably see you tomorrow." Wan said as he got up and left. I took a few minutes to update my book and to make notes on what happened this morning and who it involved. I also took two silver coins out of my savings as I had to see Sid this morning and I wanted him to give it to Lynne for me.

I left the office and walked over to the barns, walking around looking over the stock, the piglets had about doubled in size since we got them and the cows looked content. There were many people milking and I even saw three people churning butter. I also looked over the white mare we had bought, she looked great someone had been exercising and taking good care of her, I still wonder what she's for. There was also another new horse I had not seen before now, he looked similar to Blitz. He was in the same area the white mare was in; he looked magnificent standing near the mare.

I went over to Sid's office, there were no sounds of people being punished so I knocked on the door and waited for him to answer.

"Come in Davin!" He said as he opened the door. "I've just been out delivering a beautiful gown to the most beautiful sixteen year old in our village."

"Already, thank you so much, how did she respond?" I asked so quickly it sounded like I half stuttered was I was trying to say.

"Well the note said 'Love from Sid and Lynne' but I did happen to mention the mastermind behind it."

"Wow, I can't wait to see it!"

"She'll look beautiful in it I assure you, that gown is Lynne's best work. I've never seen her make such a grand gown."

I took the silver out of my pocket. "Will you give her this for me?"

"She would never accept that Davin." He pushed my hand away.

"Please, I wouldn't feel right knowing she worked so hard on it even using lace she had made herself."

He took the coins from my hand. "I have the feeling she'll be marching into your office soon to return these but I'll try, only because you look like you might cry if I don't."

"I just want to always take care of people that have helped me, and I can't express how grateful I am that she can get a gift from me for her birthday."

"We are glad to help you Davin, you have always been a good kid and we enjoy helping those who show they are good people." He said gratefully. "Speaking of good people, I heard about the terrific news about Isabell and Harry!"

"It's great news and I'm so happy they will get the children as well, the four of them have grown so close it's amazing how they have melted together like a family even before the date was set."

"Lynne and I think it's great and those children deserve someone like Isabell as much as she deserves them, she has lost so much it's great to see her patience get rewarded."

"Yes, I'm thrilled. I've always loved Isabell and now even Harry and I have grown close, it has been a good time around our cottage. I'll miss all four of them once they get bound." I had been trying hard not to think of the children leaving but I'm hoping I'll be able to be with them a lot even if they are in their own cottage.

"Well Sid, I'm off to finish some work before I have to meet everyone for mid-meal, again thank you and thank Lynne for me please."

"You're welcome from both of us now go get your work done before I have to put you in for the next whipping!"

I walked away laughing as I headed back to the Liaison's pens to get Blitz. As I mounted Blitz to head back to the cottage I noticed Wan behind the pens almost in the woods, my mother was with him. I could tell they were arguing but I couldn't hear what about. I just turned Blitz and rode away before they thought I was eaves dropping, I think it may be over something with the ceremony.

When I got to the cottage I put Blitz in his pen but I left his saddle on, I wasn't sure if I was going to need him again. I went into the cottage expecting to find Harry or Isabell with the children, but Myka was sitting with them feeding them a snack.

"Myka is anyone else here?"

"No, mother had to check on some of her patients and father is at his job. Today is my normal day off so I offered to watch the children."

"That was nice of you to spend you day off with the children." I told her as I sat down at the table by her.

"I wanted to talk with you anyway so I'm glad we get a chance to be alone."

"About what?" She asked casually.

"I've noticed how quiet and sad you seem lately, what's happening?"

"Oh, I just don't know any more. Jake is angry at me all the time, he told me yesterday he didn't even want to be my match." She told me with tears in her eyes.

"Why would he say such a mean thing?" I asked her.

"He says his family doesn't agree with the new match and he has been angry with me since I told him how happy I was over the match."

"Well it's none of their business, why should he be like that to you? Have you told mother exactly what's happening?"

"No and please don't either, she has been busy enough. This will either blow over or his parents will break the match over it. Either way I don't care I really don't want to be bound to someone so ignorant and rude anyway."

"Tell me if anything changes alright, and don't let it get you down too bad."

"Can I tell you something?" she asked me.

"You can tell me anything, you should know that by now."

"Davin I want to be matched with Eldon!" She cried desperately to me, she always hid her emotions but now I could see that she was pleading for help.

"Myka, I don't think it can be done."

"Why not, he still hasn't been matched, my match hates me and Eldon loves me. Why can't it be done?"

"Let me look into it don't go talking with mother about it just yet. Stay here with the children I'll be back shortly."

I rode Blitz back to the Liaison hoping Wan and my mother were done talking. I knew that one of the couples in the office this morning was related to Jake's family. I only wanted to let him know what was happening with Myka.

He was in his office when I got in. "Wan may I speak to you for a moment?"

"Of course, sit here with me." I shut the door and sat.

I told him of what Myka and I talked about this morning. He could see how upset it had made me that my own sister had been treated so badly.

"Well son, the match has already been broken. It happened after you left, your mother came by about the ceremony and I broke the news to her, she isn't taking it very well."

"Who broke the match?" I asked curiously.

"Jake's family is one of five families that informed us they will be out of our village by morning."

"What will become of Myka?" I asked him.

"I don't know yet, we haven't had time to discuss it."

"Can I ask you something?" I asked hoping I wouldn't be stirring another problem for him.

"Of course son, what is it?"

"What are the Liaison's plans for Eldon Dover?"

"We haven't found a match for Eldon yet, honestly were a couple girls short for the boys that age."

"I just spoke with Myka she begged me to see if she could be matched with Eldon, she says they love each other."

"I can set that match up this afternoon, I'll make it look random and you'll have to tell her to do the same." He warned me.

"I'll speak with her when I get back to the cottage."

"Your mother had patients to check on so she probably isn't back yet she has to be shocked when your mother tells her about the match breaking. I'll have your parents and the Dover's brought in the office in about an hour or so. It will take me that long to get the Liaison together."

"Thank you Wan." I said getting up.

"Don't thank me you're the one who solved this problem for us."

I rode Blitz as fast as we could go back to the cottage. Isabell and Harry's carriage was there already. I hoped Elora wasn't there yet, I didn't want her to think anything was going on and me talking with Myka alone would raise her suspicions.

"Myka!" I called from the door. "Come help me please." She ran out to join me and I had her walk with me to the river, so it can again hide another secret.

"Myka, your match was broke before I ever got back to the Liaisons."

"How did that happen?"

"Some families are moving away and Jake's is one of them." I explained.

"Listen carefully, you can't let on that we ever had this talk you must act devastated when mother and father talk with you about it. Can you do that?"

"Yes, I promise you."

"Since Eldon has never had a match and you need one, it will happen. You must also act surprised about that and you can never ever tell even Eldon that we had anything to do with it. That match has to look random to the villagers, understand?"

She threw her arms around my neck "Thank you Davin! I love you so much."

"I love you too sis, just remember our deal right here. If it ever came out the match could be broken and without Wan being a Liaison soon we would have no help."

"I Understand, I promise you'll never regret helping us. I'm so happy!"

"Just keep that happiness to yourself little lady." I warned her one last time before we headed back to the cottage.

Elora came shortly after we went in and we all had mid-meal together. We talked a lot about the ceremony, Isabell and Harry are so happy this afternoon, it's hard to believe only yesterday they were fretting over when they could be bound. After we finished eating Elora and I went out to have a private talk.

"You look happy today my love." I told her as I took her hand and had her sit on a log left from last night.

"I'm happier than I've ever been." Her smile was beautiful and she has something about her that was different, kind of like the difference I felt.

"Last night was amazing maybe we can do it again." I suggested.

"Maybe we can, for my birthday." She was using that voice again.

"That's the voice, the seductive enchantress voice!"

"You like that voice do you?"

"I love that voice it makes me feel like I'm melting."

"Maybe I should learn to be more careful with it." She teased.

"If you do I'll not use my sexy voice for you."

"You have a sexy voice?" She asked laughing at me. Why is she so mean to me sometimes?

"Well I guess I don't!" I said turning slightly away from her.

She leaned towards my ear she was so close I could feel her warm breath on my neck. "Turn back to me Davin Hewit." She used her sexiest voice so I couldn't keep my back turned on her.

"I got a present today."

"Oh really? Tell me about it."

"Davin thank you so much it's be most beautiful gown I've ever seen."

"I can't wait to see you in it."

"I'll wear it tomorrow for you." She promised.

We sat quietly for a long time enjoying the sun and the feeling of ease that was now between us. I looked up to see her parents and mine coming towards the cottage. None of them seemed unhappy so I'm assuming they have just left the Liaison's office.

"Is Myka still here?" My mother asked.

"Yes, she's in the cottage." I told her.

My father went in and asked everyone to come out. As they all piled out Eldon came walking up from his job.

"Who sent for me?" He asked looking at his parents.

"We did, we have something very important to talk about." Said my mother, she was usually the one who spoke out when our families were together.

"First I have some bad news to share, five families are moving from the village at dawn. Like that isn't bad news enough, one of them families is Jake's and they've broken your match with Jake, Myka."

Myka, like she promised let her tears fall and showed her devastation. I'll have to thank her for that later.

"But there has been some good news that has come out of this. Eldon was matched just a little while ago"

All of us asked in unison. "To who?"

"Eldon has been matched with Myka, and since Jake's family will be gone her cottage will now be built for her and Eldon." Everyone started to clap and pat Eldon on the back, he looked shocked and Myka played a good shocked look. I watched as Myka and Eldon exchanged looks of knowing to each other; looks of relief and love. How I'd never noticed what had been budding between them, maybe I've just been too distracted to notice. I felt bad, I need to be a better brother to her.

The kids brought out their new jump ropes and we all settled in to watch them play. My mother removed Maggie's arm bandages yesterday her arm looks like it should be healed now.

Myka and Eldon joined Elora and I on our log. "Congratulations to you both, seems like you're both happy now." I said to them. They both smiled and joined hands with one another I knew then that it was a perfect match.

The rest of our day calmed down a lot, we all sat out in front of the cottage for hours talking about the ceremony and the surprise conflict it bought. Harry and Isabell had a hard time trying not to take it to heart, but in their joy of being bound and being allowed to get the children their sadness was quickly washed away.

Eldon and Myka seemed very happy all evening they sat on the log just holding hands. Myka spoke softly to him he only would look her way. He was so quiet she was sure to be like my mother and speak for her family when it came to be.

Elora and I spoke about her calling tomorrow, she told me she wasn't nervous that she would enjoy whatever they sent her to do. Our village has a strong sense to work hard to make things work, we all know if one prospers we all prosper.

She has been moved around some during internships, lately she has been with the smaller children. She always seems happy when we meet at mid-meal so I assume that she is enjoying her time there. Sadly we have been so consumed by all the other things happening around us that we really don't take time to discuss the work we are doing.

Soon my mother, Mrs. Dover and Isabell were serving us supper. They made hot roast beef sandwiches with a thick brown beef gravy poured over the top. We ate around the fire that Harry had built for us and kept the chattering going long into dusk.

"After we get Isabell and Harry bound we can start our work on Myka and Eldon's cottage." My mother announced.

"Yes, it was a wonderful surprise that Eldon finally was given his match, much less that it will bind our family even closer. Myka welcome to our family, we are happy about your match with our son." Mrs. Dover said as she got up to hug Myka.

I honestly think our mothers are very enthused for the match; more because they have built such a close friendship and now even though Elora and I will be bound in a year they would still be able to meet each evening for until Myka's cottage was done. The time we spent building the cottage with Jake's family, wasn't as relaxed as when the Dover's were with my family.

I walked Elora home right after her family left for the evening. She didn't ask me to come to her window tonight which in some ways relieved me as I was exhausted, but in other ways disappointed me. Our rendezvous last night plays over and over again in my head and my desire for her is stronger than ever. I can feel that she feels the same, when she looks at me with longing in her beautiful green eyes. I've noticed tonight when we gaze at each other our bodies are drawn closer together. We have to be careful and break our gaze before we betray ourselves.

Her parents went inside their cottage and allowed us a few minutes to bid our goodnights. She looked up at me and I could see that look in her eyes again; the look that made me want to take her up into my arms and carry her down to the river. My desire for her growing stronger the longer she looked up at me. I couldn't take it any longer, I took her face into my hands and leaned down and gave her a soft kiss, instantly my breath was stolen and our kiss heated up. She let out a small cry and put her hand on the back of my neck and pulled me harder into her mouth. I slowed down our fevered kissing gently I didn't want to just pull away and hurt her again. I couldn't take the betrayed hurt look that she gave me when I've done this. Slowly we pulled apart and she quietly bid me sweet dreams as she turned and went to her cottage. Disappointed she didn't ask me to join her later I walked slowly home. I knew before I was torn at the thought of the invitation but now I was sure I wanted it more than anything.

When I got back to our cottage Harry asked me to walk with him. We walked behind the house to the river and just stood listening to the water rush past us.

"Did my talk help you any?"

"Yes Harry, Elora and I have worked things out and are able to find a happy middle ground to the misery we had been feeling."

"That's wonderful, I'm glad I could help. I'm also really happy to see you two smiling again rather than the tortured painful look you two have been carrying last week or so."

"We are happy I can't thank you enough for your help."

"Davin like I told you that day at the side show, you changed me and if it weren't for you I wouldn't be standing here right now getting ready to be bound to the most perfect lady and getting two wonderful children at the same time. Really your thanks need not be expressed."

"I'm so happy you're finding the life you have only dreamed about Harry. I've always been fond of you, I'm happy to have you here in our village and here as my friend."

"Thank you Davin that means a lot to me."

We walked slowly back around the cottage, he had his hand on my shoulder like a father would walk with a son. I was truly grateful for our friendship, and for the love he has given to the children who ripped my heart to pieces.

Harry and Isabell bid us goodnight and I went to my room to try and sleep. The children were fast asleep and I couldn't bear the hard floor again so I took my pillow and blanket and sat in the window. Hoping of course for a visitor, I sat for a long time staring into the sky at the moon and stars. I'm not sure how long I sat there before sleep took me into dreaming of the night before. Only this time we were uncontrolled, I took her over and over on the bank of the river with no reserve or worry. We rolled around the bank of the river until the sun was warming our faces. That is when I woke up feeling the sun on me realizing that I had slept through the night with no visit from my love. I went quickly to the river to bathe, before everyone noticed my body's betrayal of my dream about Elora.

CHAPTER 18

Elora's calling

I LINGERED AT THE well this morning hoping to see Elora go for her morning rations. I only ran into Eldon, he said Elora was given the day off and he would be getting the rations this morning. I ate morning meal quickly deciding I'd go wish Elora luck before she was called in to the Liaisons.

When she opened the door to greet me I felt my heart quicken at the sight of her. The gown was beautiful, Lynne had done wonderful work on it.

The dress for when the girls turned sixteen went from gowns that went all the way up to the neckline and hung loosely down the waist. Now it was tight around her upper body and the top of the gown sat snuggly around the bottom of her breast and the tight ties in the back only accentuated the shapes in her body, she wore a white under gown trimmed with lace and small green glass beads that had been sewn on it, it only covered the nipple and lower roundness of her breasts. The top of her breast now looked swollen and round and were allowed to be shown. The dark green color of the gown made her golden hair and green eyes shine.

Even when we were naked in the moonlight I don't feel as if I noticed her body being so shapely. Nor did I realize how swollen her breast appeared. The sight of her left me speechless I just stood gazing at her at unable to find the words I felt would show how much I loved her in that dress. After a few moments she finally spoke.

"Does it look terrible or something?"

"You look amazing my love, I fear your new gown shall do nothing but distract me." I said laughing and pulling her close to me. She smelled wonderful and her skin felt so soft.

"Is anyone here?" I asked hoping to steal in for a moment for a kiss. Her family had left for the day, we stepped in but left the door open and only moved away from the opening.

I took her into my arms and kissed her gently. "Happy birthday, my love."

"Thank you my love." She said as she put her hand on the back of my neck and pulled me to her lips again. Our kisses were passionate but controlled, we knew now wasn't the time to get ahead of ourselves. Slowly I pulled away and put my face down into her beautiful plump breasts and kissed them softly enjoying the smell she used to perfume herself. Her breath started to quicken with the excitement my kisses brought her. She pulled me back to her lips and we kissed again still trying to keep control of ourselves. We stepped away from each other and again I could only stand and admire how beautiful she looked.

I snapped out of my day dream when I heard horses outside we quickly moved to the view of the door but it wasn't anyone for her. "I must go to my job my love, but I'm sure I'll be there for your calling." I tried to get out quickly for if I became entranced by looking at her I'd be late. She kissed me one more time and bid me a good day.

I walked over to the Liaison's this morning I was hoping I'd be able to leave with Elora after her meeting had come to an end. I noticed the five families leaving the village as I went towards my job. When you choose to leave the village as they have you may only take the coin you have saved and some clothes. You're not to take anything else, for it came from the hard work of everyone here. They walked together slowly with a pack on their back. They couldn't even take a horse if they had ever purchased one.

After they were gone the Liaison appointed cleaners to go in and clean the cottages and put the items either to common or other areas the items might be needed in. Their cottages would be torn down and the lots left empty. The supplies that were able to be reused were taken to the construction areas, and distributed to those who were building cottages for their children or making their own larger. The reason the cottages were torn down was to show those who left them that their lives here were over, and returning to their homes was an option they gave up. It does sound harsh but it is how it's always been.

When I got to the Liaison's office the drapes were once again drawn and the building was very quiet. I went to my office and took out my book I wanted to write about the events with the five families and about Myka's new match. I wanted to express how easy it was for us to make a quick decision on the matters that had taken place. I found sometimes that waiting to hear word on a problem sometimes took longer than some would feel needed. I was trying myself to show that handling matters quickly is for the better.

Wan was at my door as I was finishing up my task. He came in and sat quietly looking like his mind was busy.

"It's about time for Elora's calling you know." He said quietly.

"Yes, I figured it would be soon, I noticed the drapes were already drawn."

"We were meeting on other things already were making a big decision that will change the way some things are done around here." He confided in me.

"When will these changes take place?" I asked curious what would be happening.

"One of them will come today, the rest will happen soon. I'll try to confide in you more when I'm sure I have full support of the others."

Jobe knocked on my door to let us know everyone had arrived for the meeting. As I walked into the main room I saw my family, Elora's family, Kyan, Leta and Kyan's family.

I can't figure out why they would be there, Kyan has a few weeks before his calling is due and Leta has two months. I wouldn't think they would have anything to do with Elora's calling.

We all took our seat and Lee rose to welcome us and begin the meeting.

"I'm sure some of you are confused why so many have been brought in today for this meeting. The reason is; we'll be doing both Kyan and Elora's callings today. The reason for this will come out soon."

"We'll start with Kyan's calling." He said and Kyan stood to face the panel of Liaison's, he looked very confused and even timid. I remember how I felt when I faced the Liaison alone, I'm sure it wasn't any easier having an audience.

"You have been chosen to fill the empty Liaison seat, the reason you have been called early is due to Wan's failing health he feels he'll not be able to continue working much longer. He would like to get to your training quickly so he may take his leave."

"Thank you Sir." Kyan said, as Lee motioned for him to take his seat.

"Elora, your new calling will be controversial for our village we ask you to have patience, the people will get used to the idea and it will be alright." We all looked confused and she was trembling.

"You'll also fill a seat as a Liaison." All the parents in the room gasped and were whispering to each other.

"Quiet please, and I'll happily explain our decision." Every one focused on Lee again and the room quieted down.

"Things have been taking change in our village as you all have noticed we even lost some families this morning. We need Elora as a woman to help make our decisions we would like the opinion of a woman in the Liaison to help us bring our village into a new era. Female opinions are softer and gentler and we all feel it will only add to better the rules the people of our village live with. We certainly feel the loss of the five families and may even lose a few more with this new decision. But in time the villagers will notice the changes that we expect Elora to help us make."

"Thank you Sir." Elora said towards the panel, and sat back down.

The calling was a surprise to all of us much like my own. I'm happy as we'll also be working together.

"Do any of you have any questions for us?" Lee asked as he took his seat.

No one spoke up, I'm not sure if it was out of shock or because Lee explained things well enough for everyone to understand.

"We'll begin your training tomorrow, I want you here in the morning and we'll tell you what is expected of you both. I just want to let you know we are working a change right now that is very big and we'll enjoy having your young fresh opinions to help us with the discussions. We are looking forward to working with both you." After he said that everyone from the Liaison's panel stood and excused us all.

I still had to remember I'm here to work and not only support Elora so I followed the Liaison's out the door in the back of the room. Lee looked happy to see that I had stayed true to my job and such a shocking calling that involved those I'm so close with. We all went to the smaller room for a meeting.

"Davin this is where your job comes into play, we want reactions good, bad and otherwise." Lee told me, I was feeling more comfortable with him as Wan told me would happen. Wan didn't look ill to me; tired maybe but he had never mentioned an illness to me. I can't bring it up to him now I'll have to wait until we are alone.

"Do as your normally would and stay close to Elora when she is out in the village I don't want her alone for the time being, we don't know how the village will react and we want no chances taken with her." Lee warned me.

"I'll be sure to let her know she needs an escort at all times."

"Thank you, please go ahead about your day and if anything else that needs to be discussed I'll be here until it's time for supper. We still have things to discuss on their training." He excused me and locked the door as I went out.

I ran out hoping to catch Elora. Everyone was still standing outside discussing what had happened in the meeting.

I walked up to Kyan and shook his hand. "Congratulations friend!"

"Thank you, I was shocked I thought I'd be making bows for the rest of my life." He laughed.

I went next to Elora and took her hand. "Are you happy with your calling?"

"I'm surprised and frightened." She admitted so I only I could hear.

"Let's get some wine so we can celebrate." I announced, I still had some coin left in pocket from going to market, I kept forgetting to tuck it away. I ran over to the common and Kyan followed to help me out. We got four jugs of wine and our little group made their way to our cottage. Isabell and Harry were already there, they seemed confused by what Elora's calling was, but they didn't seem upset about it before the situation was explained.

News was already spreading throughout the village. Some people came by to congratulate Elora and Kyan. Some came to launch complaints of how wrong it was. My poor Elora seemed so devastated when some made their opinions clear on her new calling. Harry was nice enough to tell them to leave when they started in on her. It seemed most of the younger people in our village were very supportive though, and that gave us all hope that maybe her calling was a good thing and not the curse we at first felt it may end up being.

I pulled Elora into the cottage with Harry, my father and Mr. Dover. I explained to them gently for I didn't want to put any more fear into Elora. I told them she would always need to be escorted even to go get her rations. They all understood especially after what had happened in the yard. I told them it won't always be like this and that when the villagers accept the change it would be better for her.

"Did you know anything about this Davin?" Mr. Dover asked me.

"Honestly Sir, I had no idea about Elora or Kyan being made Liaison's. I wasn't included in the meetings that took place." I told him hoping he believed me.

"I just hope this doesn't put her in any danger. This village has been a little more than upset lately I don't need this pushing them over the edge."

"The Liaison will handle those who are upset with ease, how do you think we lost five families this morning? They went to fight the Liaison over Harry and Isabell and they were told their decisions were final and if they didn't like it they could leave the village. Yes, it sounds hard but whatever changes they are making aren't going to make everybody happy."

"I'll keep my faith in the Liaison no matter what decisions they make I've always sworn to uphold their rulings and I hate feeling like I don't agree, but she's my daughter!" By this time we could tell how afraid he was.

"I love your daughter and I honestly think if the Liaison felt like they were about to put her in mortal danger they wouldn't have made the decision to put her where they did. If I for a moment I feel that she is in danger I'll fight the Liaison right beside of you."

"I appreciate your dedication Davin. I'll follow your lead unless I feel I need to step up." He told me putting his hand out to shake on the deal.

My father, Harry and Elora stood quietly while we had our exchange, it was uncomfortable for a few moments but we all knew he had to have his say.

The three men went back outside, Elora and I sat at the table holding hands. I tried my best to relax her, I begged her to be brave, I told her I was proud of her; anything to see her calm down. She was still trembling though. "You're just acting afraid because you want to see me naked again huh?" I teased her and she turned bright red and started to laugh.

"See! You do enjoy my humor."

"Of course I do my love, I'm just nervous. I wasn't expecting any of this to happen. I thought my calling would be caring for the younger children. Now I not only get laid with a responsibility that the whole town depends on, but people who I've never wronged are angry and hate me."

"No one hates you, what they hate is change. Our rules have to change they have to become modern they have to fit our village. Things will change and things will calm down for you, and I make it my personal duty to keep you safe. Even if I have to sleep under your window every night."

"Thank you Davin, you always make me feel better." She squeezed my hand, our secret way of silent communication.

"Let's go celebrate, there's wine and there's people to celebrate with. There really is something to be happy about."

"You just want to get me drunk and see me naked again don't you?" She teased me.

"Yes, I really do!" I agreed with her.

Before we stepped back out I pulled her close and kissed her very lightly. "Have I told you how beautiful you are today?"

"Nope I was beginning to think the gown made me look terrible." She teased.

"That gown makes me want to take you to the river my love." She flushed pink with that.

"How can we join the others if your bright red?" I teased her, she playfully smacked me on the arm.

"Let's go celebrate, this is a good thing I won't let anyone take us down."

"That's the spirit my love." I told her as a gave her another small kiss.

I held the door open for her and we went out to join the fun. Kyan's family had stayed to celebrate with his, his mother and father brought more wine over. Elora and I had cups of wine handed to us so often it wasn't long before we were both feeling tipsy. Leta was also here with us; she and Kyan had taken a place on a log near ours.

They didn't seem as affectionate as Elora and I. She didn't seem to be happy to be where she was. She seemed so distant Kyan tried so hard to cheer her up. After watching them for a little while I got up and asked Kyan to come walk with me. Harry seen us walk towards the river and went to sit with Elora.

"Alright what is going on with you and Leta?" I wasn't going to dance around it, they should be happy.

"Nothing's wrong, just some tension between us is all."

"Tension's about what?" I was beginning to wonder if they were going through what Elora and I had just been through.

"We just don't get to be with each other very much lately, her mother is sick and I wasn't allowed to see her for a week. It really hurt and we argued about it, that's all."

"I'm sorry to hear that, maybe I could speak with her and lighten up her mood for the fun we were all having." I suggested.

"You can try, she sure isn't saying much to me."

We walked back to the front of the cottage, and I grabbed a couple more cups of wine. Elora still had some, so I gave one to Leta and asked her to come with me.

"Leta, I know things have been hard with your mother being ill. I see how sad and distant you look, talk to me and tell me what's going on." I pleaded with her Kyan is my friend I hate to see him or his match so miserable.

"Kyan's just upset because I've been trying to help my mother so much that I don't get to spend much time with him. And I do understand where he's upset but I wish he would understand, that's my mother I need to help her get well."

"Can we maybe work out where you two can sit for short amount of time in front of your cottage together each night? That way you're still near your mother and Kyan can feel like you've made some time for him."

"I'll speak with my father, I'm sure he won't have a problem with it." Leta told me.

"As someone in the same situation as you and Kyan, it would kill me if I had to go a week without being with Elora, I can understand how he feels. We guys need to be made to feel like we are the center of attention, give him a small amount and he'll relax about it, I promise you.

"Thank you Davin, I'll do my best I do understand what your telling me. She hugged me before we turned to walk back to the cottage.

I like Leta and I know she is torn, I just hope I helped her a little bit. I don't like seeing her upset. When we got back to the front of the cottage, she asked Kyan to step away a moment with her. With so many people here I didn't think they would need an escort as they only went a few feet from us.

"What's going on?" Elora asked me.

"They are just upset over something it's nothing big see they're smiling at each other again."

I took her hand in mine and we watched as some of the adults were attempting to try the children's new jump ropes. Only problem for them was the ropes were too short and the wine was too strong. The laughter running through our group sounded great to my ears. We were all feeling the wine by the time the sun started going down and none of us had eaten supper yet.

I went in and started to put together something that would feed our group. I found two fresh loaves of bread my mother must of baked while she waited on Isabell and Harry to come be with the children. There was a beef roast that had been cooked and set aside. I assumed it was meant for our mid-meal which we all skipped celebrating with each other. Elora sliced the bread as thin as she could and I sliced up the beef. We made a platter of about fifteen sandwiches and took them outside. There was enough for everyone that wanted one, I made Elora take one I knew the wine was getting to her empty stomach. It was getting to me as well and the more sun we lost the more I found myself wanting Elora again.

I got closer to her so I could whisper to her without someone hearing. "May I come kiss you goodnight later?"

"It's my birthday I think you owe me a visit."

"I'll be there when everyone has gone to bed."

"I'm looking forward to it." She said using the voice that she knew made me want her.

I got up slowly and went in to make sure the bed was made for the children for Isabell and Harry. They followed me in with the children sleeping in their arms, looking like they had been a family all along. They told me they were leaving early this evening, that Harry had a lot to do tomorrow as he was helping to build on to Isabell's cottage.

When I walked them out, Kyan and his family was also saying their goodbye's as well. I was relieved things were dying down earlier in the evening, with all the wine I was tired but I had to be with Elora later.

After they had all left Elora's family was bidding us goodnight as well. It was a very festive feeling in the air even Elora's father had relaxed no one else had come to complain which made it easier for us all. I walked them home and they let Elora and I have a little while to say goodnight. We sat on our old log holding hands. Only it didn't feel the same as it used to, the anticipation between us was like a fire and there was only one way to put it out.

"I hope your birthday was good my love."

"I had a wonderful day and I'm hoping that our evening gets even better."

I love when she changes her voice like that, and in my mood now that's all it takes for my excitement to betray me. She hadn't noticed yet but it wasn't going to go away while we sat here and she spoke to me like that. I stood up and pulled her up to kiss me.

"I'll be here for you soon." I said never stopping our kiss.

"I'll be ready for you my love." She turned quickly and walked into her cottage.

When I went home I said goodnight to everyone and went to my room. I could still hear them up and talking but it wasn't long before my parents went to their room. I waited a small time and went into the kitchen to get more wine. There were still two full jugs and another one half full. I took the half full one and poured some into one of our empty smaller jug. I listened for a few moments and heard my father's light snore. I even made some noise to be sure no one was awake.

I again went to the river and placed a blanket and the wine down. Though I didn't think either of us needed any more wine, I was still feeling pretty light headed. I went to Elora's window she was waiting on the window sill with the window open.

"My love what took so long? I was beginning to worry." She asked sliding out the window.

I didn't even answer her; I picked her up and headed right for the river. I looked all around as I was walking there to be sure we weren't being watched. When we got to the blanket I carefully laid her down and laid gently on top of her. I pulled her new nightgown down and buried my face into her breasts and began kissing them, then I moved up to her neck, moving slowly to her lip's by the time I reached her lips she was so eager to kiss me she grabbed me around the neck and pulled me down to her. Her kisses were ravenous and so were mine, looking at her all evening had me wild. She had her legs wrapped tightly around me and her hands eagerly worked at undoing the buttons on my pants. I took her nightgown over her head and helped remove my own clothes, and I picked her up and took her into the water.

We became entwined in each other instantly our kisses were hard and demanding. She again was trying to get me to take her, I wanted to take her, I didn't want to stop. She was pushing against me with all of her might, and I was fighting so hard to keep her from succeeding. I pushed her onto the bank and began kissing her breasts, we again let our hands find where we knew the pleasure would come to us. Our cries of desire filled the air we had become frenzied with the desire that consumed us. Within only a few moments our release came together with our cries of pleasure growing into each other's and out in the river where it would forever be kept as our secret. We collapsed exhausted on the bank of the river tangled in each other.

After we calmed and caught our breathe I brought her back down in the water and cleaned her gently. I had looked around for a moment and thought I seen movement in some trees not far from where we were. I quickly pulled her out of the river and told her to dress.

"What's wrong?" She asked as she pulled her nightgown on.

"I think I saw someone, come quick I'll take you home." I carried her quickly back to her window and told her to lock the window and open the door to her room. I kissed her quickly and set her into the window. I watched for her to do as I had asked her then I turned and ran to where I seen the movement.

I started tearing through the bushes as I yelled for whoever was there to come out.

"Don't hit me!" Was all I heard as I was yelling into the bushes where I had seen the movement.

"Who's there?" I shouted the voice sounded familiar but in the dark I couldn't tell who it was.

"Davin, it's me Kyan"

"What the hell are you doing out here?" I demanded.

"I was just walking off the wine from earlier. I didn't mean to stumble across you two." He was almost shaking.

"Stay here a minute, let me go tell Elora it was nothing." I said as I ran back towards her window.

She opened her window a small ways for me. "Don't worry my love it was just a deer I got spooked is all. Sleep well my love and thank you for the wonderful evening."

She leaned out and gave me a kiss. "Sleep well my love." I didn't want to leave her but I knew I had to talk with Kyan and hope I could talk him out of going to the punishers.

I ran back to talk with Kyan, and sat down on the blanket, grabbed the jug of wine and took a big drink and offered it to Kyan. We sat quiet not speaking to each other for a long time. After a few minutes he finally broke the silence.

"What were you two doing out here?" Was all he could get out.

"We were... well what did it look like we were doing, how long were you watching us?"

"I seen it all Davin, why would you take her before you're bound?"

"I didn't take her! I wanted too but I didn't!"

"I don't understand, it looked like you were doing more than hugging Davin."

I sighed deeply as I tried to find the words. "Elora and I've had a tension building, she was really pressuring me because she wanted me and I wanted her too but I didn't want to dishonor her, and the more I denied her the worse our tension became. Harry sensed it and had a long talk with me; he told me things that would ease the tension between us without taking her. That is exactly what you saw. I swear to you I never took her!"

"I believe you Davin. Why can't you just wait until you're bound though?"

"I don't know. I felt like I was going to explode, I felt like I was in pain. She was angry she felt hurt and thought I didn't want her. So I gave in and I brought her down her a couple nights ago and did what Harry told me about. It eased our tension everything was good, we both felt better and relaxed. Then this morning she came wearing her new gown and seeing her like that drove me mad, all day all I could do was stare at her and think of being with her out here again. I asked her if we could meet again and she agreed, it's so hard to control myself though and she doesn't make any it easier for me. She knows what I'm weak to and I swear she uses it"

He laughed at that, we were still passing the jug back and forth. The wine had me so light headed I could've just slept right there.

"Will Leta and I ever be like you two?" He asked shyly.

"I don't know; some who I have talked to said the same thing. Everyone said it was almost expected of us to sneak away and explore what we were feeling. I've just promised myself that I wouldn't take her before we are bound."

"That doesn't sound right." He said unsure if I was lying to him.

"I've talked with Wan, Harry even Sid they have all said the same type of thing to me, Isabell told Elora and her mother also lets her see me alone sometimes."

"I think Leta would smack in the face if I ever tried to kiss her like that."

"She was the first to kiss me like that and when she did I felt like a different person, feelings had awakened in me that I never knew I had." I tried to explain to him.

"I just can't imagine."

"What you can't imagine is the torture you go through after those feeling are there in your body."

"It doesn't sound too pleasurable to me."

"Only when were together like that does that desire get released. It's so hard to explain, but I'm sure you and Leta's time will come."

"Sure it will. Last time I tried to kiss her she wouldn't sit with me for two days."

"She'll come around just be careful not to push her, she is delicate especially with her mother being so ill."

"I know. I won't push her. I just want time with her; it was like we were inseparable and all of a sudden she has just disappeared."

"I talked with her, it will get better I promise."

I got up to gather my blanket and the jug of wine, I have to work tomorrow and if I don't sleep soon I'm bound to still be drunk in the morning.

"Goodnight Kyan, and don't worry so much."

"Goodnight Davin thank you for our talk." He said as he headed towards his cottage.

I went through the door feeling too tired to climb through the window. Everyone was still asleep thankfully; so I didn't have to give any explanations. I put the jug away and went to my room. I got in my pallet on the floor and barley remembered lying down to fall asleep.

I woke to the sound of Luke and Maggie crawling out of the bed. I felt like I had been sleeping a very long time. My sleep was restful and I felt wonderful; which surprised me with as much wine as I had to drink last night.

CHAPTER 19

Training

I GOT READY QUICKLY this morning so I could get my chores done. I wanted to walk Elora into the Liaison this morning. I asked for permission to be excused from breakfast and I ran to Elora's cottage praying I hadn't missed her.

"Good morning Davin, here to walk Elora in this morning?" Mrs. Dover asked me as she opened the door to let me in.

They were will still eating their morning meal and Mr. Dover didn't look as pleased to see me as his wife had. Elora excused herself and went to her room to finish getting ready. She was wearing another new dress, it was yellow and it made her skin glow. It was not as fancy as the one Lynne made for her but it was still pretty and she looked wonderful in it. We stepped out into the sunshine and closed her cottage door behind us.

"Good morning, my love." She said giving me a small kiss.

All I could do was stare at her. "You look beautiful this morning, ready start your training?"

"I'm ready my love. What happened after you left me last night?"

"Honestly Elora; it was Kyan who I seen in the trees last night."

She gasped "What did he see?"

"Elora he seen everything; he thought I took you and I was sure we were in trouble."

"I can't believe he watched us, why did he follow us?"

"He said he was out walking off the wine and that he stumbled across us accidentally, and that he just froze." I tried to explain to her, I didn't want to upset her but I knew it was not right for me to keep it from her.

"What did he say, is he going to tell?" She was so afraid. I could feel her tremble and see the tears fill her eyes.

"I don't think he'll tell, I talked with him a long time. He understands that we desire each other and that we were just acting on it in a way that still kept us pure."

"I don't want to talk it about it anymore, we'll just wait and see if he tells; it's all we can do." I watched as she regained her composure.

We walked towards the Liaison slowly, enjoying the cool morning air. I held her arm properly as we didn't need any more trouble from the villagers like we had last night. Most of who saw us greeted us warmly and paid their respects over Elora's calling. I think that gave her even more confidence, which she needed today. As we got to the front of the building I noticed the drapes were drawn closed again. We walked around to the back of the building and went in. We saw Kyan sitting in the smaller office where the Liaison's met with each other, he was alone. I took Elora in and we joined Kyan. When I looked at Elora I could see she had turned red at seeing Kyan. I knew they would have to talk about it eventually.

"Good morning Kyan, what's going on so early?" I asked as we took a seat.

"Some people are in complaining of Elora's calling, they weren't making much progress when I was in there."

"I'll go see if I'm needed in there. I'll be back when I can." Not only did I need to go in there but I knew Elora needed to have words with Kyan. I closed the door as I left.

In the main hall, a married couple just older than my parents were standing before the Liaison. I heard the man yell. "I will not take orders from a woman!" As I opened the door, I took my seat quickly and saw Wan nod his approval. Lee was standing up and leading the meeting.

"You'll take whatever orders that are given from this building or you shall leave town. It's as simple as that, if you're unwilling to wait for an outcome before you make your ignorant opinion it will do you no good in here."

His wife stood looking embarrassed and I could tell she didn't agree with her husband. Though most women in our village knew they were to be passive in these types of situations, unlike the woman who had protested Harry and Isabell's marriage.

"Fine, I'll wait to see what direction this is heading in, if it's not to my liking you'll lose another family."

"So be it." Lee said and waved towards him as to dismiss him. I enjoyed seeing Lee take the position of leader, he was a very strong speaker and I've yet to see what he says make someone continue an argument.

After they left the building Lee and Wan got up and asked me to join them. We followed Lee to his office, it was about the same size as mine but there were benches cushioned with velvet rather than chairs.

"That wasn't as bad as I thought it would be." Wan said as he closed the door.

"How many have come this morning?" I asked.

"Only two, it has been quiet otherwise." Wan answered me.

"Did anything happen after you left here?" Lee asked me.

"We mostly had well wishers but there were a couple people who voiced how unhappy they were. Harry stood and told them to leave, and that was enough to show their words were unwelcome and they left us."

"Good then, we were worried it would be a lot worse, but I think the people of our village are wanting changes as much as we are wanting to make them." Lee said confirming their decisions.

"There are big changes coming, we are working everything out now and revising the rules of our village. We want them all worked out, and we will release all the new rules at one time. That was really the urgency of getting Kyan in here so quickly."

"So you're not ill?" I asked confused.

"No I'm not ill Davin. It was a ruse to explain Kyan needing to get his calling. I'm leaving Davin, as soon as we have finished the changes. I'll be going to Stormhaven, I have a twin brother and I'd like to live out my days with him." This news startled me, I liked Wan I didn't want to know he was leaving us for good.

"Why can't you have your brother come here?"

"Son, he doesn't even know if I'm still alive. I had a clerk go to Stormhaven and search him out for me."

"But you've spent years making this village what it is, how are you so willing to walk away from all your work and the people you love?"

"Davin, this is something I must do, please understand that. Please don't guilt me for I know what I've done and what I'm doing. It has not been an easy decision for me to make."

"I apologize, I just don't want you to go; you have become a good friend to me."

"I understand that Davin, but I must be with my brother before it's too late."

"If it's what you must do; I promise not to cause you any more grief over it."

I got up and left the room without being excused. I sat in my office for a long time, I wrote some in my book, but mostly I just sat staring out my little window hoping he would change his mind. Soon there was a knock on my door; it was Kyan and Elora ready to go to mid-meal.

Kyan excused himself from us as we got outside, and we walked to the kitchen to take our meal. They both had to go back after they ate.

"Did you and Kyan speak?" I asked Elora quietly.

"Yes we had a small talk he promised to keep our secret and apologized to me as well."

I took her arm and led her towards the kitchen. "Good I don't want you both to be angry with each other I have enough to worry about." I said laughing. When I'm with her I can't hold my bad mood. Her beauty, and the way she smells carries me away to another time and place. And today I'd prefer to be there then feel the hurt of Wan leaving.

We got our meals and sat at a table far away from other groups of people. "How's your training going?" I asked her as we sat down.

"It's going well. They are just explaining our duties to us. I also have to go to the tailors and get fitted for certain clothes."

"I had to do that as well. I don't care for these hot darks suits, but I love the riding outfits." I told her.

"You look very handsome in the riding outfits. I can see the outlines of your muscles in them I enjoy them as much as you enjoy my new gowns."

She made me flush bright red. I knew she seen me watching her, I didn't think it had become so obvious though. "I don't really have muscles worth looking at."

"Yes you do, when is the last time you looked at yourself?"

"I don't really look at myself. I spend all my moments picturing you in my head." It was her turn to flush red.

"You have grown into a man before my eyes Davin."

I laughed at her. "Now you know how I feel, it feels like only a little while ago we were playing in the dirt, now were rolling around it." We were both laughing.

"I want to have an agreement with you about something." Elora told me.

"What would that be?"

"We should not talk about our work when we are alone, I know both of our jobs are different and I don't want hurt feelings by either of us if we are supposed to keep our jobs private."

I'm relieved she brought this up for I feel like I had been hiding my own job from her since it begun.

"That sounds like a wonderful idea my love."

"Then it's done." She said raising her cup to me.

We settled down and enjoyed our short meal together. We didn't run into any conflict about her calling while we ate but we did notice more people looking at us. As we finished we took our dishes and put them away and left. As we walked back towards the Liaison Kyan joined back up with us.

"I'll be back in my office when you're ready to leave my love." I told Elora as I kissed her cheek and walked to the back of the building. When I got to my little office Wan was waiting for me.

"Son, I'm sorry that I've disappointed you, that was not my intention. All I can say is this situation will become clear to you as it takes place."

"I hate the feeling of mystery I seem to be stuck in." I told him.

"We are not trying to make you feel that way, but the matters we are dealing with are delicate, you don't realize how much you have already influenced what changes are taking place, and I'm not speaking about the livestock." He said with laughter in his voice.

"I'll try to be more patient and wait to see how it all comes out, I'm sorry Wan I wasn't trying to give you a hard time."

"You weren't giving me a hard time, you're doing the job I hired you for. Please know you'll not always be left out of what goes on here, just right now we want it kept between us until the time is right."

"Thank you for everything you do for me Wan"

"It's my pleasure son. Are you done sitting here alone sulking? We have some surprises for Elora and Kyan and we would like you to be there."

"Let's go!" I said feeling the excitement he wished to see out of me.

He gathered everyone up and led us all out the back door. The Mare stood brushed and saddled with a beautiful black leather saddle, and the stud stood near her and had also been saddled. Elora and Kyan gasped at how beautiful they looked.

"The white one is yours Elora the saddle was made especially for you, the tailors will finish the riding gowns we've had made for you."

She walked slowly up to the mare, she put her nose down to Elora's face and began to nuzzle her.

"Davin, my boy I think you picked the perfect horse for this young lady." Wan announced.

"She's beautiful! I love her thank you so much!" Elora said, her excitement spilling over into us all.

"Kyan, Jobe found this stud for you he's a lot of horse sitting there." Wan said as he turned to Kyan.

"He's magnificent thank you all very much. I'll take the best care of him."

"Anytime, you need to be sure to bring them here for new shoes or care. Your pens will be built but it will take some times as those who work construction are busy with finishing Isabell and Harry's cottage and taking apart the cottages of those who left the village. You can leave them here if you'd like."

"I'd prefer Elora wait for the tailors to finish her riding gowns before she take the horse out." Lee stepped in.

"I understand." She answered him.

"Now you both need to get to the tailors for your fittings, your day with us is over." Lee said as he excused them.

"Davin, you may go too we're all taking an early day." Wan told me as I had headed back to my office.

"Thank you, enjoy your time off." I said as I rejoined Elora and Kyan.

Their fittings didn't take very long. As we were leaving I reminded Elora that I had promised to take Maggie and teach her how to swim.

"I'll watch with my feet in the water then."

"Kyan will you be joining us?" I asked.

"No, I'm going to see Leta and her mother this afternoon." He told us smiling. I think our talk last night over his and Leta's problems helped both of them.

Elora and I went to my cottage where Isabell sat alone with the children. She had made both the children swimming outfits, and they were excited to see I made it back early enough so we could swim.

"How was your first day as a Liaison Elora?" Isabell asked as she picked up the dishes from the children's mid-meal.

"Overwhelming! But I learned a lot today, and they gave me a beautiful white mare!"

"I've heard tell about that stunning mare." She said as she gave me a knowing look. I hadn't known they would give the mare to Elora even after they announced her calling I hadn't thought of it.

"Where's Harry?" I asked Isabell.

"He'll be working the next couple of days helping tear down the five cottages. They finished our cottage this morning."

"So they're taking all five cottages down?"

"That's what they told us this morning." The news was upsetting and there still had been no word of our cottage.

"I'm going to change so I can take these impatient children out to swim." Maggie had been headed to the door before we ever started speaking.

I had some older pants that have become too short for me so I had my mother cut them so I could swim in them. When I came out of my room in only my shorts it was Elora's turn to get caught staring at me. I gave her a teasing nudge to wake her from her little daydream.

"Will you be joining us my love?" That was my hint for her to come out with us. She picked up Maggie, Luke took my hand and we walked to the river where I knew the water pooled on the side some so I could get Maggie comfortable in the water.

Elora pulled her boots off and laid a blanket down for her to sit on. She put her feet in the water and carefully and set Maggie into my arms. I eased her carefully into the water she was very relaxed with us. Soon I had her swimming in my arms she splashed and giggled when she realized she was almost swimming. Not long after I let her on her own and she kept her head above the water she was swimming like a little fish. Elora clapped and cheered for her and soon Maggie was swimming all over the small pool. Luke was already a strong swimmer but I made him stay in the small pool with Maggie. I waded over so I could be close to Elora and still watch the kids

"You look very handsome in only those short pants." She said quietly.

"Well I'm glad that you're enjoying them."

"Can we meet tonight?" She asked me using the voice she knew made me weak.

"We shall see how the evening goes, after last night we should be more careful."

"I know, I was sure we had been caught."

"That's just it my love, we were caught! We're just lucky at who caught us. Next time we may not be so lucky."

"I know, I was scared so bad when you carried me back home. I fretted until you returned to me."

"The ceremony is in two days, everyone will be sleepy after a long evening of celebrating and drinking. Let's meet then, sound fair to you?"

"I'll be counting the moments until you touch me again my love."

"Can I ask you something Elora?"

"You can ask me anything, I have no secrets from you."

"When we are together like that, do I leave you feeling satisfied as you leave me?"

"Davin, everything you do is perfect. When I fall into your arms breathlessly, you should know that you have done exactly as my body desires."

I was still carefully watching the children splash and play but I needed to have this private talk with Elora. I needed to be sure that I'm doing everything right.

"Why do you always try to get me to enter you?"

"Because it feels right Davin, my body just pulls to you like it knows what it needs."

"I just don't want to take you until we are bound. I want to be sure we are safe until we don't have to be."

"I understand my love I'll try not to do it again."

"It was very difficult for me to stop the other night, I'm ashamed to say this but I didn't want to." I admitted to her knowing she wouldn't hate me for it.

"I didn't want you to stop either, but we did the right thing Davin. Even you just so much as admitted that."

"I know, you're right we did do the right thing. I just don't know how much longer I can hold back. I desire to take you more every moment that I think about our time at the river."

"I desire the same thing; we just have to sustain each other the way we have been. It won't be long." She promised me with her beautiful eyes gazing down at me.

"It feels like it will never happen."

"It will happen when it's our time." She tried to assure me.

"I thought they would keep one of the unused cottages up to give to us."

"Be patient my love."

We sat and watched the children play some more, Maggie was an expert swimmer already. I had to wait few minutes so I could get out of the water; my talk with Elora had caused my excitement to become apparent yet again. These betrayals of my body were not easy to adjust to.

I lifted the children up to Elora and she set them on her blanket to dry in the sun. When I got out she gave me a kiss and told me she loved me.

After we took the children in I excused myself to get dressed. I wanted to go check on Harry and Elora could stay and help Isabell.

I went looking for Harry and found him in the first cottage. I had brought him a jar of fresh cool water. When he seen me he took a break and we sat together under a shady tree.

"So what happened to going out with the hunter's?" I asked him.

"They needed extra help out her, the men who were working on our cottage asked if I'd mind helping them do this. They got permission and here I am."

"Do you think you'll return with the hunter's?"

"I'm not sure yet, I enjoy this kind of work, I get to work my muscles out some doing this. I don't want to just lose this muscle." He said laughing as he flexed his arm.

"How did you get your muscles to start looking like that?"

"At first just all the work I was doing with the side show, scooping elephant mess is heavy, at first I just started to look strong and I grew bigger, when I was in my teen years the muscles came as fast as the height."

"I guess I just thought if you were meant to look like that you would, and if you weren't then you'd be skinny like me."

"Davin, you're not skinny you have the fine start to a muscular body and with a little hard work, they will show more. You have to remember to eat well too."

"Thank you for the advice, maybe I should start spending my afternoon's cleaning out the stables."

"It would help." He said as we both laughed.

"Are they really tearing all five cottages down?" I asked hoping someone had told him different.

"Yes, we split up into five groups and we should be done tomorrow."

"That's good because you'll be bound in two days." I said hiding my disappointment.

"Yes, I'm getting very excited. And very excited for the children as well, I'm missing them a lot today."

"I taught Maggie to swim this afternoon."

"She's doing it?" He asked surprised.

"Yes she was born to swim that little one. She was doing it by herself in only a few minutes."

"She's so wonderful. I'm excited for her now."

"She'll want to show you her skills when you come see her later."

"Then I'll try not to be too late, give them my love when you go back." I stood up to leave and promised I would.

When I got back my mother was home already, Isabell and Elora were helping her put together a little dress for Maggie to wear to the ceremony. They were talking so fast of everything they needed to finish for the ceremony. I felt like I had walked into a hen house. That's when I decided to go clean horse pens.

"Harry sends his love, and I have chores to do so I'll let you beautiful ladies get your work done."

I gave Elora a small kiss on her head and took my leave. I know how excited I am for my ceremony with Elora, I just hope I don't have to help with the planning. I went to clean the horse pens out, I emptied their water barrel and cleaned it then carried buckets of water from the river up to them. Then I fed them more so I could do it all over again tomorrow. I could still hear the ladies in the kitchen and until another man got there I wasn't safe to go back in. I just knew it wouldn't be long before one of them would have me helping them put pins in the dresses.

I walked over to Elora's cottage and took care of their horse pens as well. Carrying the water was more difficult as their cottage was further from the river than our cottage was. As I was finishing up brushing Mr. Dover's horse Eldon came around the cottage towards me.

"What are you doing Davin?" He asked watching me brush the horse.

"The women are working on the plans for the ceremony. It was horrid, so I decided all the horses could use some attention."

"I'm not going near there yet then." He laughed.

"Want to go for a swim?" I was hot and sweaty and needed to not only cool off but clean up.

"Sure, let me grab something to swim in."

"Meet me behind my cottage I have to change as well."

I ran back over to my cottage and went inside; I needed the short pants to swim in again. Normally when I went out I'd go alone so I never had a need for the short pants, but now I felt the need to use them. When Eldon and I had gone out together after the fire it was dark so I didn't feel so self conscious.

Elora looked at me when I came in, her face changed when she set her eyes on me. I could see the desire fill her. And here I thought I was repulsive in dirty work clothes wet with sweat.

"I'm going to the river with Eldon if anyone comes looking for us." I went to my room and changed into my shorts and went out to meet with Eldon. I couldn't bear to see the hurt look on Elora's face especially since we agreed not to meet later.

Eldon and I were having fun in the water. He kept trying to dunk me under but I'm so much stronger he ended up being to one to get dunked. After awhile we went to the bank and just sat soaking and enjoying the cool water.

"Are you happy that you have a match now?" I asked him, he hadn't said much to me about it.

"Honestly, I'm relieved they've finally given me a match. I'm very relieved that Myka and I were matched. I've always liked her and our families are together a lot, to me it seemed only natural for us to be matched."

"I never knew you felt like that."

"I never showed it, it wasn't proper. But when Myka had become so unhappy I had to talk to her and find out what was happening. She was so upset she couldn't imagine being forced to marry someone who she felt hated her. I finally admitted to her that I loved her, and if she was my match she would never feel that way."

"You're a very strong kid, you know that right?"

"How do you figure that?" He asked looking confused

"The fact that you have felt so strong about someone and kept it to yourself because she was matched to someone else is amazing to me."

"I had no other choice, when your mother had announced Myka and I had been matched; I had to stop myself from jumping up and down. I've wanted a match for so long and then to get matched to the one person who I knew I loved was the best thing that could've ever happened to me."

"I'm glad that you're so happy about your match. I feel the same about my match with Elora. I couldn't imagine being matched to any other; in fact no other has ever turned my head."

"Can I tell you something Davin?"

"You don't have to ask me that Eldon."

"I wanted to find Jake and hurt him when I found out how he was treating Myka. I didn't care how bad of a whipping I'd of taken from Skullmaker."

"It's alright that you felt that way, I'm glad you didn't though. I wouldn't want to be the one to rub cream on your bottom for week afterwards." We both laughed and got out of the water. I was hungry and I hope in all the women's planning that supper wasn't forgotten again.

"Eldon, thank you for wanting to protect Myka it means a lot to me."

"You're welcome, but it honestly had nothing to do with you."

"I understand." I told him as I patted his back.

He went home and I went to my own cottage, I was still afraid to go on as I could still hear all the chattering but I needed clothing and food. When I went in Elora and my mother had poor Luke trapped and they were fitting a little suit on him. The poor kid looked miserable. The one good thing going on in the kitchen now was Isabell and Myka were in the kitchen getting supper cooked. It smelled good and my stomach was growling.

I went into my room and put on fresh clothes. I chose riding clothes as I intended to take Blitz out after I ate and ride out some of my own tension. Being around Elora since she got her new gowns was like a new torture to me. Seeing her breast come out of the top of her gown all the time was driving me mad. I feel like a fool for not agreeing to meet with her tonight. I felt like I'm arguing my brain against my body all of the time.

After I left my room I started being nosey in the kitchen. I was hungry and I couldn't wait any longer. Isabell scolded me but gave me a biscuit and some venison with a promise I'd get out of the kitchen until supper was ready.

"I need to get home to my own chores." Elora said as she finished taking the suit off of Luke.

"I'll walk you home. But only because Isabell has banished me from the kitchen when I'm half starved here."

"Twenty minutes will not kill you Davin." Isabell said from the kitchen.

"How's your afternoon been my love?" I asked as I led Elora out the door.

"Busy, with all the plans that need to be made and finished. The children's clothes are done, and Isabell has finished her gown. What have you been doing?"

"I went to see Harry, then I cleaned out our horse pens and I was bored so I went and cleaned your fathers."

"That was nice, thank you Davin. I'm sure that made Eldon happy."

"Eldon is happy no matter if I had done it for him or not."

"Why do you say that?" She asked me.

"He's happy about his match, he told me today that he loves Myka and has for a long time."

"I never knew that, is Myka as happy as he is?"

"She is very happy, I guess some bad things happened with her and Jake. If he hadn't of left the village she was going to beg for the match to be broken."

"Oh my! What did he do to her?"

"Well, you know how his parents were angry over Isabell and Harry. I guess when Myka said that she was happy about it he treated her bad told her he didn't want to be her match."

"How sad for Myka, now I know why she got so quiet it must have broke her heart too be treated like that."

"She is fine now my love, don't bring it up with her she won't want to talk about it. Now you get some rest I'll pick you up in the morning."

She kissed me softly and whimpered that she loved me in my ear. "See you in the morning my love." She started to turn away then quickly turned back. "You look amazing in the riding outfit if you change your mind later you know where to find me." With that she went into her cottage.

When I got back to the cottage my father and Harry were there and it looked like Isabell was finally going to let us eat. I went out back and checked on Blitz real quick and washed up.

We all ate together outside the cottage again. After I was done I told my parents I'd be taking Blitz out for a little while.

"That's fine Davin, I have to see Mrs. Dover about what she had to work on today, and Myka you can come with me if Isabell and Harry plan to stay for a little while." My mother said picking up plates.

Harry looked happy the night wouldn't end quickly, I know he wanted to see Maggie swim this evening.

"That will be great Mrs. Hewitt. I wanted to see the children some before I left."

"They are your children stay as long as you want." She said, that made Harry's eyes fill with tears, I think it's the first time anyone had called them his children.

"I'll be back before it gets too late." I said as I went to get Blitz.

He seemed happy I was getting him ready for a ride. He kept nuzzling against me as I was trying to get his straps buckled, it made it difficult to get them done up. I mounted him and headed out towards where the side show had camped. I love that area as it's so rarely used by the people in our village. I rode out to where the river drained into the lake and started to make my way around the lake. As I came up to a shady area I seen a huge wild rose bush covered with bright yellow roses. I dismounted from Blitz and took a few off of the bush.

I wanted to show them to Isabell and my mother maybe they would want some for the ceremony. I carefully picked off the thorns and tucked them in Blitz's mane, to keep them from being smashed.

For awhile I just sat and stared at the lake, the sun was going down and the lake was a mixture of purple and red in color. When things finally calmed down I'll bring Elora out to watch the sunset here. I sat and argued with myself about seeing Elora later tonight. I want to go see her, but after the scare last night I knew it would be better to let things between calm us as much as I could. I turned Blitz around and walked him home slowly.

When I got back to the cottage I brushed him out again and refilled the water barrel. When I went in I saw that the children were already asleep and Isabell and Harry were gone. My mother was finishing Luke's suit and Myka was sewing the hem on Maggie's dress.

"I found these out on my ride." I said showing them the roses.

"Davin those are beautiful we can use them for the ceremony, where did you find them?" My mother asked taking them from me.

"I found them out past the lake, the bush is huge it has hundreds of blossoms on it."

She was thrilled with the roses. "Well before the ceremony you'll have to take some baskets out and get as many as you can carry."

"I'll be glad to get them. Do you need anything else of me tonight?"

"No son, go sleep I know you haven't been sleeping much lately." I hope she didn't know just how much sleep I had been losing.

I laid down on my pallet after I put some bed clothes on, I was thinking about trying to go see Elora when I finally made the decision I wouldn't. Not soon after I fell asleep I heard a knock on my window.

"My love I just had to see you before I could sleep." She whispered to me.

"I'm sorry I fell asleep kind of early, I guess I was more tired than I thought."

"I'm not angry I just wanted to see you for a few moments." She said, she didn't seem upset at me.

"I'll take you back to your window my love."

I jumped out of the window and picked her up in my arms and carried her to her window, when I set her down we kissed for a long time. This time our kisses didn't become frenzied, they were passionate and loving kisses. I lifted her into her window and bid her sweet dreams. She leaned down for one more kiss then closed her window and I watched as she got into her bed.

I went back to my window and got into my pallet. I laid for a long time thinking about how wonderful that was. I wish that sometimes all of our meetings were as sweet and easy at that. I fell into a deep sleep, no nightmares in fact I don't remember any dreams at all.

CHAPTER 20

Plans, Plans and more Plans

I WOKE FEELING REFRESHED and ready to face the day. The children were still sleeping so I dressed into old clothes and slipped out of the room quietly. I decided to get water for morning meal, then went out back to clean out the horse pens, they also needed more food and fresh water. When I looked back into the cottage it was still quiet so I went and did the pen at Elora's as well. They only have one horse right now so it doesn't take so long to clean the pen and feed, but I do have to go further to get water. Nobody seen me come in or leave.

I slipped quietly into my room and got my work clothes, fresh linens, and my shaving kit. I was in the river awhile enjoying the cool quiet morning. My body was a little bit achy after working in the horse pens. After talking with Harry, I got to thinking how little work I had been doing since my calling. When I saw my father go check on the horses, I decided it was time to get out. After I was dressed, I joined everyone for morning meal.

My mother kept looking up at me as I was eating breakfast. "You look very nice today Davin, are you growing a beard?"

"I thought I'd just see how it would look on me, I'd like to just keep it thin I don't want a full heavy beard."

"It looks very nice on you."

"Thank you, I'm not sure if it will stay or go yet."

Maggie reached up and rubbed my face and complained that it was scratchy. I tried to tell her it would only be that way a couple days. I'll just wait the couple days and let her feel it again. I excused myself and went to go get Elora so I could walk her to the Liaisons again.

Mr. Dover let me in and invited to me sit down. "I noticed something funny this morning." He said as he took a seat across from me.

"What's that Sir?"

"My horse has been cleaned, fed and watered for the second time since yesterday."

"Just trying to help out where I can." I told him, I was doing it because I knew once Elora's horse came it would be more chores put on them.

"I appreciate that son, but you don't have to do that."

"I don't mind Sir really I had time this morning."

When Elora came out of her room, she was wearing another new gown this one was light blue. It was just as beautiful on her as the other gowns.

"Are you ready to go to work?" I asked her.

"As ready as I can be."

I got up and put my arm out for her to take and we went on our way.

"I like your beard it makes you look so handsome."

"Thank you, I love your new dress it makes you look very beautiful. Last night was very nice my love, thank you for coming to see me."

"I missed you, I did only stand and look for a few moments but really I wanted to steal a kiss from you."

"I'm glad you woke me my love. Please be careful you know what Wan said about being out alone."

"I was careful, I promise."

"Please as much as I enjoyed our visit don't do it again until things have calmed down."

"I won't anymore, I know it was dangerous." She said with promise in her voice.

"Thank you my love I just worry, you know how I feel about you." I told her.

"I appreciate that you care so much, and you're right I do need to be more careful for the time being."

We walked into the back of the building, I went to my office and Elora went to the small meeting room. It didn't sound like there were many in yet. My pay had been put on my desk again I couldn't figure out why I was getting more, so I took out my key and dumped the small box into the secret compartment in the big box. It was more than last time but I didn't bother to count it. I needed to save what I could for when were bound. I had plans of buying our own cow and raising chickens so we could have fresh eggs.

I took up my book and updated it about the talk I had with Harry about his work. I had only filled a few pages but there was a lot written in here. I also updated on how the butter rations had increased since the new cows arrived, and I made notes on the upcoming ceremony. It was warm in my office so I got up and opened the small window this suit was heavy and uncomfortable. I'm going to ask if I can just hang a suit here and only wear it when we have meetings. I slipped the heavy jacket off and hung it on the back of the chair then I went out to the barn to see how the animals were looking.

Elora's mare really was stunning. I can't wait until I can ride along side of her with Blitz. I looked towards the area where the cattle were being milked and the workers were churning the butter. I went over and asked to try it out. One of the younger girls took an empty churn and set it up for me. She told me that now I had to finish it because she had her own butter to churn. I started moving fast, before long I had worked up a sweat, but I felt the butter getting thicker though. My arms felt sore still but I didn't mind, it was nice being out here in the cool morning air working hard.

"What are you doing out here Davin?"

I looked up to see Wan and Lee watching me. "I just felt like seeing how it is to make butter, once this fine lady had me set up she swore I had to finish what I started so that's what I'm trying real hard to do it."

They both stood and laughed. "Have you opened it to see how your butter is coming along yet?" Lee asked me.

"Not yet but it sure feels thicker, that or my arms are just getting tired."

Wan pulled the top off the churn and looked inside. "Looks like you got butter in there; look at it." He was right; there was a lump of thick creamy looking butter ready to be scooped out.

"Well then." I said looking towards the girl who had helped me. "My work here is done." I gave her a quick smile and wink and walked back towards the office with Wan and Lee.

We all went to my office and sat. "I spoke with Harry last night." I told them.

"How's he getting along?" Wan asked me.

"He's doing good, I asked him about the hunting like you asked me too. He does enjoy it when he goes out hunting with the others but he's also enjoying working with the men in construction areas. He says he likes the hard work."

"That's interesting, we'll have to spend some time talking with him, I want him placed where he's comfortable."

Lee agreed with Wan, and asked how the ceremony plans were coming. I laughed at the thought of my hiding from everyone most of the afternoon.

"I think the women have everything under control. I got busy doing some work around our pens to avoid them all." I told them.

They both laughed hard at that.

"We just wanted to let you know Elora's riding outfits and one of her work gowns are done, she'll probably need help taking them home." Lee informed me.

"That's no problem I walk her everywhere."

"We also want you to let your mother know that we are leaving at mid-meal again, so they are free to come decorate for the ceremony. I've already given her a key to use."

"Thank you, I'll let her know when we get to the cottage for mid-meal."

"Is there anything you need before we call it a day?" Wan asked me.

"Yes actually, I was just thinking about something. Would it be possible if I just kept one of these suits in my office and change into it when we have meetings? I just feel more comfortable in my normal clothes."

"Yes, the suits are rather stuffy, I think that will be fine. Maybe we'll all follow your lead on that as well."

Wan and Lee stood to leave as Elora's new clothes had arrived.

"She'll need to use your office to change if she would like to ride out." Lee told me.

"I'll go get her while she dresses I'll saddle her mare for her." I said heading for the small office to pull her away from her work.

"Your new riding outfits have been delivered, they are in my office, if you want to change there you can. I'll saddle your mare for you if you wish." I told her as we walked towards my office.

"That would be wonderful, it shouldn't take me too long to dress, but I might need some help tying the back of my gown."

"I'll be back to help in a few minutes my love."

I brought her mare out of the pens and saddled her with ease. She was a good horse and very smart. I never even had to tie her while getting her saddled. After I had her ready to go, I went to help Elora with her ties.

I was careful to leave the door standing open so no one got upset that I was helping her. She kept telling me to pull her ties tighter, I was afraid I was going to hurt her. She laughed at my reluctance to pull them tight. Her riding outfit was beautiful it matched my grey riding outfit..

I walked her out to her mare and helped her mount her and arranged her gown around the back of the horse and down her legs. Then I went in to get her other gowns so I could carry them home. They were surprisingly very heavy, and I thought my suits were heavy.

She walked her mare carefully at my side, I told her to stay on and I'd set her gowns on her bed. Now that my hands were empty I could at least lead her to my cottage. I asked her to stay mounted while I changed into my riding outfit and saddled Blitz. All I wanted to do was ride beside her and I made that very clear. She walked her mare back and forth between our cottages while she waited. She was already very good at controlling the mare.

My mother was still in when I went in to change, I gave her Wan and Lee's message and ran to change real quick.

"Where are you off to in such a hurry?" She asked when I charged out.

"Look outside mother." I said as I followed her to the window.

"Breath taking!" Was all she could say.

"What the horse or the beautiful woman on top of it?" I asked.

"Both of them, they look like they were made for each other."

"Yes they do, mind if I take a short ride with her?"

"Go to my office and grab a couple baskets; you two can go get me some of those roses."

"We'll be back soon." I promised.

I had Blitz saddled and mounted in just a few minutes, when I rode along side of Elora and her mare Blitz began to nuzzle the mare.

"They like each other!" Elora exclaimed.

"How could they not?" I said as I led her towards my mother's office. "We have to get some baskets from my mother's office she wants us to go after some roses I found last night."

"And the plans begin again." She said with a smile.

After we were done getting the baskets we walked the horses out of the village. We ran into Kyan and asked him to ride out with us. We both knew he was eager to see how his horse was as well. Besides it looked better for us having him with us. I led the way setting a good pace for the horse's it wasn't long before I found the rose bush.

"Those are beautiful, how did you find these?"

"I just went for a ride last night and this is where I ended up. We'll have to come back at sunset with Leta too, the lake changes color as the sun goes down."

I helped Elora off her horse I don't see how she'll be able to walk much the gown is longer than she is. I let her sit while Kyan helped me fill the baskets with roses. Our hands had cuts and scratches all over them from the thorns. I'm glad Elora couldn't help, for the rose's beauty beholds an uncomfortable pain.

It didn't take long to fill the baskets I didn't want to linger for too long because I was getting hungry again. I helped Elora back on her mare, this time she looked uncomfortable.

"What is wrong my love?"

"Nothing; I just think I'd do better with some pants under this dress."

"We can have the tailor make some for when you ride, I'll pay for it for you."

"Thank you my love that would help a lot, the inside of my legs are hurting me."

"Why not try sitting side saddle we'll go slowly back to the village."

Kyan turned his back while I helped her adjust in her saddle. I lifted her gown to look at her legs. They were red and looked as if they would bleed.

"I'm so sorry my love that looks terribly sore. I don't think riding in a gown is going to work out so well for you."

"I'll be fine just get me home Davin."

We walked the horses slowly back to the village. Kyan took the roses to my mother while I took Elora to her cabin and helped her off the mare, I carried her into her cottage and told her I'd put her mare in Blitz's pen for the night.

I led both the horses back to my cottage and tied them up, then I ran in to see my mother. I told her how bad Elora's legs were and begged her to go check on her. My mother dropped everything she was doing and ran to Elora's cottage she didn't knock she just went inside.

About ten minutes had passed and my mother called me in. Elora was in a long night gown. "Help me carry her to the river Davin." I picked her up with ease and walked with my mother to the river. She had me ease her into the river carefully, and told me to run to her office and get the cream she has used on the children's feet. Elora was silently letting tears fall down her face as I went for the cream. When I returned my mother had her calmed down and out of the water. She was walking a little tenderly, but she looked a lot better.

I picked her up and carried her back to the cottage. All I could do was tell her how sorry I was over and over. I never knew that would happen. I don't think any of us did, females didn't ride on horses in our village.

"Davin, she'll be fine, it's just been rubbed to hard from the leather on the saddle. She can't ride in a gown it's as simple as that. Have them come up with a better idea." My mother seemed angry about what had happened. I felt terrible and I just wanted to make her better.

"I'll go take care of the horses and come back for you." I said almost crying.

"I'll bring her to our cottage as soon as she is dressed, this cream will take the pain away and she'll be able to be up and around. It isn't as bad as it first looked. I promise she's is alright, this is not your fault son don't beat yourself up over it."

"Alright, I'll see you both at the cottage." I laid her on her bed and kissed her cheek.

All I could do with the horses was put Blitz on a tie and let Eloras horse have the pen. After I ate I'd go build a pen at her cottage for the mare.

When I was finally finished I washed up real quick at the river and went to my cottage. Like my mother promised Elora looked a lot better she was walking around as if nothing had happened.

"Sit my love; I'll bring you something to eat." She told me, Isabell had been busy cooking when I had run in to get my mother earlier.

"After I eat I'll go get the materials and build a pen at your cottage for your mare."

"Thank you Davin but really it can wait a day or two, I can walk her back to the barn until I'm ready for her."

"How about I take her back to the barn, and if I can find Wan or Lee I'll see what can be done so you can ride her."

"That sounds like a compromise." She said as she put my plate down and sat to eat with me.

I heard Isabell whisper to my mother about how much I cared for Elora and how nice it was to see. We ate quietly I asked her every few minutes if she was alright. She finally got upset and said she wouldn't talk to me if I didn't drop it. I left as soon as I finished my meal and I rode Blitz and walked the mare along side of us. I made sure she was comfortable in the barn and I went to see if Wan or Lee were still inside. They both were still inside sitting in the main room having ale and looking relaxed.

"May I speak for a moment?" I felt like I was interrupting them.

"Yes, come have an ale with us and tell us what's on your mind." Lee invited me.

"Elora, Kyan and I went for a ride outside of the village, there is a problem with Elora's riding in a gown."

They both looked surprised at what I said. "What happened?" Wan demanded.

"The saddle rubbed her legs very bad she was almost bleeding when we stopped. I had her ride sideways on the way back and my mother treated her legs with the cream she used on the children's feet."

"That's terrible, we never thought about the saddle hurting her." He said full of concern.

"I came up with an idea while I was coming here, I think maybe it would be a compromise and certainly it has never been allowed before, but then women don't normally ride.

I was thinking having riding pants made for her, and much like our own riding jackets, have one made with the top like her gowns and let it flow down to her knees so it still looks proper."

They both looked at each other and nodded. "That may work let me speak with the tailors to see if it would be possible and if it is we'll have her fitted in a couple days after the ceremony." Lee said.

"Thank you so much, I'd hate if she couldn't ride that mare for she has already taken to her."

"We agree with you, it was never our intention for her to get hurt. Please take our apologies to her." Lee asked me.

"I will and thank you again." I said as I got up to leave.

I mounted Blitz and went back to the cottage. I explained to everyone the idea for the new riding outfit for her. Everyone agreed it was a great idea, "Maybe with proper riding outfits more women could take to riding." My mother said.

"Wan and Lee send their apologies Elora, they never thought such a thing would happen, they were headed to the tailors with my idea to see how it could be done. I fed and watered your mare before I left and she'll be fine until we get your pens built."

"My love, she is comfortable there she'll be fine there is no need to overwork yourself over her."

"I know, I just want to help."

"I just want you to relax, I'm fine and she's fine."

I sat down with her to show her I was trying to relax. But I couldn't sit long I still had our horses to take care of and I was going to try to get to her father's as well. I know that everyone will be busy with decorating at the Liaison main hall this evening I just wanted to make it as easy as possible.

Someone was knocking at the door my mother went to see who was there. It was a boy from the tailors asking for me. "They would like you to bring the riding outfits back as soon as you have a free moment."

"I'll be there with them shortly." I told him.

"They also said they didn't need Elora back for another fitting, they kept her measurements from before." He told me as he turned to leave.

"Thank you, I'll be on my way soon." I told him.

"I'll be back, I have to get your outfits and take them to the tailor's. You guys keep your ceremony talk up I won't be long." I said as I kissed her lightly on her hand before I headed out.

After I left the outfits with the tailor, I rode to Elora's and took care of her father's horse. Then I went to work in our pens, since I worked on them this morning there wasn't much to take care of. I unsaddled Blitz and brushed him down before I returned him to his pen.

I knew we would be having an earlier supper, so I tried to wash up some before I went back into the cottage. When I got in I saw that Mrs. Dover had arrived and was helping get everything together.

"Davin, you look exhausted please go lay down before supper." My mother said as I tried to sit at the table.

"Your mother's right." Isabell was agreeing with her. "You look like you haven't slept for days."

"I slept fine last night I was just cleaning horse pens is all."

"I won't take no for an answer." My mother insisted.

"Alright I'll go lay down just don't let me sleep through supper." I said as I went and laid on my bed; I fell asleep quickly.

When I woke it was almost dark and the cottage was quiet. I got up quickly and noticed everyone had left. There was a note on the table that had my name on it. "Davin, I couldn't bear to wake you. I left your supper in the oven. We're at the Liaison preparing for the ceremony. Please don't be upset, come join us. With all the love I have to give, Elora."

I couldn't be mad at her I just didn't want to sleep my evening away. I opened the oven door and found my supper, it was still warm and it smelled delicious. I dined alone on wild boar, boiled carrots, potatoes and fresh bread. They left a lot of food on the plate, I was grateful as I've been so hungry the past couple days. After I finished eating I changed out of my riding clothes and put on my normal work clothes.

I walked to the Liaison's office so I could see if there was anything left to help with. The curtains were pulled open and the main door was left open. There were so many people there helping to decorate I hadn't thought there was so much support after the last few days.

I saw Elora sitting in a chair putting flowers together she truly looked beautiful surrounded by all the flowers. I walked slowly over to her and sat in the chair next to her. She never looked up from what she was doing but she knew I was there.

"Good evening my handsome love how was your rest?" She asked very quietly again never taking her eyes off the work she was doing.

"My nap was nice, someone forgot to wake me for supper and I found myself dining alone." I knew that would get her to look up at me.

"I'm sorry, you just looked so peaceful, and you really didn't look so good when you had come in. I don't want you working yourself to exhaustion I worry about you as much as you worry about me."

"Speaking of worrying about you, how are your legs?"

"They feel much better, thank you for getting your mother she helped a lot."

"I was scared when I took you down from that horse you didn't look so good."

"I think I'm just tired like you are." She told me.

"Then why are you sitting here working so hard?" I asked her, she was worse than me when it came to pushing herself to hard.

"Like you really need to ask that, I wouldn't have been able to tell you goodnight if I hadn't come here."

"You're just silly." I said laughing at her.

"I'm not silly Davin, I'm in love."

"With who?" I teased.

"I'm about to get Harry over here to beat you up!" She teased me.

"I'm just teasing with you my love, I'm glad you came too for I wanted to see you as well. I'm glad you're feeling better, I feel so bad."

"There's nothing for you to feel bad about my love."

"Thank you for leaving me something to eat, I was starving when I woke up."

"I've noticed your increasing appetite. I hope I left you enough to eat."

I was stuffed. "It was perfect." I told her.

Harry came up to us and handed us both a cup of wine. "Feeling any better Davin?" He asked as he took a seat with us.

"Yes, I must have been tired is all, I'm fine really you all don't have to worry."

"We choose to worry besides Isabell said you looked pretty bad." He said showing his concern.

"I had been working, cleaning the horse pens. I was just a little tired is all."

"If you insist, but if you're coming down sick you better let your mother know." He warned me.

"I'm not sick I promise."

The wine was good tonight and with everyone that was here was helping the mood was festive. It was nice to see our village come back together. I had a couple more cups of wine and my head was starting to feel light. The decorating was about done and people were starting to say goodnight. I was glad for one reason they let me sleep, I got to skip all the decorating stuff.

Elora and I walked around back and looked in on her mare.

"Are you going to give this mare a name?"

"I will, I just can't think of anything yet. It'll come to me when it's time."

We didn't linger long I didn't want anyone coming to check on us, nor did I want Elora to get a chance to get me wound up tonight. When we went back into the hall I picked Maggie up, her eyes were so sleepy. Luke took Elora's hand, and we headed out. I told Harry and Isabell to enjoy their evening it was our last night to be able to put the children to bed. Maggie was asleep long before we were at the cottage, and Luke was dragging his poor little feet all the way. Eldon and Myka also came back with us we let them sit on their new log while we got the children to bed. They were sound asleep before we left the room, I don't think Maggie ever did wake up.

I started a fire outside and we sat with Eldon and Myka, they talked while Elora and I enjoyed some more wine. When our parents came home they sat with us as well. It was a quiet night everyone had been working hard the last few days. I told Elora she should go home and sleep, she didn't argue just got up and bid her goodnights. I walked her to her cottage and gave her a small kiss and bid her sweet dreams.

It was unlike her to just go willingly, I had the feeling her thighs were in more pain than she was willing to tell me. She walked slowly to her door and turned around to blow me a kiss. I walked back to our cottage and had more wine it wasn't long before Kyan came up on his new horse.

"Did you get to see Leta this afternoon?" I asked him as I handed him a cup of wine.

"Yes, I had mid-meal with her and her mother."

"How's her mother doing?"

"She looks better and she is more up and around then she had been."

"I'm glad to hear that, I know she got pretty sick for awhile."

"She was, but it seems to be getting better for her. I can't stay for long tonight; I just wanted to stop by and see how the decorating went."

"I slept through it." I said and we both laughed. In our village the men were known for not wanting to help plan and decorate for a ceremony. I was no different I preferred to be out cleaning after the horses than be caught in the middle of that.

After Kyan left, everyone slowly got up and bid me goodnight. I had slept so long that I wasn't feeling tired yet so I went to the river. I stripped off my clothes and went in for a swim. The water was cool and the sky was clear. The moon light was bright and I could see very well. I just sat and enjoyed the privacy the river provided me, I heard Blitz whinny but I didn't pay him much attention. I swam back and forth across the river. The soreness in my arms started easing up and it felt good to stretch them in the cool water. After swimming back and forth for about a half an hour or so I swam to the bank and laid naked in the moonlight. I hadn't been laying there long when I heard footsteps coming towards me. I didn't even get a chance to cover myself when I heard someone begin to speak.

"What are you doing laying naked out here alone?" It was Wan, at first I was startled I almost felt as if I were doing something wrong but I've swam in the nude before and even my parents had never scolded me for it.

"I slept during the early evening and I couldn't sleep yet so I came out here to tire myself some." I answered him as I grabbed for my pants and slipped them on. "What are you doing walking out here this late?" I countered.

"I woke when Harry came in so I decide to come walk by the water."

"I'm sure that big man makes some noise coming in when he's full of wine." I said laughing.

"He does, but I like Harry a lot. I'm glad I could be of help to him, he's sure been a big help to all of us. The five cottages are down thanks to all the help he gave."

"He's a nice guy. I sure became friends with him quickly."

"I've noticed how close you two had become when you returned from you trip."

"The trip was good in more ways than being able to get the livestock. It was good to be away from my parents and make friends with people I normally wouldn't have had the opportunity to spend time with."

"I'm glad the trip was memorable for you. How is Elora feeling this evening?"

"She says she feels better and the cream my mother used on her was helping. She was tired when I was with her during the decorating party, after we put the children to bed I walked her home so she could get some rest."

"I feel so bad about what happened, we should of thought that through a little better. I gave the tailor your idea and he said he could work it out, he also said he would make her riding pants much like what the younger boys wear."

"I'm glad it worried me she may not be able to ride again."

"The tailor is very good I trust whatever he comes up with will work perfectly for her." Wan said, he sat down next to me on the bank. He was smoking a pipe and taking small draws from a jug he has was carrying.

"So have you figured out when you'll be leaving?"

"Not yet, I don't really want to talk about it I know it makes you sad and I can't seem to talk you out of those feelings." He told me with his voice full of sadness.

"I guess it's just hard for me to accept that you'll be gone for good."

"I've dedicated my life to this village Davin, I came here as a small boy on my own without my family. And I worked hard to show I belonged here, when the Liaison was assembled I was chosen and I vowed to help keep our village an enjoyable place to be. Now I have a few changes to make and once those are in place my work here will be done, there is no need for me to stay. My brother is my twin, I have dreams about him a lot and I think he needs me."

"Do you know where he is?"

"I think he's in Stormhaven but that's just what it looks like in my dreams."

"You're going to live under the Kings rule?"

"I may not have a choice Davin, if that's where I find my brother then that's where I'll have to be."

"I think you'll be missed around this village." I told him.

"It will be fine son; I promise I won't leave the village with a feeling of despair."

He handed me the jug he was drinking out of, I thought at first it was wine but when I took a big drink I realized by the fire running down my throat that it wasn't.

"What is this?" I asked trying not to show that it had made me uncomfortable.

"Whiskey, I have the kitchen make it for me. It doesn't get made often and it certainly doesn't get handed out." He handed the bottle back to me and I took another big drink, this time it went down much easier.

After we had passed the jug back and forth a few times Wan got up to leave. "Don't get in that water when you're full of whiskey it's a lot stronger than the wine and ale you're accustomed too."

"I'm done swimming for the evening. I don't even think I can walk to my bed." He laughed at me and walked away slowly.

After he was gone for awhile I got up and pulled my boots on, I put my shirt over my shoulder and went walking aimlessly. The whiskey was very strong and my head was swimming. Before I realized it I was standing at Elora's window watching her sleep. Her golden hair was flowing across her pillow. I watched as her breasts moved slowly up and down with each breath she took. I stood longing for her, wishing she would wake and come to me, but she slept peacefully not even stirring.

My mind was racing I paced from the river to her window a few times. I wanted her. I needed to be with her. I opened her window and slowly climbed into her sleeping room, I moved with careful steps to be sure she didn't stir and made sure her door was locked. I went to her bed and carefully put my lips to hers and began to kiss her, she opened her eyes and looked startled and frightened.

"It's only me my love, sshhh… Don't say anything."

I was quickly losing control of myself. I was kissing her moving up and down her shapely body. She lay silent unmoving and unresponsive to my kisses and caresses. I moved up to her lips kissing them lightly, "What's wrong my love?" I asked in between the kisses I was showering her with.

"Davin are you drunk?" She whispered trying to get up.

I was still kissing her trying to get her to return my love. "Yes, I've been drinking my love and I've also been thinking of you."

She got up and went to the window. I followed her out, picked her up and carried her to the river. She was still reluctant to return my kisses. When I set her down at the river she pushed me off of her.

"What is wrong with you?" She demanded.

"I'm in love and I want you to kiss me." I pulled her back to me, and she pushed away from me again.

"Elora don't do this to me now, you stirred this fire in me and now you treat me as a stranger." I cried to her as I fell to my knees. She came back to me and I pulled her close burying my face into her belly. I just held on to her crying, my body aching for the relief I knew only she could give me. She pulled me up to her face this time she kissed me softly; like she loved me. Her fingers ran through my hair and she said nothing. She never lost control of herself as she tried to calm me.

"I love you Davin, you've had too much to drink and you scare me."

"I didn't want to scare you. I wanted to be with you, to take you like you've been trying to get me to do. I wandered around aimlessly and still was drawn to your window I watched you sleeping and wanted you more. I still want you."

"Davin I'll not let you do something you'll hate yourself for tomorrow."

She still held onto me calmly running her hand through my hair. "I want you too my love, I want you more than anything in the world right now. But I know what you really want and I can't let you make a mistake like this."

I slowly came out of the trance I was in, and laid my head on her chest. I felt her heartbeat on my face and listened to her soothing words. "Take me back to my bed now my love." She whispered softly as she kissed the top of my head. I picked her up saying nothing and carried her back to the window. When I set her down I felt such shame I couldn't even look at her. She took my face into her hands and made me meet her gaze.

"I love you Davin; I'm not angry with you, do you understand that?"

I cried silently feeling shameful for what I had done to her. She pulled my face to hers and kissed me, the sweet kisses like the night before constantly whispering over and over that she loved me.

"I'll see you in the morning, please go home and sleep Davin. Promise me!" She demanded still holding my face forcing me to look into her eyes.

"I promise." I said trying to look away.

"I mean it go home and sleep!" She demanded.

"I will, I'm so sorry Elora please don't hate me, please." I begged her.

"I could never hate you Davin, this is as much my fault. I love you. I love you more now at this moment than I ever have." She said softly as she kissed my lips tenderly.

"I love you too will you see me in the morning?"

"Of course I'll see you after our chores are done." She pulled my face to hers again and kissed me softly and whispered. "Go to bed Davin, sweet dreams."

I set her back in her window and walked away with my head down. I felt miserable I went to my cottage but I didn't go in, I walked back to the river and screamed into it. I hated myself and I hated what I had just done to the one person who loved me so unconditionally. I don't know how long I stood screaming into the river before I fell and passed out on the bank.

I felt the warm sun on my face and stirred some but I didn't get up. I laid still and fell asleep again. I was having nightmares of what I had done to Elora only in my nightmares

I didn't stop, she was crying when I finished and I kept calling her name and telling her I was sorry.

Someone was shaking me, telling me to get up. I opened my eyes and Elora was kneeling by me. I was groggy and I heard her tell me to wake up again. I sat up quickly and looked at her not sure if I was still dreaming or not.

"Are you alright Davin? I told you to go to your bed!" I realized that I was awake and she was really there.

"What are you doing here?" I asked trying to rub away the nightmare I had just been in. The guilt I felt rushed into my head as I remembered what I had done last night.

"Myka came across you, she heard you calling out my name and she ran to get me. You're lucky she didn't go to your parents, you wouldn't want them to see you like this."

I looked down I was covered in dirt and my shirt had a big rip in it. "Elora, I'm so sorry please forgive me." I begged instantly.

"Davin, I'm not angry with you, I as much caused what happened last night as you did. There is nothing for me to forgive."

"I shouldn't have ever come to you like that."

"Listen to me for I'll only say this one time to you." She interrupted me. "You only did what all along I have encouraged you to do. You were right last night I did start the fire that burns deep inside of you. I stopped you because I knew after all the time we spent talking, after our time at the river that you would've hated yourself if you took me like that last night. I'm not angry or hurt or upset at you, I love you and I will not watch you beat yourself up over this. Do you understand me?"

I nodded as I looked into her eyes, her look for me had not changed she still looked at me as if she were drowning in our love.

"I want you to get up and get in the river and wash up. And before you get out leave all your guilt in there, let the river that holds our secrets take with it the hurt you're feeling. I will not let you apologize to me again. I will not let you explain yourself anymore. It ends before you get out of that water or I won't speak to you until it's gone." She kissed me on my cheek and walked away back towards her own cottage.

I did as she told me and got in the water with my clothes still on. I washed all the dirt away that was on me and watched it disappear into the water. I yelled some more into the water, until I felt a sense of relief come over me. I went underwater and swam for as long as my breath would allow me. When I got out of the water I restarted my day trying to do as Elora wished of me and forget what I had done to her.

I let the sun dry off my clothes and I took the shovel and cleaned the horse pens. By the time I had fed and watered them I was dry enough to go get changed and let my day begin.

CHAPTER 21

The Ceremony

EVERYBODY WAS SO BUSY preparing for the ceremony, that no one noticed when I came in. I went to my room and put on dry work clothes. I was trying hard to not think about last night. I didn't want to upset Elora again I had done enough to her. After I had changed I left the cottage and went to clean her father's pens. When I got there I noticed all our footprints from last night in the dirt under her window and I used the shovel to quickly move the dirt around so no one would notice.

I went right to work on the pen and had it cleaned quickly then I fed the horse and dumped his water. When I turned to go start hauling water back I saw Elora watching me through her window with a smile on her face. It took me four trips to the river to get the horse watered. She had opened her window and watched silently as I went back and forth. I always looked up at her and gave her a smile as I went past. When I had finished, I was all sweaty from the work. I leaned against the horse's pen and just gazed at Elora.

"Are you feeling better my love?" She asked leaning a little further out the window. I was sure her breasts would fall out of her gown at any moment.

"Yes my love, I'm just enjoying the view." I said looking towards her breasts again.

She looked down and saw how her leaning had her dangerously close to falling out of her gown. She turned red and pulled herself up some. "You're looking mighty handsome all sweaty and muscular looking out there."

"I'm glad you think so my love." I walked close to her window, I could smell her hair on the breeze.

"Did you sleep well?" She asked as if we hadn't seen each other already this morning.

"You're absolutely amazing." I said as I walked away from her towards my cottage. When I looked back at her I seen her face had gotten that look that I love so much.

I went into the cottage looking for something to eat. I was so hungry that I felt pain in my stomach. Everyone was still rushing around, packing things up and setting out things they would need when they dressed. I found biscuits still warm on the stove and a pan of venison gravy. I put three biscuits on a plate and smothered them in gravy. I took my plate outside and sat under a shady tree and ate while enjoying the fact I had gone unnoticed so far this morning. Soon Myka noticed me sitting here when she looked out the window.

"What was wrong with you this morning?" She asked me.

"I had too much wine last night." I told her hoping she would drop it.

"You're not mad I went to Elora are you?"

"No, I'm grateful you did, it was wonderful waking up to her beautiful face."

"I'm going to help Isabell dress for the ceremony I'll see you there later."

"Give her a hug for me."

"I'll, see you later." She said as she walked away headed to see Isabell.

Harry was coming up in his carriage as Myka was walking away. He walked over and joined me under the tree.

"Good morning Davin, how are you this fine day?"

"I'm a fool, but otherwise I'm just fine. Are you ready for the ceremony this afternoon?"

"I'm more than ready, I can't wait until it's over and we can get on with living. So what happened which made you think you're a fool?" He asked me, I knew I could trust Harry I was worried he would be ashamed of me though.

"Please don't get angry with me, but last night after everyone was gone I went to the river to swim and while I was down there Wan happened upon me. I drank some of his whiskey with him and got rather drunk."

"Hmm so that's where he goes when he leaves at night?"

"He leaves all the time?" I asked now fearing he may have seen Elora and I at some point out by the river.

"He has every night since I've stayed there. And why would I be angry that you had too much to drink?

"Well, that's not all that happened Harry. I was stumbling around and I found myself at Elora's window and I went in and tried to take her."

He looked surprised but not angry. "Did you take her Davin?"

"When she woke she got me away from the cottage and she was angry and wouldn't even kiss me back. I got angry because she is always trying to get me to take her then when I was trying she refused me. We argued by the river some but I didn't take her. She kept strong and spent time calming me down. She isn't angry with me she's acting as if nothing had happened."

Harry started laughing, "It's a good thing one of you always keeps their wits when you two are alone together. If she isn't angry maybe it wasn't as bad as you remember Davin."

"She won't speak about it all, she takes blame saying she has pushed me and she feels as responsible as I do."

"You two I'm sure will talk it out; right now it's fresh, today is suppose to be festive. And maybe it's exactly as she says and you should leave it at that Davin. Do you think you hurt her?"

"No, I remember even when I was angry all I could do was fall to my knees and beg for her to love me."

"She does love you Davin, anyone who has seen two together can see that."

"She just kept telling me she couldn't let me do something I'd hate myself for later."

"She is right there, I know how your mind is set on waiting to take her until you're bound, usually you're the strong one who makes her see the need to wait. Last night was her turn to be the one who knew it wasn't what either of you wanted to live with."

"I know your right, I just feel like a monster for doing that to her." I told him, the guilt still putting me in turmoil.

"You'll be fine once you busy your mind, and it wasn't you who was the monster it was that whiskey and maybe in the future you should learn to take it easy on it."

"I agree, I had only had small amounts of it in the past, last night I knew I had too much."

"And boy next time you go getting drunk and wandering around the village, I may just have to wear your hide out myself. You could've fallen in the river or something."

"I won't be doing it again, I promise. Has Wan ever mentioned Elora or I to you?"

"Not to me why do you ask?" He asked me curiously.

"Just hearing that he leaves every evening like that, we have been to the river with each other, I'm not sure if he has seen us or not."

"If he had wouldn't you both have been in trouble?" Harry asked me.

"Well I'm not so sure, I've noticed Wan has taken to me he may not say anything." I was thinking of the unusual calling I received that no one knows about. I'm even unsure if Elora and Kyan have been told.

"Come boy, quit your brooding were have a celebration coming."

I got up and followed Harry into the cottage. I was still hungry so I shoved another biscuit in my mouth while I washed my dish. The children ran up to Harry and he scooped them both up with no effort at all. It's so great to watch Harry with the children. I'm so fond of them, and I feel if I hadn't found them when I had maybe they wouldn't have had the chance to become a part of his life.

"Are we getting married today?" Maggie asked him, everyone laughed at her innocence.

"Well something like that, Isabell and I will be married. You and Luke will become our children. And we'll all live together in another cottage."

"We can't sleep in Davin's bed anymore?" She almost looked afraid.

"We built you and Luke your own beds, and we put them into your own rooms."

Maggie cheered and hugged Harry around his neck.

All morning the women rushed around trying to make sure everything they needed would be where they needed it. My father was in the front of the cottage roasting the pig that had been sent over. It has to be cooked before we go to the ceremony because it can't be left on the fire with no one to turn the spit. My mother was cooking one loaf of bread after another in between peeling vegetables and fussing at me to do something or other. Elora and Mrs. Dover were making peach tarts; a lot of them. Though they wouldn't let me have one.

Elora acted like everything was perfect between us and maybe it was. I was just having trouble shaking last night, although Harry's talk helped me understand why she wasn't as angry at me as I felt she should be. I planned on wearing my black riding outfit but I didn't want to change until it was close to time we left. I was already covered in flour from helping my mother with the bread.

Harry and Mr. Dover set up the outside of the cottage with logs for places to sit and makeshift tables for food and presents. My mother went out and placed some flower garlands they had made last night around the table that would hold the presents. On the food tables she put three jugs of wine. There was more wine under the tables. The jugs are huge so we expect twelve to be enough.

After we got everything set up I took Luke with me to the river with me to wash up before we got dressed up. I shaved around my beard it was actually filling in better than I thought it would. I left the moustache also today I just want to see Elora's reaction. I helped Luke put his little suit on and told him he had to sit and stay clean. He didn't like it, it seemed since he was finally able to get up and run around that he wanted to make up for the time we kept him down. He's a good boy, I've never heard him talk back and he uses great manners. I think his parents were doing good raising him when they were still alive.

Maggie looked beautiful in her little white dress; my mother had her hair pinned up and had put little tiny white flowers in all the pins. She looked very tiny like maybe she was only about three years old. Where Luke was filling out and looking well fed she had only really gained a healthy color. I was feeling sad that they would be leaving us after the celebration later I just kept reminding myself what a wonderful life they would be given.

My father and Mr. Dover brought the carriages over and had the horses on them by the time we were all dressed and ready. Harry had Luke and Maggie ride with him in his carriage he would be following behind our families.

It looked like most of the village showed up for the ceremony. The Liaison's building had all the drapes open with the windows open as well. They moved all the furniture out of the room for ceremonies because so many people came to see when people are bound. There was a small pulpit at the back of the room and everyone was crowded in around the sides.

Harry walked with Maggie holding one hand and Luke holding the other. Isabell was standing at the door waiting to enter with Harry and the children. Elora took my arm and we walked into the building and found a spot to stand, it was very crowded. It looked beautiful with the yellow roses and little white flowers that they had strung into garland and hung around the entire room. Lee was standing at the pulpit waiting to begin the ceremony.

Harry placed the children in the middle and he and Isabell stood on the outside they all joined hands and walked as a family together to the pulpit. A lot of us clapped happy to see such a wonderfully blessed match.

"Thank you all for coming to see Harry and Isabell be bound in marriage this fine day." Lee started the ceremony. "We're also helping Harry and Isabell welcome Luke and Maggie into their new lives as well." He had Harry and Isabell face each other and take each other's hands. "From today on you'll both live as husband and wife, you'll strive to work together in happiness and love. You'll take care of each other and be there when the other needs you. You'll learn to respect each other as well in every aspect that comes forward to you. If you both agree may you say I do now."

They both said 'I do' together as they looked lovingly at each other.

"I'd like you both to now join hands with Maggie and Luke." They were now standing in a circle. "Your dedication and love for these children says so much for your compassion. Do you agree to take Luke and Maggie as your children and swear to always treat them with love and compassion as if they were born to you?"

Harry and Isabell both swore to the children that they would be loved forever in their home.

"I now pronounce you the proud and beautiful Birch family."

Harry bent down and gave Isabell a kiss then he lifted Maggie up and kissed her cheeks. He shook Luke's hand then picked him up and hugged him tight.

Everyone that fit in the hall was clapping and cheering as they walked out officially a family to their carriage. This time they all rode together, and led all the carriages to our cottage. A lot of the villagers that were at the ceremony came to the celebration they brought gifts of every shape and size with them.

My father and Mr. Dover brought the roasted pig out and began carving it. My mother, Mrs. Dover, Elora and I carried out the vegetables, bread and peach tarts. When we had celebrations this large everyone brought their own cup to drink from and linen to set their food in. No family had enough dishes to serve this many people. Sometimes they used the main kitchen, but Harry and Isabell felt their family had become what it was in our yard and they asked to have the celebration here.

Sid brought fire wood in his carriage and quickly got the fire going. Lynne made everyone in the new family a linen with their names hand stitched on them. Elora was wearing the gown Lynne had made for us.

"She looks absolutely stunning in that gown." I told Lynne while she was standing near me.

"The gown would be nothing without her beauty."

"Thank you again Lynne."

"Seeing her wearing it is thanks enough Davin." She sighed deeply. I remember Sid telling me how much she had wanted a daughter.

I watched as everyone began to eat and drink. Elora had been so busy all day I don't even know if she has eaten anything all day. I took her by the arm and escorted her to the line so we could eat together.

"There's something different about you today Davin, I just can't figure it out." She said quietly.

I shrugged. "I'm not sure what you're talking about."

She reached up and traced my new beard and moustache with her finger. "I just can't seem to place my finger on it."

"Well is it a change you like?"

"I do very much so, my love." She whispered as she touched my upper lip.

"Maybe I'll keep it then."

We got our food and found an empty spot to stand and eat. Jobe came and delivered two barrels of ale, he said it was a gift from Lee. I noticed Wan stop by and drop off a gift at the table and leave before people noticed him. Someone brought a fiddle and began to play festive tunes and people began to dance around the fire with their loved ones. Harry led Maggie out to dance and Luke led Isabell out they danced and laughed. Elora decided to go cut in and take the kids so Harry and Isabell could have a dance for themselves. I picked Maggie up and danced her all over the yard, I asked her if she was happy and she told me it was her best day ever.

Soon Myka and Eldon took their turn and danced with the children and Elora and I danced together. The idea took a life of its own; married and matched couples alike cut in and took the children for a dance and when they were cut in on the couple merged together for a dance of their own. Even Sid and Lynne joined in, Maggie barely reached Sid's thigh so he picked her up and twirled her in his arms around the fire. I really began to realize the impact that Luke and Maggie had on all of us.

I led Elora away from the dancing and poured us both more wine. The evening was turning cool as the sun went down. We stood far from everyone and watched as everyone danced and celebrated. Isabell and Harry looked so happy, and they were constantly talking with the children and tending to their needs. They sat with them on the logs and made sure they ate enough.

"Are you enjoying yourself my love?" Elora asked me.

"Yes, although I'll be sad not to be around Luke and Maggie so much."

"We'll be with them when we can, their life will be good. The decision was for the best."

"I know it was, I guess I just didn't realize how much they meant to me until I knew this would be our last evening together." I told her.

"I'll cheer you up later if you wish."

"We shouldn't my love."

"Davin, if you're going to start about last night I'll go home right now."

"No it isn't that, before I went to you last night I had been swimming in the river. When I got out I was laying on the bank and Wan came upon me. That's where the whiskey came from. Last night I didn't think anything of it, but this morning I was talking to Harry and he mentioned that Wan leaves every night like that."

"Oh no Davin do you think he's seen us out by the river?" She asked looking terrified.

"That's what I don't know. I'm afraid if we meet again he may accidentally stumble across us like he did me last night."

"We'll not be able to meet again! I can't wait a year to be in your arms like that again." She was trembling as her eyes welled up with tears. I couldn't even hold her to ease her pain right now.

"My love, I'll figure something out I promise you. Don't be upset, I'll not let you down ever again."

"Davin I can't bear the thought that a creepy old man may have been watching us."

"I know my love let's just see what happens before we get too upset."

I took her hand in mine and squeezed it. I wanted to see her tonight, to show her I wasn't a complete fool. But I knew it would be impossible I was starting to doubt my trust in Wan. At least Kyan had been man enough to admit he had seen us.

Harry and Isabell began to load the children into their carriage they both were falling asleep near the fire. My mother offered to keep the children one more night for them but they insisted that their family be together from today on. Everyone cheered as they rode away.

"I'm going to get our fathers horses put in their pens and fed. Ask your mother maybe she'll let you walk with me."

I waited a few minutes while she went to find her mother. She came back smiling and walked with me to her father's horse first. We were very careful not to touch or kiss fearing we were being watched. We talked though Elora wouldn't speak about last night at all. I was feeling better about it. I was now more concerned over if we had been watched. I brushed her father's horse down and gave him fresh hay. Then I took the water bucket and made two trips to the river and refreshed his water.

"Why are you so determined to help my father with his horse lately?" She asked as we walked to get my father's horse taken care of.

"Promise not to laugh at me?"

"Why would I laugh?"

"I said promise not to laugh at me!"

"Alright I promise!" I could already see the smile forming on her lips.

"I was talking to Harry a few days ago and he mentioned that his muscles came from his work cleaning after the animals at the side show."

"You're doing this to get muscles?"

"You promised not to laugh at me!" I reminded her.

"My love I'm not laughing, I was just thinking how I've watched you admire Harry since we were little kids. I should've figured him being here now would only make you want to be like him."

"I don't want to be like him. I just want to look normally strong." I admitted to her.

"You're not skin and bones Davin. Just promise you'll not get a big as he is."

"I won't I promise you, just a little bit muscular is all I'm headed towards."

"I really like the beard on you but I'm not sure about your moustache yet. I'll let you know as soon as I can kiss you safely."

"I'm happy you approve so far."

She watched me as I worked in the pens. I had to bring six buckets of water to our horses. I brushed them both down and did a quick clean up for them. She helped me give them a scoop of oats. But I wouldn't let her help me give them hay I didn't want her getting itchy from it. After I finished I brought her close to me and kissed her gently.

"It's a little bit scratchy." She said as she ran her finger across my lip.

"Don't worry about it, it will soften soon then you can decide if it stays or goes." I lifted her face to mine again and gave her another kiss.

"Let's get back to what's left of the celebration. Look at me all hot and sweaty, I need some wine."

"I love looking at you after you've been working."

"I did notice you watching me this morning." I teased her.

"It was quite a nice view out my window."

"It was a very nice view in your window as well." I said recalling her leaning out of the window this morning. She flushed bright red when I reminded her.

Most of the guests were gone by the time we came around. I poured us both more wine and just looked around. Myka and Eldon were sitting far from listening ears talking a mile a minute to each other. I had two more cups of wine and began picking up things for my mother I knew she had to be tired she had worked so hard.

"Elora, do you think it would be alright if I had one of these tarts?" She almost threw her cup at me. I owed her that after her refusing me one in the kitchen this afternoon. She was helping me clean up as well. When our mothers came to help I sat both of them down and gave them more wine.

"I think you ladies have done more than your share today, call me when your cups need refilled."

"Davin, that was so sweet of you." Elora whispered as she walked past me with more dishes.

It wasn't taking us very long to clean things up. Myka was helping wash the dishes and Eldon was drying them for her. Our fathers were standing near the fire trying to empty the last barrel of ale. I checked on the ladies and I brought a jug of wine with me to refill their cups.

"Davin, you're a good young man."

"Thank you Mrs. Dover, does this mean I really can marry your daughter?" Both of them laughed out loud at me.

"I think she has belonged to you longer than she has belonged to me Davin."

"I've loved her ever since she threw the first handful of dirt at me." I joked, and again they were laughing.

As I was walking away Elora came up to me. "I never threw dirt at you!"

"No you didn't but I do recall you kicking me out of my chair when we were six." I said laughing remembering that day very clearly.

"You pulled my hair!"

"I was only trying to smell it as I've spent every day since trying to do." I said putting my face in her hair. I felt the heat of her flush and I lost myself in the magnolia scent I craved.

"You're such a charmer when you're full of wine."

"Better than when I'm full of whiskey?"

"You can trust me that the way you were last night was exciting and thrilling. But I couldn't let you do that to yourself no matter how much I wanted you."

"I know my love, thank you for taking care of me."

"I'd do anything for you."

"I would for you too." I kissed her cheek. We were out of earshot but we could still be seen.

After the mess was cleaned up I took a jug of wine and our cups and led Elora to the fire. Our parents, Eldon and Myka also joined us. I filled everyone's cup I even gave Eldon and Myka some. They weren't supposed to drink yet but I wanted to make a toast.

"To good fortunes and our families coming together." Everyone raised their cups and said, "Cheers!"

We all had a few more cups of wine. I was feeling pretty drunk as I'm sure everybody else was. I could see Myka almost falling asleep.

"Eldon help me take her to her bed." We helped her up and guided her to her bed. Eldon bent over her and kissed her lips softly and whispered "I love you" and left her to sleep. He knew I wouldn't get him into trouble.

When we got outside everyone was saying goodnight. I took Elora's arm and walked her slowly to our log. We were both wobbling as we got there, and both of us had to sit. Her parents and Eldon went into their cottage, this time with no warning not to be long.

"We could sleep right here together, they never said you had to come in." I teased her as I took her into my arms and let her lay her head on my chest.

"I wish so bad it was our ceremony today." She whispered softly to me.

"I wish for it every day my love." I told her rocking from side to side.

We just sat silently for a long time in the moonlight. I was starting to get sleepy, I lifted her face and bent my head down to her and kissed her. She responded but only in that sweet way. We were trying hard to resist the fevered kisses we both craved. I carefully helped her up and walked her to her door, everyone had gone to their beds and her cottage was silent. I went quietly in her room with her and helped her undress and get into her nightgown. She laid down in her bed, her eyes begging me not to leave her.

I pulled her covers over her and bent down and whispered for her to sleep well while I kissed her sweet lips. I turned away quickly and all but ran from the cottage. If I hadn't left when I did, I'd have never left her.

CHAPTER 22

Suspicions

I BARELY REMEMBER GETTING in my bed last night, when I woke I was sleeping naked and I was tangled in my blankets. I got up and dressed so I could get my chores done. My head felt heavy and my stomach was so hungry it hurt. I went to get the water for morning meal then I headed over to Elora's cottage to work on her fathe'rs pen. I was about halfway done cleaning the mess when I looked up and saw Elora watching me through the window. I mouthed I love you, to her and finished what I was doing.

I had everything cleaned and the horse fed and was getting the bucket so I could get his water. It took me four trips to fill his barrel this morning. Maybe I didn't get him enough water last night. I was really drunk so I may not have. As I headed to do my own pens Elora blew me a kiss.

When I had our horses done, I went in to get my clothes and linens so I could bathe in the river before morning meal. The water felt great this morning. After all the wine last night and the hard work this morning my body needed the cool water. I shaved my face touching up around my new beard and moustache.

After I ate with my family I went to get Elora to go into our work. Her parents let me in while she finished getting ready.

"You're looking very awake this morning for as much wine as you had last night." Mr. Dover said as he sat back in his chair.

"I just jumped into the river it helped clear the cobwebs in my head."

"Maybe I should try that." He said laughing at me. "Thank you for tending to my horse again this morning."

"Anytime." I said with a smile.

Elora came out wearing her yellow gown. She looked tired but beautiful, I took her arm and we were on our way.

"Thank you for putting me to bed so sweetly last night."

"You slept well then?"

"I'm not sure if I slept or passed out." She said laughing.

"I'm not sure either but when I woke I was naked and twisted in my blankets." We both laughed about it, I'm sure the picture of it she imagined was pretty funny.

"Last night was a lot of fun, even with the bad things that we may have discovered."

"I'll see if I can get any hint of it out of him today, don't worry." I told her.

"I'm trying hard not to. You know, I really thought we might get into trouble when you had me naked in my room last night."

"Well I was partly trying to redeem myself, and the other part of me didn't want us getting into any trouble."

"You don't owe me redemption Davin."

"I know I don't, but I still can try right?"

"Davin I think you would work yourself to death trying to please me."

"I'm only happy when you're happy my love."

The rest of our walk in was quiet. I don't think I have much to do this morning. I want to get my book updated on Harry and Isabelle's ceremony. I'll speak to Wan if he comes to me this morning. I don't want to be in very long as I'd like to get Elora's pen built today.

It wasn't long before Wan came to my office this morning. "Good morning Davin, how did the celebrating go last night?"

"Good morning, it went great many of the villagers came to celebrate late into the evening with us."

"So the support was good?" He asked.

"I think once the decision had time to get used to, people took the time to accept it. Maybe if the other five families had just not gotten so upset in the beginning they would still be here. Not that I wish Jake and Myka's match had been fixed. I couldn't have taken it for her to be wed to someone who could be so mean to her."

"I can understand that." He said. "How did your evening go after we parted the other evening?" Yes, he was watching us I thought to myself..

"All I remember is waking up by the river." I said watching his face closely.

"I've had a night or two like that myself." He said laughing.

All my trust in him has gone from me, but I can't let him know that, I have to keep our relationship as it was for it could cost me Elora.

"I think I'm going to leave soon. I'd like to build Elora a pen for her mare today."

"I can send men out to do that today."

"That will be nice, maybe I'll just help I've been enjoying doing labor the past few days."

"Why's that?"

"Just working out my body some; I've been feeling weaker lately."

"It's good your spending you spare time doing some hard work, you don't want to become old and weak like I have just sitting in this office for the last thirty years."

"I just want to feel like I help do my part as well, I was feeling lazy for a little while.'

"You'll find a routine I'm sure." He said to me.

"I think I'm going to walk over to Harry and Isabell's and see how the night went for the children; I know they were a little upset when they realized they would be leaving our cottage for good. I'm sure they are fine, but it would be good for them to know I'll still be seeing them.'

"Good idea, send my blessings. Let them know we'll be calling them together in a few days to let Harry know of his calling and get the children where they belong so Isabell can go back to work herself."

"I'll tell them, I was wondering when things would start getting situated for them."

"We just wanted to get the children well and then settled in their new home before we got them in with the other children."

"I won't be gone long and I'll let you know how everything is going."

I walked towards Isabell and Harry's cottage taking my time I was in no hurry to get back to my stuffy office. I felt like my attitude towards anything to do with Wan changed this morning. It bothers me that he has been watching me but I don't know what I can do other than not giving him anything to watch.

When I arrived at the cottage I could already hear the laughter inside. After I knocked Isabell opened the door and I could see Maggie getting a piggy back ride from Harry as Luke chased them around the cottage.

"Come in Davin, the children were just asking about you." Isabell said as she let me in.

Instantly Maggie was squirming to get off of Harry's back she was in my arms in mere seconds.

"Davin! I have my own room now, come see."

Her happiness was wonderful I had worried last night about her being upset and frightened for no reason. Her room was small they had built her a bed and painted it white. Her little pink blanket that Elora and I had picked out for her was neatly laid across the top. They had also built her a small chest, it was painted white and had her name carved on the top. A small wooden doll cradle also painted white was sitting in the corner, her dolls hair was about the same color of her own and the blanket inside looked like the one on her bed. The little curtain that hung in the window matched a dress that Isabell had made for her. In the other corner sat a small rocking chair that had her name carved into the back.

"Do you like it Davin?" She asked still holding onto my neck.

"Well." I teased her. "It's not nearly as beautiful as you are."

She buried her face in my chest and laughed showing her embarrassment. About that time Luke grabbed my arm and half dragged me to see his bedroom. He looked happier than I've seen him.

His room was about the same size his bed and chest were left with the natural wood. His bed was bigger than Maggie's and a new bigger thicker blanket had been placed on it, but his little yellow blanket was folded nicely next to his pillow. He also had a small desk where his little wooden animals had been set up along with his paints. There was a small chair that looked like it was built to fit his small size perfectly. His curtain matched the blanket on his bed as well as a small cushion that was on the little chair.

"Well I see you both have been busy spoiling these children already." I said as I walked up and gave Harry a pat on the back.

"We just want them to feel like they are home." Isabell said handing me a cup of ale.

"I think it's safe to say they feel at home." I told her laughing. "How was your first night as a family?"

"It's been wonderful." Harry said while he poured himself some ale.

"I'm glad you're all so happy. It was weird sleeping in bed last night I almost laid on the floor again." I said as we all laughed.

"How did things go after we left last night?" Harry asked.

"About the same as any other evening when the fire is going and the liquor is flowing. I'm supposed to let you know the Liaison will be calling in a few days to get everyone settled into their daily routines. So if you have job preference better tell me now so I can hint around at it."

"I'm fine where ever they decide to put me I learn to enjoy everything I do in the long run. That comes from doing so many different things with the side show." He said.

"That's good I just thought I'd offer just in case you had your mind set on something."

"No, I'm just happy I have Isabell and the children, anything else that comes along will be a blessing as well."

Isabell flushed red with that and turned to the kitchen. She looked like a different person today, the sad distant look she used to carry is long gone, her eyes are bright and her face always smiling.

"Well, walk me out I have to get back over there so Elora doesn't go looking for me."

I gave Isabell and Maggie a kiss on the cheek and hugged Luke and followed Harry at the door.

"Harry, remember what we talked about yesterday?"

"About Wan?"

"Yes, I think I'm right he has been watching me a lot." I told him.

"Why do you think that Davin?"

"That night we sat by the river drinking the whiskey, he knew I had too much I could barely get up when he left me. But instead of asking me if I made it to my bed or something like that he asked me how my evening went after he left."

"That's awfully strange, you better be careful Davin just in case he is."

"I'm being very careful. I even spoke with Elora about it, she is so upset."

"Well I wouldn't suggest going on your evening outings for the time being, let things calm down. If he is watching you and your not giving him anything to watch maybe he'll move on."

"I feel like any faith or trust in him is gone, I don't want him to know I think this way so I have to keep our relationship as if nothing were happening." I said feeling the anger well up inside of me.

"Davin just be sure Elora is never alone, have her put something in her window so it can't be opened from the outside. I have a funny feeling about all of this, make sure you tell her you won't be coming to her window to call on her and that she's not safe to go to yours either."

"I will Harry, I've thought of that too."

"Let me know if you need help with something, if things get too bad you both will be having me following you."

"I don't think it will come to that Harry, I'll be sure to make changes to keep her safe for now." I promised him.

"See you later Davin, I'm here if you need me for anything.

"Thank you Harry, see you later enjoy your time with your family."

I took my time getting back to the Liaisons, it was close to time for mid-meal when I got back my anger had died down some, but I wasn't going to let my guard down. I had to be sure Elora was safe and she had to know that the danger she may be in was Wan.

There were also two new black gowns that matched the material my suits were made of. They looked very heavy and uncomfortable much like I found my own suits. There was a black one and a grey one. The pants looked similar to mine but the jackets looked like small gowns that fastened in the front with ties down to her waist and split open to about her knees. Instead of wearing a white under dress each one had a white shirt that would tuck into the riding pants.

I was in my office when Elora came in to get me for mid-meal.

"Those gowns look dreary don't they?" She whispered quietly as she looked at them.

"Nothing you wear looks dreary, but the riding outfits look better." I told her hoping we could get out of the office before Wan happened upon us. "Let's go I'm starved!"

We were the first to get to the kitchen and I led her to a seat in the far back. She ate quietly while I told her what had happened this morning with Wan. I also told her about what Harry said about out meetings and her window. She agreed with me that we needed to be careful and promised she would take care of her window when she got to her cottage tonight. She was upset, but I assured her at this point we were just being extra careful, that it all may be nothing.

"I can't leave after we eat today my love."

"Why not?" I asked irritated.

"We're having a meeting and it wasn't over, they told us all to come back after we took our meal."

"Listen to me!" I demanded "You're not to be alone ever, have Kyan walk you to your cottage, tell him I insist and I'll speak with him later."

"I will Davin I promised you I'd be careful. I'll do whatever you ask, where are you going?"

"I'm going to take your clothes to your cottage. In fact I'll fix your window while I'm there, do not try to open it. Then I'm going to get the supplies and build your mare's pen. I want her out there with you, she has already taken to you and maybe she'll warn you if someone is lurking around your cottage."

We got up from our meal, feeling despair at not knowing what was happening. We knew we would see little of each other and that was difficult to accept as well. She looked as sad as I felt, I had to warn her to act normal while she was around Wan as we didn't want him to know what we were thinking. I also pulled Kyan aside and told him he was to walk Elora to her cottage and I'd explain later.

I carried her clothes to her cottage, they were heavy I felt bad she had to wear those gowns. While I was walking I found a thick branch and when I got to her cottage I adjusted it in her window so the window wouldn't slide open. I also checked it on the outside and looked around below her window to see if anyone had been out there. Last night when I did her pens I had raked under the window to cover my own tacks but now it would tell me if someone else was also coming here. There were footprints there and for some reason I wasn't surprised to see them there. I followed them down to the river where they disappeared into the water.

I went to my cottage and saddled Blitz so I could see about the wood and nails to build her pens. The men at the construction building were happy to help me they had a lot of left over materials from the cottages that had been torn down. They also had enough material to build her a small shed like mine for her saddle and tack. They loaded their lumber wagon and followed me to her cottage. It only took four of us about two hours to have the pen and shed finished. After thanking them for all their help I put Blitz in the extra pen and walked back the Liaison's barn. I saddled the mare up and looked for Elora but there was no sign of her yet. I rode her mare back to her cottage, she walked wonderfully, I enjoyed riding her as much as I enjoy riding Blitz.

I put her saddle and tack away and spent some time brushing the mare down. I was hoping to see Elora before I finished but she still hadn't come in. I finally got on Blitz and took him home cleaned our pens and fed both horses. Their water was empty again so I went back and forth to the river getting them fresh water, I was bringing up the last bucket when I seen Elora standing there with Kyan. I walked up to them after I emptied the bucket.

"Thank you Kyan I owe you a favor!"

"No way, I just paid you back for talking with Leta for me. Have a good evening, she's probably wondering where I am by now."

"Thank you again, please give Leta our love."

"Davin, how long have you been working? You look exhausted!" Elora said looking me over.

"Come my love, I have something to show you?" I said as I put my arm out for her to take.

I wasn't going to tell her about the footprints I found under her window and I made sure to rake over them again so I could check them in the morning. As we went around to the back of her cottage she saw her mare and the new pen.

"You did all of this?"

"I had some help but yes it's done and now your mare will be by you."

"Can we ride tonight since I have proper riding clothes?"

"I'm sure we can, but ask your parents I don't want them upset with me. Do you know how to saddle her up?"

"Of course I do, I've saddled my father's horse many times."

"Well great, if you can go have Eldon let me know when you're getting ready, and wear the black riding outfit I can't wait to see you in it."

"I'll send Eldon as soon as I know, I love you so much thank you for putting up my pen!" She said giving me a big hug.

"My love I've been working and I'm sweaty you shouldn't get to close to me." I warned her stepping back. "I'll hug you all you want after I get cleaned up, I hope we can ride together. Have your legs healed my love?"

"I'm healed your mother took good care of me."

I told her goodbye fighting every urge in my body to kiss her. When I got back to my cottage my mother and father were inside. I'm not sure if they had been arguing but they looked angry and my mother went into her room without a word to me.

"Did I do something wrong?" I asked my father.

"No son, she's upset with me don't worry. Did you finish your chores?"

"There's fresh water by the stove, the horses have been taken care of and I'm going to the river to clean up, I may take Elora around on her horse if her parents will allow it and if it's alright with you?"

"I think that will be fine as long as you're not out too late. Will Kyan be joining you?"

"I know he has been helping with Leta's mother. But I don't plan to take her far just enough to get her used to the horse."

"That'll be fine if her parents allow it then."

I've noticed they don't push us on escorts like before, I'm unsure if it's because were sixteen now or if they have been too busy to notice. I went to my room and got my black riding outfit and clean linens so I could bathe before we had our supper. While I was in the river Eldon came by and let my father know Elora could ride for a little while this evening after they took supper. I had saddled Blitz before I got in the river just in case her parents said yes.

Supper was very quiet; my mother was still in her room. Myka and I helped finish cooking the venison steaks and potatoes so we could eat. My mother didn't eat with us, but my father took her supper into her room. I didn't even hear them speak when he left it in there. He didn't sit down to join us for supper either. Myka asked me what was wrong and I told her I didn't know either. Not soon after we had cleaned up I heard a horse out front. Elora looked beautiful in her grey riding outfit I wasn't sure at how she would look in black.

"You look beautiful; that tailor's a genius!"

"I didn't think I'd like wearing pants but I must admit they are comfortable, and I don't feel this saddle at all." She told me.

I got on Blitz and led her towards the river. I really wanted her to see the water on the lake as the sun set but I had to hurry as it was already starting to get late. I asked her if she was up for a run and she told me to go. Her mare almost kept up to Blitz there wasn't much distance between us. She laughed as the mare ran along the river.

When we got to the lake; I helped her off the mare and tied her and Blitz to a nearby tree.

"Just right here my love I wanted you to see how the water changes colors with the sun."

We both sat silently holding hands watching the water turn brilliant shades of pink, purple and yellow. I didn't want to say much as I didn't want our conversation to lead to anything about Wan. We both knew we might have had been followed, so we didn't kiss nor touch other than our hands. I wanted to touch her hair at least but I didn't dare.

I still don't know for sure if he's watching and if he is why he was doing it. Would he try to separate us, or was he just watching from sick perverse. I feel so angry when I start thinking about him; I wish I understood what was happening. More than anything I wish Elora and I could still enjoy our blissful escapes where the river used to hide all our secrets and left us feeling safe.

I didn't want to keep her out too long, the least thing we needed was either of our parents worrying if we were doing something wrong. I helped her stand and walked her back to her mare before I lifted her up I stole a gentle kiss from her and reminded how beautiful she looked.

"Are you going to name that mare yet?" I asked as I helped her into the saddle.

"Yes, I'm going to call her Misty, she reminds me of the mist on the river during the winter months."

"Well then Misty, you ready to get beat by the stunning magnificent Blitz?" I asked as Elora laughed so hard I thought she might fall off her horse.

As I was getting situated on Blitz Elora turned Misty around and yelled. "GO!" As she ran off ahead of me. I tried to call to her that she was cheating but it didn't slow her down, she ran until she was coming into the village. I caught up and teased her about cheating but she'll keep her win. We walked the horses back to her cottage and I helped her unsaddle and brush the mare out. I also brought more water but only two buckets this time. We slowly walked around to the front of the cottage and I bid her goodnight with just a light kiss on her hand. Now that our busy nights were over it would be even harder for us to kiss goodnight.

After I got Blitz taken care of I went sullenly into the house. It was quiet, my mother and father weren't anywhere to be seen. I checked on Myka, she was sitting at her little desk writing.

"Will you take me to visit Eldon? Mother and Father won't speak to anyone and I haven't seen him today."

"I'll take you, I figured we would start working on your cottage again but I guess it won't be tonight."

As we walked over to the Dover's she asked me again what was wrong. I wish I could tell her but I didn't know what was wrong, and I'm worried, my parents don't normally get upset with each other.

Eldon and Myka sat on our usual log. Elora came out and brought me some wine while I watched my sister. Not that I felt I needed to be there, but I'm hoping they don't make the mistakes Elora and I have lately. Mr. Dover came out and joined me for another cup of wine. I wasn't trying to rush Eldon and Myka and the Dover's didn't seem to be in a hurry either.

"How did that mare look today?" He asked me.

"She looked terrific she's strong and steady on a run."

"Good, I'm glad she is a good horse she'll be good for many years."

"She sure has taken to Elora, they seem made for each other." I told him.

"Much like those two over there, how do you feel about that match?"

"I'm just happy that they like the match." Little did he know how responsible for that match I was, and I hoped it stayed between Myka and I. I'm concerned it may come out with this thing with Wan which is another reason I have to be careful.

"I'll be right back we still have many jugs of wine left from all the celebrating I'll get another. We might as well enjoy the cool evening."

When I went into the house I was careful to be quiet, I didn't want to disturb my parents. I got the wine and heard my mother, she wasn't yelling but she was upset and I heard her say Wan's name. Afraid it may actually be about me, I left quickly at least if I was to be in trouble I'd have the wine in me to soften anything I may have to face.

When I got back Elora and her mother had also come out to enjoy the evening air and have some wine with us. We talked about how the ceremony went and I let them know about my visit to the children this morning. Everyone seemed relieved that the children have adjusted so well. Eldon and Myka just kept to each other talking quietly and none of us wanted to interrupt them. I noticed my father come out of our cottage but he made no effort to come over to us. He went behind our cottage and was gone for a few minutes then went quietly back into our cottage.

"Well, I better get my sister home before they fall asleep out there." I said getting up off the ground and reached out to help Elora get up. It was nice just sitting there with her and parents. I gave her a small kiss on the cheek and called for Myka. I seen Eldon lean over and kiss her cheek as well. It was sweet to see what is becoming of their match, Eldon seems very happy and Myka is smiling again.

It was quiet again in the cottage when we got in. Myka and I put together some tarts in the kitchen. I was hungry again and needed some food on the wine I had just had. We had just got them in the oven when my father called me into the bedroom. I felt my heart pound and my stomach felt sick, all I could think was at least I got one last evening with Elora before they separated us for life.

My father asked me to sit in the chair near the bed. My mother's face looked wild with fear I could tell she had been crying. I must of really destroyed her, how could I have done this to my family?

"Davin, we need you to be honest with us about something." My father started. "Do spend any time alone with Wan?"

"Yes, he comes to talk to me every day." I certainly wasn't going to lie and get in any more trouble than I may already be in.

"What does he speak with you about?" My father asked.

"We mostly speak about things to do with my work. Sometimes he talks with me about Elora." My mother's face looked as if it would crumble she had a fear in her eyes I had never seen before.

"What about you and Elora?"

"He just asks me about how our courting is going. He also helped arrange for us to take mid-meal together when our cottage was done."

"Has he ever talked about your mother or I to you?"

"Not really, when I first began he spoke how about how much he respected you father, and the hard work you do for our village."

"And that's all, you're telling me everything?"

"Yes father, I'd never lie for anyone to you or mother."

"Alright son, go finish what you were doing with Myka."

"Thank you Sir." I said as I left the room feeling more confused than when I went in there. I poured a cup of wine for Myka and one for myself. I told her to be careful in case our parents came out. We ate our tarts in silence and soon after we finished she went to bed, I couldn't sleep there was so many things running through my head. I don't think I'm in any trouble but I don't understand what it was all about. I still had my riding outfit on so I decided to go hide in the trees between Elora's window and the river and watch for a little while.

Everything in Elora's cottage was quiet, there were no candles burning in any room that was in my view. The horses stood quietly and it seemed the world was asleep. Not long after I got hidden I noticed a shadowy figure come up the river. I could tell from where I was that it was Wan. He went by my cottage first; he was looking into my room. He stood for a few minutes then he went back to the river where the trees would hide him. I was up high so I could still see him lurking around. He was taking small cautious steps to get near to the spot where Elora and I had been. When he seen we weren't there he went carefully to her window. I watched him stand there for a few moments then step away. I think he was drunk tonight for no matter how carefully he walked he was still stumbling. He walked back to her window again and I seen him try to open it. Fortunately the stick I jammed into it stopped him. He almost ran from the window. He was just about under me and I heard him cry. "Where the hell is that boy?" I think in his drunken state he has lost his mind. He continued mumbling to himself and went back to my window he stood there again then went towards the river and disappeared. I wanted to follow him but I've never been to his cottage nor did I want to chance running into him. I was so angry I seen him looking at Elora as she slept, even trying to open her window. I think that whiskey he has been drinking has eaten his mind away.

I waited to make sure he didn't come back for a long time before climbing down and going to my own cottage. I had another cup of wine and went to bed.

The next morning my parents were up and cheerful, when I came in from doing my chores. We had morning meal together and nothing was said about what happened yesterday. I wasn't going to push it just in case I'm wrong in assuming I'm not in trouble.

I walked Elora to work, and again there wasn't much for me to do. I decided I'd go work in the barns again, the girl from before let me churn more butter with her. And I cleaned the pig stalls. The pigs have already doubled in size. We have more pigs but it was nice looking at the ones I picked out, knowing they would increase our food supply one day. Even with the betrayal I felt over Wan, I still wanted our village to prosper and do well. And now I was finding myself happy Wan would be leaving. Even without news of our cottage, I just wished he was gone. I know Harry would pitch in his spare time if I asked to help me build a quick cottage.

When we went to mid-meal Elora told me she had to go back in again. I asked her if I should be worried, she said that I shouldn't they just had a lot of backed up issues they wanted to discuss with her and Kyan. She dropped it at that though we didn't want to break our agreement. I warned her again about having someone walk her home, she told me Kyan had already spoke with her about it.

After mid-meal I went in my office for a little while but no one came to see me, so I locked my office and headed for Harry's. He was putting two little swings in a tree by the cottage for the children. Luke and Maggie were both playing with their jump ropes trying to see who could jump the most. After Harry got out of the tree, which I still have no idea how he got up there much less how the tree held such a huge man. His dark hair was soaked with sweat maybe climbing a tree was a better work out than I had thought before. Isabell brought us both some ale and we sat for a few minutes.

I talked with Harry about what happened last night. He felt as outraged as I did. He said that Wan drank too much and maybe he had been in a drunken daze, I told him that I had wondered the same thing. I helped Harry build a table outside with little benches like the ones they used at the sideshow. He told me he wanted to take some meals outside like he used to and the children and Isabell were excited about the idea. After we finished I bid him farewell and went to work on my chores. I had no idea how late it is I worked with Harry for a long time but when I left the table was finished and Maggie was already putting supper dishes on it.

It didn't take me long to finish the horses today, I think I'm getting used to the work. No one was back from working so I went for a long swim in the river.

The evening was much the same as last night, I'd decided I wouldn't say anything to Elora about last night but I reminded her to go check her window before I said goodnight to her. There was no sense in me climbing the tree and waiting again for I already knew what I needed to know.

CHAPTER 23

Time for change

THE NEXT WEEK PASSED quickly; I settled into my routine easily as I had no choice. Elora stayed beyond mid-meal at the Liaison's everyday. Wan had come to me only once and I was leaving so we didn't talk long. He did however ask me what I had been doing with all my free time and I simply told him working with the horses and helping Harry at his cottage.

Today was to be when Harry and Isabell were called in to the Liaison's for Harry's calling and the children to start their schooling. Wan asked me what I felt about Harry's calling and I repeated what Harry and I spoke about. He asked me if I had an opinion on it and I really didn't.

"Is something bothering you Davin?"

"No Sir, I have just been working hard and I've been feeling tired."

"Hard work will do that to you, would you like an extra day off?"

"No, I'm fine really just trying to get into a routine. I expect to be tired until I get used to it. I've never really spent much time doing specific internships so it has been nice finding things I enjoy doing."

"I'm glad to see you're making use of your spare time. How are things with you and Elora?" I prayed at this very moment that my face didn't betray me. I felt the anger build inside me and I've never before wanted to strike someone until this moment.

"We are fine, as you know she has been staying after mid-meal here so we haven't been able to spend much time together."

"That won't be for much longer our longer work hours are about over."

"That'll be great maybe we can fit some riding time in each day." I said and headed to the main hall to join the others for the meeting. I didn't want to be alone with Wan nor for my anger about him to show.

Harry and Isabell were already here with the children. They were a beautiful family, and Maggie looked like she may have put on some weight. I looked over at Elora she had her Liaison gown on, she really looked beautiful in black but she looked as uncomfortable as I felt. I noticed that the others who worked with us followed my lead and were only wearing their suits for meetings now as well. The atmosphere at the Liaison's was different, the clerks looked as bored as I was lately, the Liaison's, even Elora and Kyan looked tired and worried. Though I kept my promise and didn't ask Elora about what was happening.

Lee began the meeting again, Wan seems to have stepped back completely from speaking at the meetings.

"Birch family how has your first week together been?"

"We've had a great week spending time getting to know each other." Harry spoke as the leader of the family.

"Have your daily food rations been enough for the family?"

"Yes, Sir we are given plenty and the children have been putting a little weight on as well."

"That's great. It's customary if your rations need increased just come in here and let us know and we'll take care of you."

"Thank you Sir, I'll remember that." Harry told him.

"Harry we have discussed your' calling endlessly here, do you want to make a special request before we tell you what we came up with?"

"No Sir, put me where you need me. I'll be happy where I am."

"Harry we would like you to continue working with the hunters, they all spoke highly of your skills and they would like to continue working with you. But that is not all, the men you worked with tearing down the cottages also would like for you to continue working with them. So our compromise is your calling is for hunting, but if there is extra work that needs done we would like you to work with the men in construction. You'll be given time off like everyone else. We'll figure out what days Isabell gets and work it so your time off can be spent together."

"Thank you Sir."

"Now the children are to begin their schooling tomorrow. We are also going to have them watched for their future match. We still haven't made many matches in either of their age groups so there is no worry that it won't happen."

"I understand Sir, thank you"

"And please if there's any problems know we are here any time to help, we want to see your family do well. Making this work together was a big change in our village and as you both know it caused a small uproar, we now strive to show how good it has been for our village." Lee told them.

"Thank you for your faith and support, we intend on showing everyone how strong our family bond already is and will continue to be." Harry said proudly.

After the meeting Elora and I took our mid-meal with Harry and Isabell. Maggie was excited to start her schooling and Luke was very timid about it. I hope all goes well, the town kids are raised well I don't see that he'll have any problems once he gets in and makes some friends. I know the children really need to be around other children though, and if they didn't do it soon they may have problems interacting with other children.

Elora went back to her work and I was off to take care of the horses and find other meaningless things to waste my time with. I've been going in and working with my father some, he is helping me make Elora a rocking chair like the one he made for Maggie only bigger. He has been teaching me how to use carving tools and I was putting little designs throughout the chair. I wasn't in a hurry for I knew I had time to finish it. I even spent some time in with the tailor making a cushion for it. He did most of the work on it I just gave him the size and how I wanted it. It was dark green velvet with gold cording on the edges. It looked like a big square cushioned pillow when he had it done.

Before everyone finished with their days my work was always finished so I've spent a lot of time swimming in the river. My shirts are starting to get tight in the arms and shoulders so maybe the extra work I've been doing is actually working like Harry said it would. My moustache and beard have filled in, I keep it trimmed and the beard thin. I don't want a full beard just enough to make me look like a man and not a boy. Elora says she likes it so I plan on keeping it unless she changes her mind. We have not had time alone or any romantic exchanges, after seeing Wan I've been very careful about the little bit of time we do spend together. And fortunately she has not pressured me about it nor questioned my decision to not meet like we had been. I remind her every night to check her window before I'll leave her for the night. I also check under her window every morning, only one morning there has not been foot prints under her window. So I know he is still watching us. I also have been watching under my own window finding the same prints in the dirt.

While I was swimming in the river Kyan walked Elora out to the river for me. I've taken to swimming with the short pants on so she didn't come across me naked again. I got out of the water and kissed her lips I knew we were alone at least for a few minutes.

"How did the rest of your day go my love?" I asked her as I tried to dry off with my linen.

"It just got perfect my love." She was looking at my chest with longing in her eyes.

"My love, I know this past week has been difficult but let's not slip up now."

"I won't my love but you have changed so much since the last time you held me in your arms and kissed me, now I stand here looking at a stranger." She looked so sad, I felt like I had become a stranger as well. My anger towards Wan ate at me all of the time. When I worked I worked with anger. I didn't want to be like this but if I didn't I may blow at him myself and I can't take that risk right now.

"My love I'm no stranger, just growing into a man as you have grown into a woman. Look how different you look in your gowns now."

"Davin please don't change, your anger is consuming you. Don't let that old drunk do this to you. I know you're hurt and angry, but he has more than once told you he's leaving, he told us that too. Please promise when he is gone that this ends."

"I promise you my love, when I don't have to worry about him you'll have me back fully. I'll take you to the river and hold you until the sun begins to rise."

"I love you Davin, I just want to see you happy again."

"It will come, my love." I pulled her close and held her tight, no kissing, no getting excited, just the loving reassurance that I knew I owed her.

"There's a town meeting tonight my love." She told me.

"About what?"

"I can't say but will you join me after supper so we can walk in together?"

"Yes, I'll come get you when I'm ready. Do we need to dress for Liaison's?"

"I will be but it's up to you my love. I know none of the clerks were informed of the meeting until it was time to announce."

"That's what I get for leaving out of boredom."

"I'll see you after supper my love." She said as she gave me a kiss and turned to leave.

"I look forward only to seeing you."

I went in and helped with supper my parents were speaking about the meeting and asked what I knew of it. They thought it odd that I worked there but knew nothing about it. I don't care really, as long as Elora and I'll get more time together. After we had our supper I dressed in my black suit and headed over to get Elora. She seemed happy maybe the meeting would bring good news to our little village.

The people in the village were gathered in front of the Liaison's building, the pulpit had been brought outside. Town meetings were always held outside; the building wasn't big enough to hold everyone. Lee stood at the pulpit and five of the elder Liaison's stood behind him. Wan had a chair brought out and had a book in his lap which he was writing in. Jobe was with them and he also was to take notes of the meeting.

Elora and I stood with Harry and Isabell. Kyan was with his family and Leta but I didn't see her parents anywhere. My parents stood towards the back, my mother looked very uncomfortable and I still don't know what was wrong with her last week. She has been acting normal but her thoughts are far away. My father remains the same trying hard to keep her smiling, whatever has happened has caused them to grow apart though.

Lee asked for everyone to calm down so the meeting could begin. The crowd quieted very quickly, town meetings were always important and it was difficult to hear sometimes.

"We bring you here today with some big changes for our village. Some of these changes you may or may not agree with. We ask that you all let us read out the rules, they will be posted on the wall outside the kitchen and this building. We do understand not everyone will agree but we ask that during this meeting you do not interrupt us so we can finish quickly. Tomorrow we'll see anyone who feels they need to discuss the changes we'll be in the main hall until mid-meal."

He cleared his voice and looked among the people making sure they understood.

"We are striving to bring good changes to you all, we feel the rules are old and have for many years never been reconsidered for revising."

"First thing we are changing will be the work and schooling schedules, starting this week everyone in the village will work Monday through Friday. There will be no more having families having different days of rest. It's important to us that the families in our village have time to bond and keep the strength we have always prided ourselves with. We have noticed many families with the different schedules lately and we would like to bring it to an end."

The crowd stayed quiet but they seemed happy about the change. Many were smiling and nodding to show they agreed with Lee.

"I know in some areas having no workers for two days will be difficult. For the village barns we'll see those who would like to work long enough to help feed and water them quickly. We need four people for this and there will be a small amount of coin offered to those who sign up. The first four to sign up will see us and we'll explain how it will work. Again it won't take long for we don't want our families separated. Also the village guards will have to stay on their original schedules, but they are free to work things out amongst themselves that will allow them more time with their families."

Everyone again seemed happy with this.

"Now as for the way it'll affect your daily rations, we'll begin working with the common to make sure we provide enough food on Fridays to sustain families through the week's end. If milk will be needed we'll have you go get some but there will of course be limits as to how much is allowed. By this Friday we hope to have that worked out and we'll have the common inform you on how it will work. This is all I have to say about this, as time goes by we'll adjust what needs adjusted. We don't expect it to work perfectly at first so allow us time to help work through it."

Lee looked among the crowd again then turned his paper over. "Next we would like to speak about our match rules. There's not much we would like to change but we feel some rules do need to be updated. First thing we would like to discuss is about our matches being able to spend a little more time together. At the age of fourteen we'll now allow matches to take mid-meal together at the kitchens. We have experimented with this some with our older matches and it seems like they have enjoyed the time together. If anyone here feels other rules about matches need further looking into we have now placed a box with a slot in the main hall, during our work hours the box with be put into the entry of the building feel free to put what you would like looked into in the box. We ask only that you sign it, if it is not signed it will not be considered. That box will be there for any other issues as well. We are striving to better our village and all of your opinions will be considered."

Everyone again seemed pleased which prompted Lee to continue. "We also recently discussed that our young ladies of the village are commonly not involved with horse riding. Recently our tailor worked with us to create proper riding outfits. Any young lady interested in using her coin to buy a horse will now be allowed to ride. The tailor will help get the patterns for the riding outfits to anyone who needs them. Our only stipulation is no woman with child or under the age of fifteen may ride. This is another rule we have only been experimenting with, changes will be made as needed."

The girls in the village were excited by this, as were the women. There was some murmuring through the crowd and Lee again asked for quiet so he could continue.

"The final rule up for change is one of our main rules, I again ask that you let me finish and remind you of the box and the fact that we'll be here tomorrow to speak to anyone who comes to see us." He paused to be sure everyone would give him his request.

"We're changing the rules on the ages of those to be bound." I looked at Elora terrified, if they make it higher we'll have to wait even longer, she looked happy and squeezed my hand reassuringly.

"We'll now let our matches be bound as early as when the female in the match turns sixteen." The murmuring began at one, I was so excited but I only stood and gave the attention that was asked of me. When I looked back to my parents they were only looking at each other with worried looks but not saying anything. "Quiet please for I have not finished." Lee demanded. The crowd fell quiet again and stared up at Lee waiting for more.

"We know not all matches are in a hurry to be bound younger, so we have also extended the time allowed for them to be bound. Now all matches must be bound before the female turns nineteen. The time they are to be bound will be the choice of the matches. It's something they will have to work out for themselves, if they need counseling on this we'll see anyone and help them work through it. We feel it has become necessary for them to have some say in their futures. We understand this is a big change but we think the changes it will bring to our future generations will be good ones.

"That's all I have to say this evening and you're all excused, please remember before choosing to make any snap decision give these changes time to work, we are here to discuss any concerns with you all." With that Lee and the five other Liaison's, Wan and Jobe went into the building and closed the door behind them.

Everyone around us began to talk and the noise around us grew louder.

"Elora this is wonderful! We can be bound tomorrow if we choose!"

"Yes my love, but we have to have time to plan and there is still the issue of our cottage." She was smiling and looked as thrilled as I did.

"How did you keep this big secret?"

"I didn't have a choice; I just had to keep my excitement down when I was with you, which as of late has been much time at all."

"Are your long afternoons in meetings done now my love?"

"Yes, that is what was keeping me so late every day." She said taking my hand and leading me to our parents. They all knew why we were coming to them.

"Let's go to our cottage, I see we have much to discuss." My mother said. We all followed her silently to our cottage; I knew they couldn't stop us from being bound when we chose. But I also knew they would try to persuade us to wait.

"Eldon, Myka you may both sit together outside while we talk." My mother told them and held the door open for the rest of us to enter.

I got the wine and some cups I felt the need to celebrate even if our parents didn't seem to feel the same.

"Alright we know the rules have now changed, and we also know you two want to be bound as soon as possible, but plans need to be made and you still have no cottage, this is a problem would you agree?"

"Mother I've talked with Harry he'll help me build a small cottage that will sustain us until we need to make it larger." I explained.

"Alright we'll go see the Liaison in the morning and see what we'll have to do." She said.

"I know there'll be no talking these two out of what was decided the moment the new rule was allowed." Mrs. Dover said smiling at us.

"No, these two are lovesick for each other and have been since they were small children." My father said laughing.

I'm surprised they are supporting us but maybe they understood the urgency we felt. Elora was happy and never let go of my hand. Our mother talked long into the night of the ceremony plans they had. Elora and I went to the river so we could talk more.

"Are you happy my love?" I asked her.

"I couldn't be happier my love, I can't wait to become your wife."

"I'll make you happy I promise you now."

"I know you will Davin." She said to me as she pulled me closer to her.

"During all your meetings our cottage was never discussed?" I asked her hoping she had other secrets to reveal.

"Sadly no, I want to be bound to you my love I hope they have decided something. We have no choice now but to wait on the Liaison's decisions."

"But you're the Liaison now!"

"Only in opinion, there are ten other opinions above my own."

"I understand, I just want to do this quickly and begin our lives together. I want no one following us; and no one telling us when we can be together."

She pulled me into her arms and kissed me gently, our desire growing quickly. It seemed so long ago that we were able to kiss like this I almost felt she had lost her desire for me. But in this moment I knew it was there stronger than before. She slowly pulled back from me, we know now wasn't the time to lose control.

"I like the moustache my love." She said and she touched it softly with her fingers.

"Then I shall keep it for you." I kissed her one more time and led her back to the cottage. Our mothers were still talking of the plans and our father had moved outside with Eldon and Myka. They had started a fire and we joined them to enjoy the wine. We talked for another hour at least and I walked Elora home behind her parents.

"I can't wait until I no longer have to walk you home, when I can just put you in our own bed and stay with you through the night."

"My love it'll be soon, for if it isn't you'll be taking me to the river. I've missed our time together and my desire for you is maddening." It was so wonderful to hear her speak like this. Even more wonderful was knowing that we were to be bound soon.

We stood outside her cottage holding each other and kissing softly. We felt no need to rush our goodnight to each other. I reminded her to check her window three times, before I gave her my final kiss of the evening.

I went to the river and swam for a long time, I was too excited to sleep I had to wear myself out some. As I swam I seen Wan making what I now knew was his usual walk at night. He seen me in the water, I was naked so I couldn't come out to speak with him. Not that I've forgotten what angers me about him.

"How are you this evening Davin?" He asked me with a slur in his voice.

"I'm doing well, very excited about the changes."

"Are you and Elora planning to be bound quickly?"

"Well we have no cottage; but we would be bound tomorrow if we could."

He laughed and stood quietly for a few moments. I pulled myself out of the water, he intruded on me I'll feel no shame.

"We have worked something out, I assume your families will be amongst those to be in the hall tomorrow?"

"Yes our parents know we're in a hurry to be bound and that there's no trying to slow us down."

"Well you'll have to be on the panel tomorrow but when they come you and Elora both will be allowed to speak for yourself."

"I just hope we can be bound quickly and begin our lives together."

"I'm sure it'll be worked out tomorrow. Go and sleep son, I'm sure you're up for a busy week."

"Goodnight Wan; travel home safely."

My anger with Wan had subsided, now my only focus was being with Elora. I felt I've waited a lifetime for this to come. When I got into my bed I slipped into sleep quickly, I remember my dreams were of Elora standing in the hall before the pulpit making our promise to each other.

I woke before the sun had started to come up. I went to Elora's and took care of her mare and her father's horse. Both the horses knew why I was there. They began to make it difficult to clean their pens as they nuzzled up to me wanting their morning meal. I talked with them as I cleaned them up and got their food for them. I made the three trips to the river for their water and bid them goodbye. As I was leaving I saw Elora in her window, she had been watching me work. She is usually there in the mornings watching me but we don't speak as I don't want her window opened.

Taking care of our horses was quicker and I was done as the sun was warming the air. I got into the river to wash and touch up my beard and moustache and went to dress for the day. When I got into the cottage my mother was serving morning meal, she looked happier this morning then she has over the past week.

"Good morning Davin, excited to get things settled today?"

"Good morning mother, I couldn't be happier. Only thing I'm worried is for them to make us wait longer while a cottage is built for us."

"It would be nice to know their plans on that wouldn't it?" She asked as she gave me my food.

"It would be nice but honestly I haven't talked much with anyone over the last week. They were locked in that meeting room all day, and by the time they were done I was gone."

"I guess we'll know soon enough, we all plan to go in first thing this morning."

"Thank you mother, it means a lot that your trying to help us with this."

"I knew whether I helped you or not you and Elora would want to be bound as soon as possible."

I laughed at how right she was. After I finished my meal I dressed in my suit and headed to Elora's.

"Are you nervous?" I asked as we walked towards the Liaison's.

"Not at all, I have faith we'll be bound soon."

"I have faith too, I feel like we've waited too long already."

When we got to the Liaison's there were already a few families standing outside waiting for their turn to speak. Elora and I went in through the back and took our seats. Kyan and a couple other of the Liaison's weren't in yet. I quickly went to my office and grabbed my book so I could update it with everything that happened last night, and keep up with any other decisions made today. After the rest of us were seated the clerks began showing villagers in one family at a time.

The first family wanted to discuss the riding rules for girls and asked if the age could be changed to fourteen like the males. The Liaison's quickly dismissed them with a simple no.

The next family wanted to set their children to be bound when the girl turned sixteen. Neither of the families brought those to be bound and they were sent away and told when they came back to bring those who were to be bound as it was their choice as much as anyone else's. It went like this for over an hour. No one came to complain of the new rules, they had questions and suggestions but nothing was changed.

The next to be led in were my parents and the Dover's. Lee told us to take our place with our parents.

"I'm assuming we are here to discuss Davin and Elora's ceremony?" He asked us.

"Yes Sir." I said beaming.

"How soon would you like to be bound?"

"Today? Tomorrow? How long would it take to get things together?" I said still feeling on top of the world. Lee laughed at my enthusiasm.

"How about in five days? Would that be long enough for the families to have things ready for the ceremony?"

Both of our mothers said it would be enough time.

"Then it is done; in five days we'll hold your ceremony."

"Sir, not to be rude but what about our cottage?" I asked trying not to show that it upset me that it still hadn't been brought up.

"You both work here in the Liaison, the elders have spent time working on it and we can assure you it is taken care of.

Your cottage will be unveiled after you're bound and celebrate. We plan to have your carriage finished and Jobe will need both of your horses the morning of the ceremony. He'll also wait until your celebration is over to take you to your new cottage."

"Thank you Sir." I said as they excused us.

"Davin, Elora; your both excused for the day these meetings are boring and you have plans to make." Lee told us.

CHAPTER 24

Avoiding more plans

ELORA AND I WALKED to her cottage so she could change into her riding outfit. Since we had the day to ourselves we decided to spend it riding and talking about our future together. I helped her untie her gown and watched as she undressed. I was captivated by her beauty, her slim waist, the fullness in her breasts. I made no attempt to touch her I just watched in awe as she dressed for our ride.

After we had Misty saddled we walked her to my cottage and much like I had done with her, she stood and watched as I dressed in my riding clothes. We again wore our matching riding outfits. She helped me get Blitz ready and we walked the horses along the river until we reached the lake.

We tied both of the horses to a tree near the water and I helped her remove her boots. We sat with our feet in the water for a long time, there was no hurry we had nothing to do and now that our date was set everyone would be too busy to notice we were missing.

"Are you excited?" Elora asked me.

"In five days you'll finally be my wife. I'm the happiest person in the world right now."

"I think I may be happier then you're my love." She said as she smiled at me.

"Why do you think that?"

"Because, I had the deciding vote on the age change."

"I just don't know how you kept that a secret! You must have been dying for me to know." I told her, not in bitterness I still respected our different jobs within the Liaison.

"It wasn't easy my love, I'd known for three days before the meeting."

"Honestly, did Wan try to speak with you alone in the last week?" I asked her.

"No he hasn't said much to any of us. Even in the meetings he only talked when someone spoke directly to him."

"He came to the river last night while I was swimming." I told her.

"What did he say to you?"

"Nothing much, he was very casual. I still don't know how to feel about him."

"I hear he plans to take his leave soon." She told me.

"I'll be happy when he's gone honestly."

"I will too, he really makes me feel uneasy."

I took my jacket off and hung it on a branch, the weather has warmed and the summer months are here. Elora removed her jacket as well it seemed odd seeing her in pants and a shirt. We both folded the bottom of the pants to our knees and I took her hand and led her into the water. We splashed and played the water was cool and felt so good I wanted to just go in.

It wasn't long before I had splashed Elora a little too much and she gave me a push. I went down as I wasn't expecting her to push me. I fell all the way in and was soaked. As I stood she tried to get out of the water but she wasn't quick enough. I had her in my arms and brought her into the deeper water. She looked beautiful with the sun coming down onto her golden hair. The sun made her eyes look greener and her cheeks were flushed red. To me she was the most beautiful women in the world. I was so consumed with her beauty I didn't even realize I had pulled her into me and begun kissing her.

We hadn't stolen a passionate kiss since we figured out we were being watched. I unleashed a week's worth of frustrated lonely kisses on her and she responded with as much passion. I listened for our horses as I knew they would make noise if anyone was coming. She had her hand in my hair, and she kept me from pulling away from her. I had no desire to pull away I've longed to kiss her like this for many days.

Our clothes were wet and our white shirts were transparent, seeing her all wet before me was driving me to that maddening feeling of desire. I lifted her in my arms using my face to pull down her shirt. My face was buried in her breasts kissing them softly. I pulled her face back down to mine and began kissing her again. We both tried slowing down knowing we only had five days left to wait. Soon her hands were exploring my body, my riding pants are thin and tight and don't do much to hide me. She had me unbuttoned and in her hands, we were still kissing and our bodies had become tangled under the water. I had her riding pants un-buttoned, we never stopped kissing our cries of pleasure being muffled by our kisses. Our bodies were submerged in the water. I had to use one hand to hold her up as she was slipping down. Soon our release came and together we slowly relaxed our bodies, not moving at all we continued to kiss as we let ourselves calm down from the excitement. Slowly our bodies untangled and our kisses subsided. I held her tightly to me whispering I loved her between our kisses.

After a few minutes and we caught our breaths I lifted her out of the water and brought her up the bank to a sunny grassy area. We laid down in the sun letting our clothes dry.

"I've dreamed of being with you all week my love." I whispered to her.

"I've wanted to come to you every night, but I didn't want to break my promise to you."

"I know, it's been difficult but now after five days we won't have to hide our love ever again."

"I can't wait to become your wife Davin."

"I hope I'll be a good husband to you my love."

"You will be, I know it."

"How do you know such a thing?" I asked her wondering what her basis of that opinion was.

"Because; you've always been good to me. Now we'll just have all the rights as a husband and wife." She said softly.

"I'm happy I make you happy for you drive me mad my love." I told her.

"How have I driven you mad?"

"Elora, I do nothing but think of being with you, since you've started wearing your gowns I do nothing but desire you."

"Do you think it's been easy for me? Watching you work so hard seeing the sweat on your muscular arms, seeing your shirt stick to your skin showing how muscular your chest has become. Seeing you with your dark hair, damp with sweat and the determined look in your blue eyes."

"You really see all of that while I'm working?"

"Yes Davin, you've grown into a man before my eyes and in case you hadn't noticed in the water my desire for you is uncontrollable. Five days still feels like forever."

"It does to me as well my love. And I know our mothers will keep us busy before they get here. I'm happy we have this afternoon with each other; without it I may have gone mad." I said laughing.

We laid out until our clothes dried and both of our stomachs were rumbling. She let me fix her hair for her and help her tie her jacket even though it tied in the front.

"You truly are the most beautiful woman in the world." I said kissing her again.

"I'm glad you think so!"

We rode into the village slowly, there was no need to hurry we knew everyone would still be working. I helped her put Misty away and we went into her cottage so she could change. She let me watch her dress again and I helped her tie up her yellow gown. She fed me some venison from their supper from the day before. Then we went to my cottage and I put on work clothes I still wanted to take care of the horses even if we had time off. Now I just wanted to do it so she would watch and desire me. I gave her a cup of wine and one of the cherry tarts Myka had made. I left my room open as I dressed and I saw her looking at me as I had watched her dress.

"I still have work to do, would you like to come with me or wait in the cottage?" I asked her as I pulled on my boots.

"I'll come watch of course."

I worked fast and hard, it wasn't long before the heat and hard work had me soaked again. I realized my shirt did stick to my skin when I got working hard. I had the pens cleaned and animals fed and watered by the time everyone was coming in from work. I left Elora with her mother and I went to get fresh clothes so I could clean up before supper. I've never bathed this much but I always needed to after I did my work in the pens.

When I went into the cottage my mother was making supper and talking with my father about the ceremony.

"I just want to walk in and make my promises to Elora, I don't care how the room looks or how many flowers hang in it." I said throwing my arms into the air and walking to my room.

I could hear them laughing, but I really would only see one thing when we were bound and that was Elora. When she was near me I saw nothing else. And even when she wasn't near me I still saw her. My mother came to get me for supper I had fallen asleep thinking of our afternoon in the water together.

"Everyone will be here soon we better hurry." My mother said as she put supper on my plate.

"Everyone will be here for what?"

"Davin, didn't we just go through the steps of a ceremony a little over a week ago? People come and congratulate you and Elora, some will bring gifts there'll be wine, ale.and food. Are you remembering now?" She asked me looking irritated at me.

"Yes, I remember. Really can't we just do the wine with Elora here and leave the rest out?"

"Boy, your enthusiasm is amazing."

"I just want to be bound to Elora, the rest is a formality I could do without."

"Well just be polite this evening or I'll have your father whip you."

"I will mother, I'm just tired this evening is all."

"Eat, you'll feel better afterwards."

She was right; soon the villagers were making their way to our cottage. Elora and I sat together so we could thank everyone. Harry and Isabell were among the first to arrive. The children were so happy about Elora and I being bound and Maggie thought she would be marrying us like she did with Harry and Isabell. Harry brought two jugs of wine to help celebrate. I was drinking my share everyone who knows me knows how miserable I am over being the center of attention.

My father and Harry had a fire going as the sun went down. Elora and I couldn't talk much as we were constantly greeting friends and family. Harry asked me to walk with him, I was grateful to get away.

"Are you happy Davin?" Harry asked as we neared the river.

"Of course the rule change is a blessing, in five days I'll have all I've ever wanted."

"I'm glad you're so happy Davin. Have you spoken with Wan at all?"

"He came to me last night while I swam in the river it was no surprise to see him there."

"Anything come of your meeting?" He asked curiously.

"Nothing of importance, I'm just waiting for him to take his leave then all should be well."

"Has he mentioned when he would leave?" He asked as he poured more wine into my cup.

"No, but I hear that it'll be soon. I know Lee mentioned he would only spend a month helping to train his replacement, though I'm unsure if that has changed."

"I've always liked Wan; it's a shame what has been going on as of late. I think his mind is gone, I know he wanders every night drunk on whiskey." He told me. I know it's because of Wan Harry is even where he is, I can understand why he is troubled over it.

"Maybe it's better for him to leave, I know he's in pain and has been since he lost his wife many years ago in child birth. I do care about him, I just feel wronged and angry after seeing him spying on us. I can't figure out why he would be so interested, if it's because of our work in the Liaison's it's still not his business to be watching us like that."

"I understand your anger Davin; just don't let it keep consuming you as it has. I've seen the anger in your eyes maybe it's time to let it go, for Elora if not for anything else."

"I'm letting it go Elora and I spoke of it yesterday. I made her a promise and I will not break it over that old fool."

"I'm glad to hear you're coming around Davin. Any word on your cottage yet?"

"We were told today in the meeting that after the ceremony and celebration we would be driven to our cottage. Until then we can't know more than that."

"Well, it's nice to know you won't be sleeping in a tent while we try to build a cottage from the ground up!" He said laughing, relieving our talk some.

"How did the children do today?" I asked.

"They left happy, Maggie says she has a friend and Luke isn't talking much."

"Let me know if there's something I can do to help him."

"I will of course. You haven't taken Elora yet?" I laughed in embarrassment but I knew what he was getting around at.

"No, and yes I'm glad we have waited." He laughed patting me on my back.

"Let's get back to our beautiful women before they come looking for us."

"Yes, and hopefully most all have gone home."

"You're such a simpleton my boy."

"Thank you kindly Sir." We were both laughing as we walked back to join the others.

I took my seat next to Elora and she poured me more wine and took my hand.

"Are you trying to get me drunk my love?"

"No, you're already drunk. I'm simply trying to keep you that way."

I saw Jobe riding towards our cottage in his usual carriage. He brought two gifts to us and announced they were sent from the Liaison's. I found this odd I know commonly gifts from each work area were brought after the ceremony along with gifts from the villagers. Each work area would make something for the couple to be bound to welcome their new cottage. The gifts from the villagers were things like preserves and homemade wines, linens with their names on it.

Jobe handed Elora a small box which I recognized immediately, it held the necklace Wan had me purchase in Breakstone. He handed me a box that was just a little bit bigger than Elora's. We gave our thanks to him and I gestured to Elora to open hers first. She was speechless when she first opened it as was I. There was also a matching ring to go with the necklace and earrings.

"They are beautiful please send my thank you to the Liaison." She said never taking her eyes off of the jewelry.

"I'll do so." Jobe told her.

I opened my box it held an emerald ring that matched Elora's and a key which had a small emerald embedded in the top of the key.

"The key will open your cottage after you're bound, and the Liaison request that the jewelry be worn when you're bound."

"Thank you Jobe. Do take some wine with us." I invited him.

"Thank you Davin." He said accepting a cup of wine. "I was asked to let you both know you'll only have to come in tomorrow until mid-meal. Then you'll have time off to get ready for your ceremony. They also told me to let you know that you'll be given seven days of rest to begin your lives with each other. During that time either I or one of the other clerks would deliver your food rations so you can be at peace with each other.'

"Is this another new rule?" I asked him.

"This is customary when someone who works in the Liaison is bound."

"That'll be a nice rest I'm sure, thank you Jobe."

He bid us goodbye with that.

Our well wishers were bidding us goodnight soon after Jobe left us. I gave Maggie a kiss on her cheek and told her she would always be my love, and I walked Harry and his new family to their carriage and bid them good night.

Elora and I helped clean up from the celebration. We took all the gifts we received and put them into my room until we could move them to our own cottage. Our parents weren't forcing the rules of courting so much and didn't say anything when she entered my room to help put things away. Not that they were sticking much to them since the fire happened.

"There's one thing for sure my love." I told her as we walked back to get more gifts.

"What would that be?" She asked taking my hands into hers and looking into my eyes.

"We won't have to make perseveres for a long time." We both laughed and went to finish so we could take some time alone before it was time for us to say goodnight. By the time we were done our parents were saying goodnight as well. We were left alone standing in the little kitchen of my cottage. I poured her some more wine and we sat in the candle light.

"I can't wait until we don't have to leave each other at night anymore." I whispered to Elora.

"I can't wait either my love. I can't wait for a lot of things, like seeing our cottage for the first time or spending seven days alone with only you."

"It'll be seven days of heaven for me, my love. Shall I escort you home or would you like to sit here and stare at me all night?" I teased.

"We should go, we have to be in early and you know when were done our mothers will run us ragged."

I stood and put my arm out for her. We walked slowly in the moonlight and enjoyed the cool air of the night. When we got to her cottage I took her into her room and checked her window to be sure my stick was still there. Then I helped her untie her gown, kissed her softly and bid her good night.

CHAPTER 25

Waiting

I WOKE EARLY AND hurried out to do my chores. I'm excited to be getting so much time off for our ceremony. I'm not sure why we were requested to come in this morning maybe they had more instructions for us. After I finished my work in the pens I went to the river so I could clean up.

I ate with my family and then I went to get Elora. I'm still insistent that she not be alone. After Wan is gone maybe I won't feel so strongly about it, but for now she'll have an escort. "What are your plans after you're done this afternoon?" I asked her.

"My mother needs me to help her at her work so she can get done early."

"More plans I take it?" I knew it was a question I already knew the answer to.

"She wants to help me with my gown for our ceremony."

"What will you wear?"

"That's to be surprise!" She said laughing at me. "Will you wear your grey riding outfit for the ceremony?"

"If that's what you want my love. I guess I hadn't thought much about what I'd be wearing."

"What will you be doing this afternoon my love?" She asked me.

"I have some work at my father's shop to help him finish." I had thought I had time to finish the chair but now I had to really get to work on it, I want it finished so I can give it to her as a ceremony gift.

"Sounds to me like you're up to something!" She said to me.

"I guess you'll just have to wait and see my love." I pulled her close and gave her a small kiss on her cheek. "I love you Elora."

"I love you too Davin, I can't wait until we are bound."

"Neither can I my love."

We continued our walk into the Liaison's. Some of the villagers were already getting their day going, some stopped to congratulate us. I'm sure most knew once the rule changed we would be quick to be bound. We've been inseparable since we were small children, I remember many times people commenting us as we grew up.

When we reached the Liaison's building the drapes were drawn again. We went in through the back door where Jobe met us.

"They're in a meeting right now. Elora, they would like you to wait in the office, some work has been set out for you to get finished." She walked into the small meeting room and closed the door behind her.

"Davin, I was asked to have you make sure all your work is caught up before your time off." He handed me a folded piece of paper that had the Liaison's seal on it.

"This is a list of the new rules Lee would like you to update your book. He also said to put your opinions and the reaction and general atmosphere of the villagers."

"I'll have it finished before I leave. I plan to do some work with my father for a couple days if I'm needed for anything."

"I'll inform everyone." He said turning to go back into the meeting.

I went into my office my wage box had been put back on my desk. I opened it and found another five gold pieces in it with a small note that read: 'In case you need anything for your new cottage.' I already have a few gold pieces saved of my wages. And my savings from my parents will be given to me after the ceremony. Not that Isabelle would charge us if we did need anything.

I took my book and began writing the new rules out. I added small notes to the sides of the pages and gave my opinion on how the villager's reacted to the rules. I made sure to spend time making my writing nice and neat so it didn't appear that I was in hurry.

The list I had also contained the names of the matches who were choosing to be bound at sixteen, there was only two sets of matches to be bound. The other couple wasn't matched until they were about ten years old. I worked with Adam in the fields during one of my many different internships, his match Carrie worked with Elora with the small children. I didn't know either of them very well and I found it hard to comment on them choosing to be bound earlier. I just added that I thought they were a good match it was all I could think of. I had been locked in my office for about two hours when I heard Wan knocking on my door.

"Good morning Davin, getting your work caught up I see." He said as he closed the door and took his usual seat.

"Yes, I just finished up. Do you know how long until Elora will be finished?" I asked him.

"She shouldn't be much longer; I know they are just trying to get some issues with a family in the village."

"Is everything alright?"

"Yes, just details over Adam and Carrie being bound. Her father's unhappy and trying to get the Liaison to grant permission to have it stopped."

"Will the Liaison let them be bound?" I asked concerned.

"Yes, the new rule states that it's the matche's decision. There isn't much that we can do if a parent tries to fight it."

"Well it looks like it will happen even if he doesn't approve. The other parents are supportive?" I asked him.

"Yes, they are fine with it. They just requested a couple weeks time to get everything together. Then it will be announced and celebrated. Are you ready for your ceremony?"

"I've been ready for many years Wan."

"Is there anything you'll need for your cottage? We know with the fire anything that Elora had put away was ruined."

"I honestly don't know yet.. I have coin saved and if I need to we can take a quick trip to Breakstone." I told him.

"Make sure you two don't travel alone, get Sid or Harry to travel with you please." He warned me.

"I'll work it out only if I need to go. As of now I can barely walk in my room with all the gifts, I'm sure we'll be fine for some time."

"Well son, it sounds like you have everything in order. Enjoy your time off and I'll be seeing you after you're back to work."

"Thank you Wan." I stood up and shook his hand before he left.

I updated my book on the situation with Adam and Carrie. I was just getting finished when I heard Elora saying her goodbye's in the hall. I put away my book and took all the coin I had saved. I still don't know if I'd need it, but I knew I could just add it to the rest of my savings.

Elora and I had mid-meal together in the kitchens. I asked her if she was finished for the day and she told me she really hadn't had much to do. When we were finished I walked her to her mothers work and promised I'd come see her this evening.

I worked for about three hours on the chair. I used the carving tools and carved intricate vines on the arms and rockers of the chair. I carved Elora Hewit on the upper back piece and carved vines entwining each other around her name. I should have it done tomorrow.

"That's a beautiful chair son." My father said as he looked over my work.

"I hope she likes it, it would be a waste of work if she didn't."

"She'll love it, you put your heart into that chair and it will be the one gift she'll never forget."

"I just can't wait to see her in it."

"Soon son, soon. We'll get it oiled tomorrow and I'll have it brought to our cottage so you can give it to her after the ceremony."

"Thanks for your help father."

"That's what I'm here for son. Is there anything you would like to talk about before your ceremony?"

"What do you mean?"

"Do you have questions about what will happen once your bound, for example… the first night you two will spend together?"

"No." I said laughing, I felt embarrassed that he wants to talk with me like this now. "I think I'll just let it happen and enjoy learning her on my own."

"Alright son, but if you need anything you can come talk to me."

"I will father. I'm going to do my chores so I can enjoy a swim before mother gets in and starts with her plans." He laughed as I got up and excused myself.

I got the horses done quickly and went about my swim. When my mother got in she was instantly putting me to work. She ran me ragged all evening until I begged her to let me go say goodnight to Elora.

"How was your evening my love?" I asked her as we sat on our log.

"We have been busy as I'm sure your mother has kept you."

"She's torturing me, why can't we just run away right now and forget the ceremony?"

"Davin, it will be over soon and I'd never give up my day as the bride. Even if it did help you get out of all the planning." She said laughing.

We sat for a little while speaking about our future we also promised not to meet at night until our ceremony, we wanted to wait until we could be together with no shame or worries of being caught. I'd have to live with our afternoon at the lake until the night of our ceremony.

The next two days passed slowly, I worked twice as hard hoping to make the time go by faster. I had the chair finished and it looked a lot better than I thought it would seeing as I've not ever made one. My mother was still busy with her endless planning. She had jugs of wine delivered and extra food for the celebration after the ceremony.

I went to bid Elora goodnight for one last time. She looked beautiful she was wearing the green gown that Lynne had made her.

"You look beautiful this evening my love."

"You look very handsome this evening yourself."

"You know, this is the last time we'll have to sit on this log to tell each other goodnight." I told her taking her hand into mine.

"That thought makes me very happy." Hearing that she's as happy as I was relieved me a lot, in all the time I've had to myself my biggest worry has been about her happiness.

"You make me happy my love. I'll leave you now so we don't get ahead of ourselves. I love you, sweetest dreams my love."

"I love you too Davin, sleep well."

We kissed for a long moment and I let her go. I know I only had tonight to wait but I didn't want to let her go. I walked slowly back to my own cottage trying not to let my feelings get to me.

Tomorrow Elora and I'd not be allowed to see each other until the ceremony began. I still have heard nothing new on our cottage, I know they tell me it is taken care of but I worry none the less.

I couldn't fall sleep tonight over the excitement of this being my last night without Elora. I had some wine and went for a swim. I half expected Wan to stumble across me knowing he always came to see if we were together or not. I swam for over an hour and he never came by. I got out of the water and laid naked in the moonlight thinking of tomorrow. I had drunk a lot of wine hoping it would help me sleep and when I was feeling tired I went into my bed only to toss and turn until the morning.

I finally gave up and went out to clean after our horse's I knew I couldn't go take care of Elora's. I wanted to go hoping to catch a glimpse of her, but I didn't go for the fear our parents spouted of bad luck. We weren't suspicious people often but something's we didn't dare push.

Our parents had the day off so they could prepare for the ceremony. We couldn't have the decorating party last night, Lee had sent a message that they were working late. I didn't mind because it meant I didn't have to decorate. I had to take Blitz to the Liaison's so they could get our carriage ready for tonight.

I spent most of the afternoon packing up my clothes and all the gifts from the other night. I had my father's carriage set up and I loaded it with everything. He would follow us out to our cottage and leave the gifts for us to unpack tomorrow. I didn't realize how much stuff my parents had collected for us over the years until I had to load it all.

By the time I got done with that everyone had returned from decorating the hall. I was sweaty from all the work I had been doing so I went for a swim and to get dressed for the ceremony. I trimmed my moustache and shaved around my beard. I had it growing just around my jawbone and I kept it thin and trimmed short.

My parents and the Dover's were setting up in front of our cottage. They had a big makeshift table for the food and wine. And another table was set up for presents. There were garlands of flowers hung on both tables. They used a lot of green plants and a large mixture of wild flowers for the garlands. Elora's rocking chair had been set by the gift table along with presents from our parents and their workplaces. My father had made me a chair to match Elora's but it wasn't a rocker, he had also had the tailor make a matching cushion for it.

"Davin, it's time for you to get dressed for the ceremony."
My mother said as she was putting more food out.

"I'm going, did you take Elora's jewelry to her?"

"I gave it to her after we decorated, now go get ready!" I
think our mothers are more excited than we are the way they
are running around.

I went to my room and dressed in my grey riding outfit. All
I can think is how finally I'll get to be with my love forever. I
put the ring on like I was instructed to and put the large silver
cottage key with the emerald on it in my jacket pocket. I went
back outside to join my family so we could walk together to
the hall.

CHAPTER 26

Our Ceremony

THE HALL WAS FULL of villagers and many had flooded outside from lack of room. I went inside the main hall it had been decorated with the same garlands that were at the cottage. The only furniture in the room was once again the pulpit, where Lee stood waiting to begin the ceremony.

I heard the villagers cheering outside, Elora must be here now. Her parents came in the main hall and stood with my parents as she entered the doorway. She looked more beautiful than I ever remember seeing her. The gown she wore was from the dress my mother had made her it had been remade into a gown. There were tiny dark green beads sewn into the under dress around her breast. The front of her hair was pinned back; her golden curls flowed down almost to her rear end. There was a crown of white flowers with small greenery sitting on the top of her head. The emerald necklace sat snuggly in between her breasts. As she walked towards me I felt as if she were an angel, her beauty was breath taking. She joined me gracefully at the pulpit never taking her eyes off of me, her smile making me feel the happiness she felt.

"Thank you all for coming to see Davin and Elora be bound in marriage this fine day." Lee started the ceremony. "This is a special ceremony as Davin and Elora will be the youngest match ever to be bound under the new rules. It's also the first time two that work in the Liaison together will be bound."

He had us face each other and take each other's hands. "From today on you'll both live as husband and wife, you'll strive to work together in happiness and love. You'll take care of each other and be there when the other needs you. You'll learn to respect each other as well; in every aspect that comes forward to you. If you both agree may you say you do now."

We both agreed, our gazes never leaving each other.

"I now pronounce you Mr. and Mrs. Davin Hewit!"

Everyone around us was clapping and cheering. I pulled Elora closer to me and kissed her lips gently. This time no shame and no worries that we would get in trouble. The cheers around us grew louder.

We walked towards the door hand in hand and saw the carriage that was our gift from the Liaison. It was pulled by both of our horse's, they used garlands similar to the ones in the hall to decorate the carriage and horses. We got into our carriage together for the ride to my parents cottage.

"You look amazingly beautiful my wife." I said as I kissed her again.

"You look very handsome my husband."

"We are finally bound, do we have to stay and celebrate long"" My excitement for us to start our own lives together was pouring out of me.

"I hope not my love, I want to see our new cottage and be alone with my new husband." She said leaning over to kiss me again.

"I've dreamed of it all my life my love."

We arrived at the celebration with everyone following our carriage. The congratulations began as we stepped down. Harry was one of the first to come to us he had Maggie in his arms.

"You both look wonderful, congratulations!" He said giving Elora a hug.

We couldn't even get into the yard for at least five minutes as were inundated by well wishers. I finally took Elora by the hand and led her to our chairs I wanted her to see the gift I made her.

"This is what I've been up to." I said as she looked at the chair. She ran her finger around her new name carved on the chair.

"I love it Davin, you must of worked so hard on this."

"I told you I'd work myself to death to make you happy, and it looks like it's has worked. Shall we get some wine?"

I led her to the tables of food and poured both of us wine. It was cherry wine like the wine I had got from the market. We sat down and continued to greet people, thankfully Isabell brought us food and more wine since we found it difficult to get away long enough to get our own. We dined on roasted pheasant with fresh bread and roasted butternut squash. My mother had also spent all evening baking small sweet cakes with cherries and cream on top.

The table with the gifts was full and the gifts were now being put on the ground around the table. Sid and Lynne brought us linens with our names on them, Harry and Isabell gave us hand carved wooden goblets with our names on them, the tailor delivered us matching cream colored riding outfits with our initials beautifully embroidered in gold thread on the lapels of the jackets. The gifts were endless.

A man started to play a fiddle and I led Elora out to dance with her and like at Harry and Isabell's celebration people began cutting in and we were passed from person to person for a long time. I finally got back to Elora and danced with her, this time not letting anyone cut in.

After we sat to dance Harry came to me and asked me to join him for a moment.

"I just wanted to tell you, Jobe came to me after you guys got out of the carriage." Harry told me.

"What did he want?" I asked him.

"He just brought up the fact that Wan left the Liaison yesterday."

"He left without even telling me goodbye?" I was relieved to hear he had gone but also hurt in some ways.

"Well I don't think he wanted a big deal made out of it Davin."

"I'm glad he's gone I won't have to worry about him watching us anymore, I guess I'm just sad I didn't get the chance to tell him thank you for the faith he had in me when he decided on my calling."

"Don't worry yourself too much over it Davin, I just thought it would bring you some relief." He told me.

"It docs Harry, it just caught me off guard is all."

"Boy go get back there with your beautiful wife, we can talk more about this later."

"Thank you for letting me know Harry, I did need to know."

"You're welcome, go now!"

I went back and joined Elora, I whispered to her about the news Harry had given me. She only smiled at me I knew she felt the same relief I did when I heard the news.

We drank a lot as many toasted and congratulated us. The sun was starting to go down and the people were starting to leave.

"I think it's time to leave my love." I told her as I helped her up and announced we were tired.

Harry, my father, Mr. Dover and Eldon loaded all of our gifts in our carriage and filled my father's with what wouldn't fit.

I led Elora to our carriage and as we climbed in everyone cheered and waved as we pulled away. My father's carriage followed behind us, Harry and Mr. Dover joined him to help carry in the gifts.

The carriage headed towards the other side of town. We came along the other river and followed a small trail for a few minutes. I didn't see many cottages out this way. I didn't venture up this way very much and even when I did I never traveled this far, there was a never a need we had a river behind our cottage. Soon we reached a lake, it was smaller than the one that fed our river. The carriage made a sharp right and crossed a small bridge and we pulled in front of a very large cottage. It had steps that led up to a porch that was built across the front of the cottage. There were two white rockers that sat on it in front of a window. The cottage was twice as big as the cottage I had lived in all of my life. Jobe opened the carriage door for us and welcomed us home.

Together Elora and I walked up to the cottage, both of us wide eyed at how big it looked. I took the key out of my pocket and used it to open the door then I picked her up and carried her into the cottage. It was stunning and for a moment I just stood with Elora in my arms taking it all in.

To the left was a sitting room, there was two green velvet chairs and a small table with a candle sitting in a gold and emerald ornately decorated candle holder. There was a carpet in the middle of the room, handmade to match the chairs. The drapes covering the windows also matched the chairs. There was a desk under one of the windows that matched the chair my father made me.

To the right was what looked like a sleeping room, the door was closed so I couldn't see in. In front of us was a large kitchen, there was a newly built wood burning stove. A long counter was built along the wall. Shelves were also built on the walls. One of the shelves had handmade clay dishes and new pots for cooking. There was a table with four chairs in the middle of the room. On the table top there's a lace table cloth and a vase of yellow roses.

Next to the room on the left there's a hall that leads back and behind the kitchen. There are three more rooms with the doors closed. There's also a back door that leads to a smaller porch looking out on the forest and onto a barn and horse pens. It's dark and I can't see much but I thought I heard chickens out there. We walked slowly and took it all in. We didn't open the doors as everyone was now busy carrying in our gifts and I wanted to discover everything when we were alone. When they were finally done they came in to bid us farewell.

"Good night son." My father said shaking my hand.

"See you in a few days." Harry told us as he stepped outside.

Elora's father was hugging her and bid her goodnight.

"Treat her right boy." Her father said to me as he stepped out the door.

"I promise I will Sir." I tried to reassure him.

"I'll put your horses away, someone will be by tomorrow to care for them and if you need anything have him let us know." Jobe said as he left and closed the door.

"This cottage is so big!" Elora said as she looked around.

"I wasn't expecting anything like this." I told her.

We went towards the back of the house and looked into the last room. It wasn't a large room and it was empty except for a small rug that sat in the middle of the room. The next room was the same. They had a connecting fireplace and neither had drapes in the windows. The next room was bigger and it had a small baby cradle in the middle of the room. The drapes where white linen, and there was a small wooden chest sitting under it. I could see the fireplace connected with the room that must have been ours.

I opened the door to the room, there's a very big bed directly in front of us. It has four very large posts in each corner with dark green linen drapes that go over the posts and around the bed. The drapes have gold cords used to have them tied them open. The blanket on the bed is thick green velvet with gold vines hand sewn on it, and six large pillows at the head of the bed. Each side of the bed has a table with candle holders like the one in the sitting room. There is also a gold goblet on each side of the bed, around the top of each goblet there are small emeralds embedded in them. One goblet has a D and one an E, they are beautiful goblets, I've only ever seen wooden ones before now.

There's one long chest which takes up the foot of the bed where it sits. On the wall by where we stood was a small table with a mirror on it, it has three small drawers in it and a small cushioned chair. There is a silver hair brush sitting on the table with a little ceramic bowl of hair pins. The fireplace has a beautifully carved mantle above it, a new shaving set is on it along with more candles and smaller candle holders that match the others. Next to the little table with the mirror there is another simple small table that holds a water pitcher and bowl, it also holds a dish with little soaps in it and there are a few linens folded nicely sitting next to them.

"I can't believe this is our cottage!" Elora said as she walked into the room and turned in circles to look and take it all in.

"It's beautiful, I wonder if all the Liaison's live like this." I said to her. I had never been to a Liaison's cottage before I didn't even know where some of them lived.

I took the goblets and carried them to the kitchen and poured us some wine. Our kitchen and sitting room were now cluttered with all the gifts. I picked up Elora's chair and carried it to our room, and placed it near the fire place for her. I was glad whoever put this together knew the colors I used to make her chair for it matched perfectly.

We took our wine and went on our new porch. The small lake looked like it was glowing from the moonlight.

"Are you happy my love?" I asked her as I pulled her close to me.

"I'm very happy, our cottage is beautiful, we are finally bound and we have seven days to build our own world.'

I pulled her close to me and began to kiss her.. I feel as if it's been forever since I've kissed her with such passion. I showed no restraint as I consumed her with my kisses. I took her goblet out of her hand and put both of them on the rail of the porch. Still kissing her I picked her up and carried her into our cottage. I used my foot to close the door, and took her into our room.

I laid her on the bed and began the fire we didn't have to worry about putting out this time. I kissed her neck working my way down to her breasts. Her hand was on my neck pushing my face into her harder. She cried with excitement as her breath quickened, she was trying to unbutton my shirt with her other hand. I worked my lips back up to her lips and rolled onto my back pulling her on top of me. I untied the back of her gown never stopping the passionate kisses we were sharing. Her body was pressed against mine and her hips were pushing towards me. I pulled her gown trying to get it off of her, she sat up and pulled it over her head, now she was only in her under dress, shyly she removed it revealing her beautiful body to me. Only this time there was no restraint.

She reached down unbuttoning my shirt and pants I sat up with her still sitting on my legs and took off my riding jacket. She pushed my shirt down before I even got my arm out of the jacket. She was kissing my neck and face and was pushing me back down on my back. She started to pull at my pants and I helped her get them off. Our naked bodies touching, her skin was soft and warm and she smelled of the magnolias that had always haunted my dreams.

I rolled her onto her back and put myself between her legs I kissed her softly on her breasts and moved down to her belly. I kissed her hips and belly; her cries were soft and breathless. I slowly teased her with my soft kisses until she was crying for me to enter her. I worked my way with my lips back up her body this time my kisses were demanding, when I reached her lips she responded to my demanding kisses with her own. She ran her hands down my back and pushed me down towards her. Carefully I found my way to her warm opening. I entered her slowly and she let out a small cry, I tried to pull back but she used her hands to push me forward. We both cried out our pleasure as I slowly went in her. We were still kissing passionately our hips moved with each others, her hips moving faster with each thrust I took and soon our cries of pleasure filled the room. I couldn't hold my release any longer, she held me tight as our bodies shuddered in excitement and pleasure.

I held her close as our bodies relaxed, kissing her softly. When I looked down at our bodies, I noticed blood on the inside of her thigh and on me.

"You're bleeding!" I said alarmed.

"My love, that's suppose to happen, don't fret you didn't hurt me." She said reassuringly.

I picked her up off the bed and carried her out to our private lake. In the water our bodies became entangled with each other's again. I gently pushed her to the bank and in my excitement I took her again, the moonlight on her face and body had excited me and I couldn't stop myself. After we finished I brought her back into the water and washed her body, then carried her back into the cottage.

"Are you hungry my love?" I asked her as I sat her in one of the chairs.

"Yes, we didn't really get much of a chance to enjoy the food this evening."

I knew my mother had packed some of the food along with three jugs of wine for us. I got our goblets and filled them and made us both sandwiches with the pheasant from the celebration. We sat naked in our kitchen and enjoyed our first meal together.

"Are you still happy that you're my wife now?' I asked her.

"More than you'll know my love."

"I'm glad you're because I'm not about to let you go now. Are you ready to sleep?" I asked her.

"I'm very tired it has been a huge day for us."

I picked her up out of her chair and carried her to our bed. She laid her head on my chest and I held her tight as we fell into a deep sleep together. When I woke the sun was shining through the slightly opened drapes. Elora was still sleeping on my chest I started to kiss her forehead softly as she stirred. Slowly as she woke our kisses became heated and we greeted the morning with our love. After we finished we laid sleepily in each other's arms with our bodies still tangled under the blankets.

"Good morning, my love." She whispered.

"Good morning, how was your sleep?"

"It was the best sleep I've ever had. How was your sleep?"

"I slept perfectly and when I woke my beautiful wife was really in my arms."

"Davin you speak so sweetly to me, but now will you feed me for I'm famished."

"Yes my love, you stay here I'll see what I can get together."

I went into the kitchen looking at the boxes of gifts piled everywhere. Discouraged for a moment I stepped out onto the porch to get a fresh breath of air, someone had put a basket of our food rations on the porch. I was still naked so I grabbed it and went back into the cottage. Inside the basket was fresh baked bread along with food for later. I opened a jar of spiced pears someone gave to us and put them in a small bowl. I also found fresh cherries in the basket. I took a tray that someone gave us and put the bowls of fruit on it. Then I found a jar of the preserves and the fresh bread and added it to the tray. I took it into her and set it in the middle of bed, then went back to the kitchen to get a jug of wine and the two goblets.

"A meal fit for my beautiful wife!' I said as I joined her at the head of the bed.

"It looks wonderful my love, thank you." She said taking a piece of bread.

I fed her some of the cherries and she fed me the pears. We enjoyed our meal with each other not in a hurry to do anything but be with each other.

"These goblets are beautiful; and they match our jewelry." She said as she took the wine inside of it.

"Everything in this cottage is amazing I still can't believe it's ours."

"Neither can I, would you like to dress so we can see the outside of it?" She asked me.

"No, but if you insist I'll dress and we can go see it."

"I insist my love." She said smiling.

We dressed simply since we didn't have to go anywhere. We both put our cream colored riding pants on and only the undershirts with them, no jackets or boots. We went out the front of the house and looked over the lake; it was small but private and beautiful. I couldn't see another cottage anywhere. There was a well not far from the trail we came in on. Roses grew wildly all around us, the cottage was beautiful in the light, there was a lot wood and the stone work was very precisely set so that the stones were all close to the same color.

We went around to the back of the cottage to the right of the trail was a garden. The plot was big and had been planted around spring as it was in full bloom with vegetables. The barn was medium in size I could see Misty and Blitz had been penned together. We walked up taking in the barn; there was a pen that held the four pigs I bought in Breakstone. And behind that was a fenced in chicken coop. Inside there was about ten hens and a rooster walked around the outside showing us he didn't want us in there.

"I wonder if they lay." Elora said as she went in to check their nests. She came out with four eggs.

"I guess they do." I told her. "We can start separating some eggs for food and let some hatch so we can eat chicken sometimes."

We went into the barn and found two cows and plenty of hay, milking buckets and even a butter churn. Our saddles had been brought here and had their own place in the barn. Whoever was sent to feed and care for the animals had been and was long gone. It was late in the day though. I set out to get a bucket of fresh milk for us and Elora watched as she held on to her eggs like they were gold. We never really had a lot of eggs in our diet with the village being so large the only way to get eggs very often was to raise your own chickens and most just didn't bother. When we were through we took our treasures to the house and set out to make a real meal.

The oven already had a stack of wood in it so I lit it for Elora and she began to put away some of the gifts while she waited for enough heat to cook. In the basket she found a small venison roast so she prepared it and set it aside so she could put it in the oven after we ate our eggs. I helped her put some of the endless jars of preserves and fruit on the shelves. She took out a pan and mixed the eggs while they cooked, I skimmed the cream off the milk and poured us both some milk while she sat plates on the table. She scooped the hot eggs onto our plates and sliced each of us some bread.

We sat at our little table and enjoyed our mid-meal or at least I think it was about time for mid-meal. I helped her clean the mess when we finished, as she washed the dishes I went up behind her and wrapped my arms around her kissing the back of her neck. She put down the dish and turned to kiss me I picked her up and carried her back to our bed, where we spent most of the afternoon. After we had our supper we noticed that the sun was going down so we went for a swim. There was no shame for us we went naked to our private little lake, if someone came to see us I'd just have tell them to go away and not come back for six more days.

We spent the next few days inseparable, enjoying every minute together our desire for each other only a kiss away. It didn't matter what the time of day it was, if we wanted each other we let ourselves go. Our appetites grew insatiable, worse than when I was doing so much work. They left us plenty of food on our porch every morning. I still hadn't seen who had been leaving it we were usually asleep when it was left.

CHAPTER 27

Betrayal

WE SETTLED INTO OUR cottage with ease and after a few days things were starting become a little normal, we actually got out of bed and dressed today. We didn't have plans to go anywhere, but Elora wanted to put away all the gifts that have been cluttering up the cottage. There were too many jars of preserves to put on the shelves in the kitchen so Elora asked me to put them in the back room until we would need them. I took a box of them and went into the bare room. After I set it down I turned and noticed a small lump under the carpet. I moved the carpet and found a small door that led to a cellar. I went down and found jugs of wine and jugs of the whiskey that Wan had been drinking. I found a small desk in the tiny room. I lit the candle on top and looked through the desk. In a drawer I found a book, it looked like a journal.

I sat at the desk and opened what I thought was a journal. There was writing on the front page: 'My dearest Davin, I do hope in many ways that you never find this but if you do be sure you're ready to read the truths it holds.' I read, I was starting to feel a fear deep within me. I opened the next page, it read, 'This was once my cottage, I have spent years trying to make it perfect for you and Elora. I'm gone now and please never try to find me.' I took the book and went to sit on the back porch and look it over.

The third page left me feeling as if someone had ripped me into two.

'You may wonder why I'd go through so much trouble to be sure you're happy. Your job, getting the Liaison to change the rules, everything you know was done by me to ensure you a life of ease with the one that I knew you loved with all your heart. Davin you're my son, I'm sorry I never told you. Call me a coward if you will, but I couldn't live with knowing you didn't know. I swore an oath to your mother and I've waited many years, I could no longer take the heart break it has caused me knowing I have a son and could not be a part of his life.'

I sat there stunned reading the page over and over in disbelief. I knew I needed to keep reading but I was almost afraid to turn the page.

'I didn't force your mother son don't ever think I did anything to hurt her. And I'm not trying to destroy hers or your life right now. I live with the guilt every day since it happened and now all I want to do is make sure you know I've done everything I can to make it right. I wish you would not go to your mother with what I've told you, but ultimately it will be your choice.' I read on.

'After my wife and child died I was lost, I spent many evenings wandering down the river drunk. One evening I came across your mother, it was never my intention to ever be with another after I lost my wife for I loved her dearly. Your mother and I talked for a long time and before I realized what was happening I took her by the river. She didn't fight and I did not force her. She was due to be bound to the man you know as your father within the month. I don't think she ever told your father, but after you were born and I saw you for the first time I knew that you were my son. I tried over the years to convince your mother that you should know but she would never give in to me.'

I don't even know what to think or what to do. The anger and hurt makes my body shudder with pain. There is one more page and I'm not even sure if I should go on, but I have no choice I've gone this far.

'Son, I know you knew I was watching you. Please know I was only concerned you and Elora were going to get in trouble. I pushed the new rule through quicker than I had planned because I worried she may of become with child and I couldn't bare to see you ripped from her if she had. I know all too well the pain that comes from losing someone you love. Please know I do love you as my son and always have. And please accept that I'm gone and as I asked before don't search for me. I've done what I've wanted all these years which is give you a good life. Please trust in me and live it.'

I sat for a long time just holding the book in my hand. I knew my tears were falling but I didn't care. The life I thought I had is all made by someone else. My mother betrayed my father and tricked him into raising me when I'm not even his son. I don't know who to be angry at. Wan corrupted the Liaison and my family and yet he is my father and I'm just supposed to pretend I don't know. I'm not sure how long I sat crying and letting everything sink in.

"My love, what are you doing out here?" Elora asked as she stepped out onto the porch. She looked into my face and saw my tears falling." What has happened my love?" I didn't answer her, I only handed her the book. She read it silently even a couple times gasping for a breath.

"Davin, I'm so sorry I can't believe it, where did you find this?"

"I found it in the extra room, there was a door under the carpet and this was in a desk that sits down there."

She came and sat on my lap and ran her fingers through my hair forcing me to look into her face. Her face was hurt and confuse.

"I don't know what to do or say." I admitted to her.

"Come in with me I'll get you some wine."

I followed her in to our cottage that didn't feel so much like home now. I just want to take her and leave this place, this place feels like nothing but a fake life has been set out for us to live.

"I think we should leave Elora." I desperately said to her.

"Leave to where?"

"I don't know! I just want to get the hell out of here. Everything feels tainted and wrong."

"Davin, I know you feel betrayed and hurt, I think Wan was trying to help you. Do as he wished of you, which is to live your life and be happy. That seems like all he wanted for you."

"I do see that, but my mother! My father, I mean is he still my father?"

"Only you can decide that my love." She said kissing me tenderly on my hand.

"What would you do, what if this had been about you?"

"I'd do what was wished of me, why destroy your parents with the knowledge you have? Your father would be destroyed if he found out you weren't his son. Wan spent his last years here dedicating all of this to you, he did it out of love. You need to look past your anger and see the love he has for you Davin."

"So you also want me to pretend this book doesn't exist?"

"No, I want you to accept what it says and don't use it to destroy your family or us. Let us live happily as we have wished for since we were small children. Let us make our own children and our own future and not let the sins of others pasts destroy what we have."

"You're right my love, I can't use this to destroy the people I love. And I'll never let anything destroy what we have." I kissed her softly.

"Now that I think about it does it seem to you that fire at your cottage may not have been an accident?"

"You think Wan set the fire?" She asked me.

"Well it does make sense, if we already had a cottage he couldn't have arranged for us to have this cottage?"

"I can't imagine he would do it, but it does make sense. I think we should leave that thought alone for now, it can only make all of this worse in the end."

I know it has everything to do with me and I wanted nothing to do with any of it. To me it doesn't matter that Wan says he's my father, a lot of what has happened over the last month fits together like puzzle pieces in my mind. But no matter what that book says I'm still me. A boy changing into a man who wants only the simple things in life; an honorable job, the woman I've loved since I was a small boy and a chance to make my own choices and create my own fate.

I took the book and put it back down in the cellar and closed the door behind me. I feel like I've left the lies, confessions and corruption where they belong. I took Elora by the hand and led her out the front door onto our new porch and held her close as we watched the sun reflect on the lake in silence. I know now the only thing to do is begin my life with Elora and try to let go of Wan's past.

ABOUT THE AUTHOR

TERESA WHITE WAS BORN in Long Beach California in 1973. She has four daughters and currently resides in Utah with her husband Tony. She hopes to leave a legacy of hopes and dreams so her children know that sometimes it's alright to chase the end of the rainbow.